For My Daughters

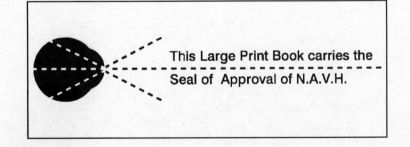

This Large Print Book carries the
Seal of Approval of N.A.V.H.

FOR MY DAUGHTERS

BARBARA DELINSKY

THORNDIKE PRESS

A part of Gale, Cengage Learning

GALE
CENGAGE Learning·

Detroit • New York • San Francisco • New Haven, Conn • Waterville, Maine • London

GALE
CENGAGE Learning®

Copyright © 1994 by Barbara Delinsky.
Thorndike Press, a part of Gale, Cengage Learning.

Thorndike Press® Large Print Famous Authors.
The text of this Large Print edition is unabridged.
Other aspects of the book may vary from the original edition.
Set in 16 pt. Plantin.

LIBRARY OF CONGRESS CATALOGING-IN-PUBLICATION DATA

Delinsky, Barbara.
  For my daughters / Barbara Delinsky. — Large print ed.
    p. cm. — (Thorndike Press large print famous authors)
    ISBN 978-1-4104-5059-3 (hardcover)— ISBN 1-4104-5059-7 (hardcover)
  1. Mothers and daughters—Fiction. 2. Women—Maine—Fiction. 3. Sisters—Fiction. 4. Maine—Fiction. 5. Domestic fiction. 6. Large type books. I. Title.
  PS3554.E4427F67 2012
  813'.54—dc23   2012019169

Published in 2012 by arrangement with HarperCollins Publishers.

Printed in the United States of America
1 2 3 4 5 6 7 16 15 14 13 12

*To Karen and Amy for fighting.
To Steve, Eric, Andrew, and Jeremy
for loving. To readers everywhere
for believing, as I do.*

FOREWORD

My last glimpse of him was as forbidden as all that had gone before, but no less precious. It was early morning. The coastal air was crisp, made tangy by the sea salt it bore. I felt its moisture on my skin and in my hair, and smelled it with an acuity that was to become an indelible splash on my memory's canvas. September had barely arrived, yet the early chill left no doubt that summer was ebbing. With it went a glow that I had never seen before nor would ever see again.

He stood in the door of the gardener's shed, framed by wood the color of the lichen-covered granite headlands that spilled to the sea beyond the bluff. The shed, like the man, had withstood many a coastal winter wind. It was where he lived, and in our summer of nights together, had proven far more a home than any larger, more elegant and pricey residence of mine.

He was a compelling figure. A good head

taller than me, he was lean, but solidly built, as befit his work. His back was straight, his shoulders level, his skin toasted. Eyes that I had initially found darkly mysterious were somber now with a mix of rebuke and desire as they held mine for the last time. Everything about him spoke of the stoicism that was the callus of life along the rugged Maine coast.

A passerby might have thought he was angry, and perhaps there was a touch of that. We had agreed that we wouldn't see each other again, that it would be too difficult after the night. But I couldn't help myself. I needed a final reference, a daylight reference, a reference to last the rest of my life.

Angry, perhaps. More likely dying inside, as I was. Torn by the sorrow of knowing that we had found something priceless and were letting it go. Of our own free will.

Our own free will.

But was one's will ever truly free? Were there ever times in any responsible person's life when choices could be made without a thought to past or future? I was, unfortunately, a responsible person. I could no more have chosen a different course than could Will Cray.

At the main house, my bags were packed

and waiting on the front porch for the battered station wagon that was Downlee's taxi. At the main house, too, was Dominick St. Clair, my husband of four years, the man I had promised to love, honor, and obey in exchange for his magnanimity — and therein lay my challenge. The summer that was to have been one of recuperation and rediscovery had been so, but in unexpected and shattering ways. My job now was to pick up the pieces of this chosen life of mine and reassemble them in some kind of acceptable manner.

I took nothing of Will with me, not the pink beach roses that he had nurtured, that I had worn and breathed, then pressed; not the photographs that had caused such a stir in tiny, parochial Downlee; not the thin leather band that he had woven and given to me to wear in the night. Today I wore a solid gold ring and its companion of emerald-cut diamonds and baguettes, symbolic as nothing else could be of the world to which I returned.

I was twenty-seven that summer, wise to life's material needs yet naive enough in the ways of the heart to think that I could be whole without him.

How wrong I was. My heart stayed with Will Cray, with the salty air, the scent of the pines and the wild honeysuckle, the crimson splash of the dahlias he grew. Tears clogged my throat as I looked on him that final time, as I clung to his warmth for a last minute and melted with the memory of it, as everything inside me cried and the parting tore at the finest, most sensitive and giving parts of me.

Fighting those tears and the doubts that I knew would plague me for years to come, I turned and started down the path. When everything before me blurred, I imagined the fog horn at Houkabee Rocks sounded its mournful warning, and still I pushed on. I stumbled once. I stumbled again, and might have called it fate and run back to him, had not my sense of duty been so strong.

In hindsight, I see that I was driven by something far less noble than duty, and for that my punishment was harsh. The tears I fought that morning as I left him behind froze in my throat, growing hard as stone, a barrier past which softness rarely crept, for in leaving Will I had sentenced myself to a life devoid of emotion.

That was what I now sought to correct.

ONE

The news wasn't good. Caroline St. Clair read the verdict on the jurors' faces well before it was passed to the judge. None of the twelve could look at her. Her client had been found guilty.

The rational part of her knew it was for the best. The man had kidnapped his ex-wife, held her hostage for three days, and repeatedly raped her. A respected state legislator with an otherwise spotless record, he would serve his term in the relative comfort of a federal prison, receive the psychiatric help he needed, and be paroled while he was still young enough to start again. In some regards an acquittal, which would have tossed him to the media and others bent on exploitation at a time when he was as bruised as his ex-wife, would have been more cruel.

But for Caroline each win was crucial. Wins generated renown, renown generated new cases, and new cases fattened the bottom line that was the obsession of the predominantly male partnership of Holten, Wills, and Duluth. Like so many of its kind, it had spent the better part of two decades in overextension, but while other firms folded, Holten, Wills, and Duluth clung to solvency. The cost was a fixation on cutting dead weight, limiting perks, and streamlining operations — and a preoccupation with accounts receivable.

Caroline was one of the newer and, even at forty, younger partners. The future of the firm rested on her shoulders, lectured her older colleagues in the same breath that they grilled her on her billable hours. They didn't like sharing the wealth. Worse, they didn't like women. Caroline had to work twice as hard and be twice as good for the same recognition. She had to be more clever in the manipulation of legal theory, more aggressive negotiating with prosecutors, more effective with juries.

She had badly, badly needed this win.

"Tough break," said one of her fellow junior partners from the door of her office. "The press opportunities would have been good, what with your man's political connections. Now you get exposure for a loss."

Caroline shot him a look that might have

been more stern had he been anyone else. But she and Doug had joined the firm at the same time, both lateral appointees, and though he had been named partner two years before her, she hadn't held it against him. She couldn't afford to. He was her strongest ally in the firm.

"Thanks," she drawled. "I needed that."

"Sorry. But it is true."

"And you think that that thought didn't keep me awake for more than a minute or two last night?" she asked, tapping the desktop with her forefinger, then her pinkie. "I knew the potential for this case when I took it. I thought we had a shot at winning."

"Proving insanity is tough."

"But aside from this one aberration John Baretta has lived an exemplary life," she argued, as she had more eloquently and in greater depth to the jury. "I thought that would count for something."

"Then you do believe he was temporarily insane?"

Caroline had had to believe it. That was the only way she could present an effective defense. With the trial behind her now, though, what would have been, "Definitely!" became, "Arguably." Her fingers kept up their alternating beat. "The man was crazy about his wife. He couldn't accept it when

13

she left him. But he has no history of violence. He's ashamed and apologetic. He isn't a danger to society. He needs therapy. That's all."

"And you need a cigarette."

She stilled her hand. "You bet, but I won't have one. I'm not going through withdrawal again, and I'm not doing anything that'll make me sick. Just think of what the firm would do to me then." She sputtered out a breath. "My friends don't understand. They think that making partner guarantees something, like if I were to become pregnant tomorrow the firm would throw me a shower. They'd throw me out, is what they'd do. They'd find a way to get around the issue of discrimination and toss me out on my tail." She sighed, feeling suddenly tired. "It's so fragile, this thing we call a partnership, this thing we call a career. Is it worth it in the end?"

"Beats me. But what else can we do?"

"I don't know. But something's wrong, Doug. I'm feeling worse for myself for losing a case than I do for my client, and he's the one who'll be doing the time. My values have gotten messed up. All of ours have."

The words had barely left her mouth when a second face appeared at the door. This one belonged to one of the senior partners.

"You allowed too many women on the jury," was his assessment. "They sided with the victim."

Doug slipped away just as Caroline said, "Gender isn't grounds for exclusion."

"You should have found a way to get them off," he answered and continued on down the hall.

She had barely begun to think up a response when another partner appeared. "You shouldn't have let him take the stand. He was looking piteous up to that point. Once he started talking, he sounded slick."

"I thought he sounded sincere."

"The jury didn't," came the chiding reply.

"We can all be brilliant tacticians after the fact," Caroline reasoned, "but the truth is that none of us knows why the jury reached the decision it did."

She was brooding about that moments later when yet another partner stopped by with as much encouragement as she would get. "Put this behind you, Caroline. You need a victory. Take a look at your caseload, pick a good one, and clobber the sucker."

Caroline glanced at the stack of folders on her desk. To each were clipped the telephone messages and memos that had gathered while she had been on trial. She was thinking that she ought to address them but that

15

she wasn't in the mood, when another partner called from the door, "Just try not to mention the name of the firm when you talk with the press, okay?"

Seconds later she found herself staring at the empty doorway feeling something akin to despair when, suddenly, messed up values seemed the least of it. There was selfishness, greed, and partisanship. Not to mention pomposity. And vanity. And condescension.

While she was at it, she threw in ruthlessness, and in that moment couldn't for the life of her understand why she wanted to be associated with these people.

Not caring that she risked the ire of the senior partners by leaving the office while the sun was still up, she filled her briefcase with the files from her desk that would be perfect reading during the wee hours when she couldn't sleep, instructed her secretary on the appointments she wanted made for the next day, and headed home.

Chicago was typically April-cold, but the wind on her face was a relief after too many tense courtroom days and stuffy office nights. Rather than take a cab, as she had in the rush of the weeks past, she buttoned her overcoat, wound her scarf around her neck, and set off on foot.

Fifteen minutes of brisk walking later, she was able to produce a smile for the doorman, who greeted her by name, held the door, then summoned the elevator while she got her mail.

Her condo was on the eighteenth floor with a view of the lake. From the vantage point of the living room sofa, she could freeze the scene at an angle that cropped out all signs of the city and left a portrait of sails in the wind. On a clear day, it was the stuff of which dreams were made.

This day was overcast. She dropped her things on the chair by the door and flipped through the mail. There was nothing of note but one piece, a thick envelope whose Philadelphia postmark was as telltale as the script on its front.

She shouldn't have been surprised. It figured that a message from her mother would arrive on a day like this. Ginny hadn't wanted her to be a lawyer, had thought it a fatal occupation for a woman. Losing a case, as Caroline had just done, would be proof of that, as would the fact that there were neither a husband nor children to greet Caroline at her door.

Caroline and Ginny St. Clair had never seen eye to eye on women's rights. They had never seen eye to eye on much of anything.

Ginny didn't like the ultrashort clip of Caroline's dark hair or the no-nonsense cut of her clothes. She didn't like the fact that Caroline's nails weren't manicured, or that she didn't wear perfume. She didn't understand why Caroline didn't have the maternal instinct of her sister Annette or the social flair of her sister Leah.

The one thing upon which they did agree was that to argue about any or all of this would be futile. So they settled into a relationship of prescribed roles and surface pleasantries. They saw each other on family occasions and chatted sometimes on the phone, and this worked well for Caroline. She had long since stopped looking to Ginny for either warmth or understanding.

With a moment's sigh for what might have been, she dropped the thick letter, along with the rest of the mail, went down the hall to her bedroom, and took off the plum-colored tailored suit that hadn't impressed the jury either. Then, barefoot, wearing jeans and an old shirt rolled to the elbows, she returned to the living room and sank onto the sofa.

The world beyond her window was cloudy and gray, even depressing, and the sleekness of her apartment, with its preponderance of chrome and glass, didn't help. She felt cold, failed, thwarted — none of which made sense on a rational level. She was a successful lawyer, partner in a prestigious firm. She had won enough cases to make today's loss an aberration, and would win plenty more down the road. There was no cause for discouragement. No cause at all. Still, she felt it.

The telephone rang. She counted the rings. With her jaw resting on her palm, she waited through her own voice for the caller to speak.

"This is Mark Spence, *Sun-Times,* wanting a quote for the morning edition. Call me at —"

She let the machine take his number, though she doubted she would use it. She had given quotes to the press outside the courtroom after the verdict had been returned, had made the obligatory mention of faith in her client, the system of justice, and the process of appeal. She had nothing to add.

The answering machine clicked off. Her front buzzer rang. She closed her eyes and willed away whoever was downstairs, but the buzzing went on. Muttering choice things about privacy and the press, she stalked to the intercom and barked, "Yes."

"Hey, pretty lady."

After a moment's pause, she smiled, put her forehead to the wall, and released the angry breath she'd been holding.

It was Ben. Her Ben. As predictably there when she needed him as her mother was not.

"Hey, Ben."

"Need a lift?"

"Don't you know it."

"Buzz me up."

She did, then sank back against the front door with a fluidity in her limbs that she hadn't felt in days. Ben Hammer, with his slow smile and easygoing way, was everything she wasn't, and while she could never take a steady diet of him, in moments of strain he was like a smooth, sweet wine.

She had the door open when he stepped from the elevator looking as loose-limbed, laid-back, and — wearing leather, with his sandy hair mussed from the motorcycle helmet he carried — disreputable as ever.

"Dangerous thing," he chided as he sauntered down the hall, "to open your door before you peek through the hole."

"No one could possibly imitate your voice," she said. It was one of the few simple truths in life. "How are you, Ben?"

He produced a bunch of daisies from behind his back. "Better'n you, I'd wager. I heard the news. Tough break."

She took the flowers, ushered his wind-chilled self inside, and closed the door. "Thanks. These are sweet. A consolation prize."

"Nuh-uh. They're congratulatory."

"But I lost the case."

"So? Win or lose, you tried a damn good one."

"Looks like it wasn't good enough," she murmured on her way to the kitchen. She put the daisies in a square vase and set them on the low slab of glass in the living room. Her decor called for something more chic than daisies, but nothing could have been more cheery.

Ben was lounging against the archway, jacket unzipped now, watching her. Watching him right back, she felt a swell of gratitude. "I should have known you'd come. You usually do, when I'm in need." She reached for his helmet.

"I take it your esteemed partners weren't thrilled."

"To say the least." She set the helmet atop her briefcase in token defiance of those esteemed partners. "Compassion isn't in the firm directory. It's a sign of weakness."

"You don't believe that."

"The partners do, and that's what counts."

21

"Not as long as you have to work there. How do you stand it?"

"I've worked hard to get where I am."

"Definitely. But you have heart. Or you would have, if your partners didn't deem it a waste. They aren't nice people. Doesn't that bother you?"

"Sure, it does. Then a case comes my way that wouldn't have come if I wasn't affiliated with the firm — or the clout of the firm gives me an edge in defending clients — and I realize that it's a tradeoff," which was precisely the conclusion she'd reached during the walk home from work. "We feed off each other, the firm and I."

"They get the better end of the deal."

"You're biased."

"Yup," he said and grinned.

The fluidity Caroline had been feeling became a honeyed melt. She wrapped her arms around his neck and sighed at the relief of it.

Ben was as close to a significant other as she had. While many another man had been scared away, in turn by her frenzy in law school, her dedication to the Cook County prosecutor's office, and her willing self-servitude at Holten, Wills, and Duluth, he had remained undaunted ever since they met, ten years before.

22

He shouldn't have liked her then. She had been the assistant district attorney who had sent his younger brother to prison for computer hacking. But she was fair, he had said with the smile that had been her undoing. When he asked her to dinner, she went, and when they ended up in bed, it seemed the most natural thing in the world.

His life was the antithesis of hers. An artist, he spent weeks traveling the world taking pictures, then months translating those images into silkscreen prints that stole Caroline's breath nearly as consistently as his smile. Art consultants bought entire sets of his prints for placement on corporate walls. Local galleries eagerly sold his work. But when Caroline suggested that he broaden his base and exhibit in San Francisco, Boston, or New York, he merely shrugged. He was as unambitious as she was driven. Each time he completed a series of prints, he spent a long stretch doing absolutely nothing.

Caroline had never done absolutely nothing. She wasn't sure she could. Likewise marriage, which he had suggested dozens of times. Dozens of times she had refused, yet he kept coming back, which was one of the reasons she loved him. He was irrepressible. He made her smile.

She was smiling now, shaking her head not in denial of the inevitable, but in amused resignation. He took a single nip of her mouth, threw an arm around her shoulder, and guided her down the hall. Once in the bedroom, he kissed her until what little tension remained in her body was gone.

As was his habit, he removed his clothes first. Caroline had always suspected that he was simply more comfortable naked when aroused, but if there was a selfishness to it, she didn't complain. Looking at him turned her on, so much so that by the time he leisurely freed her of her own clothes, she was needing far more than just a look.

He gave it to her without reservation, loving every inch of her body until she lost track of time and place for those few precious moments of orgasmic suspension. For all of their differences, in this they fit, and when it was done, when their breathing steadied and their bodies began to cool, there was the sated afterglow in which to bathe.

"Would you have still come to see me if I'd won?" she asked in a whisper that glanced off the tawny hair on his chest.

"You bet. Either way. I was glued to the tube, waiting for the verdict. Left as soon as I heard." He looked down at her. "Come back with me for the weekend?"

She shook her head. "I can't. I'm way behind."

"Bring work with you."

He lived an hour north of the city, in a cabin in the woods. Between the scent of the firs, the abundance of natural sounds, and the preponderance of glass that made the cabin a studio, she fought a losing battle. "I can't concentrate at your place."

"Because you love it there. Confess."

"I love it there."

"So why don't you move in with me? Sell this place, tell your cold-hearted partners to fuck themselves, and live off my money."

She laughed. Of the two of them, she was the one with the money. Not that he wouldn't give her everything he had. "But that's not my life. I'm a city girl."

"You're a masochist."

"I'm addicted to work."

"Not when you're with me."

"I know. You're a bad influence."

"Hah. I keep you sane."

She suspected there was some truth to that. "Yes. Well."

He sighed. "So you won't marry me?"

"Not this week. I have too much to do."

But she wasn't rushing to do anything now. She was feeling mellow in Ben's arms

25

and wasn't ready to leave.

Too soon for her taste, he gave her a warm kiss and slipped from bed. She watched him dress, threw on a robe, and walked him to the door, where she took another kiss. When his presence was nothing more than a musky scent on her skin, she steeped a pot of tea and poured a cup. She drank that, plus a second, before she felt sufficiently steeled to open the envelope her mother had sent.

Dear Caroline, wrote Virginia St. Clair. *Since I haven't heard from you or your sisters to the contrary, I assume that this letter finds you well.*

Caroline made a small, sad sound. Her sisters wouldn't have known if she was sick. She hadn't spoken to either of them in weeks.

I returned from Palm Springs last Tuesday. The weather there was beautiful and the company lovely, as always, but it was good to get home. It's more restful here. I suppose my age is finally catching up with me. I can't go from one dinner to the next the way I used to. Lillian says I'm becoming a hermit. She may be right.

Caroline doubted that. Her mother had been a social creature all her life. She spent mornings at meetings of one ladies' group

26

or another, afternoons playing golf, and evenings playing bridge. If she wasn't attending a dinner at the club, she was hosting one. The death of her husband — the girls' father, Dominick, an innocuous bear of a man — three years before had hardly caused a ripple in that social flow.

Oh, Ginny had mourned him. She had been married to Nick for forty-four years and suffered the loss of a good friend. Had she cried for days? Not quite. That wasn't her way. Nor was it Nick's. He had the complacency that came with being born into wealth. He was confident, noncombative, and undemanding.

Caroline resented him for not demanding more, just as she resented her mother for not giving more. But Nick didn't know how to demand, and Ginny's greatest giving was to social convention. Caroline couldn't imagine age slowing her down.

It was therefore with surprise that she read, *I sold my house here and will be moving in June. My new house is farther north — much farther north, actually — in a small town called Downlee, on the coast of Maine.*

Caroline didn't understand. Her mother had never spent time in Maine. Her mother didn't know anyone in Maine.

Call it a birthday gift to myself, a gift of quiet

*and rest. Do you realize that I'll be turning
seventy in June?*

Yes, Caroline realized it. There were an
even thirty years between her mother and
her, which meant that they shared big
birthday years. Some families would have
thrown joint bashes. Not the St. Clairs.

*The house itself is old and in need of work,
but the grounds are breathtaking. They over-
look the ocean and spread inland, with a
saltwater pool and gardens of heather, wild
rose, primrose, peony, and iris — ah, but flowers aren't your thing. I do know that. And I
know how busy you are, so I'll get to the point.*

*I have a favor to ask of you, Caroline, and
I'm aware that you may refuse. You feel that I
haven't given of myself as I might have to you.
So I have deliberately asked little of you in
the past. But I care a great deal about this
new house, which is why I'm writing you now.
If ever there was a time when I might cash in
on what little feeling you have for me, this is
it.*

Caroline was surprised by Ginny's insight,
and felt the tiniest stab of guilt.

I'd like you to help me settle in.

Come again?

*You have a knack for pulling things together.
I may not be quite as contemporary in my
tastes as you are, but I do admire what you've*

28

done with your apartment.

Flattery will get you nowhere, Mother. Then again . . .

Caroline read on. *You especially have an eye for art. The pieces you've chosen warm up the place. I particularly remember the oil that hangs in your living room. It was done by a friend of yours, I believe.*

Caroline's eye flew to the piece in question. It was something Ben had painted before her own eyes in a single afternoon, a large canvas with splashes of greens, blues, and golds suggestive of a meadow not far from his home. Caroline thought it symbolic of the genius of the man. She adored its simplicity and, yes, its warmth. But it was more abstract than realistic, a definite departure from Ginny's taste.

You use art to soften the harsher lines of the modern decor you favor. Those harsher lines aren't unlike those of the headlands at Downlee. I think you could work wonders with Star's End.

Caroline felt a sense of foreboding as she glanced at the still-thick envelope from which she had taken her mother's letter.

I've enclosed herewith airline tickets that will take you out of O'Hare on the fifteenth of June and return you there at the end of the month.

29

Her jaw dropped.

Yes, I know, two weeks is a long time, and you have a job. That's why I'm writing now. With two months' notice you can plan your work accordingly. Surely you've attained enough stature in your field to do that, and if not, you can always say that this is a family emergency. In a sense it is. I'm not young. I don't know how much time I have left.

"Oh, please," Caroline moaned. She let the vellum fall to her lap. A two-week absence would wreak havoc with her practice. She couldn't possibly do it, regardless of how maudlin Ginny got.

The woman had gall. Caroline had to give her that. She hadn't been much of a mother during Caroline's growing-up years, pre-occupied more often than not, physically present yet distant. She hadn't been emotionally involved enough to help when Caroline had broken up with her first boyfriend or been rejected from her top college choice, and on the day of her graduation from law school, Ginny had had the flu. Oh, she had offered to attend the ceremony anyway, but the offer had been half-hearted, so Caroline hadn't pushed.

Caroline didn't owe Ginny a thing.

Not a thing.

Then again, seventy was seventy.

And Ginny was her mother. Melodrama aside, Caroline would have to be totally unfeeling not to experience a twinge at the thought of the woman dying. She was the only parent Caroline had left.

Feeling frustrated in totally different ways than she had earlier that day, Caroline read on. Ginny, her housekeeper, and the furniture would be arriving a mere day before Caroline — which meant, though Ginny didn't say it, that Caroline would be helping unpack.

Oh, yes, Ginny was sly. And selfish. And presumptuous. She clearly felt that her needs were more vital than Caroline's work.

Caroline sighed. Given the day's verdict, maybe she was right.

Then again, maybe the day's verdict was proof that Caroline did need a vacation. The thought of spending time by the sea, away from the office, with a housekeeper to look after her and, unpacking notwithstanding, little to do but give her opinion on what should go where, held a certain appeal.

The guys might just buy a family emergency.

She hadn't taken more than three days off at a stretch since she had joined the firm. At the rate she was going, by mid-June she would amass a personal best in billable hours, and if that wasn't good enough for the senior partners of Holten, Wills, and Duluth, she didn't know what was. Besides, come late June they would be gone themselves, off to huge lakeside homes for vacations of their own.

So, resentful as she felt that her mother dared to ask for two precious weeks, there was this lure. There was also, unwelcome but inescapable, a glimmer of pride that her mother admired her taste. Ginny hadn't asked for Annette's help. Or Leah's.

And then there were her closing lines. *We haven't been close, you and I. I'd like to try to rectify that, if I might. This would be a good time for us to talk. What do you think?*

What Caroline thought was that Ginny was a cunning old bird. She had offered the one thing Caroline couldn't refuse.

If wasn't fair. It wasn't *right.* Ginny deserved to be rebuffed.

Caroline fully believed that if their positions were reversed and she had been on the inviting end, Ginny would have offered some excuse and politely refused. But she wasn't Ginny. She couldn't possibly do that. For as long as she could remember, along with wanting Ginny's attention, she had been driven by the desire to be different from Ginny. She wasn't about to change now.

Two

The last thing Annette St. Clair could ever be accused of was resembling her mother. Virginia was petite, Annette tall; Virginia was blond, Annette dark; Virginia was cool, Annette warm.

Physically, Annette most resembled her older sister Caroline, a fact that she had cursed for years. Caroline had been a straight-A student, a class leader, an achiever. Following in her footsteps had been a nightmare for Annette, whose strength wasn't so much in academics as in character. She was the Dear Abby of her class; friends turned to her for comfort and support. She listened and advised, and was adored by her crowd.

Unfortunately, prizes weren't given for peer adoration, nor was there an appropriate category for it on a résumé, which was fine. Annette had never needed a résumé. She was a full-time mom, which was, in her judgment, the most important job in the world. She took pride in doing it well, spent upwards of sixteen hours a day at it, and saw the results in a loving husband and five wonderful kids.

Caroline had none of that. For all the times as a child when Annette had envied her, she wouldn't trade places with her now.

Nor would she trade places with Leah — poor, pathetic Leah, whose life was as shallow as Ginny's. In love with the idea of being in love, Leah had rushed into marriage at nineteen and divorced at twenty, married again at twenty-two and divorced three years later. Now thirty-four, she lived for the night, but for all her partying, she remained unattached.

Annette was very definitely attached, which was why she ignored the thick envelope that lay on the kitchen counter with the mail. Between its Philadelphia postmark and the elegant script directing it to St. Louis and Mrs. Jean-Paul Maxime, there was no doubt as to its source. And it could wait. It could wait a good long time, which was how long Annette had waited for her mother to give her a hug and a soft heartfelt, "I love you."

No, Ginny hadn't earned the right to take Annette's time, not when Annette had so much else to do. She had started the morning chaperoning a field trip for twelve-year-old Thomas's class, then had stopped at Neiman Marcus to buy dresses for her sixteen-year-old twins to wear to their semi-formal two weeks hence. While she was at it, she picked up matching shoes and the appropriate underclothing, and now, with the one o'clock chimes in the front hall set to ring, she carted the bundles up the broad spiral stairs.

"Let me help, Mrs. M.," called her housekeeper, Charlene, as she dashed to catch up.

Annette yielded the packages that teetered on top and proceeded to the girls' room, where she removed the dresses and laid them out appealingly, one per bed.

Charlene was all eyes. "They're beautiful."

Annette agreed. "I think they'll be perfect — teal for Nicole and red for Devon. They'll probably want black, of course. Everyone wears black, they'll say. Fortunately, they don't have time to shop for themselves, so they may give in. If they don't, if they absolutely *detest* these, I can return them and try again, but at least we have something to start with." Satisfied, she glanced at her watch. "Let me grab a little lunch. I have an appointment with the second-grade teachers," for Nat, her youngest, "at two, and Robbie's game starts at three."

She started back down the stairs. When the phone rang, she quickened her pace to the kitchen.

"Hi, Mom, it's me."

"Robbie. I was just thinking about your game."

"That's why I'm calling. Don't come, Mom."

"Why not?"

"Because I won't be playing."

"Why *not?*"

"Because the coach just told me so."

"But you had a great season last year."

"That was JV. This is varsity."

"You're an incredible first baseman."

"Hans Dwyer is better, and he's a senior. I'm only a junior."

Annette's heart went out to her son. "Won't you play *at all?*"

"Maybe in the last innings, if we're way ahead or way behind."

"But that isn't fair."

"It happens all the time."

"Then I'll come to watch in case it happens today," Annette decided.

"Please don't, Mom."

"I don't mind," she insisted. "Really."

37

"But I do. I don't *want* you there. It's bad enough that I have to warm the bench, but doing it while you're watching is ten times worse."

"But I'll be cheering for the whole team."

"No, Mom."

"Look," she said appeasingly, "let's not argue. You go to your game and do the best you can. If I get there, I get there; if I don't, I don't." She knew that she would. She would have to be physically debilitated to miss an event in which one of her children was involved, even if, as in Robbie's case, he had little playing time. Being there for her children was how Annette defined herself. She never, never wanted them to know what it was like to see other parents in the stands and not their own.

Jean-Paul tried. He went to games and concerts and recitals whenever he could, but that wasn't often and with good reason. He was a neurosurgeon. His workday ran from seven in the morning until seven at night, and then he had reading to do at home.

So it was doubly important for Annette to attend things like baseball games. She was sure that Robbie's protestations were de rigueur for a seventeen-year-old, but that deep down he agreed.

38

For that reason, she wasn't fazed when he ignored her presence in the bleachers and ran past her with the briefest wave when the game was done. Nor did she linger; he would drive himself home when he was ready, and, besides, she had to fetch Thomas from his trumpet lesson and deliver him to his math tutor, then pick up Nat at his friend's house and get him home for dinner.

She had barely finished with that first dinner shift when the girls came in, full of chatter about the day that had been. As it happened, they weren't wild about the dresses, but not because they weren't black. "We made plans to go shopping with Susie and Beth tomorrow after school," Nicole said.

Annette couldn't see it. "You won't have time. You have two midterms the next day."

"But we've already studied," Devon assured her.

"You have?"

"Well, a little, but we can do the rest after we shop."

"Honest, Mom," Nicole insisted. "We've been planning this for ages."

"But what about these dresses?" Annette asked, gesturing toward the beds.

"They're gorgeous."

"But they're you, not us."

"They are so you," Annette argued. "They're spectacular dresses."

"But we wanted to do this ourselves."

"You don't let us do enough, Mom."

"Because I love shopping for you."

"That's because Grandma never did it for you and you missed it, but we've had it all along."

"Speaking of Grandma," Devon asked, "what did she send in the mail?"

It was a minute before Annette recalled the letter that still sat downstairs. "I don't know."

"You didn't open it?"

"Not yet."

"Aren't you curious?"

"Not awfully," Annette said with a smile and a hand out to each daughter. Touches counted. Even little ones. "You girls interest me far more. Do you want to eat now or later?"

They ate then. Annette kept them company, and did the same when Robbie came home. She didn't eat, herself, until Jean-Paul arrived, and was putting the last of the dishes in the dishwasher when the letter from Philadelphia materialized before her.

"Are you deliberately ignoring this?" Jean-Paul asked in his quiet, lightly accented voice. It was a calming voice, a reassuring voice that instilled faith in his patients and comfort in her.

"I suppose."

"Tit for tat?"

She laughed softly, ruefully.

He gave the letter a little wave. She took it between a wet thumb and forefinger and tossed it on the counter. "Later. When I've finished everything else." Her first priorities were the children. She didn't want anything marring her time with them.

Communication with her mother was bound to do that. It always did. She could more successfully push her sisters from mind, and keep them there, than she could Ginny. Too much resentment remained, sparked by memories of only token closeness and a squandered family life. Ginny had been there, without being there. Annette's major focus in life was to be there all the way.

She'd be damned if she'd let her mother thwart her now.

But she could only drag out the evening so long. In time Nat and Thomas were in bed, and the older three were either studying or on the phone. Each had kissed her an enthusiastic goodnight in a dismissal of the gentlest sort.

So Annette changed into her nightgown

and slipped into bed beside Jean-Paul. He was propped against the pillows, his reading glasses midway down the aristocratic Gallic nose that the twins had mercifully inherited, his long limbs loose and bare beneath the sheets.

Only then, with the promise of his comfort at hand, did she unfold her mother's letter and begin to read. Almost immediately she snorted.

"Quoi?" Jean-Paul asked.

"She starts off by saying that she assumes the seven of us are well, since she hasn't heard anything to the contrary from me or my sisters. Poor Mother. She still pretends that we're one big happy family. But neither Caroline nor Leah would know if one of us was sick. I haven't talked with them in weeks."

"Sad," he mused, but without criticism. "How would you feel if our children grew up to be strangers?"

"Terrible, which is why I'm raising them to be friends. They don't have to compete for my time or affection the way my sisters and I had to do for Ginny's. I have more than enough to go around."

She returned to the letter, only to grunt a minute later. "She's just back from Palm Springs, saying it's quieter in Philadelphia —"

42

She gasped. "Oh my. She's sold the house. And bought a new one in *Maine?*" She frowned at Jean-Paul. "This doesn't make sense."

"Why not?"

"Mother is first and foremost a fixture of society. She doesn't *know* anyone in Maine." She continued under her breath as she read on. "And this isn't even Portland. It's a small coastal town, something of an artists' colony, from what she says. She's turning seventy." Again Annette raised her eyes to Jean-Paul, this time for reassurance, because much as she begrudged Ginny's performance as a mother, the fact of her aging was unsettling. "Seventy is getting up there."

"Your father was older than that when he died."

"But Mother's different. She barely looks sixty."

"She's also female, so you identify with her."

"No, I don't. Not one bit." She escaped Jean-Paul's amused look by returning to the letter, but kept up a soft commentary as she read. "Star's End — that's the name of the place — is a birthday gift to herself. She says it has a beautiful garden. Leah will be thrilled. She'll be able to cut and arrange to her heart's delight. Of course, way up there in Maine there won't be anyone of import to ooh and aah over her ornamental genius."

"Annette," he chided.

But Annette had an old gripe to air. "No problem. Mother will ooh and aah. Leah was always her favorite."

"Come now."

"It's true. Leah was the only one of us who had any taste for the country club. Uh-oh. Mother says she has a favor to ask of me." She chuckled dryly. "She says she knows I may refuse. How intuitive, Ginny."

"Annette."

Finally she felt a twinge of guilt. "Sorry. I have trouble being generous where my mother is concerned." She fell silent as she read on. The silence lengthened, until Jean-Paul broke it with the rustle of his papers when he set them aside.

"Quoi?"

"The woman is amazing. Truly." She peered inside the envelope, then tossed it to the foot of the bed. "That's an airline ticket. She wants me to spend the last two weeks in June helping her settle in. She says that she's always admired the warmth in our house here. As though the decor provides the warmth. Doesn't she understand that it comes from people, not things?"

44

"She wants you to *decorate* the new house?"

"Not decorate, exactly. More like help christen the place."

"It sounds like it would be fun," Jean-Paul said so seriously that Annette twisted away and gaped up.

"I'm not going!"

"Why not?"

"I have obligations here — obligations that mean a sight more to me than doing my mother a favor. I can't just pick up and leave here for two weeks. I don't owe her that. She never did it for me. Besides, it would be one thing if she sent tickets for you and the kids, but that wouldn't occur to her. She has no idea what my family means to me."

"She probably assumed the kids would be in school."

"The fact that she assumed wrong shows how far removed she is. They'll be smack in the limbo period between school and summer plans. Thomas and Nat will be getting into mischief until camp starts, and neither Robbie nor the girls start their jobs until the very end of the month. Those two weeks would be *the* worst time for me to go. Not that I'd want to go, in any case."

"Your mother admires your taste."

"Uh-huh."

"She wouldn't ask this of you if she didn't. She isn't asking Caroline or Leah."

Annette had to admit that there was some satisfaction in that. Of the three of them, she most embodied what Ginny had tried but failed to achieve.

Jean-Paul was quiet. When he didn't return to his reading, she gave him a nudge. He set his glasses aside and said, "I think you should consider going."

"It's out of the question."

"It shouldn't be. She's asking you a favor. Yes, I know you feel you don't owe her anything, but she did give you life. If she hadn't done that, I wouldn't have had you, and our children would never have been born. She is your mother, Annette."

"But I'm needed *here*."

"Well, that's what we all believe," he said with a sigh, "but wouldn't it be nice to find that we can function without you for two weeks out of our lives."

"Of course, you can do that."

"Can we? We won't know unless we try."

"But it's such a *bad time*."

"Actually," he said slowly, "it's not a bad time at all. Rob and the girls will be around to watch Thomas and Nat. They could take turns planning activities to keep them busy."

Annette rose on an elbow and studied his face. "You're serious."

It was a minute before he offered a thoughtful, "Yes."

"But this is my *mother,* Jean-Paul. You know how I feel about her."

"Yes. I know how. But I never totally understood why. What did she do that was so awful?"

Annette pushed a pillow against the headboard. "It was what she didn't do." She collapsed back on the pillow, depriving Jean-Paul of her closeness as punishment for his doubt. "She was an automaton of a mother. She went through the right motions and did everything she was supposed to, only she was never emotionally involved. Not deeply. I told you about the bedroom incident. That's a perfect example."

"I never saw what was so wrong with what she did."

"Jean-Paul," Annette complained, "she treated me like a nothing!"

"Because she did over your bedroom while you were away at summer camp?"

"Because she didn't involve me. She didn't ask what I wanted. She didn't ask *if* I wanted a change. No, *she* decided what would be done when, and it wasn't only me. It was Caroline and Leah, too. She just swept through our bedrooms that summer without any consideration of who each of us was. We came home to find bedrooms that were all gorgeous, all nearly identical, all utterly lacking in character."

"She wanted you to have pretty things."

"She did what she wanted, not what we wanted. She couldn't be bothered with that, which is my point. She was never really into us or our lives. She always held a part of herself back from us. As children, we always felt she disapproved. We always felt we were the ones lacking for failing to interest her. We always felt we had done something wrong."

"Maybe that was just her personality. Not everyone can be warm like you. Not everyone can be as emotionally involved with her family."

"But it took a toll, that constant feeling that we couldn't please her. Caroline became obsessed with being the best lawyer in the world, and she may be that, even if she is a cold fish personally. Leah became obsessed with being loved, and she may be that, for a night here and there."

"And you became obsessed with being the best mother in the world."

"Not obsessed. That's too harsh a word."

"But accurate. It's what you want most to do."

"Maybe," she relented, "but what's wrong with that?"

"Nothing. Only you're afraid to leave us for even a few short weeks."

"Not afraid."

"I think, afraid."

Annette would have been offended if she had been less sure of Jean-Paul's love, but they were best of friends, in addition to the rest. "Explain," she said now.

It was a minute before he did so, and then his voice was gentle. "We are your life. You devote yourself solely to us. The love in this family embodies everything you missed when you were a little girl. You are afraid of losing it."

She shook her head, but he went on.

"You are afraid that if you aren't there to hand us a tissue each time we sneeze, something will be lost. You'll be negligent, like your mother. The love will vanish."

She snorted. "I'm not that bad."

"But you are afraid. You are afraid that if you aren't intimately involved in the lives of our children, they will resent you and drift away from you, the way you drifted away from your mother."

"Every woman fears the day when her

children leave the nest."

"But you don't have to," he said more insistently now. "Your children love you. They know how much you love them, and they know how much you do for them. Their experience with you is totally different from your experience with Virginia. They are bound to you, Annette. If you are not here, they will miss you."

"There you have it. That's why I'm not doing Mother's bidding."

His voice lowered gravely. "But they need to know that they can miss you and still survive without you. That's part of growing up. They need to be able to do without you, then feel joy when they have you back."

"But why go without when you don't have to?"

"You do have to. You're too involved sometimes, Annette. You need to let the children breathe."

"And you?" she asked with a qualm. "Do you need to breathe, too?"

He smiled. "Oh, I breathe fine with you by my side." The smile grew sad. "But you need to breathe, yourself."

"I breathe when I'm here with my family."

"You need to see yourself as an individual. Everyone needs that. I can do it at work.

But with you, work is home and home is work and there isn't any separation, any way to put it all into perspective. And then there's your mother. You are right. She's getting up there. Reaching seventy is a gift in itself. You don't know how much longer she has."

"That's what she said," Annette muttered. "Preying on my sympathies."

"You ought to make peace with her."

"We're at peace."

He studied her, slowly shook his head, said nothing.

"Well, it's a kind of peace," Annette allowed, though she couldn't seem to shake Ginny's closing words. *We haven't been close in the past, but that doesn't mean we can't find common ground. It would be nice to spend time together. We might talk.*

"You can improve it."

"But I don't want to go."

He sighed. "I know." He reached for her and drew her against him. She didn't resist. "Think about it, though? Think about how you would feel if you were seventy and I was gone —"

She covered his mouth. "Don't even think it."

He removed her hand and held it tight. "But it may be one day. Think if you were

51

seventy and asked this of one of your children. How would you feel if that child refused?"

"I'd be *crushed,* but my mother isn't me. I doubt she cares deeply one way or the other whether I go."

"She went so far as to send you the tickets. She cares."

Annette suspected he was right, which was the bitch of it all. He was usually right, Jean-Paul was, in those very few times when he disagreed with her, but he did it in such a nice way that she loved him all the more.

Of *course,* the children could survive without her. Of *course,* they wouldn't suddenly hate her for spending two weeks with her aging mother. It was a one-time shot. There weren't any proms or recitals or playoff games during those weeks. She would be back before they knew it. Of *course,* their love wouldn't die.

Her head knew all this, but her heart? Ah, that was something else. And he was right about that, too, Jean-Paul was. She was afraid. Just a little. Of being like her mother.

THREE

Leah St. Clair lived in fashionable Woodley Park. On any given day, her travel around town took her past embassies, the State Department, the White House, and the Capitol. On any given night, she hobnobbed with people associated with those buildings. They were her friends, her social circle. Theirs wasn't the only social circle in Washington, or the most elite, but it was exclusive. Membership was prescribed, attendance at parties predictable, whether those parties' purposes were political, charitable, or social. At any time Leah knew whom she would see and what she would say. She could run through the conversation in her sleep.

This evening she had hosted twenty-four for dinner. With the last of those guests now gone and the caterers packing up in the kitchen, she combed the living room, scooping up crumbs, wiping away condensation rings, erasing spills from marble, glass, and wood.

Great party, Leah. Great food. Gorgeous flowers.

She took a minute to admire the tall scarlet-and-white lilies that spiked from crystal bowls in elegant trios. Moving closer, she wrapped herself in their scent. It wasn't her favorite; she was more a lilac, even a honeysuckle person. But she preferred a lily bouquet to the memory of cigars that clung stalely to the corners of the room.

She resisted the urge to open the windows. It would be a futile effort. The April night air was warm and humid, not at all the clean, dry, bracing air she craved.

She removed stubs of candles from sterling candlesticks and picked at waxy drips, sweeping them into her palm along with the glitter that had decorated the table.

Stunning presentation, Leah. Simple but festive. Shiny. Sophisticated.

And the food had been *great* — the tenderloin butter-soft, the béarnaise perfectly piquant. Even the fiddlehead ferns, on whose preparation she had had to tutor the chef herself, had been divine.

She frowned at a splotch of pink on the Indian oriental in the den. What had once been a fine red Bordeaux was on its way to becoming a permanent stain. Loath to let that happen, she fetched the proper solution, hiked up her long gown, and knelt. She sprayed and blotted, sprayed and blotted. Gradually the stain began to fade. She continued to spray and blot until it was little more than a shadow, then she sat back in triumph.

"We're leaving now, Ms. St. Clair," called the caterer.

She gave a satisfied smile and a wave, but didn't rise. She had already thanked him and tipped his staff accordingly. Experience told her that a hefty bill would be in the mail the very next morning.

The door closed. In the sudden silence, her contentment waned.

She went at the stain on the rug once more for good measure, then stood and looked around. This was her home, yet, in the wake of the invasion of the night's strangers, not so. The emptiness was stark, the remains of the party few but grating. She felt deserted, stranded in a place of frozen smiles.

A good cleaning would remedy the situation. By the time her woman was done the next day, the party would be history, the cigar smoke gone, home would be home, and Leah would relax.

She returned a displaced side chair to its proper position, straightened picture frames, disposed of several crushed cocktail napkins that the caterers had missed.

It had been a great party. A great party. Conversation had flowed, intriguing at times, amusing at others. The bores of the group had been pleasantly quiet. She tried to pick out the high point of the evening, but details blurred with other parties on other nights.

Feeling suddenly muddled and in need of escape, she flipped off the lights and climbed the two flights of stairs to her bedroom. There, in the dark, she slipped out of the long white gown that had given elegance to her waifishness, and, wearing only the silk teddy that had been beneath it, stood at the window's edge. Far below, the courtyard was an amber glow through the spray of budding branches, a diffused portrait of a wrought-iron bench and chairs set to advantage in an urban garden.

The thought of working in the garden that weekend brought her a measure of calm.

She sank onto the window seat with her back to the hunter green wall. She loved this room, with its preponderance of white wicker on hunter, loved this spot with its garden view. When her neighbors complained about the smallness of their third-floor rooms, she never joined in. The smallness here gave her comfort. The coziness warmed her. The walls defined a segment of the world that was wholly familiar and blessedly safe.

Gingerly she shifted her head against the wall, then brought it forward and pulled out the pins that had held her hair in a tidy knot for so many long hours. When they lay in a neat pile, she ran her fingers through her hair. Like a dry sponge watered, the blond mane took on volume and curl such that it pillowed her head when she sat back again.

She thought of the party. She looked at the courtyard. She listened to the silence.

She sighed once, then again, and when her vision blurred, she closed her eyes. She was tired. That was all. And expecting her period, which always made her weepy. Then, of course, there was the inevitable letdown after a party. All the work done. Nothing more to do but plan another.

She opened her eyes to a lovely idea. She would redecorate. That was always good for a lift. The living room could use new wall-covering. No, the kitchen. A new stove. A larger one this time, a professional one. She loved cooking. If she had three small dinners for eight, rather than a big bash for twenty-four, she could do the cooking herself.

Not that her friends would appreciate it. The women among them might actually be threatened, which would be a surefire way of drawing catty comments. Leah didn't need that. She had insecurities enough.

Still, she might invest in that stove. She could cook for herself. Or, hell, for the local soup kitchen.

Pushing up from the window seat, she crossed to the corner armchair. A cashmere shawl was draped on its back. She transferred it to her own, sank into the deep cushions of the chair, and drew in her arms and feet. She adjusted the shawl until it covered all of her but her head.

Perhaps a stove.

Then again, the stove could wait. Summer was coming, and she was going away — assuming she could decide on a destination. She had given thought to her travel agent's suggestions, but Hong Kong was too busy, Costa Rica too hot, Paris too coupled. Alaska was a possibility; the cruiseship the travel agent proposed was small and personal. She might not feel as lost as she would on something larger.

What she really wanted was to go on a cattle drive. The romance of the Old West held a certain appeal.

But she had never been one for horseback riding, or for roughing it, and doubted she could survive a cattle drive, even *with* a friend, though none of hers wanted to go. She suspected that things like cattle drives, even luxury ones of the type she was considering, were better dreamed of than lived through.

Still there wasn't any harm in looking into it. She had sent for information. She wondered when it would arrive.

With that thought came the realization that she hadn't yet seen the day's mail. It had arrived late that afternoon, when she was caught up in preparation for the evening.

Holding the shawl tightly closed, she went barefoot down the two flights of stairs to the kitchen, where the mail stood propped between bright copper canisters. Anticipation lifted her spirits. She loved getting mail. There was always the chance that someone new might call or write, that something totally unexpected might happen. For all she knew, her life was about to take an exciting twist.

She flipped through. The information on the cattle drive hadn't come. Nor had a letter from a secret admirer who had just now decided to declare himself. The only communication to arrive that day with any element of surprise was from her mother.

Experience told Leah that there would be little sweet-talking from that source. But hope died hard, even after years of neglect. Excited in spite of herself, she tore open the thick envelope and read the letter inside. She paused midway to peek at the airline tickets. When she had finished the letter, she tucked it back into the envelope with the tickets and took it upstairs. After turning on the low lamp beside the bed, she snuggled under the comforter, took the letter out, and read it again.

Not sweet-talking, exactly. But surely a compliment, and, in that, flattering. Virginia St. Clair didn't hand out compliments easily, though not because of arrogance, pride, or impossibly high standards. Only recently had Leah come to understand that. The truth was that when flattery might have been appropriate, her mother's mind was off somewhere else.

Leah refused to consider all the reasons why she shouldn't go to Maine. Rather, she fell asleep thinking about Virginia's request and slept the night through lulled by hopes and dreams.

Excitement woke her at eight the next

morning. She laughed at her startled cleaning woman, who was accustomed to letting herself in and not seeing Leah until later, let alone bright-eyed and bushy-tailed. But Leah was buoyant. She knotted her hair back, put on a silk lounging suit, and indulged in a bowl of raspberries and cream at the table on the edge of the courtyard. She sipped coffee while she read the paper, and bided her time with varying degrees of good-natured impatience until ten o'clock arrived. Only then did she dare phone her mother.

Virginia was out.

"This *early?*" Leah asked in dismay.

"She's at the hair shop," Gwen said. Gwen was more than a housekeeper. She was Virginia's right hand. "I expect she'll be there until noon."

Leah refused to be deflated. "Then I'll try her at twelve-fifteen."

"She's going straight from the hair shop to the club."

"Lunch can't last very long," she insisted. "I'll try back at two or so."

"After lunch she's playing bridge."

Echoes of the past burst into sound. If it wasn't one thing it was another. "And after that?" Leah asked, wary now.

"I believe," Gwen said apologetically, "that

she'll be at the dressmaker's. The Robinsons are having a dinner party tonight, and the new dress your mother ordered was late in arriving."

"Ahhh," Leah said. New dresses for dinner parties did take precedence over daughters. Any fool knew that.

She supposed she might have caught Virginia at home for the few minutes when she was preparing for the party, but it suddenly didn't seem worth the effort. After telling Gwen that there was no message, she pressed the disconnect button and punched out another number. She hadn't called this one in a while either.

Several hours later, tucked in an old familiar corner of Ellen McKenna's leather loveseat, she unburdened her heart. "I spent all of last night being excited, thinking that maybe Mother really does find comfort in me, that maybe she really does need me, that maybe she really *does* want to be with me. Then I tried to call her today, and she's out doing all of the other things that mean more to her than me. Okay. I can accept it. Nothing's changed — which makes this all so absurd."

"What all?"

"Her letter. The fact that she's sold the house, which is a huge change. Mother is a

62

social creature. I can't believe she's removing herself from civilization."

"Is she?" Ellen asked in her gentle, non-judgmental way. She was nearly as petite as Leah, though twenty years older and silver-haired. The fact that in those basics she resembled Virginia, was something they had discussed at length. "What do you know about Downlee?"

"Only what she wrote in her letter, that it's a small town. But Mother isn't the small-town type. She's lived all her life in the city."

"Maybe she's always dreamed of living elsewhere."

Leah considered that. As improbable as it sounded, she couldn't rule it out. Virginia's dream world, if one did exist, was a mystery to Leah. "But if that had been at the back of her mind," she thought aloud, "wouldn't something of it have slipped out last year? We spent hours sitting together in doctors' offices. If that wasn't a time for thinking about mortality and dreams that may or may not come true, I don't know what is."

Ellen remained silent.

After several minutes, Leah said, "I know. She was never a sharer. After keeping her thoughts to herself all those years, this shouldn't surprise me. It's just that I thought — I thought —" She tried to stand back, as Ellen had taught her to do in four years of therapy, and view her expectations and emotions from a distance and hence with greater objectivity. "I had hoped that last year might have made a difference. I was there for her then. And she did thank me. But once the worst was over, that was it. She went her own way. She was her usual, detached self."

"What might you have liked?" Ellen asked quietly.

"A bouquet of flowers, a call now and then, an invitation to Palm Springs. Hell —" Leah threw up a hand. "I don't know. I'd like to have gone to lunch with her and talked." She frowned at the letter that lay open on her lap. "She says something here. At the very end. She says she regrets that we've never done that — really talked — and that she's hoping we can do it in Maine. She says that she's looking forward to spending time with me." She gave the letter a despairing nudge. "Can a leopard change its spots?"

"This may be a belated bow to last year's brush with mortality," Ellen offered.

"I could have bought that, if she'd been at home waiting for my phone call. Or if she'd told Gwen to ask if I was coming. Gwen does whatever Mother wants. But Mother was out. Like it really doesn't matter, one way or the other, whether I take her up on her invitation or not." She sighed. "Okay. So she wants to talk. But Mother is shallow. Substantive discussions scare the heeby-jeebies out of her. She avoids them like the plague."

That didn't explain the words she had written, words Leah clung to against her better judgment. "Maybe she does want to talk. Maybe she'll actually try. Then again," more realistically, "maybe these tickets are her way of thanking me for last year. I mean, it's me she's invited to Maine, not Caroline or Annette."

"Have you spoken with either of them?"

"Not since I got this letter."

That wasn't what I was asking, Ellen's arched brows said.

Leah sighed. "It's been a while."

"Still not comfortable doing it?"

She shook her head. "When I think of calling Caroline, I picture her snowed under with work of some critical nature. She thinks I'm a ditz. She'll resent my interrupting her. And when I think of calling Annette, I just *know* that she'll be busy with the kids."

"That doesn't mean she wouldn't like to hear from you."

65

"She doesn't call me."

"Maybe she thinks you don't want to hear from her."

"That's no excuse. She's older than I am. She should take the lead. Besides, she's the family-oriented one. If she considered me family, she would call."

"She may be thinking the same about you. She may be thinking that you have more time than she does."

"No doubt she thinks that. She thinks my life is a waste."

"Has she ever said that?"

"Not in as many words, but I know she's thinking it."

"How do you know?"

There were facial expressions and tones of voice. There were comments of the type women made, that were indirectly direct. And, to Leah's chagrin, there was her own hypersensitivity, which Ellen had helped her see, though not quite overcome.

"I think," she said with a sheepish smile, "that we've had this discussion before."

"But not for a while. It's been months since I've seen you, Leah. I take it there have been no major upheavals in your life?"

"No major upheavals." Or she would have called Ellen sooner. Ellen knew more about her than any soul on earth, and if there was sadness in having to pay someone to listen to one's woes, Leah didn't care. Ellen was an insurance policy on sanity. She was worth far more than she charged.

"All is serene?"

"Serene is one word for it."

"Give me another."

"Uneventful."

"And another."

"Boring." The word hung in the air.

"Is boring bad?" Ellen finally prompted.

Leah considered that. "I don't know. Boring isn't traumatic. It isn't threatening. Well, maybe it is."

"In what way?"

She tried to pin it down. "Frightening. To think that the life I have now may be the life I'll have for the rest of my life."

"You don't want that?"

"Part of me does. I've been named chairperson for next year's Cancer Society benefit. It's an honor. I've worked a long time to get it."

"So what's frightening?"

"After that. *Beyond* that." She sighed. "I know, I know. If I don't like my life, I can change it. I have that power." She and Ellen had discussed this at length during their last few sessions together. Nothing had changed since then — neither Leah's reluctance to take that power into her own hands, nor Ellen's inability to do it for her. As her therapist, Ellen could only take her so far. It was up to Leah to do the rest.

"I'm looking," Leah said now. "I'm waiting for the right time. When I see a change for the better, I'll go for it." She frowned. "Assuming I can recognize that it's for the better. My record isn't great. First Ron, then Charlie. Face it. I've made some lousy mistakes."

"Not lately. Not for a while. Don't condemn yourself for things that happened years ago. You were younger then, and naive. I dare say that if you met either Ron or Charlie now, you wouldn't be in the least bit interested."

"Lord, I hope not. But then there are those times when I'm feeling desperate and thinking that anyone would be better than no one. Thank God, those times always pass, but they leave me doubly cautious. Maybe too much so. Caution can be paralyzing."

After a bit, Ellen said, "Is that what you're feeling today? Paralysis?"

"Some. I'm confused. I need to talk with someone who knows me well."

"You have friends."

Leah studied her hands. "It's hard to

confide in the kind of people I know. Gossip is . . . well, it's a way of life. When you see the same people night after night, you eventually run out of things to say, so you pass on something you heard. You don't intend to say it — well, the kind friends don't. It just slips out to fill a lull in the conversation." She looked up. "I'm not justifying it. I hate it. But I can't condemn everyone who does it. I can't say that my friends are bad people just because they let something slip once in a while." She knew she sounded defensive, but she had a point to make. "I like my friends. I just want to be careful about what I share with them, that's all." She grinned. "You, on the other hand, are bound by ethical considerations, so I can tell you anything and everything I want."

Ellen smiled. With that momentary softening and brightening of her face, she was the mother Leah had always wanted. Virginia had never, to Leah's memory, looked soft and bright. Virginia had never listened to her woes.

"I don't know what to do, Ellen. If I go to Maine, I'll be giving in to the old insane need for Mother's approval. If I don't, I'll risk alienating her forever."

Ellen nodded her own approval, which

was, in part, what Leah had come for. "That seems to sum it up. You do have a grip on the situation, Leah."

"I should after all this time, don't you think? Yes, I want her approval — I've always wanted it — and yes, I'm aware that I do, but that doesn't make it go away. Hence, the dilemma. I mean, Mother isn't inviting me there to fawn over me. Sure, she says she wants to spend time with me, but I think she says that because she knows it's the one thing that would get me there, but when push comes to shove, she doesn't really *need* me there."

"Perhaps, given her health problems and your knowledge of them, she feels more comfortable with you around."

"But she's fine, now. The doctor said so. It was really a false alarm that got blown out of proportion by her own fear, which she kept firmly locked inside and denies to this day. And her housekeeper will be with her — Gwen does *everything* — not to mention the movers, who'll have the unpacking all done, and whatever other hired help the place comes with. So I'm flattered. But skeptical."

Ellen grew thoughtful. "Why do you think she wrote, rather than called?"

"Cowardice. She thought I'd refuse, so

she wrote and sent the tickets to give it the feeling of a done deed. Either that," Leah added, "or it's sheer gall, a command performance. I can't decide which."

"Does one make you feel better about going than the other?"

"*Neither* makes me feel terribly good. I like being here. I'm used to being here. I know the people here, and they know me."

Ellen heard all that Leah hadn't said. "There will be new people in Maine."

"I'm not good with new people."

"But you're bored here."

"Bored, but comfortable. Besides, seeing Mother makes me angry. She's always so perfectly calm and composed. Even during the heart business, it was like she was resigned to her fate. Okay, so she was suppressing her fear, but I swear that deep down I was still more scared than she was. I half think that's why she wanted me along — to express the emotion she couldn't, so that the doctors and nurses would think she was being calm for my sake and, hence, normal. She's a tough lady. And ballsy." Leah couldn't help it, the venom escaped. "I mean, if she wants to relocate in her old age, that's fine, but she has some nerve asking me to take two weeks out of my life to help her do it. She never took two weeks

71

out for *me,* not even that summer when I was so sick."

Leah had been fifteen and bulimic in the days before bulimia was in style. After collapsing one day, she was rushed to the hospital, where she had remained for a month. Virginia had been oblivious to any problem in the days preceding the collapse, and in the days after, she had been attentive — but not so much that her normal routine had been upset. She hadn't missed one round of the golf tournament in which she had been competing at the time.

"Did you ever discuss that when you were together last year?" Ellen asked.

"No. It wasn't the appropriate time for me to be angry with her. I wanted to be supportive and helpful."

"Everything she never was, and in that, your revenge?"

Leah made a face. "Something like that. Not that it worked. Mother isn't the intuitive type. My motives went right over her head — and they will this time, too, if I go to Maine. I shouldn't go. Really I shouldn't. I should mail the tickets right back to her with a polite thanks but no thanks. I should tell her that I just can't spare the time." She wanted to do that in the very worst way, but the bald truth was that she had the time.

She had those two weeks and more. Unless she decided to redo the kitchen. Or take a trip. It would serve Virginia right, if Leah were to turn her down flat.

Despairingly, she faced Ellen. "But I won't do that, will I? I'll go there for those two weeks, even though I don't know a soul there, and I'll play the dutiful daughter, even though she won't begin to appreciate it."

"She may, Leah. She's approaching a milestone of a birthday. That might be having an effect on her. You may be surprised."

"That would be nice. I suppose it's one reason for going."

"Give me another."

"She's my mother."

"And another."

"She asked me, not Caroline or Annette."

"And another."

"She's almost seventy and could die tomorrow and leave me feeling guilty for the rest of my life, and when all is said and done, I want her approval. This may be my last chance." Last chance. A heavy thought. "She says she wants to spend time with me. She says she wants to talk. It's what I've always wanted. How can I say no?" She tried to think of a way, but couldn't. "That's it in a nutshell, I guess. I don't want to go.

But I can't *not* go." She rose from the sofa.

Ellen walked her to the door. "There's more, Leah. The thing about being with new people — you can handle it. You'll prove to yourself that you can. And more — you're still not into thinking as highly of yourself as you should, but the fact is that you'll go to Maine because you're a good person. You really are. You're not like your mother one bit. You care, and you aren't afraid to let it show. That's healthy."

"Yeah, and at the end of the two weeks, when she smiles and pats me on the head and sends me home like she's always done in the past, what then?"

"Then you'll know you've tried your best and have nothing to regret. You'll have had a two-week vacation, you'll have survived in a new environment, and you'll be back here with nothing lost. Your eyes are open, Leah. You know what to expect and what not to expect. You'll do just fine."

In the weeks that followed, Leah clung to that thought, even as she tried to find a compelling reason not to use the tickets Virginia had sent.

She called Susie MacMillan, whose third husband was a former ambassador with ongoing ties to the diplomatic corps. They were mainstays at Leah's parties. "Hi, Susie. It's Leah. How are you?"

"On my way out the door," Susie said breathlessly. "Mac and I are heading for dinner at the embassy, then taking off for Newport."

"I was thinking of throwing something wonderful at the end of the month," Leah tried. "Will you be back?"

"Barely. Better count us out, Leah. Maybe another time."

Leah tried Jill Prince. She and Jill worked Cancer Society functions together. Jill's husband was the head of a prominent Washington think tank. "Hi, Jill. It's Leah. What's doing?"

"God, Leah, life is hectic. The kids are finishing up the school year, so there are cookouts, banquets, recitals, you name it, and in the middle of it all, I'm trying to get them ready for camp. What's doing with you?"

"Not much. I thought maybe we could do lunch next week."

Jill sighed. "I can't, Leah. I can't plan anything until the kids are gone, and once we drop them at camp, we're continuing on to Quebec. Maybe when I get back?"

Leah tried Monica Savins. Monica didn't have a husband or kids. But she did have boyfriends. "I'd *love* driving out to the spa with you, Leah, but it's not a good time." Her voice grew confidential. "I'm seeing Phillip Dorian." When Leah didn't immediately react, she said, "He's with the National Symphony? Plays violin? He has *the* most incredible hands." She sucked in a breath and let it out in a rapturous sigh. "Another time. Gotta go, now. Howard's taking me to lunch. You know Howard. He's with CNN." Her voice lowered again. "Howard doesn't know about Phillip, and I'm trying to keep it that way. You won't breathe a word to anyone, will you?"

Leah promised that she wouldn't, and it was a promise that was easy enough to keep, given that Monica's social life embarrassed her. Besides, she had her own agenda. She called a handful of other friends, but those two weeks in June were shaping up to be a total void where social happenings were concerned. People were either traveling, or moving to summer homes, or visiting friends.

Leah, on the other hand, would be in steamy Washington with no one but the censorious ghost of her mother, unless she flew to Maine.

Some things seemed preordained. This was one.

Besides, her life was stalled. It struck her that Virginia might be the unfinished business that prevented her from moving on.

And she did want to move on. Truly. Quickly. Desperately.

FOUR

Caroline was hoping that engine trouble might force a cancellation of her flight. When that didn't happen and her plane took off on time, she hung her hopes on the possibility that air traffic or fog would cause a delay or, better still, force a landing in an airport other than Portland. She would happily set herself up in a hotel room in Boston, Providence, or Hartford, and, using the computer notebook she had with her and a rented fax machine, work nearly as productively as if she were in her Chicago office.

To her consternation, the plane touched down at the Portland Jetport quietly, smoothly, and five minutes early. Moreover, the one small bag she had brought — that she might have easily carried on board but had checked, daring the airline to lose it — was one of the first to appear on the carousel.

She hoisted it to her shoulder. The briefcase that held her files and the computer was heavier. Gripping it firmly, she crossed to the nearest phone bank and called the office.

"Hi, Janice," she said to her secretary. "I'm in Portland. Just wanted to find out what's doing there."

Janice was ten years older than Caroline, a whiz of a legal secretary, and annoyingly intuitive. "Not much since you called from O'Hare," she chided. "Timothy's still working on Westmore and Beth on Lundt."

Timothy and Beth were the associates Caroline shared with Doug. She had left both with mounds of work to do in her absence.

"Have there been any calls?" Caroline asked.

"No. We told everyone that you were going away."

"Mmm. Well. If anyone does call, you know where to reach me, don't you?"

"I have your mother's number right here."

Caroline checked her watch. "It's just about two. I'll be leaving as soon as the driver from Downlee arrives." She had a clear view of the taxi stand and saw nothing resembling the wood-paneled station wagon Virginia had described. "We'll be driving for two hours. It's too much to hope that there'll be a phone in the car, so if you need me during that time, leave a message at Star's End. I'll check back with you as soon as I get there. Is Doug around?"

"Hold on."

Doug came on the line a minute later. "Long time no see."

"I just want you to know," Caroline announced, "that I may be out of state, but I'm far from out of touch."

"Your mother's number hasn't moved from where you plastered it yesterday."

"Good. Be sure to call if anything comes up. This is a working vacation — working being the operative word. I have notes enough with me to do the Baretta brief, but if I'm needed there, I can be back in a matter of hours."

"Everything's under control," Doug said.

That was what she feared. "Even if it's something small, don't hesitate to call."

"Caroline."

"I'm going. Just remember. I'm here." She hung up the phone, before adding under her breath, "To my everlasting dismay." She scanned the taxi stand but still saw no wood-sided wagon. So she picked up the phone again.

"Hi," she sighed moments later. The sound of Ben's voice, even the briefest hello, was a balm.

"Hey, babe. Are you there already?"

"I'm in Portland waiting for the damn taxi. This was a mistake, Ben. I shouldn't be here. Why did I let you convince me to come?"

"You didn't. You were the one who sat here the other night listing the reasons you were going."

"And you let me. You didn't argue. You let me go without a peep. You should have stopped me, Ben. You knew I didn't want to go."

"I also knew that you'd never forgive yourself if you hadn't. Come on. It won't be so bad."

"Fine for you to say," she grumbled. "You're not the one who's missing God-only-knows-what in the office for two weeks."

"So you brought work with you. Just think. You'll be able to do it all while you sit on the beach."

"I don't think there is a beach. This is Maine. I think it's all rocks."

"Then you'll sit at the pool. That's even better. You won't get sand in your briefs." He chuckled.

"Hah, hah."

"Seriously. You'll work and relax. The

81

change of scenery will do you good. Just think. No snide words from your partners, no seductive ones from me."

"I like your seductive ones. That's why I invited you to come along." She had thought it a brainstorm. Ben hadn't.

"You invited me to come along because you wanted a buffer. But your mother didn't invite me. She invited you. You need to do this, babe."

"What I need to do," Caroline said, "is have a cigarette. So help me, if that taxi isn't here in five minutes I'm buying a pack."

"No, you're not."

"If this is a sample of Maine-style service, I may last all of two days."

"Like you never have to wait for things in Chicago."

"I *always* have to wait for things, but at least the things I'm waiting for are of my own choosing. This isn't. It would have been easier if I'd simply rented a car and driven myself. But Ginny said someone would be here to meet me. I've been waiting now for twenty minutes."

"That's not very long."

"It's long enough for everyone else from my plane to have picked up their luggage and left. The people I'm looking at now are from a later plane." She studied them.

"What a weird group."

"Weird how?"

"Motley. All ages, all sizes, all styles. There are even — hard to believe, but true — men wearing business suits." She focused on the electronic board behind the carousel. "From St. Louis via Boston. That explains it. Almost." She caught her breath. "Oh, God."

"What's wrong?"

"There's a woman who looks like my sister, but it can't be. Mother didn't say anything about inviting Annette."

"*Is* it her?"

"I can't tell. Her back is to me now. The hair's the same — dark and shoulder length — but for all I know Annette's had hers cut and colored since I saw her last. She always wanted to be a blonde."

"Is it Annette?"

"I can't tell. It could be. She's wearing walking shorts and a blouse. Very tailored, like Annette. But it can't be her," Caroline decided. "It's the power of suggestion, what with that plane having come from St. Louis and me being in my nightmare mode. Ginny wouldn't do that to me."

"Did she specifically say you were the only one coming?"

"No. But she implied it. She kept referring to me in the singular."

The woman by the carousel glanced at her watch, then glanced back, full face, toward the bank of phones where Caroline stood.

Caroline turned away, praying she hadn't been seen. She needed time to gather her wits. "If it isn't her," she told Ben, "it's a clone. God damn it, Mother screwed me. God *damn* it, Ben."

"Relax, honey. It isn't that bad."

But Caroline was furious. "She deliberately misled me, because she knew that if I thought either of the others would be here, I wouldn't come. The draw was that she invited me and not them. But if she has Annette here, she doesn't need me. I'd much prefer to be back in the office. This is an incredible imposition. I have a career."

"Your career will be here when you get back."

"I have an *important* career. If one of my clients gets into trouble, I have to be there."

"Your partners will cover for you. That's why you're in a firm. Your clients will do just fine without you."

"Thanks a lot."

He sighed. "Come on, Caroline. You know what I mean."

"I sure do. You've said it enough in the last few weeks. I'm just another swelled-headed lawyer who is, in the final analysis, expendable."

"That's what you hear, not what I say. I say that you mean the world to your clients, but that their needs aren't the be-all and end-all in life. They don't own you. You have a right to take off once in a while. You *deserve* a break."

"If I wanted a break, I'd go somewhere good. I wouldn't choose to be with Ginny." She lowered her voice. "Or with *Annette.* Why in the world did she invite Annette?"

"She may have thought Annette needed a break from the kids."

"It's manipulation. Pure and simple. A power struggle. A struggle for control. Ginny wants us together so she gets us together. She pretends that we all get along. She refuses to see that we have nothing in common."

"You have her in common."

Caroline snorted. "That's about it."

"But that's why you're there. Think about it. You're there because she's your mother and because she asked. So she invited one of your sisters."

Caroline had a terrible thought. "What if she invited both? What if it's a fucking family reunion?"

"That wouldn't change your basic reason for going."

Caroline didn't like the idea of a family reunion at all. "Maybe I'm wrong," she said. "Maybe it isn't Annette after all." She shot another look toward the carousel. The object of her scrutiny was studying her watch, then heading straight for the phone bank at which Caroline stood.

All hope fled. She whirled away, muttering to Ben, "It is Annette. No mistaking it. The perfect little mother. The perfect little wife. She and I have *nothing* in common."

"So she'll sit by the pool while you climb on the rocks."

"You're missing the *point*," Caroline whispered insistently. She peered out. Annette was using the booth four down from hers. "The point is that Mother should have been straightforward. She should have told me exactly what she had planned."

"Tell her that."

"I intend to. And I'll tell *you* something," Caroline said with a burst of self-righteous determination. "She'd better have a perfectly good explanation for having misled me this way, or I'll be back in Chicago tomorrow. Mark my words, Ben. I'll be back."

Annette was uneasy. She had been that way since dawn, when Jean-Paul had drawn her reluctant person from bed. No. She had been that way for weeks, ever since she had been railroaded into making this trip — but how could she have said no, with five children and their father insisting that she couldn't let Ginny down? What kind of example would she be setting if she didn't go? What kind of message would she be sending the children?

She had considered every possible emergency that might arise during her absence, had left memos addressing each, and even then had spent hours discussing contingency plans with Robbie and the twins. She had left numbers listed by each phone. She had taped step-by-step instructions on the microwave, the coffee maker, and the washer and dryer, because even though Charlene knew how to work each, Charlene was prone to allergy attacks that kept her home at least one day a week.

Annette had left nothing to chance.

Now, though, while she waited for her luggage to arrive, she worried. Robbie was taking Thomas and Nat canoeing in Forest Park, and although all three boys were good swimmers, the younger ones were novices in a canoe. Annette had visions of one of them swinging a paddle and knocking the other into the water, of Robbie going in after him, of the canoe capsizing in his absence. She should have insisted that they wait for the weekend and Jean-Paul. But Thomas and Nat had been ecstatic about going with Robbie, whom they adored, and Annette's yielding to their ecstasy had made her feel less guilty about leaving.

"Hi, Charlene. It's me. I've just landed in Portland. Are the boys back yet?"

"Not yet, Mrs. M."

"But it's one-fifteen there. They were planning to be on the water by ten. They should have been back long before now. Are you sure they didn't call?"

"They didn't call."

"Are either of the girls there?"

"No. They're at Lauren Kelby's pool."

Annette moaned. "Okay, Charlene. I'll try them again once I get to my mother's place." She hung up the phone and quickly punched out Jean-Paul's office, but he was in the operating room.

"Would you like me to send in a message?" his secretary asked.

But Annette couldn't call the situation an emergency. Not yet. "Don't bother him now. When he's done, though, would you ask him to give the boys a call and make sure they've returned from the lake?" When she had exacted a promise to that effect,

88

Annette dialed a final number. This one belonged to Lauren Kelby and was answered on what Annette guessed to be a portable phone beside the pool, if the mix of fuzz and background laughter was any indication.

"Hi, Lauren. It's Mrs. Maxime. Could I speak with one of my girls?"

"Sure," Lauren said. "Devon, Nicole, it's your mom!"

A breathless Nicole took the call. "Mom! Where are you?"

"At the airport in Portland. Nicole, I'm worried about the boys. I called home and Charlene hadn't heard from them. They were just going to the lake. They should have been back by now."

"They were having lunch afterward at Union Station. Thomas and Nat wanted to go to a sports store there. How was your flight?"

"Just fine." Lunch at Union Station hadn't been part of the plan. "When did they decide to do this?"

"At breakfast, after you left."

She let out a breath. "I've been worried."

"They're fine, Mom. What's the weather like there?"

Annette glanced outside. "Uh, nice, I guess. I haven't been out yet. I'm waiting for my luggage."

"Are you with Grandma?"

"No. I won't see her until I get to Star's End. Ah. Here comes the luggage. Finally. Do me a favor, sweetie? Call Charlene and tell her where the boys are, because I just called your father."

"Oh, Mom, you didn't."

"He was in surgery, but he'll be calling home to check as soon as he's free."

"They're *fine.* We're *all* fine. Really."

Annette sighed, then smiled. "I'm just not used to being away. Okay, there's my bag. I have to run. I'll call when I get to Star's End."

"You don't have to —"

"Talk with you then." She tossed two kisses into the phone and hung up in time to run to the carousel and snatch off the larger of her bags. The smaller one was slower in coming. Only when she had both did she head for the door. She had barely cleared the baggage claim area when she stopped short.

Ten feet ahead, looking at her in a way that precluded mistaken identity, was her sister.

"Caroline! What on earth — ?"

Caroline gave a thin smile. "How are you, Annette?"

"Fine, uh, surprised. I hadn't expected to see you. What are you doing here?"

Caroline studied her for a minute, then sighed. "Same thing as you, I guess."

"But I thought —" She had thought *she* was the one Ginny wanted to be with.

"So did I. It looks like Ginny's playing games."

Annette was stunned. "I guess so. I had no idea." If she had, she wouldn't have come. She would have stayed with her family, where she belonged, rather than subjecting herself to the emotional turmoil that being with Caroline caused.

Caroline was the consummate professional. Even now, in jeans and a silk blouse with her hair short and sleek, she looked sophisticated in ways that Annette, at her most classy, never looked.

She was glad she had worn linen today. Linen wasn't as sophisticated as silk. But it was smarter than cotton — which was irrelevant, but typical of what being with Caroline did to her, which was why she didn't want to be here. Ginny should have said something, damn it.

"Did you just land?" she asked for lack of anything better to say.

"A little while ago." Caroline looked over her shoulder. "I've been waiting for the car

Ginny promised to send, but it looks like — is that it? Ahhhh. Yes. Finally." Her returning gaze fell on the larger of Annette's bulging bags.

"I wasn't sure what kind of clothing to bring," Annette explained defensively and instantly regretted it. She shot a withering look at Caroline's lone bag. "Is that *it*?"

"Yup," Caroline said. She wheeled around and made for the taxi stand.

It struck Annette that nothing had changed. Caroline was as arrogant as ever. She rushed to catch up. "Caroline, wait." There was no time to waste. If she entered the Downlee taxi, all would be lost. "I was under the impression that Mother would be alone here. That's the only reason I came. But since you're here, I don't need to be. I'm sure I can catch a flight back to St. Louis."

Caroline was focusing on the tall stick-of-a-man who had unfolded himself from the wood-paneled wagon. "Are you from Downlee?"

"Yup." He released the tailgate.

"Caroline?"

Caroline slung her bag into the back of the wagon. "If either of us catches a flight back, it's going to be me." More carefully she placed her briefcase beside her bag. "I can't tell you how much this trip is putting me out."

"My kids are on vacation," Annette said, helplessly watching the driver put the larger of her bags into the car. "If ever there was a time when I like being with them, this is it. I think," she cautioned the man, "that I'd better have that back."

But Caroline was taking the second bag from her hand. "Since neither of us wants to stay, the only fair thing is if we both do, at least until Ginny explains herself. I don't know about you, but I'm feeling slightly used."

Annette was feeling slightly desperate. Downlee was two hours away. She didn't see how she could travel there, talk with Ginny, and return to Portland in time to catch a sameday flight to St. Louis.

"Climb in," Caroline said, but more gently. "The sooner we get there, the sooner we leave."

Annette looked back once, wistfully, at the airport, before sliding into the car. The seats were velour and looked new. The car itself looked new. She was surprised.

Caroline read her mind. "I know," she murmured as the driver left the terminal. "I was expecting something dusty and run-down."

"Do you think the house is?" Annette murmured back.

"Mother likes the best, so I can't imagine it, but then, I wouldn't have imagined her moving here, period."

"Why is she, do you think?"

"She said this was a gift."

"But why would she want a gift like this?"

"She wrote that she wanted something quieter."

"What's the *real* reason?"

"Who knows."

"You haven't spoken with her?"

"No." Caroline shot her a look. "Have you?"

"No." And she was cursing herself for it. Had she talked with Ginny, she might have learned that Caroline was coming and saved herself the trip.

But it was done. She was there, at least for the time being. There was nothing to do but take in the sights.

"So," Caroline said. "How are the kids?"

Annette smiled. This was home turf. The kids were her favorite topic. "They're great. Getting bigger. Rob's going into his senior year."

"Little Rob?"

"You haven't seen him since Dad's funeral. He's six-one now."

"Really?"

Annette nodded. Her children were a source of pride and strength, none of which Caroline would understand. "How's work?"

"Busy. But good."

"You look tired."

"That's from burning the candle at both ends getting ready for this trip." She faced the window, but the tightness in her jaw was telling. She was as peeved as Annette was. "How's Jean-Paul?"

Annette drew in a breath. "On my shit list, as we speak. He's the one who kept telling me I should come here."

"Same with Ben."

"You're still seeing him?"

"Yup."

Annette had met Ben at the funeral. "I liked him. He looked like he was wild about you."

"He is." Caroline held up a hand. "Don't ask. I turned him down. I'm not ready for marriage."

If not now, when? Annette wondered but didn't ask. Marriage was one of the things about which she and her sister disagreed vehemently. There was no point in renewing the argument now, not when they were confined in a small space with nowhere to flee, not with new territory whipping past.

95

Annette leaned forward. "I'm Annette Maxime. What's your name?"

"Cal."

Cal had faded skin, a sparse gray crew cut, and a flat tone of voice, and while nothing about him invited approach, Annette needed a diversion. "Are we still in Portland?"

"Yup."

"For how much longer?"

"A bit."

"All on the highway?"

" 'Til Falmouth."

"What then?"

"We go on up the coast road a ways."

Annette sat back. "I wonder if it gets picturesque. I mean, the trees here are pretty, but I was hoping for charm."

"Ben said there was charm. I guess it doesn't come until we hit the shore."

Mention of the shore, with its image of waves, made Annette think of the boys in their canoe on the lake. She looked at her watch and wondered if they'd come home, or called home, at least. Leaning forward again, she searched the front.

"No phone," Caroline murmured. "I looked."

Annette sat back. "I feel out of touch."

"Tell me about it. So. You have a phone in your car?"

"In all of them. For safety. If the kids are in an accident, I like knowing they can call for help. How about you? Do you have one?"

"You bet." She hesitated. "Think Leah does?"

"Actually," Annette mused, "I think her insurance company gave up on her." Leah was the master of fender-benders. "She doesn't own a car now. When she has places to go, she takes a cab."

"Wise move."

"Mmm. Caroline? Do you think she's coming, too?"

"I don't know," Caroline said and turned back to the window.

Annette could see Ginny doing it, inviting each and implying that she was the only one. Was it an honest mistake? Not likely. Ginny lived life in a deliberate way. Of course, if Annette had said that to Jean-Paul he would have called her a cynic. She was the bad guy, where her mother was concerned. Poor Jean-Paul. He couldn't possibly understand. He hadn't grown up in a world of benign neglect.

Hating herself for even that single, self-pitying thought, she leaned forward again. "So, Cal. Are you a native of Downlee?"

"Yup."

"What's it like?"

"Small."

"How many people?"

"Couple hundred year 'round. Twice that in summer."

"Then it's crowded there now?"

"Not crowded. Just family and friends."

"And tourists?"

"Nope."

To Caroline, Annette said, "That's a relief. There are times on Hilton Head when we're stuck waiting in traffic to get to the store to buy milk. I hate that. But the kids love it there. We rent the same place every year."

Caroline nodded. Her eyes remained on the window. Annette guessed that either her mind was miles away, or she was bored. Probably bored. She had no interest in Annette's life. Which made conversation a mite tricky.

So she hit on Cal again. "Are you familiar with Star's End?"

"Yup."

"What's it like?"

"Nice."

"Mother wrote that there was work to be done. Are we talking electricity and plumbing?"

"Oh, it has bathrooms. Lights, too."

Annette heard dryness in his voice. He thought her rich and spoiled. She wondered

98

if everyone in Downlee would. "How big is the estate?"

"Fifty acres, give or take."

"Are there other estates in Downlee?"

"Nope. Lotsa interest in this sale."

She didn't know whether that was good or bad. "Who did Mother buy from?"

"Mathew Pierce. Nice fellow, 'til he died."

"When was that?"

"Year ago. Lived alone, so the place was shabby, is what your mother probably meant. Lotta work's already been done."

"Really?" Annette looked at Caroline, who was similarly surprised.

"What work?" Caroline asked.

"Walls, floors."

"When?"

"All spring, starting in January."

"January," Annette mouthed to a wide-eyed Caroline. In a low voice, she said, "When she wrote me in April, she said that it 'needed' work, future tense implied."

"She's good at implying things."

Annette returned to Cal. "Who's been supervising the work?"

"A decorator from Boston. Nice lady. Uses locals."

"Ahh. Well, that's good, at least." More quietly again, she asked Caroline, "If she has a decorator, why does she need us?"

Caroline grunted.

Annette was feeling the heat of a slow boil. "She wrote me that she wanted help settling in."

"Same here. And that she wanted to spend time with me."

"Same here. She dragged us away under false pretenses."

"Deliberately."

"But we're adults, not children. She can't control us this way. Whatever is in the woman's mind?"

"I can't wait to hear."

"It had better be good," Annette swore, "because if it isn't, I'll share a cab with you back to the airport, and we can *both* fly out. It would serve her right to suddenly find herself alone."

Caroline sent her a wary look. "Either alone, or with Leah."

Annette closed her eyes. She shook her head, then bowed it. "Or with Leah," she murmured and sighed. "Right."

FIVE

Leah took a long, deep breath that carried with it wisps of ocean, beach roses, and spruce. Curling into the lounge chair, she tightened the afghan around her. Beneath it she wore a bathing suit and a bright silk sarong, appropriate attire for an afternoon by the pool had the sun been stronger. But the breeze off the ocean was a cool one. Thanks to the afghan, it was delightful.

She felt content, even lazy, which was one of the reasons why she didn't return to the house to get dressed. Another reason was that her clothes were all wrong. They were too fine, too fitted, too chic. They had worked for her when she had visited friends on the Maryland shore or in Newport. But Star's End was different. As elegant as the house and the flower beds were, they were also unpretentious, raw, and exceedingly real.

The moistness in the air wreaked havoc

with her hair, but she loved it. That moist air invigorated, the beach roses comforted, the spruce scent excited. She felt contented.

Give me another word.

Gratified.

And another.

At home.

None of the three made much sense. Given the circumstances, she ought to be feeling unsettled. Things hadn't gone quite the way she'd planned.

She had left Washington the morning before, a full day ahead of schedule, but there hadn't been any point in waiting. She had nothing left to do in the city. Besides, she liked the idea of surprising Virginia, indeed had spent much of the flight anticipating it.

After renting a car in Portland, she headed north, but a bit more nervously now. She wasn't the best of drivers, the sun was setting, and the roads were foreign to her. Once she left the highway there were several tricky spots that the rental agent's directions had failed to mention. She made one wrong turn, realized her mistake, and corrected it, but she lost half an hour in the process. A second wrong turn was even worse, and she ended on an unpaved road at the end of nowhere in the pitch-black. By the time she had turned the car around and headed back, an overextended something she hadn't seen had put a two-foot scratch on the side of the car.

Shaken, she stopped at a roadside diner. Once out of the car, she relaxed and grew excited again. That excitement built when she returned to the road, armed with more detailed directions this time, courtesy of the owner of the diner. The closer she came to Star's End, the greater her anticipation.

She loved surprises. She just knew Virginia would be pleased.

It was ten o'clock when she hit Downlee, and five minutes past that when she realized she had. The town center was a single main street ribbed with parallel storefronts, all lit by nothing more than pale shafts of a low-slung moon. She drove through once, hit a stretch of widely spaced homes, turned around, and drove through again.

The place looked asleep. She hated to have to wake up a stranger. She hated to have to *approach* a stranger. But she needed help.

She was idling in the middle of the road trying to decide what to do, when a cruiser appeared out of nowhere and slowly approached. Relieved, she rolled down her window. The ocean air brushed her cheeks.

"Evening," said the cop with a tip of his hat. He had a round face and looked to be a friendly sort. "Having car trouble?"

"I'm looking for Star's End," she said. "I have no idea where to find it."

"Why Star's End?"

"I'm Leah St. Clair. My mother's the new owner."

He stuck out his head for a closer look. "You're her daughter?"

"That's right."

"I didn't know she had a daughter."

"She has three, actually."

"How old are you?"

Leah wasn't sure her age was relevant, so she simply said, "I'm the youngest. I live in Washington. I've never been up this way before. Is the house far?"

"Not far. The moving van was there today. Stayed awhile. She must have lots of things." His head was back in the cruiser, but his eyes stayed on her. "So she's a widow now?"

"Mother? That's right. She's not expecting me until tomorrow. I would have been here long ago if I hadn't gotten lost. I'd really like to reach Star's End before she goes to bed. Which way do I go?"

"Up Hullman Road."

"I don't know where that is."

"So you're the youngest daughter. How

old's the oldest?"

Telling herself that questions went with the territory when one was dealing with the law, she said, "Just turned forty. Is Hullman Road marked?"

"Follow me."

She trailed the cruiser down the road. After several minutes, its brake lights came on. She drew alongside.

"That's Hullman Road," he said, pointing to the right. "Follow it to the end." With the touch of a finger to his hat, he swung the cruiser around her and left.

Hullman Road was dark, the trees on either side too dense to let moonlight pass through. She closed her window and locked the doors. With her high beams leading the way, she touched the gas. The car crept forward.

The road went this way and that and up and down for what seemed an eternity. Eyes wide, Leah clutched the wheel. She was beginning to fear she had taken another wrong turn, when the trees gave way to an open patch, then a more select cluster of trees and shrubs. It was only when the drive swung broadly around, though, that her headlights found the house.

She caught her breath in delight. The sprawling Victorian was large and two-tiered, part wood, part stone, with gabled windows, an arched porte cochere, and a turret that anchored a wraparound porch. From within came the warm glow of lamps.

She parked on the circular drive and stepped from the car into a swirl of cool, moist air. From nearby came the crash of the tide against the rocks, and around and above it, the smell of salt, sea, and something faintly sweet, lovely, and familiar.

The lure of it drew her forward, over crunching pebbles, under the porte cochere, and up a broad set of stone steps. She tried the front door, but it was locked, so she rang the bell, then waited, hoping that the lights weren't just a show and that someone was awake. She heard footsteps, though she guessed the sound might as easily have been her heart. Excitement had it pounding. She loved surprises.

Gwen's face appeared at the sidelight. Within seconds, the door swung open. "My word, girl, you frightened me. I had no idea who'd be calling at this hour in this place. I know what demons to expect in the city, but this is all new. We weren't expecting you until tomorrow."

Leah couldn't keep the grin from her face or the excitement from her voice. "Hi, Gwen. Sorry about that, but I hadn't planned to be so late. I thought I'd surprise Mother. Has she gone to bed?"

"She isn't here," Gwen said, but more gently now.

Leah's heart fell. "I thought she was coming with you."

"She decided to let me organize things first." Gwen Nmumbi wasn't the usual housekeeper. More a submistress of the house, she did all the things Virginia couldn't or wouldn't do. She was paid handsomely enough to preclude her ever returning to the secretarial pool from which she'd come, and she liked her work. She cooked, made beds, and paid bills. She hired and supervised more lowly workers as she saw fit, but she was tireless, herself, and strong. She was also sensitive, which explained the apology in her voice. "She's still in Philadelphia."

"Oh."

"She may be up tomorrow, though. She said she'd give a call."

Leah let out a breath. Then there wouldn't be a surprise, in spite of the effort she'd made — but if she was discouraged, it was her own fault. She should have known not to count on Ginny.

"Well then," she said, "I guess I'll just have to wait to see her." She peered inside. "Wow.

Everything looks new."

Gwen drew her in for a better look. "Everything is, just about. They've been working on it for months."

"Months? I thought she just bought the place."

"She bought it last fall, as soon as it went on the market. She'd had her eye on it for a while."

So much for sharing dreams, Leah mused, feeling wounded, but not for long. Her spirits refused to be trampled. There was something about Star's End that was uplifting.

Gwen took her arm. "Come. We'll get your things and I'll show you to your room, then you can explore the house on your own. These old bones of mine are starting to ache. It's been a long day."

Leah knew she must have spent endless hours unpacking, still, wearing a blouse and pants, with a sweater draped across her shoulders, she looked clean and composed. Gwen was like that. Tall, slim, and ruler-straight even at sixty, she had a natural elegance. The only possible betrayal of the work she'd done that day was the moist gathering of wiry tufts of gray hair on a pale black brow.

At the trunk of Leah's rented car, Gwen gaped.

"I didn't know what to bring," Leah explained quickly. "Sweaters take lots of room — and then there are evening clothes — I didn't want to crush anything — and makeup and contact lens stuff and hair stuff — and books. I have most of last week's *Washington Post* list. Must be in the know when I return."

Gwen gave her a droll look along with two of the bags. She took the other three herself, one per shoulder and one in her hand. "You may go through the books, but the evening stuff won't see much use. No one dresses here."

"There must be nice restaurants."

"*No* one dresses here."

"Ahh," Leah said with a sigh and turned her attention to the house.

The front hall was large. The walls, which were newly painted and bare, cried for art, but a stunning oval rug lay on the wide-planked floors and a long marble piece nested beneath the sweep of the stairs.

Guided by a gleaming mahogany banister, they wound their way up those stairs and down the hall. Gwen opened a door and reached inside, simultaneously turning on a pair of shaded floor lamps and a high Casablanca fan. "Your mother thought you'd like this room."

Leah did. It held an oversized four-poster bed, with matching nightstands and a dresser, and a sitting area with a loveseat, a clothed table, and two chairs. Everything had been done up in lavender and white with dashes of green, different from her bedroom in D.C. yet not so. There was the same sense of coziness here — which struck Leah as odd, since this room was much larger and more open. In D.C. a single small bay window looked out on the courtyard. Here, four huge windows looked out on the ocean. Four. She should have felt exposed and vulnerable, but she didn't.

Gwen broke into her thoughts to show her the bathroom. "It connects your room with the next. You'll find towels and soap, everything you need."

"A jacuzzi," Leah observed.

"All of them are, don't you know. Your mamma don't skimp, when she does things up."

"Do tell."

But Gwen was done. She was, in the final analysis, ever faithful to Ginny. "My room is at the very end of the hall, just at the top of the back stairs. I'll be heading there now, unless there's anything else you want."

Leah assured her that there wasn't and turned back to the wall of windows and, beyond, the ocean. The play of the moon on the water was dazzling, the rhythm of the waves hypnotic. Pushing the sash up to allow for a rush of fresh air, she set her forearms on the sill and listened to the waves and to the fog horn at Houkabee Rocks, droning its presence in long, deep, nasal blasts. She breathed the salt air and enjoyed the moment. In time, smiling, she straightened. The thought of being lulled to sleep by the surf was a tempting one, but for later. She wasn't at all sleepy now.

The house had six bedrooms on the second floor and on the first two large parlors, a library in the turret, and — to Leah's delight — a huge new kitchen that opened onto a family room filled with furniture of the sink-into type. Like her bedroom, this room faced the ocean. She imagined it would be spectacular by day.

French doors in the kitchen opened onto a wide deck, which she presumed was the tail end of the wraparound porch. The deck, in turn, opened onto the salt-water pool Virginia had written about. As Leah faced the pool, trees were on her left, open land straight ahead, bluff on her right.

She was enchanted. She walked to the

edge of the bluff and stood for a time, lost in the same kind of pervasive sensation, the scent of sea and spring growth, that had caught her up when she'd first stepped from the car. The few thoughts that sought a foothold in her mind were blown away by the same breeze that gave her body form and strength. It was a paradox she didn't try to understand. The feeling was enough. The pleasure. The comfort.

In time she returned to the pool, but the thought of continuing on into the house wasn't as enticing as staying outside. So she sank down on a long, cushioned swing that hung from the wide arm of a singular oak. There was a woodsy smell here, along with the ever-present salty and sweet. The blend was rich.

Any tension that remained in Leah, either from the wisdom of this trip, its length and stress, or the disappointment of finding Virginia absent, drained away. Her limbs grew light along with her heart. She stretched out on the swing with her head on its cushioned arm, only to straighten again seconds later and pull the pins from her hair. She ran her fingers through the un-bound strands, feeling them start to curl and, for once, not caring. By the time she lay back on the swing, her head was cushioned by a riot of waves, nearly as lush as the breeze that propelled the swing ever so gently forward and back, forward and back.

She closed her eyes and took a deep, deep breath.

The next thing she knew it was morning. To her astonishment, she was still on the swing, feeling not at all cramped, but more rested than she had in weeks. Nothing at all felt odd; from the minute she opened her eyes she knew where she was. There was pleasure and contentment, even familiarity.

The air on her face was cooler than it had been the night before, but the rest of her was delightfully warm under a large knit afghan. She didn't remember it from her mother's house, though Virginia might well have received it as a gift once upon a time and stashed it away. If so, she had been wise to take it out now. Its patchwork quilt design fit the setting.

She gathered it to her chin and lingered for a few last, lazy minutes. The afghan smelled of wool and something else new and pleasant. She wondered when Gwen had brought it out.

Gwen was nowhere in sight, but there was clear evidence that she had been up and about. Leah's bags were unpacked, her

113

clothes neatly hung in the closet, her books stacked, her toiletries arranged by the pale green marble sink. She showered and put on a sweater and white jeans — which were the most casual pants she had brought and even then seemed wrong — folded the afghan over the back of the loveseat in a statement of ownership, and went downstairs.

A note anchored by a basket of warm sweet rolls on the granite island in the kitchen said that Gwen had gone grocery shopping. Leah helped herself to one of the rolls, then turned and gasped. Beyond the tall windows of the family room, in beds lying between the edge of the porch and the sea, were a profusion of flowers. She crossed to the windows and stared. There were daylilies and asters, purple iris, white phlox, towering blue lupines. She swung around to the pool side to find sundrops blooming beside baby's breath — and, unbelievably, poppies — bright scarlet poppies.

She went out the French doors and along the porch toward the front of the house. Creating a foil for the circular drive, looking casual and perfectly at home, were lavish bursts of pink and white, blue and yellow. She saw peonies and bleeding hearts. She saw the first of the hollyhocks and the last

114

of the columbines. She saw newly planted dahlias, their crimson blooms little yet but a promise.

She continued around to the very front of the house, where alyssum billowed low and white against green-gray shrubs, but her nose led her on, off the porch now and across the lawn, to the sea again and the point where the bluff began. There she found beach roses. They were in full bloom and fragrant beneath the sun in ways that had only been suggested the night before. Their scent was as familiar to Leah as her own.

She had plucked one from its vine and was breathing it in, looking dazedly toward the sea, when a movement far down the bluff caused her pulse to trip. A man was there. He was working among the irises, deadheading blooms that had gone by. She guessed him to be the gardener, though the distance precluded her guessing much more. She could see that he was tall and, given the ease with which he worked, bending and reaching, bending and reaching, limber. She could see that he wore jeans and a dark shirt, and had dark hair. But that was all.

She thought to approach him and compliment him on his work, but something held her back. So she lingered with the roses, then wandered back toward the front of the house. She was crossing the drive when she came upon him again, and again her pulse tripped. He was closer this time, unscrewing a hose from a spigot at the corner of the house.

The shirt was denim and rolled to his elbows, baring forearms the color of a new tan, more brick than brown. His hair was windblown, his jaw shadowed, his hands large and dirty. She watched the way his shoulders moved as he gathered up coils of hose, the way ropy muscles in his forearms rhythmically bunched and eased.

He wasn't handsome in the classic sense, was too large and blunt for that, but therein lay an odd beauty. He was as physical a man as she had ever seen. She couldn't take her eyes from him.

She guessed him to be nearing forty. In theory, they could be friends. If she could only speak. But her mouth had gone dry.

She didn't know whether to pass him or go back, and was trying to decide which, when he raised his eyes from his work.

She smiled a dumb smile and raised an open hand in greeting. For a minute, seeming startled, he just stared. Then he blinked, nodded solemnly, opened his hand in a brief returning wave. He looked at her a minute longer, then took the hose and set off across the grass.

She went the other way, fairly flying around the house and reentering the kitchen. Her heart was beating up a storm. She grinned when she saw Gwen, who must have returned while she was out on the bluff. "The flowers are spectacular," she gasped. "I'm amazed that they grow here."

"Oh, they're coaxed," Gwen said as she filled the refrigerator. "The gardener is quite good. Have you seen him?"

"I just did. Does he work here full-time?"

"Believe it, with fifty acres of land."

"Much of that is forest."

"Much isn't. You saw the flowers, girl. You know what kind of care they demand."

Leah certainly did. Flowers were her thing. "Did he come with the house, or did Mother hire him new?"

"He came with it. From what I hear, if it hadn't been for his keeping an eye on things when the last owner died, the house would have fallen to ruin. He lives right here on the grounds, in a cottage at the edge of the woods. There's a small greenhouse beside it." She busied herself washing blueberries. "Mmmm-*mmmm,* but he's a well-made man. I tell you, honey, if he were fifteen years older and of color, those sweet rolls over there would'a gone from my oven to his cottage first thing."

Leah laughed.

"Don't laugh," said Gwen.

"Sorry. Has Mother called?"

"Not yet."

"She must think I'm on my way. Maybe I ought to call her and tell her I'm here. She isn't still at the house, is she?"

"Lord, no. Not with all the furniture gone. Not with me gone. She's with Lillian."

"Ahh. Saying her goodbyes. I won't bother her then."

"She won't mind."

But Leah wasn't inviting disappointment. She wasn't taking the chance that Virginia would find some compelling reason not to come to the phone. "When she calls," she told Gwen, "tell her that I'm here and that I'm impressed. I'm taking a book out to the pool."

That was precisely what she did, but she didn't read more than the occasional page. Sounds kept distracting her, and sights. She walked along the flower beds by the pool side of the house. She wandered to the bluff and watched the surf. She lay idly on the lounge chair with the book face down on her lap and thought about absolutely nothing at all.

The sun climbed toward noon, then past. Just when she was wishing it, Gwen brought a tray with a tall glass of iced tea and a chicken salad sandwich.

"This looks great. Mother hasn't called yet?"

"Not yet."

"Did she say she would call before she left, or on the way?"

"She didn't specify."

"Which do you think?"

"Your guess is as good as mine. She may not be in a rush. She knows I have a handle on things."

"She also knows I was to be arriving today," Leah said a bit sharply. "Why did she ask me here, do you think?"

"She wanted to share the place with you. She knew you'd love it."

"But that wasn't why she bought it. She must love it herself. Funny, I wouldn't have thought it. It's different from her usual."

"Maybe that was the appeal."

"At her age?"

"A lady is never too old," Gwen said pointedly.

"Sorry." Leah debated how best to handle the situation. "I'd try Mother myself, except that she must be on her way by now if she's

119

planning on getting here today, and I don't really feel like talking with Lillian. So I guess I have no choice but to wait."

The waiting should have been painful; she felt impatience galore. But that was in her mind, and only in fits and starts, and as for her body, it wasn't having any part of pain. It relaxed by the pool. It spent untold time on the bluff. It explored more of the gardens.

She was sitting on the neatly mowed grass beside one of those gardens, trying but failing to remember what she had been doing two days before, at that very hour, in Washington, when she felt his approach. He seemed absurdly tall. It occurred to her to stand up, but she couldn't move.

Instead she just smiled. "Hi."

"Hi," he said back. His voice was deep. Close up, his face was strong, not startled anymore, but solemn.

She gestured toward the flowers. "These are gorgeous."

He followed her gesture, but only for a minute. When he spoke, he was looking at her again. His words flowed in a way that softened his expression. "It's the air and the soil. Most everything grows well here, what with the moisture and all."

"The growing season must be short."

He gave a one-shouldered shrug. "The climate is milder here than inland."

"But doesn't the wind hurt the blooms?"

"They're strong." He hunkered down, tugged at a weed, gently tamped the soil with fingers that were long, lean, and blunt-tipped. "The delphinium are past their best. You should have seen them last week."

"They're still wonderful," she said. She guessed that if he lived in the city, he would have been a two-shave-a-day man, his beard was that dark. "Will you cut them back?"

"No. They'll be stronger next year if they die back naturally. I shaped the phlox, though, so they'll come in broader and thicker."

Leah dragged her gaze from his face and skimmed the beds. They were lush, healthy to a one. "Everything works."

"Now, yes. I've tried some things that haven't, and I've had to take them out."

She was back to looking at his face. His eyes were brown and oddly warm given his solemnity — but that solemnity was odd, too. From close up, she could see creases at the corners of his eyes and grooves around his mouth. He did smile, on occasion. Somewhere. Somehow.

Her mouth was dry again. She wasn't used to strange new men. She wasn't used to men who sweated, or men who smelled like men, and this one did both.

But he was looking at her, awaiting an answer. Feeling the fool, she cleared her throat and managed what she hoped was an insightful, "You must have color all summer."

"Try to. The beds dovetail. By the time one flower is by, another's in bloom."

"That's great."

"It's scientific. Planned out on paper."

"You sound formally trained."

"I am, some."

"And the rest?"

"I learned from my father."

Something about his response — the personal element in it, perhaps — gave Leah the strength to stand. She brushed the seat of her pants with one hand and extended the other. "I'm Leah St. Clair. I'm the new owner's daughter."

His fingers closed around hers. "Jesse Cray."

She nodded, swallowed. Warm fingers, strong hand, deep, soulful eyes. Close up, he was as natural and raw as Star's End itself. She was thoroughly intimidated, but intrigued. It struck her that he was refreshing.

"Are you helping unpack?" he asked in

the easy way he had of speaking.

"Between Gwen and the movers, most everything's been done. I'm just waiting for my mother to arrive."

"When is she due?"

"Yesterday. Now today."

"Did she sell her house in Philadelphia?"

"Uh-huh."

"Then this will be her major residence?"

"Apparently."

"Does she look like you?"

Leah frowned. "You haven't met her?"

He shook his head.

"But I thought you lived here."

"I do."

"And you didn't meet her when she bought the place?"

"She didn't come."

Leah was startled. "Not at all?"

"I'd have known if she had," he said so simply that she knew it was the truth.

"That's strange. Unbelievable, actually, that she'd buy a house she's never seen." Forget the money. To make such a momentous commitment blindly, boggled Leah's mind.

She was trying to make sense of it when Jesse said, "She didn't have to come personally. They use videos now, the realtors do,

123

and her decorator must have reported back."

"Still." Leah had never known Virginia to be impulsive. Then again, Jesse was right. She might have seen a video. "I didn't learn she'd bought it until recently," Leah felt called upon to say, but one explanation led to another. "We're not very close." Then another, a more self-conscious one. "We don't see each other often. I live in Washington."

His eyes said that he understood, and that she didn't have to say more, which was good, because the way those eyes held hers made thinking harder. Which was pathetic. She was from the city. She was supposed to be socially adept — and within her own circle, among people of her kind whom she had known for years, she was. But this wasn't one of her do-it-in-your-sleep conversations. This was *real.*

She forced a blink, cleared her throat, and yielded to curiosity. "I understand you're a native of Downlee."

"Yes."

"You don't sound it. I expected an accent, a Maine kind of thing." But he had none of that. His voice had depth, resonance.

"It comes out sometimes, when I'm angry or upset."

She couldn't begin to imagine a temper. "Why not all the time?"

"In this day and age, an accent would be more of an affectation than not. I spend my winters traveling. I go to movies and watch television. Most of the people I hear in the course of a day don't speak Down East." He cast a wistful glance toward the bluffs. "Sad, in a way, the passing of something unique. It does have a charm to it, authentic Down East talk. There's nothing like sitting on the steps of the barbershop and listening to the granddaddies go at it. It's like an old song." His eyes met hers, sad, gentle. "They don't make music like that anymore."

Leah couldn't remember any old song that was quite as lyrical as his voice. She took a shallow breath. "No."

It was a minute before he shifted his gaze and said, "Well. I'd better get back to work."

She stared after him. His backside was tight, his legs long, his stride fluid. As gardeners went, he was unusual.

"Jesse?" she called. He looked back. "Would you mind if I cut delphinium for the house?"

A slick city guy would have said, "I'd be honored," or, "Be my guest," or even, wryly, "That's what they're for." All Jesse Cray said was, "Nope," and with a nod of farewell was off.

Leah hurried back to the house for the clippers.

"There you are," Gwen scolded. "I've been looking all over for you."

"I was out in the flower beds," she said, and one part of her was out there still. The other, less distracted part gasped. "Mother called?"

Gwen nodded.

"Is she in Portland yet? I could pick her up there. It's not a bad drive. I suppose I should have thought of it sooner. If she's already there, it's probably too late — no, she can make herself comfortable in the Admiral's Club —"

"She's still in Philadelphia."

"Philadelphia? You're *kidding*," Leah cried. "What's the problem?"

"No problem. She just wanted to spend a little more time there."

"With her friends." Leah didn't add, *as opposed to her daughter,* though her tone was duly frustrated.

"This is a big move for her," Gwen tried to explain. "I think she sees a finality in it."

"But she'll be seeing her friends again. They'll visit here, and she'll visit there, and

126

they'll all be together in Palm Springs come winter."

"Still, this is a big move."

"Maybe she shouldn't be doing it. Maybe it's a mistake. Did you know that she hasn't ever actually come up here and seen the place? But of course, you know it. You're the one who makes her travel arrangements." She threw a hand in the air. "I don't understand the woman. It's as simple as that. I'm going upstairs."

She thought of calling Ellen. *I knew I shouldn't have come. I set myself up to be knocked right back down. She does it every time.* But she didn't call Ellen, because there wasn't anything Ellen could say that she hadn't already said.

Leah slipped off the white jeans — grass-stained now, damn it, from sitting by the gardens — put on her bathing suit, and knotted a sarong around her hips. Taking a different book from the one that had bored her earlier, she went down to the pool.

She sat prettily for ten minutes. During the entire time, her skin was covered with goose bumps. Then it struck her that with Virginia not coming that day, there was no need for her to try to impress. So she went right back upstairs, unknotted her hair and let it spill down her back, wrapped herself in the patchwork afghan, and went down again.

That was when the hurt began to fade. Likewise disappointment and frustration. They went the way of the wind, along with the rest of her thoughts, leaving room only for long, deep breaths of a heady potpourri, the mix of ocean air, beach roses, and spruce that charmed her so.

She lay quiet and content. She dozed off. She awoke, stretched, smiled.

Things could be worse, she mused. Star's End could be a dump. It could be on an island miles at sea, connected to the mainland by a leaky mailboat. It could be infested with bats. It could lie on drab, barren ground. It could be cared for by trolls, instead of an intriguing gardener with solemn brown eyes.

Things could be worse, she thought again, and took another long, deep breath. This one caught in her throat, though, when two figures suddenly emerged from around the back of the house and came to stand between her and the sea.

SIX

Leah sat straighter in the lounge chair. "What are you doing here?"

Caroline walked right over to her side. "Ginny didn't tell you?"

"Not a word."

Annette came to stand beside Caroline and said in a slow, deliberate, mocking way, "We're helping her settle in and make the place special. We're bringing warmth."

"More important," Caroline added similarly, "we're spending quality time with her — time she regrets she hasn't spent before." Her voice straightened. "Are you sure you didn't know anything about this?"

Leah had grown increasingly dismayed by the familiarity of the words. "How would I know? She doesn't confide in me."

"You see her more than we do."

"I knew nothing about this house, let alone either of you." And she wasn't pleased at all. She had been relaxed sitting alone by the pool, warm beneath the afghan, with her hair blowing loose. Now she felt self-conscious, and it was all Virginia's fault. "She sent me a letter along with the tickets. She told me the same things she told you. She had it all scripted out."

Caroline scowled. "I'll say."

"What a *witch* she is," Annette cried and glanced at her watch. "I'm calling home. I don't believe this. Is there a phone out here?"

Leah pointed toward the kitchen. She pulled the afghan tighter, gave her hair a twist and stuck it between her head and the back of the chair. She looked up at Caroline. "Did you two come together?"

"In the taxi. We met in Portland. Ginny must have coordinated our flights. How about you? When did you get here?"

"Last night. The flight I was originally booked on would have gotten me in at two-ten this afternoon."

"Right after me and before Annette." Caroline looked away. "She implied I was the only one coming. Same with Annette."

"And with me. Why's Annette in such a rush to call home? Is there a problem?"

Caroline's mouth twisted. "She thinks her family can't live without her."

"More likely it's the reverse. Her family is

130

her life. I'm surprised she's here without them. Are you sure they aren't out front?"

"I'm sure," Caroline said with a small, but halfway natural smile this time.

It was an attractive smile, Leah mused, but then, Caroline was an attractive woman. Leah didn't usually care for the way she dressed — too sleek and hard — though she did look good now. Leah wished she looked half as good herself, but even if she was dressed, she wouldn't be dressed right. The closest she could come to appropriate pants were white jeans that now had a grass-stained seat.

But white jeans weren't right. Star's End was a blue jeans kind of place. Definitely a blue jeans kind of place. Caroline had known that.

"So where is the matriarch?" Caroline asked. "I can't imagine she's playing cards in town. Why isn't she out here with you?"

"She isn't here."

Annette materialized in time to ask, "Where is she?"

"She hasn't left Philadelphia yet."

"You're *kidding*," both of them cried.

"Why isn't she here?"

"What's she waiting for?"

"When's she coming?"

If there was any solace to be had, it was in

Leah's being the one in the know — or, as much in the know as Virginia allowed. "She could be up tomorrow. Then again, she was supposed to be up today and changed her mind. Gwen says she's having trouble saying goodbye. Wouldn't it be a kicker if she changed her mind about leaving?"

"But she sold the house."

"She can buy another."

"But she dragged the three of us up here!" Annette argued. "I don't know about you, Leah, but this is the *worst* time for me to be away."

Leah was thinking that she had nothing better to do, when Caroline turned to her and said, "Speaking of which, have there been any calls for me?"

"Not that I know of."

"I'm going inside to phone the office."

Leah watched her go, then asked Annette, "Is there a problem there?"

Annette made a sound. "Caroline may want to think so. To hear her talk, her practice is going to hell in a handbasket without her. You'd think her clients were infants."

"Her clients and your family," Leah murmured. Her sisters never failed to make her feel aimless and nonproductive. Add to that unappealing — which infuriated her. She had been feeling so good before they'd arrived.

"Excuse me?"

"Nothing."

But the damage had been done. "I know my family can get along without me," Annette argued. "It's just that I like being with them. There's no better time for that than when the children are out of school." She looked around in bewilderment. "So what am I doing here?" She seemed about to say something, then looked around again. "I have to say, it happens to be a pretty place." She frowned. "There's something familiar about it — but it isn't like any place I've ever been. The kitchen's wonderful. How's the rest of the house?"

"Beautiful."

"Unpacked and settled?"

"Relatively so."

"Then why did she want us here? If all she wanted was to get us together, she could have picked a better time."

"There is no better time."

"Maybe not for you. The social season is done."

Leah bristled. "What I meant was that it wouldn't matter *when* she invited us, none of us would have wanted to come. Our family isn't the get-together type."

"Well put," Caroline remarked, lowering herself to the lounge beside Leah's. She sat on its edge with her elbows on her knees. "I can't believe Ginny did this. I just can't believe it. You'd think we had nothing better to do."

Okay, Leah reasoned, so she had nothing better to do in D.C. But she didn't have to be here either. She didn't have to put her mental health on the line in an effort to win Ginny's approval — and there wasn't a chance in hell of impressing Ginny now, not with Caroline and Annette here. Beside them, she paled.

"The boys got home safe and sound," Annette told Caroline.

"Did you doubt they would?"

"They were very late. A mother worries."

"Ginny never did. I doubt she is now. She's probably playing cards at the club as we speak, feeling no guilt whatsoever for disrupting our lives. She's heartless."

"Heartless, thoughtless, self-absorbed — what else is new?"

"More to the point, where does that leave us? What are we going to do?" Caroline looked off toward the bluff. "I really ought to leave."

Annette shot her a look. "Me, too."

But Leah wasn't in a rush. "I think I'll

stay. After she went to the effort of sending us tickets, I'd hate for her to arrive and find all of us gone."

"Good girl," Caroline mocked. "You'll get points for that."

"I happen to like it here." At least, she had before her sisters had shown up. She wouldn't be at all disappointed if they flew out the next morning. Hell, she'd drive them to Portland herself.

"When we were kids," Caroline persisted, "you were the one of us who most wanted to please her. Some things don't change."

"You still look like a kid," Annette remarked, then added a dry, "That's a compliment."

At thirty-four, Leah took it as such, though compliments coming from her sisters were rare. "It's my hair," which, without the restraint of pins, refused to stay put behind her head. "It hasn't grown up yet. It's hopeless."

"I always wanted curly hair. I always wanted *blond* hair. I'd have bleached my hair and had a permanent if Mother had let me, but she couldn't be bothered. She thought my own hair was gorgeous."

"It is," Leah insisted. "It shines. It swings. You're not held hostage to humidity." She twisted her hair back behind her head again,

135

but it curled right back out. "There's nothing I can do with this. It's a lost cause."

"Did Gwen know?" Caroline asked, bringing the conversation back to the subject at hand.

Leah assumed she must have. "She makes all of Mother's travel arrangements. She must have booked our flights." With dawning awareness, she added, "There are bedrooms furnished and ready for the three of us. That should have tipped me off, but all I was thinking was that Gwen was incredibly efficient."

"Mother didn't say *anything* about us in her letter to you?"

"*Nothing,* Caroline. Trust me. I'm not any happier to see you here than you are to see me. If I'd known you were coming, I might have turned around and driven back to Portland first thing this morning."

"You drove here from Portland?" Annette asked in surprise.

"That's my rental car out front."

"But I thought you'd given up driving."

"I gave up a car. I don't need one in the city. That doesn't mean I don't rent from time to time."

Annette cleared her throat. "It's a good thing they gave you one that's already scratched."

Leah was saved from saying anything by Caroline, who was looking around with a bemused expression. "There's something about this place. I feel like I should be remembering it."

Annette stood. "Show us around, Leah. Let's see what Ginny spent her money on."

Leah figured that showing them around was as convenient a way as any of getting to her room. She wanted to get dressed and do something with her hair. Then she wouldn't feel so gauche.

The afghan parted when she stood.

Caroline caught the edge and held it aside. "A silk sarong. Pretty. So this is the latest style?"

"I suppose," Leah said, feeling frivolous.

"You're as thin as ever," Annette remarked. "Are you eating?"

"Yes, I'm eating. My weight is right in the middle of what it should be for my height."

"Why are you thinner than me?"

"Because I haven't had any children. You've had five."

"Four pregnancies."

"That's four more than Caroline or me," Leah said, then added, because it was the truth, "You're not so bad, Annette." Tugging the edge of the afghan from Caroline's hand, she led the way into the house.

They explored the rooms on the first floor to a quiet chorus of comments. "Pretty." "Nice turret." "Interesting molding." "Great floors."

Upstairs, Leah excused herself at her own room and did what she could to restore her sophisticated self. When she felt reasonably put together, she met her sisters back downstairs, outside, on the front steps.

"What do you think?" she asked.

"It's a beautiful house," Annette admitted.

Caroline agreed. "All it needs is a little art on the walls."

"Accessories here and there."

"The icing," Leah said, leading the way across the drive to the lawn.

"You must adore the flowers."

"I do." She thought of the gardener and wondered where he'd gone. She didn't mention him to her sisters. He was her secret for now.

"What *is* it that feels so familiar?" Caroline asked.

"The roses."

"What roses?"

Leah led them to the bluff. The scent grew stronger as they approached, and once there, the burst of pink spoke for itself.

"Beach roses." Annette took one in her hand.

"We never had roses," Caroline argued.

"No," Leah said, "but smell them. Close your eyes. Say the first thing that comes to mind."

"Mother."

"Mother."

"This is her perfume," Leah explained. "She's been special ordering it for as long as I can remember. She still does."

"The roses must have been the selling point of the house," Annette mused.

"They would have been, if she'd smelled them here." Leah told them, without revealing her source, what she'd learned from Jesse Cray.

"She bought Star's End *sight unseen?*" Annette asked.

"Apparently."

"Is she starting to lose it? Senility? The first stages of Alzheimer's?"

"I don't think so."

"She's just decided to retire to a house she's never seen?"

"Looks it," Leah said.

Caroline folded her arms. "She's nuts. That's all there is to it. No sane individual would suddenly give up the life she's always known to move to a strange house in the middle of nowhere."

"This isn't the middle of nowhere," Leah said, feeling an unexplainable urge to defend Star's End.

"It's a strange town in a strange state."

"We adopted a cat once," Annette mused aloud. "She was pretty old when we got her, but she loved us. She was always in the room where we were. If the kids annoyed her, she'd just separate herself, walk off a little ways, and plop down again. She never went far from the action, even if she wasn't actively involved. Like Mother, in a sense, there but not."

"What's the point?" Caroline asked.

Annette met her eye. "The point is that our cat never strayed far until it came time for her to die, then she went off by herself. If I didn't know better, I'd say that's what Mother is doing."

"That's ridiculous," Caroline scoffed. "Mother isn't a cat. She's a social creature. She's been with people all her life. Besides, it's not like she has a terminal disease."

"Life is a terminal disease."

"She's only seventy. And she's in great health."

"Not completely," Leah put in. When her sisters turned to stare at her, she reminded them of the heart scare the fall before.

Caroline looked stunned. "What heart scare?"

"You know. The tests she had."

"She never said a word about any tests to me," Caroline swore and turned to Annette. "Did you know about them?"

"Never." As stunned as Caroline, Annette turned to Leah. "What tests?"

Leah told them.

"Why didn't you tell us before?"

"That wasn't my job. It was Mother's, and I thought she had told you. I thought you knew."

Annette shook her head. "Though I don't know why I'm surprised. She always identified with you. It's natural that you'd be the one she told."

"She told me because she wanted someone to sit with her through it all."

"Gwen could have sat with her. Gwen does most everything else."

"It's not the same," Leah insisted. "She wanted family."

Caroline had her arms folded again. "Did she say that?"

"She didn't have to. It's common sense."

"Or wishful thinking."

"Common sense," Leah repeated, irked now. She hated it when Caroline was imperious. This time, she refused to be put down. "You have your career, and Annette has her family. Of the three of us, I'm the only one with the free time to sit in doctors' offices with her."

But Caroline was shaking her head. "It's another power play. Ginny's good at those. She likes giving to one of us and withholding from the others. Like when I announced that I didn't want a coming out party, she took the two of you off to New York for a weekend of theater and left me at home to stew."

Annette nodded. "Like when I complained that she was never around when I came home from school, she made a point of being out of my reach for the next week straight."

"Like when I said I didn't want to go to private school," Leah put in, because she had gripes too, "she bought *you* guys new clothes, as though what I wore didn't matter anymore. Okay, so that was her way of punishing us. But I'm telling you, she wasn't thinking that last fall. She needed someone with her who was family and could talk with the doctors, and I was the most convenient one. If you think it was fun, think again. If you think she was *grateful,* think again."

Annette sighed. "So nothing's changed."

"Except," Leah was on a roll, "that we're

up here, the three of us, in a place we don't want to be. So. Are you guys leaving in the morning or not?"

"She would have liked it if we'd said yes," Caroline told Ben later that night. "She'd like to have the place all to herself. She'd like to have Ginny all to herself." She thought about that, then, in a quieter voice, admitted, "We all would, I guess. When you come right down to it, that was the root of the rivalry between us."

"Was, or is?"

"Was. We're not competing now."

Ben hummed a few random notes.

"Well, not really," Caroline conceded. "Maybe there's a little of it left, but that isn't the main reason I'm staying. I want to be here when Ginny arrives." Ginny was the major object of Caroline's anger. "She owes us an explanation. I want to hear it."

"You could fly home, and then call your sisters in a day or two to find out what Ginny said."

"I want to hear it from her mouth. I mean, what could it be —" she asked as she had so often in the past few hours, "one more day? Maybe two? Besides, I'm already here, and I have to admit, the place is nice. Gwen made a great dinner, no doubt by way of apology for her part in the deception. I've been checking in with the office. Things are under control there."

"Well, now, *that's* a relief."

"Don't be smug. If something comes up, I'm on the first plane out."

"If something comes up with me, would you, too?"

"In a minute."

"But you won't marry me."

"Ben."

He sighed, then grumbled. "You're too far away."

"That's silly. We wouldn't be together tonight even if I was in Chicago."

"An hour away is better than twenty."

"*You* told me to come."

"Not really. But maybe. Do you miss me?"

"A lot." His voice calmed her so. It was incredible. Before the call, she had been feeling out of her element, unsure and on edge. But he grounded her, just by being on the other end of the line. "I'm going looking for art in the morning," she told him. "The walls here are bare. I'm counting on the town being the artists' colony you said it was. Ginny needs something fast."

It occurred to her to have Ben send a canvas of his, but Caroline needed something to do. She couldn't see herself sitting by the pool talking about kids with Annette or haute couture with Leah. Shopping for several good pieces of art might do the trick.

"We had a lovely dinner," Jean-Paul insisted when, worried, Annette asked a second time. "The casserole you left was perfect."

"Nat sounded down."

"You caught him minutes after he lost an argument with Thomas about who would be holding the remote control tonight. Don't worry. He'll be fine. He'll have his turn tomorrow."

"Nicole sounded in a rush to get off the phone."

"She and Devon are already out the door. Didn't they tell you that they were going to the movies?"

"Yes, but I imagine all kinds of things when I hear that tone of voice."

"She was in a rush to leave. That's all."

"I should be there," Annette said, agonizing over it still. "But Ginny hasn't come. I want to wait and see her, even if only for a little while. Leah's staying, and since she's staying, Caroline won't leave. How can I leave, if they're both staying?"

There was a pause, then a gentle, "You can't."

"I heard that smile, Jean-Paul, and it *isn't*

a competitive thing. It's this business with her heart. Leah says it's nothing. She says the doctor was the top heart man in Philadelphia, and that even then they got a second opinion. Can you check on it? Ask around? See if this man really is the best? At least, then, I'll feel like I'm doing something — although, Ginny was right. The house needs warmth. I thought I'd shop around and see what little local things I can buy to put here and there for effect. There isn't much else I can do while I wait for her to get here."

"How are your sisters?"

Annette sighed. "Caroline's just the same. Arrogant as ever. Convinced that she is the embodiment of the modern woman."

"What about Leah?"

"Gorgeous. I almost didn't recognize her at first. She looked entirely different."

"How so?"

"Relaxed. Unsophisticated. Very unsocietylike. Her hair was wild and loose — just beautiful. She was wrapped in an afghan, out by the pool."

"Was she polite?"

"For the most part. But that's her forte. Light social chatter. She talked about flowers through most of dinner, which was just as well. I'm not sure what I'd have had to say if she hadn't kept the conversation going." When Jean-Paul didn't say anything, she asked, "What are you thinking?"

"I'm thinking that you're good with people. You can hold your own in any social group. I don't understand why you would have trouble making talk with your sisters."

"Because they're my sisters. They're not like other people. I know that sounds bizarre, but you'd understand, if you had any siblings. Your relationship with a sibling is *different*."

"You're not friends."

"Exactly. You don't choose them."

"But is there something that says you can't be friends? Even for a short time? For two weeks?"

Yes, there is, the threatened part of her wanted to cry. The family-oriented part of her simply sighed. "After years of distance, I don't know. We're three entirely different people. It's not just me, Jean-Paul. They feel the same way."

"Did they say so?"

"No. But I can tell. They're as uncomfortable with me as I am with them. I'll wait until Mother gets here. Then, unless she offers some compelling reason why I should stay, I'm gone."

■ ■ ■ ■

Leah wanted Star's End to herself. She kept remembering how delightful she had been feeling until her sisters showed up. They brought tension with them — Caroline taking everything seriously and Annette always with an opinion. Each of them thought her way was the only way. And Leah? She thought her way was just fine.

Try again.

Not bad.

Once more.

Empty. Next to her sisters, she had little direction in life, which might well explain why she felt so at home at Star's End. It was a world in itself, a world of sights and smells and sounds, so rich in sensation as to guarantee contentment. The concept of a direction in life was irrelevant here. This was the end of the world, a direction in and of itself.

That was why she'd come back downstairs. Caroline and Annette were in their rooms and assumed she was in hers, so she had taken off on a secret mission to recapture contentment.

She huddled in an Adirondack chair in a corner of the porch. A long white nightgown covered her, neck to ankle, and was in turn covered by the afghan, but she was sheltered enough from the breeze to leave it loose. She inhaled, closed her eyes, and listened to the surf.

Her muscles relaxed and went soft. She didn't think of Caroline, Annette, or Virginia. She didn't think of having to tell the agency about the scratch in the side of the rental car. She didn't think of Washington.

She fancied that the beach roses emitted a sedative, and an addictive one at that. Without the sun's light, the scent was more subtle, but richer, somehow, even seductive.

When she heard a splash that broke the rhythm of the tide, she opened her eyes. It was a minute before she realized that someone was in the pool and another before she ruled out someone having come from the house. She would have heard the French door opening. She would have heard footsteps on the deck. Besides, she couldn't imagine either of her sisters — much less Gwen — taking a midnight swim.

It was the gardener, Jesse Cray, who lived in a cottage by the woods. His wet arms glistened as they cut through the water. His dark head turned for air on alternate strokes. Between the rush of the waves against the rocks beneath the bluff, she could hear the rhythmic beat of his breath and his stroke.

She felt a flutter inside. He was a remarkably attractive man — rough compared to those she knew at home, but with magic hands and soulful brown eyes.

She wondered if he swam every night. She wondered how long he did it. She wondered what he was wearing.

He continued for fifteen minutes or so, back and forth in steady laps, then swam to the far side of the pool and propped his elbows on the deck. He stayed there for several more minutes, his dark head bent, before hauling himself out.

She wasn't prepared for that swift movement. It was smooth and strong. He reached for a towel and ran it over his head. She looked lower. He was wearing something that was dark and clung wetly to the contours of his hips.

The flutter inside her gained strength, even more so when he raised his head and looked around. She hadn't moved, but, incredibly, he sensed her presence. Toweling his arms now, he slowly approached.

"Is someone there?" he asked quietly.

"Just me," she said, drawing the afghan close. "Leah."

He came to where she sat and hunkered

down. "I didn't realize you were here."

"It's okay. I was just sitting. It's a beautiful spot."

He ran the towel over his chest. She tried her best not to look there.

"Do you swim every night?" she asked.

"In season. The pool isn't heated. It can be cold." He looked over his shoulder. "It's different at night. More intense, in some ways. When you can't see, you hear more and smell more."

That was just what she had been experiencing, sitting there with her eyes closed. "It fills you up."

"Pretty much," he said, looking at her again.

The towel hung from his hands. His hair was slicked back, his shoulders glistened. She imagined that he might be feeling a chill if he were out by the pool. In her sheltered spot, there was no chill at all.

"Do you swim?" he asked.

"I know how. I've never done much of it, though. Where I come from, pools are more decorative than not. Wasteful, huh?"

"I can't imagine a pool no one uses."

"Oh, they use it, just not for swimming. It serves a social purpose, a place for people to sit near to talk and be seen, but when it comes to getting wet, forget it. The men

151

might dive in, but the women wouldn't risk ruining their makeup."

He brushed her cheek. "You're not wearing makeup."

For an instant she couldn't breathe, absolutely couldn't breathe. Then she forced her lungs to function. "I was in bed. Upstairs. I couldn't sleep. So I came down."

He touched the collar of her nightgown, a pretty lace strip, white, almost luminescent in the night, above the amber drape of her makeshift shawl. He drew the afghan a little higher before dropping his hand.

Leah thought she would die. The gentleness of him boggled her mind, right along with his size and his shape. And his Adam's apple. So very male.

"Any more word on when your mother is coming?"

Her mother? Her mother. "Umm, no. Maybe tomorrow. Maybe not."

"How long are you staying?"

Her legs felt boneless. She couldn't possibly stand, much less make it back into the house. "Another few minutes."

He chuckled. She tried to see a smile, but it was too dark. "At Star's End, I meant," he said.

She laughed. She couldn't help it — and it wasn't that she was embarrassed at having misunderstood him — it was the suddenly light-headed way she felt. "Two weeks."

He nodded, and for an instant she felt the touch of his gaze, warm and intent, in the dark. Then, in the same smooth motion with which he had pulled himself from the pool, he stood. "I'll be heading home. Morning comes early."

She looked up, swallowed a vague disappointment. "What time?"

"Five, give or take. I like to water the beds before the sun rises high. Sleep well." He moved off.

Leah watched him meld into the darkness beyond the pool, and even then she held her breath. The darkness was dense. Wide-eyed, she watched it for another minute, but he was gone.

She exhaled a whispered, "Jesus," and hugged her knees to her chest. Then she smiled against the inside of her elbow and waited for the trembling inside her to still.

SEVEN

Wendell Coombs shuffled across the porch of the general store and lowered himself onto the left end of the long wooden bench. He always sat on the left end, which was nearest to the east end of town, where he lived. The west end of town was represented by Clarence Hart, his friend of seventy-odd years, who occupied the right end of the bench.

Four feet separated them. Four feet always separated them. Wendell didn't like the smell of Clarence's pipe; Clarence didn't like the smell of Wendell's coffee. No one ever filled the empty space between them, with the exception of the occasional child who didn't know better. Those four feet were the channel along which town gossip passed, east to west and back.

"Clarence," Wendell said by way of greeting.

Clarence nodded. "Wendell."

"Good wethah comin'."

"Ayuh."

Wendell sipped his coffee and made a face. It was too sweet again. What had that sign said? If it wasn't vanilla something, it was nutty-putty something else. Mavis never served coffee like that in her diner. A sad day it was when she'd closed the place down. No one knew how to brew a cup of good old-fashioned coffee anymore.

The problem was computers. The town was being overrun by them. People kept inventory on them; they kept folks' accounts on them; they ordered all kinds of fancy coffee beans on them. No one did anything the old-fashioned way anymore — except the artsies, and they were *another* whole can of worms.

Setting the mug on his thigh, he looked out over Main Street. All seemed well. All looked the same. But he knew not to trust "seemed" and "looked." He took another grimacing sip of the coffee, returned the mug to his thigh, and said to the morning air and Clarence, "I heea we got company."

"Ayuh."

He glowered at Clarence. "How'd you know?"

"Cal. Picked 'em up at Pawtland."

"How many?"

155

"Two outta three."

"Third one's a'ready in," Wendell said with relief. He didn't like it when Clarence knew more than he did. "Came in night b'foa last. Chief had to show'a the road." He chuckled. "Not too smaht."

Clarence pulled out his pipe. "Cal says they don't want to be heea."

"Good. Let 'em leave."

"Says they don't like each othuh."

Wendell wasn't surprised. Rich families always fought. He wasn't feeling too bad for them. Pity, though, to have civil war up at Star's End. "Chief says th' oldest is fawty. Wonda if it's true. Wonda if she's fawty-three."

Clarence studied his pipe.

"Chief checked," Wendell said. "She's a Chicago lawya. Worked for someone named Baretta."

Clarence knew what Wendell was thinking. The whole town was thinking it, least-ways everyone who'd talked with Chief yesterday. The last thing Downlee needed was a mob lawyer running around. "Cal says she's got a boyfriend. Says he's the one made'a come heea."

Wendell chewed on that a while. "He could be mob. Could be a pusha. We don't want none'a *that*."

156

Clarence opened his pouch and was nudging tobacco into the bowl of his pipe when Callie Dalton came up the steps. He touched the tip of his hat with the crook of his finger. "Mawnin', Callie."

"Mawnin', Clarence."

Wendell looked the other way. Callie Dalton was married to a traitor. After the whole town had agreed to stick together against unsavory elements, George Dalton had gone and rented good houses to artsies. Artsies were loose people. Everyone knew it. Women lived with women, and men lived with men, and when women lived with men they rarely saw fit to tie the knot in the eyes of the Lord and the State of Maine. Everyone knew they should be kicked out of Downlee.

The only problem was that there were more of them now, than of the rest, and their money was green. Wendell wondered how long that would last. They'd been changing everything else in town. The color of money might well be next.

Clarence finished filling his pipe. "Cal says the one from St. Louis got husband trouble."

"Don't want none'a that eithah," Wendell decided. Artists and city women, the whole lot of them too loose for their own good. "If

157

she thinks she's gonna play with Downlee men, she got anothuh think comin'." He raised a hand in greeting when Hackmore Wainwright rolled by in his pickup and turned off toward the dock. "Youngest'll be the problem, if y'ask me. Chief says she's got that blond, helpless look."

Clarence knew that look. He had fallen for it hard. 'Course, his June was a Maine girl, so it wasn't too bad. Still, she'd been a surprise. She hadn't been one bit helpless. In fifty-one years of marriage, he'd had to bargain for every single thing. Take sitting on the steps of the general store. She let him do it, long as he was home by noon to carry the wash to the line.

"Jesse betta be wawned," Wendell advised.

Clarence wondered if it would do any good.

"Whole *town* betta be wawned," Wendell added. "Don't need fast women, 'specially ones runnin' drugs."

Clarence thought about the drugs. Even with the artists coming in droves, Downlee had stayed pretty clean. "Think Chief knows 'bout the drugs?"

"He will," Wendell promised.

"And the mothuh?"

"Don't know if she's doin' it. 'Coss, bein' rich, she prob'ly is. They all do it." Wendell

158

shuddered to think of that kind of element in Downlee. The artists worked, at least. Well, in their way, they did. He doubted Virginia St. Clair had ever done a stitch of work *any* way. "Don't know why she bought Stah's End. Don't know who she thinks is gonna come to pahties heea."

Clarence clamped his pipe between his teeth and imagined parties at Star's End. He imagined lights and music and laughter. The place was missing that kind of thing. "What does Elmira say?"

Wendell reluctantly thought of his wife. He snorted in the next breath. "Elmira says she's come heea to die, but what does Elmira know. Damn shame, I say. Stah's End should'a been bought by someone else." He took another drink of his coffee, a bigger one, now that it had cooled some, but the gulp took him aback. He made a face to match the size of the gulp. "Damned coffee," he sputtered. "The problem's computahs, I say, computahs."

EIGHT

Caroline's body was operating on Chicago time, which meant that when she awoke at her usual six, it was seven in Maine. Needing tea, she went down to the kitchen to find that Leah had already steeped a pot. She steeled herself for the worst.

But the tea was good. Better than good, actually. "What kind of tea is this?"

Leah was reading the newspaper. "Darjeeling? No, Earl Grey. I think. I'm not sure. There were several tins in the cabinet."

"Of loose tea leaves?" What she was drinking was rich and full. It couldn't possibly have come from bags, and Leah didn't deny it. "I'm impressed."

Leah gave a small shrug. "I cook, too. Even we socialites have to live."

"You said that, not me," Caroline warned. "I'm not good at repartee before two cups of tea, at least." She studied her sister curiously. "Are you always up this early?"

Leah set down the paper. "I don't go to parties every night, Caroline. You can only sleep so much. Besides, sunrise here is spectacular."

Caroline was startled. "You saw it?"

"Our bedrooms face east. I left my drapes open."

"I closed mine without even thinking. It's habit."

Leah's mood seemed to warm. "I did the same thing yesterday. Then I realized what I'd missed, so I made up my mind not to make the same mistake twice. The sun is breathtaking skipping over the water, and when it hits the bluff and then the flowers —" She made a sound of pleasure.

Caroline's eye fell on the vase that stood at the center of the table. It was filled with brilliant blue stalks. "Delphinium?"

"Uh-huh. From the yard. I had to cut them shorter than I would have liked — I left them longer in the other rooms — but they were so spectacular that I had to put some here. They'll be gone before long."

Caroline sipped her tea, which remained remarkable even halfway through the cup, which was remarkable in and of itself. She wondered if it had to do with the setting. With the French doors and windows open, the outside came in, creating something as

161

rich as the tea, but also loose, lazy, and free. The feel of it was worlds away from Chicago, and though the details varied, it reminded her of Ben's place.

Thinking of Ben made her feel lonely. "I thought I'd go gallery-hopping in Downlee this morning. What are your plans?"

"I thought I'd read."

That was actually fine with Caroline. She would just as soon wander at her own speed and in her own time. But Leah looked small and young, fragile somehow, and Caroline couldn't help but remember when they had been eleven and five, then twelve and six, and she had taken Leah along with her to play. Then adolescence had widened the gap between them, and by the time adolescence was done, they had taken different roads. Caroline studied; Leah partied. They competed with the other for Ginny's affection.

But Caroline didn't feel competitive now. Star's End was too peaceful to allow for it. Kindly, she asked, "Do you want to come along with me?"

Leah smiled but shook her head. "I'll stay here."

Caroline didn't push. Instead she read the front section of the newspaper over her second cup of tea. It wasn't the *Sun-Times,* but it gave her the news. When she was

162

done, she went upstairs and dressed. She came back down in time to find Annette on the phone.

"Yes, Devon, I understand that, but if Thomas has a stomachache, going up the arch isn't a good idea." She covered the mouthpiece and murmured to Caroline, "There's a slight glitch." She returned to the mouthpiece. "No. Not a riverboat, either. You ought to stay on dry ground. Try the Sports Hall of Fame." She looked up. "Are you going to town, Caroline? — that's a *great* idea, Devon. I'm sure he'd love it."

"I'm taking the Volvo," Caroline said. The keys were right where Gwen had said they'd be.

"Wait! I'm coming! Devon, I have to run now, but I'll give a call after lunch. Whatever you do, do not let Thomas eat spicy food. I'd put money on the fact that his stomachache is from the chili dogs they had for lunch yesterday. Get him to eat something bland, like bananas, or cheese toast, okay, honey?"

Caroline waited at the door until Annette joined her. "It must be nice having a doctor for a husband. He isn't thrown by things like stomachaches."

"That's the problem," Annette complained. "Stomachaches are so insignificant compared to what he sees every day that he takes them for granted. I might have known someone would get sick while I was gone."

"It's just a stomachache. You don't have to be there for that."

"Maybe not," Annette said, but she didn't sound convinced.

Caroline drove, carefully negotiating the twists and turns of the road. "I wouldn't want to be driving this on a rainy night with a beer or two under my belt." She was thinking of the DWIs she often defended, well-to-do Chicagoans with legal woes up to their ears, who tried to dull the worry with drink and ended up making things worse.

"Remember when we had chicken pox?" Annette asked.

Chicken pox. Caroline shot her a quizzical look. "Sure. I was nine."

"I was six and Leah three. Mother decided that it would be more convenient if we were all sick at the same time, so she drove us over to see a little boy in Leah's nursery school and get us exposed. Sure enough, within three weeks we all had spots. And where was Ginny?"

"In and out, doing the same things she always did."

"She brought us coloring books — identical ones, even though we were three different kids at three different age levels with three different interests. I remember her sitting in that chair in the corner of her bedroom, holding Leah."

"She held you, too," Caroline said.

"No. Not me. Only Leah."

But Caroline remembered it clearly, remembered the hurt. "You *and* Leah. I'm sure. When I didn't take to the coloring book, she gave me one of the *National Geographics* from the bookshelf in the den. She said I'd enjoy looking through it. And I did. But it wasn't what I wanted."

Annette faced her. "You wanted *her,* and she wasn't there. Or if she was there, she wasn't there enough. She'd tuck us in, sit with us for too short a time, give us a pat on the head and a peck on the cheek. She'd say all the right things, but I never truly believed she felt bad that I was sick. She was cavalier about it. She'd say, 'You aren't the first to have chicken pox, and you won't be the last.' Life was one long methodical string of events. Nothing was extraordinary. Everything was beige."

Caroline knew what she meant. Ginny never delved into red, purple, or orange. On occasion things were taupe or ivory, maybe even, once in a great while, pink or pale

165

green, but a solid, neutral beige was the norm.

"I wanted her to feel for me," Annette went on. "I wanted her to itch a little, and cry a little, and sweat because I was sweating."

"Ginny was never emotional."

"She was never *involved*. It was like she had a list of the things that mothers were supposed to do, so she did each thing because it was what was expected, and checked it off. Her job was then done. Her obligation was fulfilled. She never went above and beyond the call of duty. She certainly never put herself in our skin. But I do it all the time, Caroline. I feel for my kids. So is it wrong for me to be concerned if Thomas doesn't feel well?"

Of course not, Caroline thought. Annette was right on the nose in her assessment of Ginny as a mother, even if she herself went overboard in the other direction. "It's admirable. But it isn't grounds for flying home. The others can take care of Thomas. He knows you're thinking of him. You've always been there for him. He knows you'd be there now if it weren't for this business with Ginny. He won't stop loving you."

"I know."

"Love for a mother is the most enduring

kind. You cannot like your mother and still love her. When I worked for the county, I saw battered children who should have run away from their mothers and never looked back, but they didn't. They stayed."

"Love wasn't the only reason."

"No, but it's the strongest. When you're a child, you can't give it a name. When you're an adolescent, you rebel against it. When you finally leave home, you think you've outgrown it. But you haven't. You can pretend it doesn't exist, but when you see your mother after an absence, you notice that her neck is creased and that there are liver spots on her hands, and you're unsettled. Then when she writes and says she's turning seventy, you can't pretend anymore. You feel something, this little something inside that's kind of like fear."

Quietly, Annette finished the thought. "So you take the tickets she sent and you use them, even though it's the last thing in the world you want to do."

Caroline shot her a smile, gratified that they were on the same wavelength on this, at least. Then she turned her attention to the tiny town center coming into view.

The main street boasted stores for the everyday necessities — hardware, medicine, postage stamps, books, food. She left

Annette at the general store to shop for trinkets for the kids, and continued around the corner to the waterfront. There, tucked between fishing shacks and supply and repair shops, were the cavernous lofts that were simultaneously workspaces and galleries. She counted four from the street, though the old salt who directed her insisted there were more "behind and on down."

She picked one at random, pushed at the warped wood door until it opened, and nearly stumbled when the floor was two inches below the door.

"Watch your step," called a voice after the fact.

Had Caroline been in Chicago, she would have asked that voice why there wasn't a warning sign on the door and told it that the lack thereof, if cited by an injured party, begged a lawsuit. Because she was in Downlee, where the surroundings were gentler and more innocent, she didn't say a word. She just looked around.

The gallery consisted of paintings hung on crude wood walls, beneath which canvases were stacked one before the other. She saw landscapes, seascapes, and still lifes. The colors were stunning.

The voice came again. "Looking for anything special?"

"Could be," Caroline said. "I'll know it when I see it."

She might have already. Her eye had quickly spotted, and kept being drawn back to, one of the canvases on the wall. It was a loose depiction of a meadow filled with flowers the color of the sea. She could see it in Ginny's front hall.

"Are you just passing through?" the voice asked, nearer now.

"Actually, I'm here for two weeks," she said, still looking at the painting. Then she turned and extended her hand to a blue-jeaned, lightly bearded, paint-speckled man who looked to be well into his fifties. "Caroline St. Clair. My mother is the new owner of Star's End."

The man's hand was slow in meeting hers, as though he wasn't used to shaking hands, particularly with women. But his eyes were curious. "Jack Ivy. You're the new owner's daughter?"

She nodded. "I arrived late yesterday."

"Your mother, too?"

"No. She'll be up today or tomorrow."

"Word has it she's living here year 'round."

Caroline was about to nod, then caught herself. She had been shocked enough that her mother was moving here, period, not to give the other much thought. "Actually, I'm not sure. She may. Then again, she may want warm weather in winter." She pointed to the piece that kept drawing her back. "This is a beautiful painting. Did you do it?"

"Yup."

"Is everything here yours?"

"Not all. There's lots of artists who come here to paint, and then leave. I take the best of their work on consignment."

"Do you sell mostly to tourists?"

He chuckled. "I'd starve if I relied on them. No, there are folks who cart my things over and around. They get me good money."

Caroline could imagine. Not that the man looked to be greedy. He struck her as a happiest-in-my-oldest-clothes kind of guy who surrounded himself with similarly broken-in things. She saw a worn easel that held his work in progress, a desk made of a large door on saw horses, and a single small machine that could presumably turn out a sales slip. The studio was unadorned, even to a startling lack of lights. She assumed his workday coincided with the sun's. And his rent couldn't possibly be high.

"What's she like, your mother?" he asked.

Caroline swung around a little too fast.

"No offense meant," he said quickly. "Just

curious. It isn't often someone moves up here out of the blue. Either you're born here, leave, and move back, or you move here to be with family."

Put that way, she could see his point. Still, she wasn't about to pour out her heart to a stranger. Nor was she about to disparage her mother, despite her differences with the woman. So she simply said, "She's a nice person."

"Is she pretty?"

"Is that relevant?" the feminist in her asked.

"Whoa, you're prickly," he said. "No, it's not relevant. I was just curious."

Jack Ivy was curious, and Caroline was a product of the city. Worse, she was the product of a career where ulterior motives were common and paranoia was a way of life. It was sad to be so distrustful in such a blunt and unadorned kind of place.

Caroline sighed. "Yes, she's pretty." She returned to the painting. "Is this a local scene?"

"It's bits and snatches of lots of local scenes. Most of what I do is. I can't just sit and copy what's in front of me. I have to give it my own twist."

"You take it in your mouth, chew it up, spit it back out on the canvas," she said, "to

171

quote a friend of mine. He's an artist, too."

"He got it right. Where does he live?"

"North of Chicago."

"That where you live, too?"

"I live in the city."

"And your mother? I hear she's from Philadelphia."

"That's right."

"And that she's a widow now. When did her husband die?"

Caroline's caution resurfaced. She wasn't used to answering personal questions. But this fellow seemed innocent enough in his interest. And it was a matter of public record. "He died three years ago."

"Was he your father?"

It was a minute before she got his drift. "Yes."

He gave a low whistle. "They stayed married all that time."

"I'm not *that* old," Caroline drawled and studied him. "The stereotype says you people are insular and laconic. Is this curiosity peculiar to you, or is the stereotype wrong?"

He smiled. "The stereotype ain't all wrong. We keep to ourselves. But like I said before, your mother buying Star's End surprised us."

Caroline recalled the discussion she'd had

in the taxi with Cal. "Will she be considered an oddity and held at arm's length?"

"Not necessarily. But it's up to her. We're not mean folk. Just cautious." He grinned. "And curious."

His grin was so innocent that she couldn't be angry — or maybe it was being surrounded by the familiar smell of oils, which made her think of Ben, that put her at ease. But she stayed awhile, looking through every one of the paintings in Jack Ivy's studio. She bought one, the first one, which had attracted her so. Then she moved on to the next studio.

This one housed the work of three women. Two of them were at easels when she entered; one of those joined her and talked. Her name was Joy, she was originally from Nevada, and she wanted to know anything and everything about the new owner of Star's End. Amused, Caroline parried her questions, giving away little more than she had told Jack.

The same happened at her next stop. This one was a smaller studio on a side street cutting back from the dock. Inside were portraits and the husband and wife who made them. "We work by mail," they explained. "You send your picture, we paint a portrait." But that was all they said about themselves. They, too, wanted to know about Ginny.

Caroline was beginning to feel like something of a celebrity. Still, she gave little by way of concrete information. She figured it wasn't her job to tell all. It was Ginny's.

Annette was by nature a more chatty sort, particularly when she found something to be chatty about. She had branched off from the center of town onto side streets dotted with crafts shops, and she was astounded. She had never seen as many exquisite items in one place at one time — quilts, woven pillows, wall hangings, and rugs, one more striking than the next. The artists who had made them were there, willing to answer questions about their work until Annette introduced herself. Then they became the questioners.

"Why did your mother decide to buy Star's End?" one asked.

"Who'll be living with her in the house?" another asked.

"What's she like?" a third asked, and while Annette had answered the first two in single sentences, she gave this answer more thought. She wasn't about to speak ill of Ginny. She was too loyal for that.

"She's a social person. I'm sure she'll be

in and out of these shops all the time. She likes talking with people."

"Is she lonely, now that your father has passed on?"

"She misses him. But she has lots of friends. They give her comfort."

"Will her friends be coming here?"

"I'm sure they'll visit," Annette said with what she hoped was reassurance. Ginny might start out on better footing with these people if they thought she would be good for business.

Less for the sake of business, though, than for the sake of Ginny's family room, Annette bought a lap blanket in shades of navy and turquoise, and carried it with her to the next shop. This one was a showplace for workers in clay, and quite a showplace it was. Annette was struck so by the vibrancy of the pieces that she brushed aside questions about herself and commented on it.

"There must be something about the air here, that you people produce art like this. It's the same at each place I stop. There's a wildness to these things. A passion. I see the colors of the sea and the flowers at my mother's place, all magnified."

"That's no mystery," she was told. "Star's End is something of a legend in these parts."

Annette was intrigued. "A legend?"

"A romantic inspiration. It's said to be a place where people fall in love."

"That's so *nice*," Annette mused, smiling. "Because of the setting?"

"Yup."

She could see it. There *was* something enchanting about the place. She wondered if Ginny had known that, or if she cared. Ginny had never been prone to fancy.

She understood now, though, why the townsfolk were so curious about the new owner of Star's End. Sure enough, when she went to the next shop, the questions began again. She was more generous with her answers this time, offering bits about Ginny's life in Philadelphia, a trip she had recently taken, a charity she worked for.

"Has she been happy?"

The question struck Annette as odd. "What do you mean?"

"Has she led a happy life?"

The question came from Edie Stillman, a weaver who looked to be several years older than Ginny and shared the shop with her grown daughter. When Annette had first entered, a granddaughter was there, all country simplicity and smiles. It was clearly a close family, which, Annette decided, had prompted the question.

"Yes, she's led a happy life," she answered,

though it struck her that she couldn't say that for sure. Ginny had seemed happy. She hadn't complained.

Was their home in Philadelphia like Star's End?

"No. It was larger and more formal, beautiful also, but in different ways from Star's End."

"Did she ever talk about Star's End?"

"You mean, about buying something like it? Actually," Annette shot for the truth without revealing more than necessary of it, "Mother is an independent sort. She kind of popped this on us as a surprise. She loves surprises. You do know that these pillows are spectacular, don't you?" Their covers were woven in yarns that ran the gamut from pale pink to fuschia. "They're what Mother's parlor needs to give it life."

She bought six in different sizes and diplomatically took her leave.

Leah bought three pairs of blue jeans, a pair of denim cutoffs, three white and three colored T-shirts, an oversized sweatshirt, and a pair of sneakers. The blue jeans were Caroline, the T-shirts Annette. She figured a combination of the two looks was perfect for Star's End.

Lest either of them was there when she

arrived, she drove home wearing one of the new outfits, but the Volvo hadn't returned. So she hurried her bundles upstairs, tore off price tags, and hung the clothes in the closet, mixed well with the familiar and chic.

She had to admit that she looked great in jeans and a white T-shirt. Very in. Very Gap.

Except for her hair. It had been neatly anchored when she had left that morning, but the moist air was sly. Waves had appeared where sleekness had once been. Worse, random strands that had escaped and coiled.

She pulled out the pins and rubbed her aching scalp, then shook her head until the weight of her hair hit the center of her back. Watching herself in the mirror, she scooped the long curls first to one side, then the other. On impulse, she wet her brush and ran it through her hair, once, a second time, and a third. The wetness was all the encouragement her curls needed. They blossomed.

She stood back. It struck her that she didn't look bad at all. Curly hair suited jeans and a T-shirt far more than knotted-back hair — and it was rather nice not to have pins digging into her scalp.

Thinking that her hairdresser, who adored her curls and was always begging her to wear them loose, would be thrilled, she went downstairs and outside, to the edge of the bluff where the breeze might blow her hair dry. She slipped her hands in the back pockets of her jeans, shook her head, felt startlingly free.

In time she turned away from the sea. Savoring fresh air and freedom, she strolled through the flower beds and down along the edge of the woods until a small cottage came into view. Its clapboards were a weathered gray against a backdrop of robust green oaks, but it had the look of something loved and well kept. Black shutters hung neatly beside a pair of screened windows on the first floor and a single dormer above. The bubble of a greenhouse protruded from its side, facing the sea and the morning sun.

She stood for what seemed an eternity before curiosity got the best of her. Approaching the open front door, she shielded her eyes against the screen.

"Hello?" She ignored a quickening inside, and waited in silence. "Hello?"

She saw a sofa and chairs on one side, and an eating area on the other. Straight ahead and above was a sleeping loft, and over the whole of it, whirring softly, a large paddle fan.

The insides of the cottage could easily fit into the first of the three floors of her townhouse, yet it looked comfortable and complete. Snug. And safe. It also smelled lovely — of spruce that backed on the oaks, of wood that had burned in the fireplace on a cool evening not long before. She imagined, too, that it smelled of something male. This was his home. He was strange to her, off-limits but intriguing.

She set off this time at a faster pace, striding back toward the house and beyond to explore areas of the estate that she hadn't yet seen. The scent of the beach roses swelled and ebbed as she walked past. On their far side, she stopped. She had been within sight of this stretch of the headland before, both alone and with her sisters, but her eyes were more open now, her head clearer, and what had earlier seemed a random outcropping of shrubs now looked less random.

It was a heather garden, she suddenly realized, and beautiful in an exquisitely subtle way. The plants varied in height from thick clumps to low carpets to bulbous cushions, and in color from gray to dark green to bright green to lime. Rocks lay bare between them, darker at spots, bleached at others, higher and lower as the headland rolled.

Her eye followed the garden to the very edge of the bluff, where a dark head spiked with damp hair appeared, followed by a pair of broad shoulders, lean hips, and long legs. The hips and legs were covered with denim, but the sweat-darkened work shirt that covered the shoulders flapped open.

She felt the thud of her heart, then the spread of a slow honey inside, all the more so when he saw her and smiled. His smile took her places. It was helpless, and inevitable as it settled into its rightful place on his face.

"Hi," he said.

Her answering smile was just as helpless and inevitable. "How are you?"

"Warm. Sun's strong today." He shot it a squinting glance, mopped his brow with his arm, and returned to her. "You look nice."

"Thank you," she said, feeling inordinately pleased. She nearly added, So do you. But he was the gardener. He was dirty and sweaty. A comment like that might be taken the wrong way. So she gestured toward the heather. "I'm impressed. Again. Still. Did you do this all yourself?"

His eyes held hers. "Took four years. The whole place was so covered with brush you could barely see the ledge. I had to clear it away little by little before I planted."

"It's different from the other gardens."

"Meant to be. Star's End is like a gem. It

has facets. You've seen the flower beds, and the woods, and now this. There's also a wildflower meadow."

The sound of it suggested something idyllic and pure. Excited, she asked, "Where?"

He cocked his head off toward the woods. "In there. It's just starting for the season. So are these heathers. By August the blooms will run from white and pink to rose and raspberry. Come fall the colors will mirror the woods, all golds and reds."

"Heather. So pretty. I never imagined."

"Most people don't. They think it's a boring little plant. It's indigenous to Great Britain, so it thrives in the cool, moist climate here. When it's sited well and cared for, the results are worth the effort."

She darted a questioning look at the pail he had set down when he'd come up from the rocks.

"Seaweed," he said. "It makes a good mulch. It's organic. And it's free."

"You just go down on the rocks and gather it?"

"Yup."

That explained the pitchfork he carried, but the pitchfork didn't hold her attention for long. She was drawn to the patches of sweat on his shirt and, between its gaping front, his chest. It was broad, muscled, lightly haired. He was well built. Her lungs labored over that fact.

She tried to remember the last time she had been so struck by a man, and couldn't. It was remarkable, really. She saw men all the time. She saw attractive men all the time. She saw attractive men in swim trunks, and even, with the demise of the occasional pool party, a drunken man nude. But she hadn't caught her breath in years and years.

Not since Charlie, who had been good-looking in an intellectual way, with curly hair, wire-rimmed glasses, and an ego the size of Texas. Before Charlie there had been Ron, but as right as he was for her on paper, he hadn't caused much of a spark.

Jesse Cray didn't cause a spark. He caused dozens and, in so doing, made her feel like a woman — and it wasn't his looks, in the traditional sense. He was more craggy than handsome, more spit than polish, and though he was a solemn man, his smile was a killer.

She wondered if it was the infrequency of it that made it so rewarding, but his smile wasn't all that warmed her. There was the gentle, direct way he talked to her. He wasn't pretentious or coy. He wasn't flirting. He was just there, a man appreciating her for just being there, too.

At least, she thought that was it. Not that she was the greatest judge, where men were concerned. She might be wrong. Still, she liked the way she felt.

So she smiled. "Well." She rubbed her hands together. "I should let you get to work."

He grew solemn again. "Will your mother be coming today?"

"I'm not sure. My sisters are furious that she isn't here already."

"How about you?"

"I'm disappointed. I've been looking forward to seeing her. She implied that she'd be here when I arrived."

"Is she sick?"

"No. Just lingering, I guess."

"Is she getting cold feet about living here?"

Leah considered that, but she had no idea what her mother was thinking. Ginny was a mystery — a very pleasant, very proper and correct woman who kept her inner thoughts to herself. "Beats me," she said finally.

"I can understand why she might."

"I can't." At that moment, on that matter, she had no doubt. "This is the most delightful place I've ever been to. It's beautiful. It's refreshing. It's exciting."

"There are people who'd disagree with you on that last one. They'd call it boring."

She shook her head. "I brought a pile of books with me, but each time I sit down to read, my mind wanders off, and before I know it, I'm up doing something else."

"Have you been in town yet?"

She shook her head.

"You should go. It's nice."

"Do you go often?"

"Every day. For food or supplies. It's a surprising place."

She was bemused. "Surprising?"

"Not backwoods like you'd think. The artists are a sophisticated bunch, and because of it, the support services are, too. The general store sells croissants. And the hardware store carries cappuccino makers."

"Does it sell any?"

He shot her a crooked smile. "Sure. Artists love cappuccino. There's a restaurant called Julia's that specializes in seafood, but it has other interesting things, too. You should stop there. The owner is about your age. She moved here from New York three years ago. You'd like her."

"Sounds nice," Leah said, though she wasn't wild about running into town. She was feeling safe and content at Star's End.

"If you ever want to hitch a ride, give a yell."

Now *that* was a temptation, she thought,

185

and smiled. "I will." She started backing off. "Good talking with you. Mulch well."

She turned and walked as casually as she could toward the house. It was a challenge. She was flying high on something or other that had to do with curly hair and jeans, salty ocean air, and a heather garden planted with love.

She had breezed past the pool and was approaching the French doors when Caroline's angry voice brought her fast back to earth.

NINE

Annette was talking on the telephone, covering her free ear, while Caroline waved a piece of paper nearby.

"This isn't the time to be calling home, Annette! We have to decide what to do!" She whirled around when Leah came in. "Leah! Did you see this?"

Leah took the paper from her hand. It was a note from Gwen. She had barely begun to read it when Caroline cried, "She isn't coming today or tomorrow! Maybe Thursday, she says!" She whipped the paper from Leah's hands. "The woman is selfish, arrogant, and deceitful. She's *impossible.* What is wrong with her? Doesn't she want to come? Was buying this place a big *hoax?* Doesn't she realize that the only reason we're here is because we thought *she'd* be here? She's stringing us along, Leah, letting us dangle. This will go on for days. I just know it."

Leah was feeling a let-down, but none of the anger Caroline did. "Have you asked Gwen about this?"

"Hah. Good question. Gwen was waiting on the front porch to take off with the Volvo the minute we got back. She didn't so much as mention this. The lady knows which side her bread is buttered on. Where were you when Ginny called?"

"I went for a ride," Leah said, which was technically true. She wasn't about to say she had gone shopping for clothes. She wanted her sisters to think that she had known all along the very best look for Star's End.

Annette had hung up the phone and joined them, looking exasperated. "What's wrong with Mother? Why is she doing this? Doesn't she have any respect at all for the fact that we have our own lives?"

"Is Thomas feeling better?" Leah asked.

"For now. God knows what'll be in an hour."

Caroline drummed her fingers on the counter. "If we ever dared do something like this to her, we'd never hear the end of it." In a mocking singsong, she said, "Punctuality is important, girls. *Reliability* is important. People judge you on those things." Her voice leveled. "Do you know that I'm usually early for appointments? It's a joke around the office, but I loathe being late. Loathe? No, that tells only half the story. I can't *bear* it. I start sweating if I think I'm running late. I tell myself it's stupid, that the rest of the world doesn't give a damn if I'm late because that's the way life is, but so help me I can't change."

Leah knew the feeling. She had to deliberately hold herself back, had to actually sit home for a few minutes, fully dressed and watching the clock, lest she arrive at a party at the prescribed time, which was more often than not before her hosts were ready.

Annette said, "It's been bred into us. When my kids have dentist appointments, we're always there on time, even though I know we'll have to wait to be seen. I get angry then, and I curse Mother, and I want to tell my kids, 'What the hell, be as late as you want, if people want your company or time or *money,* they'll want it regardless,' but I can't do it."

"So what do you do?" Leah asked. Since reconciling her own instincts with those of her mother was an ongoing issue for her, she welcomed suggestions.

"I shoot for a happy medium," Annette said. "I teach the kids that they shouldn't keep people waiting, but I don't make them crazy about it. We call the dentist's office before we leave the house to see if she's running on time. In the rare instance when we're running late ourselves, rather than panic we call to alert them that we'll be right along. Usually they tell us to take our time."

"Mother should have given us that choice," Caroline grumbled, pushing her fingers through her hair. "I need a cigarette. Does anyone have one?"

"Not me."

"Nuh-uh."

"Swell." She twisted toward the French doors, then twisted right back. "How long does she think we can hang around here waiting for her to come? We've already been here for one day, now she says she won't arrive for another two, maybe more. What are we supposed to be doing?"

"Spending her money," Annette answered, grinning her way to the sofa and a mountain of bags. "I found some great things in town. Look at these." Discarding bags, she draped a navy and turquoise lap quilt over the back of the sofa, and tossed pillows strategically about. "And this," she said, more carefully removing newsprint to unveil a ceramic bowl glazed in a starburst of blues. "For fruit or candy." She set it on a low ivory cube by one of the chairs.

Leah thought the purchases were wonderful, and told her so.

Caroline agreed, less angry at last. "They are incredible. So's my painting." She led them to the front hall, lifted the canvas, and held it to the wall.

Leah came closer. "Un-believable. The colors are the colors of Star's End. Absolutely perfect for this room." She sighed, feeling no small amount of chagrin. "You two were busy."

"Ben told me Downlee was an artists' colony," Caroline mused, "but I thought he was being polite. I never expected to see work of this caliber."

Annette remained effusive. "You didn't see the crafts I did, and I didn't see the half of it. There must be eight more shops that I didn't have time to visit. Downlee is full of surprises."

Leah thought of what Jesse had said. The fact that her sisters validated it was a validation of him, which made her smile. Feeling high again — in a state of reprieve, what with Ginny further delayed, and more relaxed — she looked from one sister to the other. "I think we should celebrate."

"Celebrate what?" Caroline asked. "Ginny still isn't coming."

191

"Okay, so she isn't coming. That's her loss. She's missing out on us, and she's missing out on our discoveries, and besides, we're spending her money. I think we should celebrate successful shopping."

Caroline made a face, but it had an affectionate twist. "You would."

Leah wasn't being deflated. "I know it's late, but have you had lunch?"

"No."

"No."

"Want some?"

"Gwen's out."

"We can munch on chips."

But Leah didn't want to munch on chips. "There's good stuff to be had. I'll make something."

"Really?"

"Are you serious?"

Leah was already heading back to the kitchen, where she uncorked a bottle of white wine and filled three glasses.

"I never drink during the day," Caroline declared. "I can't concentrate on work."

Annette was warily eyeing the wine. "The last thing I want the kids to think is that I need a drink in the middle of the day."

"You don't need it," Leah proposed. "You're having it because it's a fun thing to do when you're on vacation. The kids aren't around to see. And you don't have to concentrate on work, Caroline. You left people doing it for you back in Chicago."

"Yeah, and I'd put money on the fact that they'll mess up. Somewhere, somehow, they will. I did not get a good feeling when I called there before." Still, she raised her glass. "Cheers."

A short time later, Leah refilled their glasses. They were in bathing suits now, enjoying the midafternoon sun on the back deck, while they worked leisurely at the *salade Nicoise* she had made.

"This is very good," Annette remarked. "You did well."

"I like to cook. Not that this is cooking, really —"

"It's cooking," Caroline insisted. "You boiled potatoes and green beans, and you made the dressing from scratch. Do you do this a lot?"

"Nah. It's not much fun doing it for one."

"That's why I usually bring in take-out."

"But you have a valid excuse to do that," Leah pointed out. "You've been in an office all day. I'm around the house more, so it's silly not to cook. But it's more fun doing it here. Mother's kitchen is a dream."

"Just stay away from the fattening stuff," Annette warned. "My thighs are gross."

Leah laughed. "They are not."

"They're fat."

"Not fat," said Caroline. "Just not eighteen anymore. Mine are the same. The Stairmaster can only do so much."

Leah studied her thighs, then her sisters'. "Objectively speaking, none of ours are bad. We wouldn't embarrass Ginny if she had friends here."

Caroline snorted. "Not on the issue of thighs, at least. Lord knows theirs wouldn't win any prizes."

"They'd be wearing bathing suits with skirts," Annette drawled, but dropped the drawl in the next breath. "Look at us. We have a sleek maillot, a sexy bikini, and one that's sedate and diagonally draped." She sighed. "I'm glad Jean-Paul isn't here. He'd be looking at you two, not me."

"That's not true," Caroline said.

Leah agreed, with no small amount of envy. "He worships the ground you walk on. And if Mother were here, she'd approve of your suit long before she'd approve of Caroline's or mine. She might ask us to change into something more decent, if she was expecting friends."

"Even if she wasn't," Caroline remarked. "Ginny is a prude."

Annette elaborated. "She has a narrow

view of what's proper. That view would say you have too much thigh showing, too much cleavage, too much *nipple.* She worries about what people think of her. She fears what they may say behind her back."

Leah thought back to childhood agonies. As painful as they had been at the time, she could smile about them now. "Remember when we were kids, how uptight she always was before we went to visit her parents?"

"She wanted us to be the perfect little girls," Annette began.

"With dresses from Saks," Caroline picked up, "and new shoes and our hair just so. Rollers — I remember rollers in my hair, which was, is, and always will be stick straight, which is why I wear it cut short like this, though Mother can't understand that. I remember sleeping in rollers with sharp pink picks and wire middles digging into my scalp. What a nightmare."

"But the way we looked made a statement about her life," Leah said. "If we looked beautiful, she had done something right. Same thing if we looked rich."

"We were rich anyway," Caroline asserted, "so what was the point?"

"The point," Leah argued, "was that our grandparents were richer. Money was a big issue with them. Mother wanted to show

195

them that she had married well."

"At our expense, no pun intended."

"Maybe."

"Maybe?" Annette echoed. "Leah, she made you so nuts about the way you looked that you became bulimic. Don't defend her."

"I'm not. I'm just trying to understand her. She wanted her parents' approval. Is that any different from what we want? I mean, why else are we here?"

"I'm here," Caroline said, sucking a black olive, "because Ben told me that if I didn't come, I'd suffer the guilt for the rest of my life. He has a conscience. And he's gorgeous, to boot."

"Speaking of gorgeous," Annette mused, "has anyone taken a good look at the gardener?"

Leah choked on a piece of tuna. She coughed, caught her breath, and took a mouthful of wine.

"What's wrong?"

Holding a hand to her chest, she said, "Mother would die if she thought you were lusting after the gardener."

"It's an innocent observation. He is gorgeous."

"He's not bad," Caroline remarked, sprawled comfortably in her chair now. "A little on the rough side."

"Gorgeous," Annette insisted.

"What about Jean-Paul?"

"Jean-Paul is magnificent. This guy's gorgeous."

"What's the difference?"

"Magnificent involves the whole person. Gorgeous is just the facade. Jean-Paul is bright, talented, *and* gorgeous."

"So's Ben. He's beautiful through and through. This fellow is just the gardener."

"I think," Leah said quietly, "that he's a horticulturist. I've talked with him. He's incredibly knowledgeable."

"He certainly fits in here," Caroline reflected. "Ginny would do well to keep him on. He goes with the land — literally and figuratively."

"Like the pieces we bought today," Annette said. "They capture something. I was talking with the craftspeople about it. They say it has to do with Star's End."

Leah was intrigued. "In what way?"

"This is the prettiest place around. Artists come here for inspiration."

"Really?" she asked with a smile. The idea of it carried a certain richness.

"I got that feeling, too," Caroline mused. "I kept getting glimpses of Star's End in what I saw. The piece I bought was one of dozens, and that was only at the first gallery I went to. Everywhere I stopped, I caught the same feeling, the same energy, the same —" she struggled for the word, "the same passion." Looking from Leah to Annette and back, she added a defensive, "That's what I felt."

"Same here," Annette admitted.

"I wanted to talk more with the artists, but they only wanted to talk about Ginny."

"Same here! Wherever I went, they asked questions. It was eerie after a while."

"Not eerie. Annoying."

Leah thought of the policeman who had shown her to Star's End that first night. He had been curious, too. "I suppose it's natural. Downlee is a small place. Mother is a newcomer. They're wondering what she'll be like."

Caroline grunted. "At the rate she's going, they may never know. When is she coming, for God's sake?"

The question was rhetorical. Leah knew nothing more than Caroline or Annette. They were all three in the same boat. It struck Leah that they hadn't been that way in a very long time.

Nor had they sat together, just the three of them, having lunch together, in a very long time.

Or talked for so long without personal attacks.

It struck Leah as rather nice. She guessed it had something to do with age. Maybe they had mellowed. Certainly they shared a dilemma — shared an enemy, so to speak — which was always good for unity. But they shared a past, too. That had to account for something.

"So," she said, "what are you guys going to do? Are you staying or leaving?"

She expected Caroline to speak first, but Caroline simply took another sip of her wine.

Annette said, "I don't think my family wants me home yet."

"Of course, they want you home."

"No. They're annoyed I've been calling. They want me to give it a rest. They have something to prove."

Quietly, Caroline said, "I'm getting the same thing from my office. And from Ben." She looked off into the distance. "When I talked with him a little while ago, he suggested that I was the dependent one, having to call home all the time."

Leah held her tongue.

They sat without talking for a while, picking at their food, sipping their wine, letting the sound of the surf on the rocks far below soothe over the rough edges of their predicaments.

Leah felt for them. Their lives were more complex than hers — which wasn't to say that all was forgiven. Caroline was still too high-handed about her work, and Annette took motherhood to the extreme. But apparently Leah wasn't the only one who believed that, and the others who did were making themselves known. The fact that her sisters were struggling with their feelings said that they weren't as insensitive as she might like to believe.

Besides, they weren't dumping on her. She wasn't feeling as worthless as she usually did when she was with them. Maybe it was because she'd made them lunch.

"I'll stay a little longer," Annette finally said. "It's a good exercise, I guess."

"There's one part of me that hopes they trip up," Caroline groused, "then they'll miss me more. But I'll feel foolish running back now." She drained the last of her wine and looked at her sisters. "Besides, I want to see those other galleries. There's some fine artwork to be had. Ginny needs *a lot.*"

Aside from brief spells when one or another of them wandered off, they spent the rest of the afternoon by the pool. Leah brought a third book down, since the second hadn't grabbed her any more than the first. When Caroline told her she'd read it, her hackles went up, but then Caroline related information about the author that enhanced the reading tenfold.

Caroline commandeered one of her other books and began to read.

Annette found a Scrabble set and cajoled them into a game.

The sun crept westward and lowered. The breeze picked up. The air cooled.

"I'm getting hungry again," Caroline announced.

Annette set aside her crossword puzzle. "Don't look at me. If this is my vacation, I'm not cooking dinner."

"You wouldn't want *me* to," Caroline advised.

They both looked at Leah. "Okay," she said.

But Caroline was already reconsidering. With a belligerent frown, she said, "Then again, there's Gwen. Let's make her do it. It'd serve her right, being so sneaky about Ginny."

Leah had a better idea. "I heard there was a good restaurant in town. Julia's. Did either of you see it today?"

"Not me."

"No."

"Her specialty is seafood, but the menu is interesting." Caroline looked dubious.

"How interesting can seafood be?" Annette asked.

"She's a transplanted New Yorker," Leah said.

Caroline closed her book and smiled. "When do we leave?"

"I know, Ben. I call too much. But I had to tell you the most amazing thing. I had dinner with my sisters tonight. Granted, I'd been drinking wine all afternoon, so I was fortified, but it was actually nice."

"Just the three of you?"

She could hear the surprise in his voice and was glad she'd called. Smugly, she said, "Just the three of us. Not that we had much choice. Mother is still hiding out wherever, and Gwen is in the dog house for being in collusion with her, and since we don't know a hell of a lot of other people up here, we were stuck with each other. It could have been awkward, but it wasn't. You would have been proud of me. I was totally agreeable."

"Amazing."

"It *was*," she insisted. "We're three very different people."

"So what did you talk about?"

"The restaurant. It was an adorable place. Could as easily have been in Chicago as not."

"People in Maine eat, too."

"I know, but this place was upscale."

"You're a snob," he said, but fondly. "What else did you talk about?"

"Books. Movies. Music. The time passed quickly. And you'll be pleased to know that I didn't leave the table once to call the office."

"You waited 'til you got home."

"Not even then. I'm proving that you're wrong. I am not dependent on anyone there."

"Except me."

"You don't count. I don't have to keep tabs on you. It's my practice that I worry about."

"Your practice will be fine."

"Maybe. It's just that I like knowing what's happening."

"You like being in control."

"Don't you? How would you like someone squeegeeing an odd layer of color on one of your prints?"

"Uh-uh, babe. The analogy's no good. An artist is, by definition, a single practitioner. But you work in a firm, which, by definition, means that you work in a team."

"So? My work can be done wrong. I can be stabbed in the back."

"But you choose to work in a firm."

"Because that's where the security is. And the prestige. Especially for a woman. I wouldn't have the kind of practice I do without the firm."

"So? So what if you represented fewer clients and nicer bad guys? It wouldn't mean you were any less self-sufficient. That's what this boils down to, Caroline. You've always wanted to be *the* best, *the* toughest, *the* busiest lawyer in town. God forbid anyone should think you're dependent on a man, or your friends, or your place in society the way your mother was. But you aren't. You've already proven that ten times over, and as far as control is concerned, you'd have far more control in your own small law firm, if you ask me."

"I didn't ask you," she snapped, then said more quietly, "Where did all this come from?"

Ben was silent for a bit. "It's the same old thing. I'm just thinking about it more, with you gone. Maybe you should, too."

Caroline had the unsettling sense that she'd been given an ultimatum. She and Ben had been together on and off for ten years. He'd been patient. He'd been indulgent. But he was human, too. He wouldn't wait forever.

She wanted to yell at him. She wanted to tell him that she'd never promised him a thing, and that if *he* had a problem with their relationship, it wasn't her fault. But she couldn't say that. Too much of what he said made sense.

"I have to go now," she said around the lump in her throat, and hung up the phone.

Annette waited until ten to call home. She figured that by then Robbie and the twins would be with friends, Nat and Thomas would be asleep, and Jean-Paul would be lonely enough to forgive her the call.

No one answered the phone. She punched out the number a second time, with the same result.

Assuming that Jean-Paul must have taken the little ones to a movie, she finished her crossword puzzle, then tried again. Still there was no answer. So she opened a book and began to read, trying the number every fifteen minutes, then every ten, then every five. She had worked herself into a state when Jean-Paul finally picked up.

"Jean-Paul! Thank goodness! I've been worried! Where have you been?"

"We were out, the children and me," he said calmly. "You know how they can be. One thing finishes, and they think of something else to do. By the way, I did make calls about your mother's doctor. His credentials are good."

"Did you talk with him?"

"Yes. He confirmed what Leah said."

Annette caught a tiny hesitation that one who didn't know Jean-Paul as well might have missed. "Tell me, Jean-Paul."

"The initial tests found a minimum of problem. In a subsequent visit, though, he felt some concern." When Annette gasped, he said, "Her blood pressure was up. He prescribed medication, and suggested that she watch her diet and avoid undue upset."

"Is there a problem with her heart?"

"The EKG showed a small irregularity. Had she been ten years younger, he might have suggested a pacemaker. He did, indeed, give her that option. She declined it. Since the case was marginal, he let it go."

"Would you have let it go?" Annette asked.

"I can't say, since this isn't my specialty. It is, in the end, though, the patient's choice. He has suggested that she see someone on a regular basis. I have the name of a man in Portland."

"Well, that's good, at least," Annette said.

"Of course, you heard none of this from me," Jean-Paul cautioned. "Doctors do not like to discuss patients with a third party."

"You're a fellow doctor."

"I am also the patient's son-in-law, telling the patient's daughter something that the patient, whatever her reasons, has chosen not to reveal."

"I will be very subtle when I ask about her health," Annette promised, though she did plan to ask. Given what Jean-Paul had told her, she felt a responsibility toward Ginny, which was startling given their history, not at all so given Annette's personality. She feared that it was her destiny to take people's problems to heart.

On a lighter vein, she asked, "So, what kept you out so late?"

"We stopped for ice cream."

"At eleven-thirty?"

"Thomas was hungry. He didn't have much all day."

"He wasn't *feeling* well all day." She sighed in dismay. "Ice cream." With his father a doctor. She didn't know whether to laugh or cry. She felt foolish for having worried.

It suddenly struck her that, at the rate she was going, before she turned fifty she would have wrinkles from frowning and an ulcer from worrying, while everyone else in her family went along his or her carefree way. It didn't seem fair.

It *wasn't* fair.

"Ice cream," she repeated. "Okay. Did he have it with marshmallow fluff, chocolate sauce, and nuts?" Jean-Paul didn't see fit to worry; let *him* clean up when Thomas was sick.

"Just chocolate sauce."

"You'd better leave the bedroom door open, in case he doesn't make it through the night."

"Not to worry."

"Oh, I won't worry," she snapped. "I'm here, and you're there, so if it's anyone's worry, it's yours."

"Are you angry?"

She was furious. "What makes you ask that?"

"You don't sound like you."

"Well, how would you sound if your family told you to buzz off?"

"No one told you that."

"Not in as many words, but almost. The kids are impatient each time I call, and you keep telling me not to worry, like I'm being a total pest."

"You're reading into things, Annette. You aren't a pest."

"Then why can't I call? I *miss* you all. Don't you miss me?"

"Very much. But we aren't paralyzed without you. That's a tribute to you. You trained us, and you did it well."

Her fury gave way to hurt. "That's great. I've loved you all so well that I've enabled you to not need my love at all."

"We'll always need your love. Just not crammed down our throats."

"Jean-Paul!"

She heard a soft, "*Merde.* I am not handling this right."

"Maybe you are. If you're saying what you feel."

"It's not coming out right. I don't like talking on the phone this way. This discussion would be better saved for your return."

"We've already *had* this discussion," she argued, but she was feeling as though a hole had been carved out of her center. "Many times. You say I don't give you breathing space. Okay. I'm giving you breathing space. Ginny keeps putting off her arrival, and I can't leave until she gets here, and besides, I'm actually having a nice time with my sisters. So I'll leave everything there to you. If something comes up, you can call."

Jean-Paul was silent.

She wanted to cry. She didn't understand

why they were disagreeing on this, when they rarely disagreed on anything. She didn't understand why Jean-Paul wasn't hurting the very same way she was. She didn't understand why he wasn't *missing* her more.

She was a majority of one, it seemed, when it came to defining motherhood and love. Devastated, she said, "I'm hanging up the phone now. Goodnight, Jean-Paul."

She waited for him to call back, but the phone didn't ring.

TEN

Midnight found Leah sitting out on the bluff, wrapped in the afghan, engrossed in the sea. The air was dark and full. Moonshine tipped the water a silvery black, and far below, where she couldn't see but could only hear, waves met the rocks with an explosion of spume.

Everywhere she went at Star's End she found richness, and this was no exception. There was beauty in the night, a wealth of sensation that should have filled her to overflowing. Still, a small, lonely part of her ached.

She turned around until she faced the house. The dark expanse of the pool was broken only by the rhythmic movement of a pair of ropy arms. She had been on the bluff for an hour. He had been swimming for nearly twenty minutes. If past nights were a precedent, he would be finishing soon.

No more than two minutes later he set his

elbows on the deck. He rested for a bit before hoisting himself up and out. After drying off, he draped the towel around his neck and stood with his back to her, a lone, dark figure in the night. Her heart began to thud. He turned her way.

She held her breath as he approached. When he was just beyond arm's reach, he lowered himself to the rocks.

"Been here long?" he asked gently.

"No. Yes. It's nice. Peaceful."

"Are you warm enough?"

"Uh-huh." Between the afghan and her nightgown, she was adequately covered, which explained warmth. It didn't explain why her insides hummed. Being with Jesse Cray did that. She was drawn to him — to his honesty, his kindness, and, oh yes, his body. The force of the attraction was startling. It evoked curiosity and yearning. She ached to touch him.

No doubt because he wasn't her type at all.

"We ate at Julia's tonight," she said, and worked harder to steady her voice. "I enjoyed it. Thanks for the recommendation."

"My pleasure." He wiped his face with the end of the towel. "Did your sisters like it, too?"

"Uh-huh. You had prepared me for what

I'd find there, but they were surprised. They're used to the city. Caroline lives in Chicago, Annette in St. Louis. Caroline is a lawyer."

"And Annette?"

"Wife and mother. Her husband is a neurosurgeon. They have five kids."

Jesse settled down on the rocks. "What about you?"

"No kids. No husband."

"How do you spend your time?" It was diplomatically put, but without studied tact. His seemed a natural sensitivity.

"I work for charities and the like. I am," she drawled, "what they call a professional volunteer."

"Nothing wrong with that."

No, nothing wrong with it. Except the lack of a paycheck — or a pack of children — to show that she'd done something. And then there was the loneliness at night.

"Is Caroline married?" he asked.

"No. She's too busy. Or so she says."

"Are you too busy?"

"Oh, I've been married," she said without pride. "Twice. It didn't work out either time."

"I'm sorry."

"So was I at the time. At both times," and Ginny had been furious. She had liked

Charlie *and* Ron, each being well-rooted, successful, and able to support Leah in the style Ginny wanted them to — which might have been fine with Leah, too, if there hadn't been an awful hole where the heart of those relationships should have been.

"Things that ought to be right, sometimes, just aren't," she told Jesse. "What looks right in theory can be a bust in fact. The needs of the mind don't always jibe with those of the heart."

"You didn't love them?"

"I did. Just not the right way." She had loved intellectually, but without the sustenance of passion. She had been far more in love with the idea of being in love, than with the men themselves.

"They must have been upset."

She gave a self-deprecating laugh. "They weren't. Neither marriage lasted long. Both breakups were mutual. Since there weren't any children, we just went our separate ways. That sounds cold, I know. I don't mean it to. I liked being married."

"Just not to those guys."

She nodded. "So now you know. I'm a big failure in the love department."

"I'll bet you date a lot."

She turned until she faced the sea, wrapped her arms around her knees, and

214

said, "I hate dating. It's awkward and embarrassing. I avoid it whenever possible." She dared a look at him. "How about you?"

He shrugged. "I see women. Nothing serious."

"Ever?"

"I've been waiting for the right one. I'm a dreamer."

A dreamer. So different.

He tossed his chin toward the waves. "It's a wild night down there."

"Sounds it." So different. So *refreshing.* So physical.

"Want to go down?"

"Over the bluff?" she asked in surprise. "I didn't think I could."

"There are steps. Not really steps, but rocks that serve the purpose. I could take you down. It's a sight, when you're right in the middle of it."

She was on her feet in a minute, clutching the afghan. "I'd love to, but I'm not dressed right. Either I'll freeze, or this'll get wet."

He rolled to his feet. "I have old sweaters at my place. They've been wet so many times once more won't matter, but they'll keep us warm. I'll run back." He paused. "Or walk. Want to come?"

Leah hesitated only as long as it took to realize that while Ginny might be shocked

215

by what her youngest was doing in the middle of the night with the gardener — a nobody in proper society and a pauper, to boot, but more man than most women met in a lifetime — the fact of the matter was that Ginny wasn't there.

"Sure," she said with a smile and set off beside him.

The cottage was an amber glow that grew and beckoned with their approach. Jesse held the door and followed her in.

"Be right down," he said and took the stairs to the loft two at a time. With a single lamp lit below, the loft was shadowed, but not so deeply that Leah couldn't see him tug sweaters from a closet, then open a dresser drawer, strip down, and pull on dry shorts.

Leah suffered a sudden hot flash and looked away. The large woven throw that hung over the loft rail prevented her from seeing anything of him from the waist down, but her imagination wasn't as obliging. It painted his body in large, bold, bare strokes, and had her heart pulsing in record time.

"Still there?" he called.

"Still here," she answered in an absurdly high voice. To make it sound less absurd and more deliberate, as though the highness was necessary for projection to the loft, she called in a voice not much lower, "I like your place." Her periphery registered photographs on the walls, though she didn't have the wherewithal to approach them. "It looks very comfortable."

He trotted down the stairs, wearing jeans and one sweater and carrying another, which he gently pulled over her head. She released her hold on the afghan and slipped her arms into the sleeves. He rolled them back to her wrists, then began freeing her hair from the neckline, one handful after another.

Leah's heart was on a runaway track. "Sorry. There's so much. It's unruly."

But his eyes were appreciative, his voice deep. "It's beautiful. I've never seen anything like it." He admired it for another minute, then said quietly, "All set?"

She nodded. He guided her outside and led her toward a point farther down the bluff. At its edge, he took her hand.

They worked their way over the rocks and down a path that was steep, but worn by the years into a tiered decline. Negotiating it in bare feet was the easy part. The tough part was experiencing close-up the shock of the ocean as it rushed forward, crashed against the rocks and shot skyward, then fell, foamed, and ebbed. Leah felt small and helpless. The feeling increased the lower they went and the more deeply the crashing echoed inside her.

She should have been frightened — certainly would have been, had she been alone, even in broad daylight. But Jesse had her hand. He was her protector, the difference between terror and awe.

He led her to a sprawling boulder that would keep them out of the spray, but just, and drew her down between his legs. Around them the tide surged and fled, swirled, burst, and retreated, seeming far more a tempest than it had from above and, in that, fascinating. She tucked her feet under her nightgown, which was largely covered by Jesse's sweater, and gave in to mesmerism.

"Doin' okay?" came a gentle breath by her ear.

She sighed. "Oh, yes."

"Warm enough?"

"Perfect."

He drew her back once, laughing, with an arm around her waist, when the tide threatened to wet them — then again, a while later, and each time she landed more snugly against him. Later still, when a third move became imminent, he suggested they head back.

Leah would have stayed there all night. She was thoroughly enjoying herself — exhilarated by the sea and by being near Jesse. But though she had nothing better to do than to sleep in that day, the same couldn't be said for him. So she took the hand he offered and trailed him up over the rocks. When they reached the bluff and started across the grass, their hands remained linked.

"That was special," she said. "Do you go there often?"

"Not as often as I'd like. It can be lonely sitting out there. It's best seeing it with someone else."

As they walked, she realized how pleased she was that he had asked her. He hadn't had to. He might have just climbed out of the pool and gone off to bed, which was what the men at home would have done. They weren't into going out of their way to share something purely for the fun or the beauty of it, and in the instances when they did, there was an ulterior motive. That motive was usually less than noble.

A cynic would have said that Jesse Cray had a less than noble motive. Leah was the boss's daughter, and loaded.

But she wasn't a cynic. She believed that Jesse was his own man. He didn't have to punch in a time clock or brown-nose for the sake of a promotion. He didn't have to impress anyone. His work spoke for itself, and what he did on his own time was his own business. He chose the way he lived.

And he had chosen to show her the midnight sea.

"Thank you for taking me."

He squeezed her hand. "Thanks for coming."

They walked on. The grass was soft under her feet, as seductive as the tide had been hypnotic. The breeze lifted her hair and whispered against her neck. Jesse's hand held hers.

She heard a sound from the woods.

"Owl," he said. "It's their time."

Which brought reality home. "It's very late. I'll change back into my afghan and leave. You'll want to sleep."

"I don't need much."

"But you start work so early."

"This is worth being tired for."

The farther they walked from the sea, the quieter the night, and by contrast the louder the echo of the sea within. She felt stirred — heart hammering, pulse racing — because Jesse was close. None of it had ebbed

220

by the time they reached the cottage.

He held the door for her, and, once inside, eased the sweater over her head.

She looked up at him then. He was wearing his solemn face, but there, stark amid the gravity, she saw desire and need, even fear — everything she was feeling — and it was suddenly too much to resist.

His mouth brushed her cheek. She turned toward it. Their lips touched once, then again, sweetly. She sighed — in relief, pleasure, excitement. He tasted just the way he smelled, pure and male, and when he drew her close and moved her against him, she thought she would die. His body was large and hard. He excited her beyond belief.

He kissed her again, but she needed more. She had from the start — and only in part because her loneliness craved it. The loneliness was nothing new. Nor was the availability of a man. Over the years she had had opportunities aplenty, but she had never taken any, until now.

Jesse Cray fascinated her. He was unpolished. He was physical. He was forbidden. He was also virile and aroused, and she wanted him.

More. He looked at her as though she were special, precious, one of a kind. She wanted to be those things, too.

She slipped her arms around his neck at the same time that he caught her up, and the sheer relief of the full physical contact made her cry out. He was strong and hard, so intent on holding her that his body trembled.

He held her back only to take her face in his hands, and when he kissed her this time, it was no simple touch of the lips. It was deep, wet, and long, a statement of a raw, carnal need.

It never occurred to Leah to break it off — not then, or when he led her up the stairs to the loft, removed her nightgown, and touched her first with his eyes then his hands, or when he tore off his own clothes and lowered his naked body to hers. He was an icon of grace and power, all long legs, hair-spattered skin, and magic hands that took her to the point of release and beyond, then, even before she had caught her breath, began again. He was a highly physical man with fluid moves and bold thrusts that lifted her up and away from the woman she'd once been in ways that would have been ter-rifying, had he not stayed with her. He kissed her eyes. He touched her face. He drew her hands to his chest and moaned his encouragement when they lowered. At his most untamed, when he reared back, drove her higher, then higher still, and threw back his head, her name was the sound on his lips.

She rested, curled against him. She might have even slept, but when he turned to her again, she was ready. There was a starved spot inside, it seemed, that hungered for everything he did, and he fed her — fed her with wet kisses, hands on her breasts and between her thighs, and an erection that stretched her and filled her and lasted forever.

Shortly before dawn, he walked her back across the lawn, an arm around her shoulder, holding her close.

"So," he said, "what do you think?"

She didn't pretend not to know what he meant. "I think that this has been the most improbable night I've ever spent."

"Are you sorry?"

"No. A little confused, maybe."

"Because I'm not the kind of man you're used to?"

"Partly. Mostly because what I felt was so strong."

"Felt, past tense?"

"Feel." She stopped walking, slipped one arm around his waist and another down his thigh — and there was nothing coy in the gesture. She loved the feel of him beneath her hand — better bare than through jeans, but through jeans was better than nothing. "*I* wanted more. You were the one who said we should get up."

"It'll be light soon. You need to be back in your own bed, and I need to work." He took her face in his hands. They were large, work-roughened hands that held her with exquisite care. His voice rumbled from a place deep inside. "Remember when you asked if I'd ever been seriously involved with anyone?"

"Yes."

"And I told you that the right one hadn't come along?" His eyes were intent. "She has now."

Leah caught her breath. He meant it. She could see. One part of her could even agree. The other part had her shaking her head in denial, but he held it still.

"I believe that for every man there's one woman, for every woman one man — only one, who grabs you, body and soul. Most people go through life without ever finding that one. They look around and experiment and settle for second best without knowing what they're missing. You're it for me, Leah."

"How do you know?" she cried, terrified

mostly because what he said struck a chord. She had felt the pull, had felt it the first time she'd seen him. It was like nothing else ever in her life.

"I just know," he said with conviction. "When was the last time you were with a man?"

"I — I don't know."

"It's been a while. And you've never done it after knowing a guy just two days. You're not loose."

"No, but —"

"You've been married twice. Did you ever have a night with either of them like the one we just had?"

"Sex doesn't make a relationship."

"What we did does."

She knew what he meant — which was totally unnerving. Jesse Cray was a gardener. He might be intelligent and articulate, but he had neither a pedigree, nor a formal education. He lived in a one-room cottage on his employer's property, indeed at his employer's will. He was the antithesis of the kind of man she had been looking for.

But he was the most exciting one she had ever found, the most frank, the most gentle, the most passionate, and when she thought about the way he made her feel — not only in bed, but on the bluff, in the heather garden, among the flowers — she could almost believe what he said about there being only one for one. She had never felt so — loved — in all of her thirty-four years.

Eleven

Wendell Coombs ambled across the porch of the general store and lowered himself onto the long wooden bench.

"Clarence," he said by way of greeting to the man who sat at the other end.

"Wendell," came the reply.

Wendell warily sniffed the contents of his coffee mug. The coffee that day had been made from beans grown in a place he couldn't pronounce, much less pin on a map. Not on his map, leastways. *His* map was thirty-seven years old. It didn't have places he couldn't pronounce.

Not up for taking a sip just yet, he set the mug on his thigh, where it might do some good warming the spot that ached. "World's goin' to pot," he grumbled. "Nothin's the same, lately. Can't get a cup'a coffee like Mavis used to make. Can't get a sandwich on white bread."

"Wheat's fine."

Wendell made a sound that said what he thought of wheat, and of coffee made from beans from countries he couldn't pronounce. "Doesn't seem to bothuh them up at Stah's End. That lady — Gwen — was buyin' all the fancy stuff." He grunted. "Gotta rememba who she's cookin' foah, I s'pose."

"I heea she ain't the cook. They cook themselves."

"*Who* said that?"

"My June. She was talkin' with Sally Goode, who was talkin' with'a cousin, Molly, who was talkin' with that lady. Gwen."

"So what's Gwen *do?*" Wendell barked.

"Manages the house."

"That's fancy fa keepin' the books. Lawd knows what's on those books to make so much money. The two oldest been throwin' it around in town, all flashy and hoity-toity."

Clarence took his pipe from his mouth and turned it this way and that, studying the stem, before putting it back between his teeth. "I heard different."

Wendell stared.

Clarence took his tobacco pouch from his pocket. He dipped the pipe inside and pushed tobacco into the bowl. When he had it tamped to his satisfaction, he said, "Heard they was nice."

Wendell's stare became a glare. "*Who* said that?"

"Edie Stillman. She was talkin' with the one from St. Louis."

Wendell sputtered. "Edie Stillman."

Clarence liked Edie. She had lived in Maine all her life. Sure, she was an artist, but there was nothing loose about her, like Wendell wanted to think. If she hadn't been an artist, she might have moved away long ago. Most of them did, who wanted to do things that needed people around. So artists came to Downlee because there were other artists there, and because it was a fine place to work. Town could do worse.

"What'd she say about the mothuh?" Wendell asked.

Clarence put the pipe in his mouth. "Said she was livin' in a mansion in the city."

"Yes, suh. That's flashy."

Clarence tucked the pouch in the pocket of his canvas jacket in exchange for a match. "Could be just fact."

"I'll tell you fact. Fact is the one from Chicago has mob friends *and* ahtsy friends. Simon says so. We got trouble."

Clarence put a flame to the tobacco and drew on the pipe until the tobacco caught. "Only if the friends come," he said through the smoke that escaped.

"And anothuh fact," Wendell stated. "The fathuh's been dead three yeahs. That's all it took f'ha to turn around and sell everythin' he had. I tell ya, she's lookin' for somethin'."

"How can she be lookin' for somethin' if she ain't even heea?"

"And why ain't she heea?" Wendell asked.

Clarence's sources had various theories, none of which had him convinced. There was the idea she was partying so much she didn't have time to come, but none of the people Clarence talked with could imagine a woman their own age carrying on like that. More likely she was taking it easy. "Mebbe she's leavin' all the movin' in to the daughtuhs."

"Movin' in's all done, and she still ain't heea."

"Mebbe she's seein' friends."

"While the daughtuhs wait?"

"What's Elmira say?"

Wendell glowered. "Elmira says the woman's scared'a comin' here, but what does Elmira know. I'm tellin' you, Ginny St. Clayah's lookin' fa somethin'."

Clarence chuckled. "Ain't much to find at Stah's End, but flowahs and Jesse."

Wendell liked Jesse. Feeling stronger at

the mere thought of the man, he put the coffee mug to his mouth and took a drink, swallowed it, shivered. When the spasm had passed, he said, "Jesse's one'a us. No doubt whose side *he*'d be on, if it came to keepin' dignity at Stah's End. He loves the place."

Clarence couldn't argue with that. He touched the tip of his cap when Callie Dalton came up the steps. "Mawnin', Callie."

"Mawnin', Clarence."

Wendell stared straight ahead until Callie Dalton, wife of a turncoat, was inside the store, but his thoughts were in a stir. With relish, he said, "Jesse'll hate those women. Flashy stuff don't fool him. He's seen t'all."

Quietly, Clarence said, "They don't look flashy, Wendell."

"Whadda *you* know."

"I seen 'em. Walkin' 'round town. They look just like the rest'a us."

"Looks can fool a fool."

"They ain't loud, not even last night at Julia's."

Wendell grunted. "Talk'a trouble, Julia's it."

Clarence wasn't so sure. He and June had had a fair lunch at Julia's the week before. If he ignored the funny look to some of the food, and the fancy names, and just concentrated on the taste, he had to admit that it wasn't bad at all.

Not that he'd tell that to June. She and Sally were thinking of updating the Church Ladies' Cookbook. They were thinking of asking Julia to be their advisor. He didn't know about Sally, but June was already putting sprouts on her salad.

Not that he'd tell that to Wendell, who would start grouping June with the St. Clair women. But she wasn't in the same group at all. She was quiet and loyal and polite and hard-working and bossy.

"Got somethin' to say?" Wendell asked.

Clarence pulled deeply on his pipe and let the smoke out in a stream. "Nope."

"Gawd, that smoke stinks."

"So's that coffee. Like somethin' dahk and evil."

"Leastways we agree on that," Wendell said with a snort. "Town's goin' to pot, if y'ask me. Next thing y'know, they'll be havin' us put papah in one bin and tin in anothuh."

Clarence chuckled.

"Got somethin' to say?" Wendell asked.

"Already doin' it."

"Not me. Not my brothuh Bahney, not my cousin Haskell, not the Chief. Not Hackmoah, eithuh," he tacked on when the man in question rolled by in his pickup and turned off toward the dock. "You can bet they won't be doin' it up at Stah's End."

But Clarence wasn't a betting man. The world was changing.

A few years back, the old mill up the road was eaten by termites no one knew about, until one day the flooring collapsed. Clarence figured change would come to Downlee that way, stealing up and eating away until the damage was done for good.

Listening to Wendell sometimes, Clarence figured a new floor wouldn't be so bad.

TWELVE

Annette was up early, ready to leave the house and get busy. Unfortunately, Caroline wasn't ready. So she went looking for Gwen. She found her in the first-floor laundry room, removing warm towels from the dryer.

Annette leaned against the washer. "Tell me about Mother."

Gwen shot her a bemused look, before folding the towel she held in vertical halves, then horizontal thirds. "What would you like to know?" she asked, making another vertical fold and setting the towel on top of the dryer.

"For starters, why isn't she here?"

Gwen's look turned droll. "You'd have to ask *her.*"

"I would if I could, but since she isn't here, and since you're the only one who seems to be communicating with her on any kind of regular basis, I'm asking you. We

234

know that she's still in Philadelphia, and that she's stringing us along. I want to know why."

"Now, I never thought of her as stringing you along."

"Putting us off. She keeps postponing her arrival. Is it her health?"

Gwen frowned at Annette and reached for another towel. "Her health is just fine."

"I know about her blood pressure, Gwen. And her medication, and the irregularity in her EKG. What I want to know is whether feeling poorly is what's keeping her from joining us."

Gwen folded the second towel in vertical halves. "Not that I know of." She glanced at Annette. "And that's the truth, though the woman can be stubborn as a mule. I suggested that she let me handle the move and then when all was settled here, go back for her, but she said she was fine on her own. I truly expected she'd be here last Sunday, like she said she would."

"Then, you didn't know of any plan to strand the three of us here, together, without her?"

"I don't know of *no* plan," Gwen drawled and finished folding the towel with a flourish. "She may be stubborn *and* wily."

"And her health?"

Gwen hesitated. "She tires faster than she used to. But she is seventy."

"Does she take her medication?"

"Yes."

"And watch her diet?"

Gwen arched a brow. "Do you remember a time when she didn't?"

Annette smiled ruefully. Ginny had been a sensible eater all her life — at least, as long as Annette could remember — no, come to think of it, since Leah had been sick. Part of Leah's recovery had entailed working with a nutritionist, at which time Ginny had cleaned out the kitchen pantry and stocked it with a balanced selection of foods. Likewise, their meals had become more balanced.

Funny, how the chronology of that had slipped Annette's mind. Over the years she had come to blame a preoccupation with the menu on Ginny's fascination with slimness. She wondered now whether the preoccupation hadn't been with Leah's health. Maybe even Caroline's and Annette's.

Annette could identify with that, but she hadn't suspected it of Ginny. Unconvinced, but curious, she asked Gwen, "What's it like, working for her?"

Gwen gave a lopsided grin. "It's like being wealthy without the headaches."

"Is she nice to you?"

"Always."

"Warm?"

"Uhhh —"

"The truth," Annette prompted.

"I'm trying, but it's not a simple question. She isn't touchy-feely, if you know what I mean, but she isn't that way with anyone. She is friendly. She is concerned. Yes, I'd call her warm."

"When you say she's 'concerned,' do you mean she's sympathetic when you have a cold?"

"Oh, it's more than that. She's been good to my family."

Annette was intrigued. "In what ways?"

Gwen took another towel, folded it in halves, then thirds, then halves again. She held it to her chest. "Sometimes I've needed help with my son. My girls have done all right for themselves. Both of them went to college. Both of them are married and have careers and kids, and the kids are in college now." She pursed her lips. "Jackson is something else. That boy's been in and out of trouble since the day his daddy left, and that was thirty-one years ago."

"Legal trouble?"

"That, and every other kind. It started with truancy and a little car theft. In the middle of that, he got a girl pregnant and nearly got her killed getting an abortion she had no business getting, then he disappeared. He does that," she remarked dryly, "for little breathers from time to time, only he always returns with worse up his sleeve. He's been in and out of relationships with women. He's been in and out of jail. He's been in and out of college and business. Jackson is an upwardly mobile black man gone wrong. He has dabbled in things I don't even want to *think* about, much less pay the price to get him out of, but I'm his mother, so I do it."

As Annette would, for her own children if, God forbid, they were in trouble. "What has Ginny done?"

"She's helped him get jobs — good jobs — good *white-collar* jobs. She's helped him get loans. More often than not, he defaults on the loans and loses the house, the car, whatever, but bless her, she's always willing to go to bat for him again. She says that he'll get himself straightened out one of these times, but I'm not so sure. He's thirty-six years old, for goodness sake!"

"Where is he now?"

"As we speak?" Gwen sighed, the towel against her forgotten. "He's serving time for embezzlement. He stole money from his employer, who happened to be your mother's friend. You'd think your mother wouldn't want another thing to do with him — or with me, for that matter — but don't you know, she has another job lined up for him when he gets out? She is an eternal optimist."

Annette was touched. "That's really lovely."

"She's a fine lady. There are times when I wish I could do more for her. But like I said, she's stubborn."

"Quite," Annette said, thinking of misleading letters and absenteeism. She was turning to leave when Gwen touched her arm.

"There is one thing that I did know about," she confessed quietly. "When your mother originally discussed her plans for this move, she suggested that once everything was unpacked and you girls were here, I should leave. She figured the four of you could manage. She wanted time alone with you, she really did. I'm just as surprised as you that she's late, much less this late."

"Had you made plans?"

"Only to visit Jackson."

"Why don't you?"

Gwen looked horrified. "Oh, no. Not until your mama comes."

"But she's apt to be days. And everything

is settled here. Really, Gwen. I can fold towels as well as you can, and if I get tired of it, I'll make Caroline do it. Leah likes to cook. You've already hired someone to come in to do the heavy cleaning, and we can do the dusting ourselves. What more do we need?"

But Gwen was adamant. "I really couldn't. Not until I've seen with my own two eyes that your mother is here and settled. That's my job."

Annette detected a note of worry, which gave her something to think about other than the phone call Jean-Paul hadn't made. "Well," she said with a sigh, "think about it, will you? Mother may yet be a while."

It was nearly noon when Leah woke up. Appalled, she quickly showered and dressed, stole downstairs, and sped away from Star's End before her sisters could call her on sleeping so late. Unfortunately, once off Hullman Road, she wasn't sure where to go. For lack of anything more familiar, she headed for Julia's. There, in a quiet corner table that gave her an unobtrusive view of the rest of the place, she ordered a cup of tea. It wasn't delivered by the waitress who had taken her order, but by a slender woman who looked to be close to her own

240

age. She wore a lightweight sweater over a long, flowing skirt, and had dark, wavy hair that burst from a ribbon at the crown of her head. There was something open about her that put Leah immediately at ease.

"I'm Julia Waterman," she said, setting down the pot of tea. "I wanted to meet you last night, but there was a slight emergency in the kitchen, and by the time it was settled, you and your sisters had left." She set a bread basket beside the tea, pulled up a chair, and smiled warmly. "Welcome to Downlee. Want a friend?"

This was so bluntly put that Leah couldn't resist. Left alone, she would have been self-conscious. Worse, she would have felt obligated to brood, which she wasn't in the mood to do at all. She was feeling suddenly light-hearted. The dilemma of Jesse Cray would have to wait. Besides, Julia had come well recommended.

"I understand you're from Washington. I used to live there, in Cleveland Park."

Leah grinned. "I'm right next door, in Woodley."

"Ahhh, what a *great* area. I had a hairdresser there who gave me cuts like I've never had since. I mean, my hair is *impossible*. He was the only one who could manage it."

"Aubrey."

"He's still there? That's incredible! Do you *love* that man? After Washington, I lived in New York, and I couldn't find anyone half as good. I can't tell you how many times I've been tempted to fly down just for a haircut. So he's still there?"

"Still there."

"And the Tabbard Inn? Cafe la Ruche? The Tombs?"

Leah kept nodding and grinning. "All there," and spots she loved, even if they were too young and interesting for some of her crowd.

"Wow," Julia sighed. "I forget sometimes how great Washington is."

"Why did you leave?"

"I got married. Alan was a White House staffer until the president lost his job, so we moved to New York where he could be a consultant at three times the pay. By the time the next election was over and done, the marriage was, too."

"I'm sorry."

"I'm not. I used my divorce settlement to move here and open this place, which was what I'd dreamed of doing since I was a child, and I haven't looked back once."

"You don't miss the city?"

"Only when I need a haircut. Everyone

here is friendly. And *hungry.* That's very important."

Leah laughed. "Dinner last night was wonderful." She sampled the bread. "Mmmm. Dill?"

"You bet." Julia lit up. "I have a pâté that works well with it —" She started to rise, then paused. "Only if you want the company. I'm starved. I need a break. But maybe you'd rather sit quietly?"

Leah didn't hesitate. Anyone who loved the Tombs was worth pursuing. "Get the pâté. I'll wait."

Julia returned with not one, but two varieties of pâté, a basket of tempura vegetables, and a bottle of San Pellegrino. "I really am starved. I slept through breakfast and barely got here in time to set up for lunch."

"Where do you live?"

"Down the street. My house is ancient, but it has charm. Crummy kitchen. But charm." She reached for the bread. "I hear Star's End has a great one."

Leah chuckled. "Don't tell me. One of your regular customers is the sister-in-law of the man who put in the cabinets."

"Close. Here. Try this bread. It's different from the other. It's honey-walnut." She topped it with a smear of pâté. "Breads are my specialty. What do you think?"

Leah thought it was divine and told Julia so with the roll of her eyes.

"When I was a kid," Julia said, "I remember having warm anadama bread at church bake sales. Mind you, this tempura is great, so's the pâté, but for happiness all I need is bread. Warm, naked bread."

Forget Jesse, Leah thought. She'd found her soulmate in Julia. Warm, naked bread. Her own true love. "My freezer in Washington is full of maple-curry bread. I make it by the dozen loaves."

Julia gasped. "Maple-curry? Sounds *wonderful*."

"One slice with a piece of cheese is lunch." Just one slice, carefully controlled, so that she didn't get into the bind of her teenage years. "And if not lunch, then breakfast. Or dinner."

"Sheer heaven," Julia hummed. "If you feel like making some while you're at Star's End, bring it in. I'd love to taste it. I'd love to *serve* it. You could do that, you know, make some up for the lunch crowd. It's something to do. Two weeks is a long time."

Leah smiled. So Julia knew the length of her stay. "What else did the grapevine tell you?"

"That you're attractive, that you're nice, that you're single. What do you think of

Star's End?"

"It's enchanting."

"It is, isn't it? Aside from a few old reactionaries, it's an incredibly romantic place — and that's not even counting Jesse Cray. What a love he is. We're in the same book group. You've heard the stories about Star's End, haven't you?"

Indeed Leah had, though, in view of the night past, she was taking them in a new light. "Annette says it inspires artists."

"Not only artists. Men and women."

Leah wanted to hear more, but Julia was busy eating. To get her going again, she asked, "Is it the air, do you think?" There had to be a rational explanation to offset the one Jesse offered. "Something about the ocean that makes people wild? A down-to-earth, raw something?" All of which she still felt. Her insides were echoing with the same warm Jesse-hum.

Julia swallowed what she was eating. "A *something* something, that's for sure. Who knows what it is. Do you know when your mother is coming?"

"Not yet. She may call later."

"We're all impatient."

"So are *we*," Leah said. But she didn't want to talk about Ginny. And she was afraid to ask more about romantic goings-on at Star's End, lest she come to think she was bewitched herself. Better to talk about Julia, with whom she felt an instant rapport, but about whom she knew next to nothing. "Where did you learn how to do what you do?"

"Here and there. I've always loved cooking."

"Did you go to culinary school?"

"No, but I have friends who did. They let me hang around their places and watch. I'm a quick study. And I've always been one to experiment with different recipes, so I opened this place using the best of them, then expanded the menu little by little. People expect to find different things here from one week to the next."

"Do you ever run out of ideas?"

"Once in a while. At those times I get in my car and drive down the coast. There are several great kitchens run by ex-Manhattanites. I spy."

Leah laughed. "You what?"

"Wear dark glasses, study the menu until I have it memorized, and order several of the most unusual things there. Then I drive home and try to duplicate what I've tasted. What I end up with may be totally different from what I had, but it's always interesting and usually good."

She glanced at the blackboard on the wall, with its chalked-in menu. "I'm due for a trip. I haven't had anything really new in a while." She brightened. "Maybe you'll come? I'd love that, Leah. It's much nicer when I go with someone — and not so awkward when I order more than one dish. I usually bring my significant other, but he's with his mother in Kansas. She's wheelchair-bound and frail, and needs to be in a nursing home, but she's fighting it tooth and claw. It's been a nightmare for Howell."

She looked across the room. "Uh-oh. They're giving me the high sign." She rose. "Will you think about it? We could go next week. All I need is a day's notice to arrange for extra help here while I'm gone." She gave Leah's shoulder a squeeze. "See you in a bit." She started off, then turned back. "And I do want to taste your maple-curry bread. Make a loaf?"

It took Leah a while to gather everything she needed — not because she needed much, but because the people of Downlee liked to talk. Everything was owner-run. Everyone had a finger in the town's goings-on. Had she not known better, she would have thought that the local economy hinged on the fate of Star's End. To see the look on people's faces, Ginny might have been a mystical creature coming to inhabit a fantasy home.

Leah had a package in both arms and was heading for her car when Caroline emerged from a side street and nearly bumped into her.

"Hey!" she said and peered into one of the bags. "What did you buy?"

"Baking stuff. I'm doing bread."

Caroline took one of the bags and fell into step beside her. "We missed you this morning. Are you feeling okay?"

"Fine. Great, actually." Leah raised her nose. "I think it's the air. So much freshness is zapping my system." It was always possible. "Ginny hasn't called today, has she?"

"Not yet."

"Caroline?"

"Hmm?"

"Why haven't you married Ben?"

Caroline shot her a warning look. "That's a question we usually fight about."

But Leah was feeling daring. "*Annette* usually fights you about it. Not me."

"Why do you want to know?"

"Because after so long, I'd have thought you'd either be married or broken up. But here you are, calling him every day. Do you love him?"

"Probably."

"Will you stay with him?"

"For the foreseeable future."

"Then why not marriage?"

"It's hard to be married with a career like mine."

"But your relationship with Ben isn't much different from the way many marriages work."

Caroline shot her a dubious glance. "Long-distance?"

"He visits you during the week, and you spend weekends together."

"Unless I'm on trial, in which case I spend weekends in the office."

"Married people do that, too, when their work demands it. Ron did it."

"And look what happened."

Leah dug in her pocket for the car keys. "His work hours didn't cause the divorce."

"What did?"

"Boredom." She opened the door, set her bundle inside, and reached for the bag Caroline held. "On the surface, Ron was perfect. He was everything Mother wanted me to have in a husband. Beneath the surface, we're talking serious hang-ups. He was twenty-nine going on fifty. He couldn't stand change. He wanted lamb chops for dinner on Monday, fish on Tuesday, chicken on Wednesday, and, so help me, even if we ate out, that's what he'd have. He was a computer genius. Too much so. He was programmed to the hilt."

"Did he make love that way, too?"

"In a fashion." But in the next breath Leah wasn't thinking of Ron in bed. She was thinking of Jesse, who let one feeling inspire the next in a carnal stream-of-consciousness. Ellen McKenna would adore him. Not sexually, of course.

"Ben is an inventive lover," Caroline said.

Leah tore her mind from Jesse's body and said with as much poise as she could, "That figures. He's an artist. He's creative."

Caroline made a sound that held a hint of longing and desire, and reflected what Leah was trying so desperately not to feel.

"So why don't you marry him?" she asked sharply.

"Why should I? What can a marriage license offer that I don't already have?"

"Aren't you afraid you might lose him?"

"Ben adores me. He wants to spend the rest of his life with me."

"Then why not marriage?"

"You *are* as bad as Annette," Caroline charged. "What is so all-fired important about marriage? I could understand it, if Ben and I wanted kids. But I'd be a lousy

250

mother, having had a lousy example, and, anyway, I don't have time to have kids. So that's one argument down the tubes. And another — I don't need Ben's money. And another — I don't need his name. *Why* marriage? is more the question."

Leah closed the door on the bundles and leaned against the car. "Is it that he doesn't fit the image?"

"The image of what?"

"Of what Ginny wants in a son-in-law?"

Caroline barked out a laugh. "I do what I want, not what Ginny wants."

"Yes," Leah said, "that's what we tell ourselves, only it isn't always true. We *think* we're doing what we want — like when I moved to Washington to rebuild my life after my second divorce. Since I'd married the kind of man Mother wanted twice, and failed, I was declaring my independence. So what did I do? Being a stranger in a strange town, I gravitated toward people who just happened to be related to people Ginny knew, which was how I knew them in the first place. I found them acceptable, because they were prominent, wealthy, and well connected. Those were the things I'd been taught to value. So I ended up with the same friends Ginny would have chosen for me — even though I had myself convinced that I was doing my own thing."

"I *am* doing my own thing," Caroline insisted. "Ben's being so different proves it."

Leah was suddenly impatient. "But you won't marry him. What I'm asking is whether the problem is that he isn't what we were taught to want."

Caroline shook her head. "No. Definitely not. That isn't the case here. My not marrying Ben has nothing to do with prominence, wealth, or connections. It's me. That's all."

"You don't think Ginny would make a fuss if you married him?"

"She'd find it far preferable to my dying an old maid. Of course, she'd insist on a prenuptial agreement. But that's Ginny."

"Would you draw one up?"

"No."

"Strange, coming from a lawyer."

"No. I know Ben. I know how he lives and what he wants in life. He has far more pride than greed."

Leah continued to look at her sister's face for a thoughtful moment, then shook her head in amazement.

"What's the matter?" Caroline asked.

"You're so sure, and about so many good things. You're very lucky." And Leah was very envious. She started around the car.

"Need a ride back?"

"Thanks, but I'm just starting here. Annette and I spent the morning at the mall. She bought T-shirts and jeans. She says she doesn't wear them at home because she wants to look more wifely, but since Jean-Paul sent her here, to hell with that. She's rebelling."

"Poor Annette," Leah said, then grinned dryly. "Never thought I'd say *that*. I must be going soft." She opened the driver's door. "I'm heading back. See you later."

Leah loved baking bread. She loved kneading dough and watching it rise. She loved punching it down, dividing it, and braiding it. Mostly she loved the smell when the hot bread came from the oven.

The smell this time was robustly maple with something exotic thrown in.

She made six loaves. By the time the first four had been wrapped and the last two set on racks to cool, clouds had rolled in from the west, and Caroline and Annette had returned.

"Smells divine," Annette said and tasted the slice Leah offered. "Mmmmm. *Tastes* divine."

"Where are you going?" Caroline asked as Leah pulled on a sweater.

"I promised Julia a loaf."

"*The* Julia?"

"The very one." She glanced at the clouds. "Think I'll make it there and back before the rains come?"

"Nope."

But Leah wanted to try. Carrying three loaves, she dashed for the car and slid in. She was buckling her seatbelt when the first raindrop hit her windshield. By the time she had figured out how to turn on the wipers, she needed them.

She started slowly down the drive, wondering whether she wanted to drive into town after all. Julia didn't need the bread tonight. Besides, only two of the loaves were for her.

At the twist of the drive, just out of sight of the house, she turned onto a rutted path. Several minutes later, she pulled up behind Jesse's pickup.

Sheltering one of the loaves under her sweater, she made a run for the back door and let herself into a small outer room that was home to boots, shovels, rain gear, hurricane lanterns, and a neat stack of chopped wood. A second door led into the cottage.

She was drawn into the room. Even without Jesse, warm feelings touched her. She didn't know whether it was the soft brown-

and-russet tones that did it, or the nature photographs on the wall, or the woodsy smell, or the compactness. But she felt comfortable here, completely at home, even excited.

She refused to think that it was destiny. She was simply taking life one step at a time.

"Hi," he said softly.

She whirled around, blushing. "Hi. I — your door wasn't locked."

"It never is." He approached, looking oddly unsure. "Wet outside?"

She nodded, which was about all she could do. She didn't understand how she could be so drawn to a man as to be speechless, but she was. Jesse did that to her — the dark spikes of hair on his brow, the thick shadow on a square jaw, the way he stood with his weight on one hip, the veins on his forearm. She couldn't believe that this incredible man had been inside her. His presence took her breath away.

He sniffed. "What smells so good?"

Blushing still and breathless, she produced the forgotten loaf from under her sweater. "I made maple-curry bread. It's my best."

"And still warm."

"Vaguely. I have two loaves in the car for Julia, but I don't know if I want to drive into town in the rain."

255

"I'll drive you."

"Oh, no, I couldn't —"

He kissed her then, and whatever protest she had been about to make was forgotten. She was in heaven — tasting him, smelling him, feeling him.

When he released her mouth, she kept her head tipped up, eyes closed, breathing soft and shallow. "I wasn't sure if it was real. I was my old self again today. I kept thinking I'd dreamed it all up."

"You didn't."

She wrapped her arms round his neck. "You smell good." She opened her eyes. "A little like dirt."

"It's my hands. They've been in the greenhouse."

"It's a healthy smell."

Holding her face with those healthy-smelling hands, he kissed her more deeply. She was feeling weak-kneed when he said, "Let me clean up. Then I'll drive you to Julia's."

She followed him into the kitchen, watching him walk, watching him stop before the sink, watching him reach for the soap.

He shot her a self-conscious smile.

She swallowed and cleared her throat. "I love your photographs. Did a local artist take them?"

256

"You could say that."

"*You* did?"

He nodded. "They're keepsakes from my trips." He lathered his hands. "The canals are in St. Petersburg. The crocs are in Tanzania. The fishing trawler is in the Bering Strait."

"You took them *yourself?*"

"Why so surprised?"

"They're very professional. Do you sell them?"

"No. It's just a hobby."

"I don't see lots of equipment."

"I don't own lots of equipment. Just a camera."

Charlie had been into photography. He had state-of-the-art equipment, plus every imaginable gadget, yet he couldn't have produced a photograph like one of Jesse's if his life had depended on it.

"Just a camera," Leah echoed with the release of a breath.

Jesse rinsed his hands. "So, what did you think of Downlee?"

Nosy was the first word that came to mind, and, a day or two before, she might have used it. But it seemed too harsh now. "It's curious, in a friendly kind of way. What was it like growing up here?"

"Intimate. Everyone knows everyone else's

257

business."

"That can be devastating."

"It wasn't. My mother left when I was little. Since everyone knew it, they all mothered me."

Leah was horrified. "Why did she leave?"

"She and my father had differences."

"How awful for you."

He smiled sadly. "Children adapt. There were other people who loved me."

"Certainly your father."

"In his way." He was shooting her bemused glances as he wiped his hands. "I can't picture you in the city."

She leaned against the counter, coincidentally coming closer to him. "Why not?"

"You're not hard-looking."

"I was."

"No. I saw you when you first got here. Not even then."

She had an odd thought. "When was it, that first time?"

"Late at night. I'd gone for a swim. You were asleep on the swing."

"You covered me with your afghan." It made utter sense. A patchwork afghan fit Jesse far more than Virginia. She could see it folded over the plump arm of his leather sofa.

"It was a cool night," Jesse admitted, then

more quietly, "The afghan's never looked better. My mother made it. It's the only thing of hers that I own."

Leah was more touched than she could imagine.

"I told you," he said, returning the towel to its hook, "I've been waiting for you. One look, and I knew."

"Don't say that," she begged. "It scares me." There were implications from declarations like his, none of which she was ready to face. "Maybe we ought to go?"

He smiled, stroked her mouth with his thumb, and gestured her toward the back door.

Riding in Jesse's pickup was a whole other experience. It was a man's vehicle, roomy enough for his long frame, but still a vehicle, and, in that, confining. Worse, it had a bench seat. Leah wasn't prepared for a bench seat — or the ease it allowed in sitting close to the driver.

Downlee looked different, more friendly and familiar, from under the protection of Jesse's long arm. Once parked in front of Julia's, Leah pulled on his hooded slicker, dashed inside, dropped off the loaves, and dashed back to the truck. He had the door open. She quickly slid in, nestling closer and closer during the return to Star's End. By the time he pulled up behind his cottage, she had an arm around his waist and her face against his throat.

She couldn't get enough of him — of touching him, feeling him, smelling him. She wanted to stay with him. But she knew her sisters would be wondering where she was.

He killed the engine, brought her up, and kissed her, and though the best of intentions gave her the strength to break away once, then a second time, she couldn't make it stick. He tasted too good, and she was hungry again.

With surprising ease, she straddled him, and the kisses went on, joined by a hand on her breast, her hip, her thigh. Her insides quickened and warmed. "Ummmm, Jesse," she whispered.

"Feel good?"

"Does it ever."

He unzipped her jeans, pulled out her T-shirt, and slipped his hands underneath.

She groaned. "I have to get back to the house."

He stemmed the thought with his mouth and kissed her until she was too busy to protest. Her hands combed his hair, rubbed his shoulders, slipped down his sides — using the realness of his body to ward off whimsical thoughts, like destiny. She whispered his name, begging for more, and, to the tune of the rain on the roof and the rustle of oilskins, he gave it.

His fingers brought her to a first, shuddering orgasm. She paused only to catch her breath before kicking off her jeans, opening his shorts, and impaling herself. She didn't move, content to savor his thickness inside her. Her breath came soft and short. Her eyes held his.

He whispered a smug, "Nice, huh?"

"Umm-hmmm. You make me shameless."

"Everyone should have someone who does that. To be shameless is to be free."

"I feel free."

He moved his hands over her, stroking her breasts, her belly, her backside. Her breathing quickened. She rested her forehead on his.

"I could stay like this for a month," he said, more hoarsely now.

She gave a short, high laugh. "Yes, I think you could."

"Would you mind?"

Mind? The slightest movement — even that laugh — caused a ripple of sensation. When he slipped his hands under her bottom, the ripples increased.

"Make that two months," came his hoarse whisper.

"I have to be back in Washington in two weeks."

"For what?"

"Cancer Society meetings." She gasped when he raised his hips and came higher inside her. "Ahhhhh, Jesse, that feels good."

"What if you missed the meetings?" he rasped.

"I couldn't co-chair the fund-raiser."

"What if you didn't?"

"Didn't what? I can't think, Jesse. How can *you*?"

"Not . . . easily," he ground out. In the next breath he made a guttural sound and thrust impossibly upward into a release that shook his body.

Leah coiled her arms around his neck and hung on through her own orgasm. When it was done, they stayed locked together. Finally, lowering a hand to touch his belly — such a vulnerable spot, it seemed — she sighed. "I have to go."

He didn't release her.

"They'll want to do something for dinner."

"I'd have made dinner for you here."

"You cook, too?"

"I'm a Renaissance man," he said with a

self-mocking grin.

She was wondering if he wasn't just that — master gardener, world traveler, skilled photographer, cook, lover. She was also wondering where he fit into her life. She couldn't see making love to him on the bench in the courtyard behind her Woodley Park townhouse, not like they'd just made love in the cab of his truck.

Then again, she couldn't see *not* making love to him, there or anywhere else. The attraction between them wasn't to be denied. One look, and she wanted him, and the reward went beyond the orgasmic. In Jesse's arms she felt totally loved, and, in that, sated at last.

It was almost, almost as though he was right when he said that they were meant to be together. It was a scary, scary thought.

Jesse helped her dress and ran her through the rain to her own car. When she had trouble backing up, he slid into the driver's seat, turned the car around until it faced forward, then sent her off.

She pulled up under the porte cochere, careful to leave his slicker in the car. She might blame her lateness on Julia's chatter, and the mess of her hair on the weather, but the slicker would be harder to explain.

Her sisters must have been waiting, because she had no sooner run up the stone steps and burst through the screen door into the front hall when they ambushed her, one on either side, their faces intent.

"Congratulations," Caroline said. "It's unanimous. You're our choice."

"For what?"

"To call Ginny. Now."

THIRTEEN

I've never liked goodbyes, not since that summer in Maine so long ago when the pain wouldn't die. I decided then that I simply wouldn't say them, but would skirt parting scenes any way I could and thereby minimize the hurt.

To some extent I succeeded. When Caroline first started college, I used dropping her at her dormitory as a springboard for a trip to Paris, where I wouldn't be able to dwell on her absence. Likewise when Annette married Jean-Paul. The busier I was with details of the wedding — seating arrangements, flowers, food — the more numbed I was when Nick walked my second-born down the aisle and gave her away. And Leah — dear, Leah — who kept coming in from Washington last year to face the doctors with me — how could I make a ceremony of her leaving each time, when I never knew if I would live to see her again?

Far easier to simply pretend that I'd be see-ing her the next day.

My daughters resented me, I knew. They thought me cold and selfish. I wondered what they would think if they saw me now, wandering about an empty house for the fourth day in a row, trying to say goodbye to the place that harbored so much of my life, and not knowing quite how.

We assumed that with older came wiser, but it wasn't always so. As often as not, age brought an understanding of one's very lack of wisdom.

I hadn't prepared myself well for this time. Perhaps I assumed that it wouldn't come, that I would simply go to sleep one night, as Nick did, and not wake up. Perhaps I wished it. There would have been no pain in a parting like that.

But I kept waking up, a little older and slower of body each day, a little more aware that life was a double-edged sword. Those of us who were blessed with longevity were the ones who would suffer the approach of death.

I had, indeed, been blessed. These empty rooms were once rich and overflowing with people and things. Even as I sat now in the bare bay window of the living room, I felt the velvet drapes behind me, saw the grand piano at the far end of the room, heard the murmur of guests seated before the marble fireplace. The dining room was cavernous without furniture, yet it was filled with the memory of a table set for sixteen, sideboards covered with my mother's silver service and trays bearing a sumptuous Sunday brunch.

The girls hadn't cared much for Sunday brunch. From the time they were old enough to want to be elsewhere, they had thought it confining. I had considered it family time, and do, to this day. Sunday noon was when I most often thought of the girls. Annette would be home, serving brunch to her own family. Caroline would be either at the office or with her artist. Leah would be . . . wherever.

I worried about Leah. She was the most fragile of my girls, the one who always seemed a little lost. I wished I could have helped her, but that was another of the shortcomings that I had come to recognize with age. I had never been a communicator, for to be one was to open oneself to discussions one might not like. Far better, I had always thought, to tell myself that Leah was stronger than I thought, than to talk with her and learn that in fact she wasn't.

Of course, as was a mother's prerogative, I worried about her anyway.

She loved this house. I remember her scrunching up right here on the bottom step, at the curl of the banister, watching the comings and goings. A small, agile child, she would skip up the stairs and down the hall. She loved her room, too, all those bright, oversized flowers on the wall, their warm colors scattered like petals on the bedspread, the carpet, the chair. She never forgave me my summer of redecoration.

Ah, dear. None of them did. And I was so proud of what I'd done.

You didn't ask us what we wanted, they cried. Well, of course I didn't ask. My mother didn't ask. She just *did.* She knew what was best, and we didn't question it.

But the rules suddenly changed, and I was unprepared. My daughters left me behind in the dust — my fault as much as theirs. I preferred the old rules. I still do. Life under those rules was simpler. It was more clearly defined.

I dare say that had I been of my daughters' generation, I could never have done what I did that summer in Maine. Oh, I'd have had the affair. Will always insisted that it was destined, and I agreed. But had I been of my daughters' generation, I would never have returned to the city with Nick at summer's end. I'd have given up everything

268

material, lived with Will in the gardener's shed, and had his babies.

Would my life have been happier? I don't know. I do know that it would have been different. Had I stayed with Will, I wouldn't have been walking these echoing halls.

Was that an echo? Or the phone?

The phone, I thought, and set off.

Foolishly, I let the movers take every phone but the one in the kitchen. I hurried in that direction, but the halls were longer than they used to be, the stairway more steeply wound. I held tightly to the banister lest I got dizzy and fell. What a *terrifying* thought, to lie broken at the bottom of the stairs, unable to move, unable to summon help, feeling life ebb and being helpless to stop it.

I was seventy, which was relatively young in an age of obituary pages devoted to ninety-year-olds. Still, I felt old.

The telephone was on its fourth ring. "I'm coming!" I called and in the next short breath damned my ankles for their stiffness. Like my elbows on damp mornings, they betrayed the active woman I once was.

Don't hang up! I'm coming!

It occurred to me that I shouldn't bother to answer. Everyone knew I'd moved. It was probably a solicitation of some sort.

No, it was probably Lillian. She had been a dear to house me and loan me her car. I had her worried, spending hours like this in my big old empty house.

Breathless, I snatched up the phone. "Hello?"

"Mother! You *are* there. It's Leah!"

"Good gracious, Leah!" I pressed my heaving chest. My heart was racing — traitorous heart — from both the dash I'd made, and from a sudden, intense fear. Cautiously, I asked, "Why are you calling me here?"

"When there was no answer at Lillian's, I played a hunch. Why are you there?"

She didn't sound upset. Perhaps she didn't know yet.

Telling my heart to behave just a little longer, I did my best to sound casual. "There were one or two things I had to check on. Things I promised the realtor. For the buyers."

"Didn't Gwen take care of everything?"

"These are last-minute things. They're done now. I was about to leave. Two more minutes and you'd have missed me."

"Then I'm glad I called now. We were starting to worry. When are you coming?"

So they didn't know yet. They didn't hate me yet. I breathed a little easier. "Didn't

270

Gwen give you my messages?"

"They've been vague."

"Well, of course they have. I can't say exactly when I'll be there. There's more to moving than hiring a van. I have to meet with lawyers and accountants. I have to close up memberships and say goodbye to friends. Those things take time."

There was a pause, then a measured, "Mother, you wrote us letters saying that you wanted to spend time with us. If your business there takes much longer, our two weeks will be up before you arrive."

"No, no, it won't. I'll be there. I'll be there very soon."

"Tomorrow?"

"The day after."

"Mother," she chided, "we're *waiting* for you."

"Aren't you having a good time?"

Leah repeated the question to her sisters. I tried to make out their response, but couldn't. I desperately wanted them to be enjoying themselves. I desperately wanted them to be enjoying *each other.* It was a great sadness of mine that they weren't close.

"We're having a wonderful time," she said, and while I wasn't convinced, I didn't push my luck.

"What do you think of Star's End?"

"Spectacular!" she breathed, this time without consulting her sisters. I felt the loosening of a huge knot inside me. "It's an incredibly beautiful place," she said. "I can't believe you haven't seen it."

I bit my tongue, but only for a minute. There was too much I wanted to know. "Is the house in good shape?"

"Perfect."

"And the work in the kitchen done?"

"Completely."

"Tell me about the porch."

"It wraps around from the front and widens in back. That's where we spend most of our time." Which was precisely what I'd hoped.

"And the flower gardens?"

"Are unbelievable."

The knot loosened a little more. I couldn't help but smile. Leah loved the place. That was important, a first hurdle cleared. Relieved, I asked, "Have you spent much time in town?"

"Not as much as Caroline and Annette. They're spending all your money."

"Are they buying good things?"

Leah repeated this question. I could hear Annette and Caroline talking at once. Over their voices, Leah said, "*Very* good things.

272

There are serious artists here. Did you know that?"

"Yes. I did."

"Caroline says that if you don't get here soon, she's packing up the paintings she bought and shipping them home to Chicago."

"She likes them that much?"

"She has an appreciation for fine art, and this is fine art. How are you feeling?"

"I'm fine," I answered as though there were no such thing as a chest pain or palpitations. "Why do you ask?"

"You were breathless before."

"I had to run for the phone. But I'm fine, Leah. Do me a favor, will you? It suddenly occurred to me that poor Gwen is waiting for my arrival. I had promised her some time off. Please tell her to take it now. It sounds to me as though you girls have everything in hand. Well, that's all, Leah. I'm going to hang up now, because Lillian is having friends over. She'll be upset if I don't get there soon."

"We'll be upset if you don't get *here* soon. Have you made flight reservations?"

"Not yet."

"Mother."

"I can get them on an hour's notice."

"We need more notice than that if we're

going to meet you in Portland."

"No need to do that. I'll take a cab."

"Give us *two* hours' notice, and we'll be there."

"Really, Leah. A cab will be fine. I'm hanging up the phone now. I'll see you soon."

I replaced the phone softly, timidly, half-expecting someone to walk out of the butler's pantry and call me a coward. For I was that. Yes, the girls were waiting, but I wasn't ready for Star's End yet — and it wasn't only that I feared for my emotional state when I saw that place again. It was this damnable goodbye that I had to face first.

The pain of it tore through me. I told myself that my decision was made, that all that remained was to walk out the door on the arm of these wonderful memories. I remembered that other goodbye. The two were similarly painful, similarly final.

"You'll be back," Lillian had said with a wave of dismissal, more times than I could count, and I sympathized with her intent. It was easier to think that than to think the other.

But I wouldn't be back. I knew this, as I'd known few other things in life. Nor could I complain. I had lived long and well. Even without Will. I had, indeed, been blessed.

FOURTEEN

Caroline wasn't herself.

For starters, she had just enjoyed breakfast with Leah and Annette, *enjoyed* being the shocker. Annette had made omelets, Leah tea and toast, Caroline fresh-squeezed orange juice. They had eaten on the deck in the morning mist without an unpleasant word exchanged.

Caroline was relaxed, *relaxed* being a second shocker. She had no business being relaxed. Her single call to the office the day before had been brief and uninformative, which should have made her wary, but hadn't. She felt distant from the office, so much so that she hadn't taken a single look at the papers she'd brought along.

She didn't feel distant from Ben, though she hadn't heard his voice in over a day. The sound of him was all over her thoughts, telling her that she had to make a choice.

That alone should have had her tied up in knots.

And then there was Ginny. She should have been *furious* at Ginny. But she wasn't.

She felt calm. She didn't even want a cigarette. She could picture one — could mentally go through the motions of taking one between her fingers, putting it in her mouth, striking a match, and taking that first, deep draw that filled her lungs with something evil but divine. She should have been *dying* for that drag. But she wasn't.

Caroline had never been superstitious. She prided herself on having a grasp of the facts — Ben was the first to say that she was grounded in reason — but something was happening to her here. Harsh thoughts couldn't be sustained; anger fizzled; worry was mild and brief. She felt mellow.

Crazy though it sounded, she was almost willing to believe that there was indeed something powerful in the air at Star's End, which was why she was in Downlee at ten in the morning, sitting on the stoop of Simon Fallon's wood shop.

Simon was a carpenter. He specialized in making grandfather clocks, or so her sources said, but those sources — artists with whom she had talked the day before — hadn't mentioned his name in the context of clocks.

Simon was in his eighties. If there was a story to be told about Star's End, he was the one to tell it.

Or so they claimed. Caroline wanted to think they were full of hooey, but the skeptic in her didn't have a chance against the woman who had to know more.

She sat straighter when a small old man appeared on the lane, and rose when he came toward the shop. "Are you Simon?"

He tipped a forefinger off his temple. "You must be Caroline," he said in a voice as wrinkled as his face. "They said you'd come."

"They knew better than me," she mused.

He pushed at the door of his shop and motioned her to follow. Inside, like a group of friends in varying states of undress, were four clocks in the making. Caroline was enchanted.

"Figured you'd get here sooner or later," Simon said, but she was moving from one to another of the clocks.

"These are wonderful."

"I sell to kings."

"Do you really?"

"And movie stars. Not many people can meet my price."

"That steep?"

"For one-of-a-kind."

278

Caroline touched the head of one, the throat of another. Ben's thing was paint, not wood, which meant that she was no expert on the latter, but she didn't have to be an expert to recognize the quality of Simon's work.

Then again, her sensitivities were at a high, which was why she had sought Simon out. She turned to find him leaning against his workbench, waiting.

"I was told that you've lived here longer than most," she said.

He gave a tiny nod. "Eighty-seven years."

"And that you're familiar with Star's End."

"I ride out there now 'n' again."

"Will you tell me the story?"

He chuckled. "Which one? Place like that's full of stories."

"The one about the legend. The lovers."

"Ahhhh. That one. Why'd you want to know?"

"It seems important."

He studied her for a minute, then shrugged. "Could be." He fell silent.

Caroline figured that two could play the game. So she sat down on the floor amidst Simon's clocks and scattered sawdust, and smiled. She could wait. Along with mellow-ness had come infinite patience.

Simon responded with another shrug. "It was always a place of fancy, always bigger than anythin' else in town, set out there on the bluff like somethin' in a book."

She kept smiling.

"The stuff of dreams, they always said. It's natural there'd be stories."

"Is the lore pure imagination, then?"

"Some. Not all."

Still smiling, still patient, she said, "Tell me the 'not all' part."

He tucked his hands behind his overalls' bib and warned, "If you're looking to hear a happy story, I can't tell it. This one's sad."

"That's okay. I want to hear anyway."

"They met one summer."

"When?"

"Way back. B'fore you were born. She was mistress of Star's End for those months. He worked there."

"And they fell in love?"

"Yup. Caused one heck of a scandal."

"Because of their social differences?"

"Because she was married."

Caroline caught in a breath, then let it out. "Oh."

"You're right to say that, missy. Husband was coming here every weekend and going back to the city on Mondays. While he was gone, she slept with the groundskeeper."

Caroline pictured Jesse Cray. But of course, this was before Jesse's time. "What happened?"

"Someone took a picture of them together and put it in the newspaper."

"Was it a compromising picture?"

"Like you'd know it, no. In my day, a woman only had to look at a man with that kind of devotion, and if he wasn't the right man, she was condemned. Her husband saw the picture."

"What did he do?" Caroline asked.

"Said they should go home. It was the end of the summer anyway."

"That's all?" She had been imagining a duel at dawn on the bluff. "No confrontation?"

"He wasn't that sort. Leastways, that's what they said. Me, I didn't know the husband. Knew the groundskeeper, though. Whole town did. Liked him a lot."

"He must have been a rogue."

"No. Just a nice fellow who fell head-over in love with a woman who was already taken. Near broke his heart when she left."

"But why did she? If she loved him, why didn't she stay?"

"She never told us. We never saw her again."

"Never?"

"Never."

Caroline thought of lovers sharing a single summer, then parting and never seeing each other again. She was no romantic. Still she was touched. "You're right. That's a sad story."

And it stuck with her. More than stuck. Haunted. She figured it had to do with the fact that she loved Ben and couldn't think of never seeing him again — which she had no intention of telling him, on principle alone, after the ultimatum he'd given her. She didn't like ultimatums. He could sit and stew until she was good and ready to call.

Still, she thought of Simon's lovers and felt a devastating emptiness.

"They *never* saw each other again?" Annette asked. She and her sisters were out on the deck again, working on iced tea and sandwiches this time. The tea had bits of orange and lemon in it, and was incredibly good, as was the lobster salad, which was mixed lightly with lemon mayonnaise and piled onto slices of broad boule bread. Tea, salad, and bread were all Leah's doing, and would have amazed Annette even more had she not been hanging on Caroline's every word. A gentle breeze came off the ocean and over the rocks to where they sat, carrying with it the scents of Star's End and, in so doing, rendering the story much more real.

Annette was caught up in it. Given all she felt for Jean-Paul, she identified with the lovers. Their fate saddened her.

Granted, she was in the mood to be saddened. She hadn't talked with him since the night before last, an eternity in her lifetime with him. Oh, he'd sent flowers yesterday morning with a card that said, simply, *"Je t'aime."* And he'd called yesterday afternoon while she'd been in Downlee, and left a sweet message with Gwen. But nothing could substitute for the sound of his voice.

"Never," Caroline repeated. "According to Simon, she never returned to Downlee."

"What did she do?"

"I assume that if she went so far as to follow her husband home, she stayed with him. Women didn't divorce freely in those days."

"What about her lover?" Leah asked.

"Simon says he was never the same."

"Did he ever marry?"

"I didn't ask."

"I hope not," Annette decided. "I can't imagine he had much left to give to another woman, not loving the first one that way."

"Wouldn't he eventually get over her?"

"*I* don't believe it. If something happened to Jean-Paul, I'd never get over it."

"That's because you and Jean-Paul are married," Caroline reasoned. "You've been with him for nearly twenty years. You have kids. He's an indelible part of your life. But what if something had happened to him before all that?"

"Even then," Annette insisted.

"Really?"

She hesitated. To say more was to tread on shaky ground at a time when she and her sisters were enjoying a truce of sorts. They could either end up arguing, or understanding each other better.

She decided to take the risk. "I know neither of you want to believe this," she said quietly, "but with Jean-Paul and me, it was love at first sight. One look, and I was hooked. Same with him. You call me a hopeless romantic, but that's how it was. If something had happened to him before we were married, I'd have felt the loss for the rest of my life. I might have married someone else, but that someone else would have always suffered in comparison to Jean-Paul."

"What if that someone else was even better than Jean-Paul?" Caroline asked.

Annette shook her head. "No one could be better for me than Jean-Paul." Her eyes watered. "Another kind of man might be better for you, or for you, Leah, but Jean-Paul is it for me." She wished he would call. Oh, she knew they were all fine without her. She just wanted to hear Jean-Paul's voice.

"You don't think it's possible to love more than one man?" Leah asked.

Annette took a moment to recompose herself. "Not the same way. You may love another man for his companionship, or his intellect, or his body, but the whole package only comes once."

"That is very scary," Caroline said.

Leah's stricken look said she agreed.

"But it's also lovely," Annette added. "It means that if you're lucky enough to land the package, you experience something unique."

"Unique," Caroline mused. "Go on."

"Jean-Paul and I share a vision. We agree on what we want in life and how to get it. We're partners on the same team. What I lack, he has, and vice versa. We complement each other."

"Do you ever argue?"

Annette thought of her last conversation with Jean-Paul. "Yell and scream and storm out the door? No. But we do disagree sometimes. Like about my calling home from here." She felt her eyes tearing again. "Jean-Paul thinks I shouldn't do it so much.

He says I'm ramming my love down their throats." She looked at her sisters, waiting for criticism. When it didn't come, she said, "I never thought it was possible to love too much."

Leah gave her knee a reassuring touch, but it was Caroline, with surprising gentleness, who spoke. "He's saying you're over-attentive. That doesn't mean you're wrong in the fact that you love them."

"They mean the world to me," Annette swore. "If I bore you when I talk about them, I'm sorry, but they're my life. They're what I do. I'm a wife and a mother before I'm anything else in this world."

"I know."

"And I'm dying," she rushed on, because she felt that a window was open on sympathy, and she was desperate for encouragement. "I told Jean-Paul that I wouldn't call again, and that he should call me if there was a problem, and it's not that I want there to be a problem, but I really want him to call."

"He has called," Leah pointed out, "just not when you're here."

That was small solace, as far as Annette was concerned. "We've always been so close. We haven't *ever* been separated this way before."

"Chances are," Caroline offered, "that he's overwhelmed taking care of the kids after a full day of work. He'll appreciate you far more for this, Annette. And in the meantime, you're taking a well-deserved vacation."

"But I miss him. He's my husband."

"You can still have a separate identity."

"I don't *want* a separate identity. I don't want to be a lawyer. I don't want to chair some big charity function."

"I'm not talking about your being something else," Caroline said. "I'm talking about your being you." She sat back in her chair and included Leah in the field of a grin. "Right now, I'm no one's lawyer. I'm no one's lover. I'm just me. Sitting here. Relaxing. Breathing. I'm not thinking about the brief I'm supposed to be putting together. I'm not thinking about the decisions Ben wants me to make. I'm not thinking about my law firm and who may or may not be stealing my work." She sighed. "I'm having lunch on a deck that someone else has to clean. Call it selfish if you will. But everyone needs to be selfish once in a while." She stared at Annette. "That's what you have to learn how to do. Be selfish."

Annette looked at Leah. "Is she right?"

Leah was slow in answering. She seemed

to pull herself in from a distance when she took a deep breath and smiled. "Much as I hate to give her satisfaction by admitting it, she is. Jean-Paul loves you. You know that. He sent flowers, and he's called. So, you haven't connected on the phone. That's okay. He's back in St. Louis keeping tabs on things while you spend time with your mother." She made a face. "Granted, she hasn't quite shown up, but we're here. So relax and enjoy doing nothing. It won't last for long."

Annette agreed with that, at least. "I should, I suppose. They were the ones who told me to come."

"You've paid your dues," Caroline added. "You've shouldered nonstop responsibility for years. You've earned a break."

Annette followed the flight of a gull along the bluff. She sighed and settled more comfortably into her chair. She hadn't been lazy in years. She wasn't sure she knew how to be lazy. Her eyes lit on the pool, the flower beds beside and beyond, then the bluffs. "It is beautiful here — peaceful. I could do worse."

The portable phone rang. Annette sat up straight — forgetting beauty and peace and relaxation — and held her breath while Caroline answered. Only when her eyes, then the telephone, went to Leah, did Annette release the breath and sink back.

They were right, she supposed. She was going to have to learn to relax. After all, the children were getting older. Before long, they would be going off to college and beyond. And then what would she do? Sit by the phone waiting for them to call? Imagine that everything she read about in the newspapers was happening to *them?* Butt into their lives?

She couldn't. Nor could she call Jean-Paul every few minutes just to hear the sound of his voice. She'd have to go to work. Either that, or she'd have to learn to be a lady of leisure.

Like Ginny.

It was an absurd thought. She couldn't do nothing. It wasn't in her nature. Then again, Caroline was right. She'd paid her dues. She'd earned a break.

"That was Julia," Leah said excitedly. "She says my bread went fast. She wants more."

Annette could see how pleased she was and wondered whether anyone in her super-slick world ever made her feel pleased that way. "That's great," she said enthusiastically.

Caroline turned her face to the sun. "This

is your vacation. You're not supposed to work."

"Baking isn't work. It's fun. Like making lunch. It's such a treat."

"I think you should do it," Annette said.

"Mistake," Caroline mumbled.

"Look at it this way," Leah told Caroline, rising and scooping up her plate. "You think I do nothing in Washington —"

"I didn't say that."

"You think it. So look at my baking bread for Julia as a vacation from doing nothing."

"Leah —" Annette called when she started off. The argument was an echo of the past. But she didn't want to return to the ill will that had characterized the past with her sisters. She liked the camaraderie that had sprung up between them.

She turned on Caroline, furious at her for having disturbed their lovely balance, but Caroline was already out of her lounge, going after Leah. And then the phone rang again.

Annette's pulse skipped. She slipped from her chair to the one Caroline had left, beside which lay the phone. "Hello?"

"Hi, Mom."

"Nat?" Maternal instinct surged back with its monumental world of fears. Nat was her baby, eight years old and wearing out Nikes

290

every three months. The sound of his little-boy voice made her own crack. "What's wrong, sweetie?"

"Thomas is being mean."

Annette let out a long, relieved sigh. Only then did she realize that Leah and Caroline were crowding close. She shot them apologetic looks. "Are you guys fighting?" she asked Nat.

"He won't let me play with his Game Boy."

"What Game Boy?"

"The one Daddy bought him yesterday. Daddy said I could use it, too, but Thomas isn't sharing. Will you tell him he has to, Mom?"

"Back up a minute, Nat. Game Boy was supposed to be Thomas's birthday gift." To Caroline and Leah, she said, "He's been begging for it since last Christmas, when two of his best friends got it. We agreed on November, when he turns thirteen." She asked Nat, "Why did Daddy buy it now?"

"Because Thomas is bored."

"Bored? Good gracious, I left a whole schedule there with practically every minute planned out."

"But Daddy didn't think Nicky and Dev should take us to the club, and the VCR wasn't working right, so the only thing we

could think of to do was to go to the movies, but the movies *they* wanted to see
weren't the movies *we* wanted to see, so we
decided to stay home, and Thomas was
bored."

Annette was having trouble buying into
the dilemma. For one thing, the basic
premise was wrong. "Why didn't Daddy
want you at the club?"

"Because Thomas can't go swimming,"
Nat said impatiently.

"Whyever *not?*"

"Because he can't get his cast wet!"

"What cast?" Annette demanded, chalking
one up for maternal instinct, indeed.

"The *one on his arm.* Mom, he won't
share!"

"What did Thomas do to his arm?"

"Easy, Annette," Caroline murmured.

Leah whispered, "Jean-Paul would have
called if it were anything serious."

Annette took a steadying breath and more
quietly repeated the question. But Nat was
suddenly talking to someone else, sounding
angry, then defensive, and within seconds
Devon came on the line. "Nat can be such
a little jerk. He wasn't supposed to say
anything. Thomas is fine, Mom. He just
broke his arm."

"Just broke it?" Annette asked in disbelief.

"He was riding his mountain bike on the trail in the woods behind school —"

"That trail is notorious for spills. He wasn't supposed to be riding there." And he wouldn't have, if she'd been home. She'd *known* it was a lousy time for her to be gone. She'd *told* Jean-Paul so.

"Thomas knows that," Devon said, sounding calm, sensible, and mature. "So this is his punishment."

Annette rubbed her forehead. "What happened, exactly?"

"He fell and skidded down a bumpy little hill. It was a simple break. He didn't need an operation or anything."

"When did it happen?"

"Day before yesterday. Right before supper."

"And you were at the hospital most of the evening," which explained why she hadn't been able to get through until late.

"It was awhile before Thomas made it home," Devon explained, "and then we had to wait a long time at the hospital because Dad didn't want anyone but Dr. Olmstead putting on the cast, and he was out to dinner with his wife. Thomas wanted to call you from the hospital, but Daddy said you'd only worry. You're lucky you're not here, Mom. Thomas is being a brat."

"Is he in pain?"

"Yes, he's a pain. He thinks everyone should be waiting on him just because he broke his arm."

"Which arm?"

"His right. He complains that he can't do things, but school's out, so he doesn't have to write, and he can just as easily stuff food in his mouth with his left hand. So he can't go swimming until the cast hardens more. So what. That's his problem. *He* was the one riding his bike where he wasn't supposed to." Her voice shifted direction. "It's the truth, Thomas. Dad said so. Yes, I *know* you were wearing a helmet, but that didn't make it okay."

"Put him on," Annette said and seconds later heard Thomas's voice. It was low in the way of prepubescent twelve-year-olds who imagined themselves men.

"It wasn't my fault, Mom. Someone left empty beer cans up there, and I swerved so I wouldn't hit them. It's not like *I* put them there."

"Thank heaven for that," Annette remarked. He didn't sound terribly hurt. Defensive, yes. Defiant, yes. But hurt? "How does your arm feel?"

"It aches. Robbie's gone to rent videos —"

"I thought the VCR was broken?"

"The guy just fixed it, and Nicole's making popcorn to eat while we watch, but all Nat wants to do is play with my Game Boy." In a voice that was suddenly twelve again, he said, "It's *awesome,* Mom. Wait'll you see it. No, you *can't* play with it, Nat!"

Squabbling was part of family life. But it struck Annette that, just then, she was glad *not* to be there. "Let him play," she urged.

"Devon wants to talk again."

"Are you having fun, Mom?"

Annette looked at her sisters, then beyond, at the deck where the shadows were starting to lengthen. She thought of laziness and selfishness, of the cry of gulls and the roar of the surf. When she opened herself to those thoughts, she felt removed from the chaos back home. "Actually, I am."

"Is Grandma there yet?"

"No. Maybe Saturday."

"Are you being nice to the aunts?"

She looked at Caroline and Leah. "Very nice."

"That's good. *Stop it, guys.* I have to run, Mom. Thomas and Nat are fighting. Wouldn't it be smarter if I just bought Nat his own Game Boy? I'll put it on the Visa —"

"*Don't* put it on the Visa. I left that for

emergencies. Buying a second Game Boy is not an emergency. Find something else for Nat to do. Be inventive. It's good training for the time when you're a mother, yourself."

"This isn't mothering. It's refereeing."

"So now you know," Annette said, smiling, pleased indeed not to be there just then. "Be good, sweetie. Kiss everyone for me. Love you."

"Love you, too, Mom."

Annette hung up the phone. She stared at it for a minute, then swung a wary glance at her sisters. "Maybe I should fly home."

"No!" they both said at once.

"You talked with Thomas," Caroline reasoned. "You know that he's fine."

"He broke his arm."

"So did you, as I recall, when you were eight, and you survived."

"But he and Nat are fighting. It's not fair to the others to have to deal with that." The words were right. She wanted to be talked out of guilt.

"Why shouldn't they have to deal with it?" Caroline asked. "They're all part of the family. Squabbles go with the territory."

"They were the ones who told you to come up here," Leah pointed out. "They insisted they could manage on their own, so let them do it. Jean-Paul will be home in a few hours. Let him deal with the squabbles."

"I should," Annette said. "It'd serve him right. It was eleven-thirty when I reached him the other night. They must have just walked in from the hospital, and he didn't say a word about it, the rat."

"He was trying to protect you."

"Yeah, and how much more is he hiding? Did Thomas do permanent damage to his hand? Will he get full dexterity back? What *else* is happening that they're not saying?"

Caroline snorted. "Given how good Nat is at keeping secrets, I can't imagine there's much."

Annette suspected she was right, and, anyway, it seemed they were all surviving the broken arm. Devon sounded annoyed with her brothers but otherwise composed, and cheery Nicole was close-by in the kitchen, and then there was trusty Rob and good old levelheaded Jean-Paul.

Jean-Paul would have seen that Thomas had the best of medical care. It wasn't worth Annette's time to even *begin* to worry on that score.

But old habits died hard. The more she thought, the worse it was. "I feel guilty. I should be there."

"Because Ginny never was?" Leah asked.

"Yes, and because I like being there when my kids need me."

Leah and Caroline exchanged a glance.

Annette sighed. "You're thinking that the kids don't need me right now. Well, maybe they don't. Let me rephrase that. It's *my* need to be there when my kids are sick or hurt. Sometimes there's nothing to be done but hold a hand, or plump a pillow, or sit in the chair by the window and read, but it's satisfying. If either of you had children, you'd know what I mean."

The words had inadvertently slipped out, with instant regret. Comments like that had started arguments in the past. Her sisters had always assumed condescension, though that hadn't been Annette's intent at all.

"You don't have to have children to understand," Caroline surprised her by saying. "I was a child once. I could have used moral support from time to time."

"Ditto," Leah said.

Annette eyed them warily. "We agree?"

Leah looked at Caroline, who shrugged. "We do on the issue of moral support. Not on running home to St. Louis. You've been there for them in the past, and you'll be there for them in the future. It's our turn now. We need you here."

Annette was too stunned to argue.

■ ■ ■ ■

Leah had no intention of meeting Jesse that night. She wasn't addicted to him. Not by a long shot. When it came time to leave Star's End, she would do so without a care.

For a time, she sat in the dark of her bedroom. She thought about Washington and the life she had built there, but the images were pale. She thought about Julia, who loved her bread and had extracted a promise for more. She thought about dinner, a *boeuf bourguignon* she'd made, that Caroline and Annette had sworn they wouldn't eat because of the presence of red meat, then had proceeded to devour. She thought about the people she had met in town, who had been warm and not at all exclusionary. She thought, sadly, about the lovers of Star's End.

Inevitably she thought of Jesse. She imagined him hauling himself from the pool and looking for her. But he would be looking for a lover, not a coward. She owed him an explanation.

She crept down the stairs and went out to the pool, but he wasn't there. She walked its perimeter with an eye in the moonlight for a puddle and footprints. There were none.

He hadn't come. So much for owing explanations. Feeling dejected in spite of herself, she started back toward the house.

"Leah?"

She stopped. Her hopes soared. She squelched them. They soared again.

He came from behind and gently turned her around. He wasn't dressed for swimming, any more than she was dressed for bed. His voice was deep and raw with feeling. "I thought I'd test out not coming. Wanted to prove it didn't matter if I saw you tonight or not, but it does."

"My life is in Washington," the squelcher inside her said. "It's who I am."

"Not when you're here."

"I'm someone else here."

"Which one's the real you?"

She started to answer, then stopped. Washington was what she did with herself, but whether it was what she wanted or was most suited for was something else. She rather enjoyed wearing jeans and letting her hair go wild, and her skin was responding to the ocean air with a glow no makeup could give.

But three hundred and sixty-five days a year?

He drew her to him. They stood for the longest time, just holding each other.

"Want a cappuccino?" he finally asked.

"Mmmm."

He took her back to the cottage and made her a cup using the machine he had bought not at the hardware store in Downlee, but in Harvard Square several years before — but Cambridge was the tamest of his winter stops, it seemed. While the cappuccino brewed, he walked her past the photographs on the wall, telling of those trips and others. He had gone places she didn't dare go. She was humbled, and more than a little envious.

They carried their cappuccinos into the greenhouse, where the air was lush with the smell of rich soil and new growth. Leah was into the café scene, but she couldn't remember one as atmospheric, all the more so when Jesse lit a candle and set it nearby. He pulled out a bench. They straddled it, facing each other, with the cappuccinos in the short space between them.

Leah sighed. "This is unfairly romantic."

"Some would call it damp and uncomfortable."

"Nah. Not here. The whole of Star's End is romantic. It has a charm that changes things. Take my sisters and me. We've been at each other's throats through the bulk of our adult lives, but up here we get along. They've actually been pleasant. Caroline isn't being superior, and Annette isn't being maternal."

"And you?"

"I'm not acting like fluff."

He looked amused. "How does one act like fluff?"

"By letting Caroline and Annette believe that I go to parties every night, sleep late every morning, and spend afternoons either shopping or having my hair and nails done."

"Why would you want them to believe that?"

"Because it says that I'm different from them. It warns them away from making comparisons. I don't like being compared to my sisters. I always come out on the short end."

"I'm not drawn to either of them."

"No. You're not." She didn't know whether to laugh or cry, because if he was drawn to one of them, her own dilemma would be different. "But they've done more in life than I have. Caroline is partner in a high-power law firm, and Annette has five kids. Not one or two. Five, and I can ridicule her for being supermom to the extreme, but the fact is that she's great at what she does."

"Do you want to have children?"

She nodded. "But I'd probably make a terrible mother."

He shook his head, slowly and with conviction.

"You're biased," she said.

He nodded.

He loved her. She saw it in the warmth of his eyes and felt it in the gentleness of his hands. She heard it in the fierce sounds he made when he was inside her, sounds that said he needed to be closer than even that. He insisted they were made for each other, and one part of Leah believed it. The other part wondered if it wasn't simply the charm of Star's End at work.

"Caroline heard a story in Downlee today," she said, "one about star-crossed lovers here at Star's End. Do you know it?"

"Depends which one you mean."

"The one about the married woman and the groundskeeper."

"I know it."

"Is it true?"

He nodded.

"They never saw each other again after that summer?"

"No."

"Never wrote, never called?"

"No."

"The story says they were in love."

"Very much."

"Then why did she leave? Was it just because her husband told her to?"

"He didn't. The decision was hers."

"Did she love her husband?"

"I wouldn't know."

"But she did love the groundskeeper."

"Yes."

"And he loved her. It's very sad. Did you know him?"

"Everyone in town did."

"Is he still around?"

"No. He died a while back."

"How?"

"His heart just stopped beating."

"It was broken," Leah said because it seemed the obvious thing. Then she caught herself. "Forget that. It's not scientific."

"It was broken. She had taken a piece of it and it never grew back. He tried to manage without it, but he couldn't."

"This is all speculative, of course. He was probably clinically depressed."

"Call it what you will, but he never recovered."

"Did he ever go after her?"

"No."

"Why not?"

"Pride. And love. She had made her decision. He had to respect it. He feared that showing up on her doorstep would only make things harder for her. Besides, he didn't have much to offer. She was a woman of means. He had nothing."

Leah tore her eyes from his and concentrated on her cappuccino. "What would you have done in his shoes?"

"Just what he did."

"You wouldn't have fought for her?"

"Not given the circumstances."

She looked at him then. "Even if you believed she was the only one in the world for you?"

"Even then," he said quietly and with the same solemnity she had seen in him at the start. "There's love, and there's life. Sometimes the two clash. It did in their case." His eyes gripped hers. "But I'm not in his shoes. I have an education. I have savings. I could live elsewhere if I choose. I choose to live here."

She had always known that. She loved him all the more for it. But it didn't change anything.

Fighting a painful lump in her throat, she rose from the bench and carried her cup back through the cottage to the kitchen. She was rinsing it when he came up behind her. He put a hand on the counter on either side of the sink, hemming her in.

"I've seen the world, Leah, and the more I see, the more I realize how much I love it here. I'm not being stubborn. It's just a conviction I have. I could live in D.C. I could work at the Botanic Gardens. I have a contact there, someone I went to school with, but I wouldn't be happy. And if I wasn't happy, I'd make you miserable."

But that's my home, Leah wanted to cry. She closed her eyes and leaned back. Behind her, he was strong and supportive, wrapping his arms around her even before she could ask, and suddenly she didn't want to think of the future.

He touched her. He opened her clothing. He defined her body with his hands, and his mouth, making it something that was only for him.

They made love there in the kitchen, then again after he carried her to bed, because only through passion could she say all she felt. When she awoke, he was at the window, his nudity profiled by the dawn's early light and more strikingly male than anything a mortal could paint. She was no more able to stay away from him than she was to stop breathing. Approaching, she slipped splayed hands up over his chest and, with her cheek pressed to his back, held him close.

They bathed together, dressed, and returned to the main house, so that she could leave a note telling her sisters she'd gone for a walk. Then Jesse showed her his wildflower meadow. It was a special place framed by the lush green of the June woods, a riotous canvas of primary colors, of lupines, Indian blanket, and thistle.

"God's kaleidoscope," Jesse said in the lyrical way that vouched for his love of the land. "A twist of the weather, a shift of the month, and the colors change."

Leah lay beside him among the blooms. The smell of morning dew and warm, weedy sunshine surrounded her, but what captivated her most was his face. She rolled to her side and traced the creases by his eyes. His skin showed healthy signs of weathering. The years wouldn't make him look older, but more compelling, she knew.

Several hours later she was thinking about that as she studied the faces of the locals having breakfast at Julia's, when Julia slipped into the seat Jesse had vacated moments before.

"Where'd he go?"

"The hardware store. He's thinking of putting in a sprinkling system. He needs pricing on pipe."

Julia sighed. "I do love Jesse." She broke

307

off a blueberry muffin crumb and put it in her mouth. "He's one of the most sensitive men I've ever met. There are times when I think I'm crazy not to make a play for him." She reached for another crumb. "But I have Howell, and Jesse isn't interested in me. He's interested in you."

"Do you think so?" Leah asked. She wondered just how obvious it was.

Julia looked smug. "I saw how he was looking at you just now. He doesn't look at anyone else that way, and I'm not the only one who noticed. In the last forty minutes, three different people have directed my attention this way."

"Oh, dear."

Julia grinned. "Not to worry. You guys look great together. Of course, everyone's looking for it. I mean, there's an irony to it, after what happened with your mother."

"Irony?"

"It must be in your genes, something that reacts to being away from civilization. Then again, cerebral men are stiffs. Men who work with their hands are *good* with their hands, if you know what I mean. Leah? Leah, are you with me?"

Leah was stunned. She knew the answer because it made shocking sense, still she had to ask the question. "What happened with my mother?"

Julia looked suddenly unsure. "You knew, didn't you?"

"What happened?"

"Shit."

"Tell me, Julia."

"I shouldn't be the one. Damn it, didn't she tell you herself? Why else would she be buying Star's End?"

"I need to hear the words. Please."

Julia looked regretful. Finally, she sighed. "She was the one, Leah. She and the groundskeeper."

FIFTEEN

Wendell reached the porch of the general store earlier than usual and in a snit. He didn't bother to stop inside for his morning coffee. He was too annoyed.

It didn't help that Clarence was late, ambling on down the street, taking his own sweet time about climbing the steps and moving along down the bench.

" 'Bout time," Wendell announced in a grumble.

Clarence eased himself down on the bench and offered his customary, "Wendell."

Wendell planted his hands on his thighs. He looked out over Main Street, grim as could be. "Jesse's foolin' around with the youngest. D'ya know that?"

Clarence had heard they'd been seen together, and that they looked taken with each other. He'd taken a look at the girl, himself. Couldn't say he blamed Jesse.

"Saw'm togethuh myself," Wendell said,

"up t'all kinds'a no-good."

Clarence put his pipe between his teeth.

Wendell looked at him. "Well?"

Clarence reached for his tobacco pouch. "Well what?"

"It ain't right, sittin' nearly on his lap while he's drivin' down the street."

"No law 'gainst it."

"Should be."

"We did it once."

"No mattuh. It doesn't look good. I'm tellin' ya, Stah's End's in trouble, and the mothuh's no wheya in sight."

Clarence took the pipe from his mouth, pushed it into the pouch, and scooped tobacco into the bowl.

"Malcolm says she's dead," Wendell announced.

"Gus says she's in New Yawk."

"Dead," Wendell insisted. "Been dead a long time."

Clarence knew that if Virginia St. Clair was dead, the town would have known it long ago. They had a vested interest in the woman. "What's Elmira say?"

Wendell snorted. "Elmira says she's on'a way, but what does Elmira know. I say she's dead."

"If she's dead, who bought Stah's End?"

"Daughtuhs, most likely."

Clarence didn't believe it. "Why would they do that? Stah's End's doesn't mean anathin' to them. They didn't even know about the mothuh and Will."

Wendell shot a look down the bench. "Who told you that?"

"The young one was talkin' with Julia. When Julia let it slip, she went papuh white."

Wendell eyed him straight on. "How d'you know that?"

"I saw," Clarence said and stuck the pipe back in his mouth.

"How d'you *see?*"

"I was at Julia's."

"Why were ya *theya?*" Julia's was enemy territory. Clarence had no business going to Julia's. Wendell couldn't trust *anyone* anymore.

"She makes good muffins," Clarence said. He struck a match and touched it to the tobacco.

"Know what goes inta those muffins?"

"Flowah — buttuh — nuts," Clarence said between puffs, until he felt the fullness of the draw.

"Evuh wonduh why ya like 'em so much?"

Clarence regarded Wendell dryly.

"Yes, suh," Wendell said with a smug nod. "She's up to no good with those muffins."

312

"You just don't like Julia."

"She ain't *one'a* us."

"Been heea three yeahs."

"That don't mattuh. You shouldn't be givin'a business."

Clarence stretched out his legs.

"We agreed," Wendell charged.

"You agreed."

Wendell glared at him for a minute before shifting his glare to the street.

"And anothuh thing," Clarence added. "I don't see nuthin' wrong with Jesse seein' Leah. That's the youngest. Leah."

"She's trouble. Th' apple don't fall fah."

"She has nice haya."

"But she ain't one'a us."

"Well, *hell,* Wendell, few is, nowadays. Town's changin', like it aw not."

Wendell fumed for a minute, before pushing himself up. "I'm gettin' coffee," he growled and went inside.

Clarence draped an arm along the back of the bench. He took a deep draw of his pipe and blew the smoke out in a thick line. When Callie Dalton came up the steps, he touched his finger to the bill of his cap. "Mawnin', Callie."

"Mawnin', Clarence."

"Look out fa Wendell."

Callie peered cautiously through the

screened front door. She stepped quickly aside when Wendell pushed it open and came through, then vanished inside.

"Irish creme," Wendell sneered, sniffing the contents of his mug with distaste. "Don't know what's wrong with just plain coffee."

"What's wrong," Clarence said, "is that it's borin'. Got no flavah."

Wendell grunted.

"And anothuh thing," Clarence said. "Town could use a new romance. Old one's gettin' stale."

Wendell stared at him.

Clarence puffed on his pipe. After a bit, when Wendell's eyes remained on him, he met the look.

"Smoke's rottin' ya brain."

"Nah. Those two look good with each othuh, is all."

"She'll kill 'im, like the mothuh killed Will. Damn shame, I say. Jesse's the best hope we got."

"Hope a what? Savin' the past? Nah. Jesse's movin' ahead. He's smahta than you an' me t'gethuh."

"He's as native as us."

"Town's changin'. Bettuh face it, Wendell. Julia's gonna keep sellin' muffins. Church Ladies' Cookbook is gonna have a spaghetti

chaptuh. Coffee's gonna get even moah different."

Wendell made a sputtering sound.

"Way I see it," Clarence went on, "we got
a choice. We can go along with 'em aw we
can die. Me, I'm not dyin' so fast. I don't
care what Julia's puttin' in those muffins,
long's they taste good. Fact is, I nevuh did
like those dried up old rolls Mavis used to
serve with the coffee you loved."

SIXTEEN

Caroline was sure she had heard wrong. Calmly holding the phone to her ear, she asked Doug to repeat himself.

"You've seen the news, haven't you?" he asked first.

"No. We don't watch it here."

"That explains it, then. I knew there had to be a reason why you didn't call."

"I'm calling now, and I'm wondering why no one called me." She felt a burst of indignation. "Luther Hines is my client, not Walker Housman's. I've been working with Luther and his son for three years now."

"He blew it, Caroline. He killed the kid."

Caroline found the words no easier to swallow the second time around. This time, though, she began to feel queasy. She had spent untold hours with Luther trying to deal with the boy, first when he was charged with sexually harassing one of his high school teachers, and later, in college, when he was charged with statutory rape. In both instances, she had managed to plea bargain for probation and psychotherapy. There had been several subsequent drunk driving charges, which had resulted in fines and the suspension of his license, and several loud and physical fights with his father, which had resulted in no police action at all.

Caroline had never imagined it would come to this. "What *happened?*"

"Luther claims it was self-defense. They were arguing. The boy came at him with a knife. Unfortunately, it wasn't the knife that killed the boy."

"What did?"

"He was strangled."

"By *Luther?* Impossible."

"Luther was the only one there. He called the police. He gave a confession."

Caroline knew that Luther had a temper — Jason hadn't come into it by chance — but she had never seen him lose it to the point of violence. Yes, he was exasperated with Jason, but exasperation was a far cry from hate, or whatever the emotion was that would incite him to murder. She supposed it could have been fear. But Luther *loved* his son. God only knew — as did the partners of Holten, Wills, and Duluth — the sums he had paid Caroline in the past to help the boy.

Swallowing down her emotions, she said, "He had the right to make one phone call when he was arrested. Who did he call?"

"You, but you weren't around, so Walker took it. We're talking the middle of the night, Caroline. Walker got out of bed to meet him at the police station, then stood beside him in court yesterday morning."

"Just long enough to establish himself as the lawyer of record," she said in disbelief. "I called in yesterday, Doug, but no one breathed a word of this." She felt betrayed.

"Because it's not your case. It's Walker's."

"But Luther is my client," Caroline said, trying to stay cool. "I'm the one who should be defending him."

"You weren't here."

"If Walker had called me, I'd have taken the first plane back. I could have been there in time for the arraignment. Partners are not supposed to steal cases from partners."

"Come on, Caroline. You're making a big deal out of nothing. The fact is that Walker Housman has defended a helluva lot more murder suspects than you have."

"Not by much, if you count the ones I prosecuted."

"Defense work is different."

Caroline was feeling *doubly* betrayed.

Doug had always been on her side. "Are you suggesting that Walker will do a better job than I could?"

"I'm suggesting that you leave it alone. Luther Hines will be well represented. Isn't that the most important thing?"

"But I *know* Luther in ways Walker doesn't. I've worked with him. I believe in his innocence."

"Caroline, he confessed."

"He's not a murderer, Doug. He's a decent person who may have acted in self-defense, may have acted out of fear-driven terror, may have been momentarily insane. I believe in the man. I also believe that he must be in agony now. Pure guilt may have him agreeing to a greater punishment than he deserves."

"Luther Hines? Are you kidding? He knows when to be cool. He's a successful businessman because he plays his cards right."

"He's also running for mayor — or was — which means that whoever tries this case will be in the limelight. You don't suppose Walker wanted that limelight for himself, do you?"

Doug was too slow in answering.

"While I'm out of town. He's a snake. Tell him that for me, will you, Doug?" She slammed down the phone, strode into the family room, and sank into a chair. To Annette, who was on the sofa, she said, "One of my partners just robbed me of a major case."

"That sounds illegal."

"Not illegal. Only unethical. Damn it, it *is*," she cried and, bolting up out of the chair, strode back into the kitchen. Within minutes, she had Walker Housman's secretary on the line.

"He's in a meeting, Ms. St. Clair."

"This is important. It won't take long."

She was put on hold, but it was the secretary's voice, not Walker's, that returned. "I'm sorry. He can't take your call now."

"It's about the Hines case. Would you tell him that?"

She truly expected Walker to come on talking a blue streak in defense of his taking the case, but, again, the secretary was the one who returned. "He'll have to speak with you another time."

"When?" Caroline asked, drumming the counter. She could use a cigarette. Then again, no. She wasn't letting the likes of Walker Housman re-hook her.

"Let me see," the secretary said. "Well, he has meetings most of today. Maybe late afternoon — no, that's bad."

Caroline simmered. "Just put me through to him now."

"Why don't you give me the number where you are, and I'll give him the message."

Caroline didn't know which was worse — the secretary running interference, or Walker putting her off. She knew what he'd do with her message. He'd ball it up and slamdunk it into the nearest wastebasket.

But there was more than one way to skin a cat.

Docilely, she reeled off her phone number. Then she disconnected the call. Then she dialed again. This time, she connected.

Graham Howard was on the firm's executive committee, and hence part of the management team. If she was to make a protest, this was the place to do it.

Graham had always been cordial to her. This day was no exception. "How are you enjoying your vacation, Caroline?" he asked.

"I was enjoying it just fine until a little while ago, when I learned about Luther Hines. I just tried to reach Walker, but he won't take my call. I have to say, Graham, I'm appalled by what Walker's done."

Graham didn't pretend not to know what had happened, though he gave it his own twist. "I can understand your disappointment. It will be an interesting case to try."

"Luther is my client. It's my case."

There was a pause. Then, a still polite, "I think not. Walker is the lawyer of record. Luther has agreed to it."

"Was Luther given a choice?"

"That, I don't know. You'd have to ask Walker."

"I would have, if he'd agreed to talk with me. But he refused. He must have known why I was calling. Graham, this isn't right."

"Of course it is, Caroline. Walker is an experienced defense attorney. He'll give Luther the best possible representation."

"He won't do a better job than I would, and Luther is my client."

"But you were away. I really don't know why you're so upset."

She fisted her hand in a bid for self-control. "I'm upset," she said deliberately, "because I have been Luther Hines's lawyer for three years now. I have cultivated a relationship with him, and I've worked hard at it, all of which benefits the firm. The firm owes me this case."

"No. It doesn't. Walker will try the case. The firm will benefit from that. Really, Caroline, there's no need to carry on."

"I'm not carrying on," she said in her

most sensible voice.

"Yes, you are. Walker hasn't done anything wrong. Partners work together."

"If that were so, wouldn't he have called me prior to the arraignment? Wouldn't he have wanted to update me on the fate of my client? Wouldn't he have wanted to consult with me about the best defense?"

"Walker knows the best defense," Graham announced. "It's going to be temporary insanity. Now, you know as well as I do, Caroline, that you haven't done very well with that particular defense. The Baretta case was an embarrassment. Let Walker try this one. It'll be better, all around."

Caroline was dumbstruck. It was a minute before she could think, and another before she could speak. Within a matter of seconds, she was raging mad. "I want you to know," she said in a tremorous voice, "that I find what you just said to be totally offensive."

Graham sighed. "That problem is yours, not ours. If you want to play in the big league, you have to be able to rise above things like that. Professionalism is called for."

"I'm talking ethics. I'm talking mutual respect. I'm talking scrupulousness."

"That sounds like an accusation."

"If the shoe fits," she suggested.

"I'm going to forget you said that. You're upset. You're saying things that you'd think better of saying, if you were thinking more clearly. It's good you're away, Caroline. Clearly, you need this vacation. Now, I have another call coming in. We'll talk more when you return."

Caroline turned away from the phone, stalked across the room, and threw herself into the chair. "I don't *believe* that man. He says *I'm* the one with the problem. Was I 'carrying on'?"

"I thought you sounded very reasonable," Annette said.

"So did I. There are stereotypes of women that some men cling to, even when they see proof to the contrary staring them in the face. I am *totally* offended." She blew out a breath.

"Is there anything you can do?"

Fly home, she thought. Take the very next plane back to Chicago, she thought. But, damn it, she didn't want to have to do that. She didn't *want* to fly home. She had earned her vacation. She had a right to spend time with her family.

With another sigh, her anger gave way to resignation. "I can launch a protest before the executive committee of the firm, but it's apt to do as much harm as good. If my conversation with Graham told me anything, it was that. If I were a man, I'd be perceived as standing up for my rights. As a woman, I'll be considered a whiner. *And* a sore sport. The fact is that I wasn't there when Luther Hines called. Walker Housman was."

Annette turned her head on the sofa arm. "Are you angry?"

"Furious."

"You don't sound it."

Caroline was aware of that. She couldn't muster the strength to rant and rave, with Chicago so far away. "But intellectually it's there. I feel betrayed. This is the first vacation of any length that I've taken since I joined the firm. Why did I know something like this would happen?"

The question was no sooner out, when she gave the answer herself. "Because I work in a dog-eat-dog world, and my partners are curs. They're successful because they're ruthless. Unfortunately, the ruthlessness doesn't always stop where it should."

"You're not like that."

"Thank you."

"I'm serious."

"So am I," Caroline said. Damn it, she *didn't* feel like rushing back to Holten, Wills, and Duluth. "Thank you."

"You're welcome. So why do you work there? How can you stand it?"

"That's what Ben always asks." She missed him with a sudden, sharp ache, missed his voice, missed the sounding board he was and his down-to-earth, grass-roots perspective. She missed knowing that he might just show up, and the melting inside when he did.

She had tried to call him last night. He hadn't been home.

"He thinks I should open my own firm, a smaller, kinder one."

"Why don't you?"

Caroline drew a sudden blank. She had to think about it for a minute, but even then she felt bewildered. "I don't know. I always wanted a partnership in the biggest, strongest firm." Was it habit, then?

"So now you have it. You're the first female partner. But it doesn't sound like it's so great."

Caroline crossed her knees and began swinging a leg. "Want to know something? It's *pitiful.* Those men play games, Annette. They compete with each other for billable hours, for women, for appointments to the boards of foundations and club memberships, and when there's a break during partners' meetings, know what they discuss? Cars! Not their kids. Not family leave. Not putting together a gift for the retiring business manager. Cars." She threw an exasperated hand in the air. "I don't know *why* I stay there! Sitting here, right now, it doesn't make any sense at all!"

"Hey, guys."

Caroline's leg stopped mid-swing. She came forward. "Good God, Leah. You look like you've seen a ghost."

Leah had, in a way. With Julia's words still raw in her ears, she was trying to grasp them, trying to understand why Ginny had never said anything, trying to understand why *Jesse* hadn't let on, trying to understand what in the world was going on in her life. She was feeling shocked and hurt.

She lowered herself to the part of the sofa that was still warm from Annette's legs. She was grateful her sisters were there. Past, present, and future seemed suddenly in flux. They were the only ones who shared enough to help.

"You won't believe what I just learned," she said in a shaky voice. "Mother's been here before, after all. She and Daddy rented Star's End one summer. It was several years before you were born, Caroline. While she

327

was here, she had an affair with the grounds-keeper."

Both faces were blank. Then Caroline said, "And I'm the pope."

"She did."

"That's *absurd*," said Annette.

Caroline nodded. "You have the *wrrrong* woman."

"If that's the kind of gossip this town loves —"

"Ginny would be better off elsewhere."

They were staring at her, challenging her to take back what she'd said. All she could do was to stare right back. She hadn't wanted to believe it. Her initial response had been much the same as theirs — until she had started to think.

Apparently Annette was doing the same, because her stare wavered. "She was *that* woman?"

Caroline remained adamant. "Impossible. Not Ginny. She wouldn't have had an affair. She was too proper. She wouldn't have *dared.*"

"She had the perfect set-up," Leah went on. "Daddy used to commute. He'd spend five days in Philadelphia and the other two here."

"Who told you this?"

"Julia. I know — she's only been here

three years, herself, so how would she know, but the natives talk. They go to her place, and they talk. The talk started the minute Mother bought this place, and it hasn't stopped. Think about it. The curiosity about her. It's *intense.*"

"And understandable," Caroline reasoned. "Suddenly a stranger is the single largest landowner in town."

"But think about the questions," Leah urged. "They're not asking how rich she is, or what improvements she'll make to the land, or whether she'll sell off a parcel for development. They're wanting to know what her life was like in Philadelphia, whether she stayed married to Daddy, whether she was happy."

Jesse had asked questions like that. He had known who Virginia was. Just the night before, Leah had asked him about the legend. They had been in the greenhouse. He hadn't let on what he knew.

She wondered why, if he loved her.

"They're just nosy in an intimate way," Caroline said in dismissal.

But Annette was looking worried. "Are they? I remember how startled I was when I first read her letter to me. I couldn't believe she was writing, not calling, about something as momentous as selling the house where we all grew up. I couldn't understand why she would pack up and move to a strange place with strange people at this point in her life. I kept thinking there had to be a better reason than simply wanting to rest. This would explain it."

"How so?" Caroline argued. "Even if she *was* that woman, why would she come back? If she'd been involved in a scandal, the *last* thing she'd want to do is show her face here."

"Maybe she couldn't help herself," Leah offered. "Maybe she was drawn here over every rational impulse." She could understand that all too well. People often did things that made no sense at all. "Maybe she needed closure," which was one of the very reasons Leah had accepted Ginny's invitation and come to Star's End, herself.

Closure? Hah! The visit had opened a Pandora's box!

Annette's eyes were wide. "The compulsion to return would almost make sense — if it's true and she was madly in love."

"Mother madly in love?" Caroline muttered. "Right." She scowled off toward the deck, then scowled right back again. "You're making two rather improbable assumptions. The first is that straight-arrow Ginny would defy society by having an extramarital affair. The second is that she was *capable* of having an affair. I don't know about either of you, but the last word I would ever associate with our mother is *passion*."

Annette was holding very still. "My kids feel that way about Jean-Paul and me. It's taken them awhile to accept that if the bedroom door is shut, they shouldn't barge in."

"No, it's *not* just that she's my mother," Caroline insisted. "It's spending a lifetime watching her. She wasn't passionate toward Daddy. She wasn't passionate toward us. She wasn't passionate toward her friends, or the club, or even the *living room* when she had it redecorated a while back. She busies herself with all the things she deems right, but nothing deeply moves her."

Leah thought of herself, of the woman she was in Washington, an icon of social grace, all sleek lines and smooth responses. Was she passionate there? No. Was she passionate here? Yes. More than yes. Jesse destroyed her inhibitions. In his arms she was a creature she didn't know. But it was emotional, too. She was involved at Star's End in ways that she had never been involved before. At that moment her heartstrings were tied up in knots.

"What about the beach roses?" she cried,

331

because she couldn't stop thinking about them. They seemed as conclusive evidence as any that what Julia had told her was true. "All those years Mother special-ordered her perfume. Do you ever remember her wearing anything else?"

"No, but —"

"Once, I found a similar scent," Leah pressed on. "It was in a really pretty bottle, so I bought it for her birthday. Years later it was still sitting, full, on her dressing table tray. I told myself that she was so pleased with it that she wanted to save it, but the truth was that she didn't want it, period. She wanted the purest scent, the same one that permeates this place. Is it pure coincidence that she bought property that smells like her perfume? Or does she wear that perfume because it smells like the property she just bought? If she was that woman who was madly in love, but left at the end of the summer and never returned, maybe she needed something of this place to help her through life."

Annette gasped. "Help? I'd think the constant reminder would have been agonizingly painful for her."

"And for Daddy," Caroline said. She was sitting forward, hands clenched hard between her knees. She looked suddenly vulnerable as Leah had never seen her. "I can deal with most anything in life. God knows, I've had to, what with the professional shit that's come my way over the years, but as long as I felt I had an element of control, I was okay. This has been some day. First Chicago, now —" she screwed up her face in disbelief, *"Mother?"*

"What happened in Chicago?" Leah asked, and Annette explained. "Oh, Caroline, I'm sorry." The tragedy wasn't the loss of the case, but the betrayal of her partners. Viewing Caroline through kinder eyes now, Leah could see that.

"It's funny," Caroline said without cracking a smile. "Chicago happened. I'm angry. I'm hurt. But that's there, and I'm here, and I'm finding this far more upsetting. It's more important. It has to do with certain very basic beliefs." She swallowed. "Suppose — just suppose — that Mother did have a passionate love affair early in her marriage. That throws other things into question."

Leah had been too stunned by Julia's revelation to think of those ramifications, but with Caroline's cue, her mind began to whir. "Like her feelings for Daddy and her feelings for us —"

"And her primness," Annette cut in, "and

her preoccupation with appearances and with social position."

"It makes you wonder," Caroline ventured, "why she wanted us here and why she's so late in coming, herself. It sheds new light on lots of things. Assuming it's true."

"We can check," Leah said and she wasn't thinking of Jesse. She couldn't put her relationship with him into any kind of context until she learned more about Ginny. "If there were pictures in the paper, there must be old copies filed somewhere. The *Daily* still exists. The office is right in town."

The *Downlee Daily* was established in 1897. Its earliest issues were little more than a single sheet of local gossip. By the 1920s it had expanded to four pages to include war news, and by the time the war was done, county news took its place. By the 1950s, the *Daily* was a twelve-page weekly containing a lively combination of news and sports, gossip, and cartoons.

To the publisher's credit, the picture wasn't on the front page, but even buried on page five, it was striking. Caroline held the opened paper, which was yellowed now and parched at the edges, and stared. There was no mistaking Virginia, but a very different Virginia this was from the one she had known. She felt betrayed.

Annette and Leah flanked her, whispering back and forth to keep their thoughts from the front room and the woman who had shown them to the archives.

"She looks so young."

"She was."

"But younger even than her wedding picture, and that was taken before this."

"It's her hair. It's messy."

"And long. She must have had it cut right after that and never let it grow again. Look at her face."

"Look at *his* face. Mother's lover."

"That sounds odd."

Caroline was suffering. She had always regarded Virginia as a dependent sort, a boring woman who lacked the courage to stand out from the crowd. This Ginny had stood out from the crowd, all right. She also had a secret life that she had never cared to share with her children.

Caroline was Ginny's firstborn. For three years she had been her only child. Rationally, that didn't give her any rights over Annette or Leah. Irrationally, she felt the slight. The Ginny in the picture was deeply in love. Caroline felt robbed.

"Simon called it devotion, that look," she muttered.

335

"She never looked at Daddy that way."

"She never looked at *us* that way."

"He's very good-looking."

"Good God, they're holding hands."

"In the middle of town?"

"Behind the church," Caroline said and read, " 'The Annual Downlee Harvest Festival was held last Friday in the baseball field behind the First Congregational Church. Virginia St. Clair, Star's End's summer mistress, was there enjoying the festivities with her groundskeeper, Will Cray.' "

Leah grabbed the paper from Caroline's hands. "Who?"

"Jesse's father?" Annette asked.

"Must be." Caroline couldn't make out the resemblance, feature by feature, though this man was attractive in the same rugged way. "The write-up wouldn't be incriminating if it weren't for the picture. Forget the hands. Simon was right. The way she was looking at him leaves no doubt."

"Will *Cray?*" Leah repeated miserably. She handed the paper back.

"What do you think happened?" Annette murmured. "Did she make an agreement with Daddy to avoid a divorce? My God, I don't believe this. Mother is the last person I'd have dreamed had an affair. She certainly never strayed once we were born."

Caroline was trying to imagine her having strayed in the years before. She was having trouble reconciling the vibrant woman in the picture with the detached one who had raised her. The vibrant woman made mockery of the detached one. The vibrant woman made mockery of the emotions Caroline had grown up with.

Frustrated, she tossed the paper aside. "I still think this is a lie."

"How *can* it be?" Annette cried. "It's right here in black and white."

But Caroline dealt with this kind of thing often in court.

"Black and white can be misleading. Taken out of context, something can look totally different from how it really is."

"You're deluding yourself, Caroline."

"I'm trying to see the whole picture. That photo —" she jabbed the paper, "doesn't fit."

"Are you saying it isn't a picture of Mother?"

"Oh, it's her, all right," Caroline said, aware that their voices were rising enough to be overheard, and half-wanting that, to refute the allegations against Ginny, "but we may be misinterpreting her expression. For all we know, she was telling Will Cray about Daddy."

"I've *never* associated that kind of look with Daddy."

Neither had Caroline. Still. "Absence makes the heart grow fonder. He was gone five days out of every seven. She might have missed him."

"Caroline, she's *holding hands with Will Cray.*"

"So? Six months ago I tried a case whose preparation required meeting with the DA. He's my former boss. More, he's my friend. I was entering the lobby one day when he was returning from lunch. He said something. We laughed. He took my hand and pulled me into the elevator. Someone might have taken a picture of us at that point and assumed we were having an affair, but we sure as hell weren't. Why are you so ready to assume Mother was? We don't have proof."

"The *whole town* knows!"

"Did anyone catch them in bed together?" Caroline demanded. "So there's gossip. So there's a *legend.* That's the kind of juicy stuff that keeps a small town going. It may be pure fantasy, all of it."

"It wasn't," came a low voice from the door. Caroline's first thought was that it was Leah, who was standing in that direction with her arms crossed over her middle, but it wasn't Leah's face beneath the doorframe.

Martha Snowe was the current editor of the *Downlee Daily*. She was wide, dowdy, and ruddy-cheeked. Her manner spoke of reluctance, despite the slow certainty in her voice. It struck Caroline that she hadn't wanted to intrude but had felt bound to, which gave a certain credence to what she had to say.

"Were you living here then?"

"Yes. I was seventeen."

"Go on."

"Your parents' coming here for the summer was big news. We were more provincial back then, and they were rich and attractive. My friends and I would watch your mother walking down Main Street and dream of being like her one day. She was refined. She walked just so and talked just so. And she was nice. Everyone liked her. So she was invited to town picnics and such, and it made sense that Will would drive her over."

She paused. Caroline urged her on again.

Very quietly, she said, "He started driving her more — not only to town things, but whenever she left Star's End."

"There's nothing wrong with that."

Even more quietly. "They were seen driving through town late at night."

"He was her chauffeur."

In little more than a whisper. "She wasn't sitting in back."

Caroline began to get the picture. "How close were they, exactly?"

"Very close."

"Who reported this?"

"Different people. At different times. And the police chief."

Annette was looking anxious, Leah was ashen, and Caroline was running clear out of excuses. "Is that the basis for the legend? Two people sitting close in a car?"

Martha shook her head. "They were seen together in the woods at Star's End."

"In a compromising position?"

"Very."

"By trespassers," Caroline charged. "Interlopers on Mother's property."

"The town has always had an understanding with the owners of Star's End. Our people can go up there long as they don't go to party and they stay out of sight of the house. The people who were up there that night weren't doing anything wrong."

"Teenagers?"

"Artists."

Caroline stuck her hands in her back

pockets. The artists she had met in Downlee reminded her of Ben. While not quite
eccentric, they marched to the beat of their
own drummer. They wouldn't have been
shocked seeing Ginny and Will in the woods,
any more than they would have returned to
town to spread unfounded dirt.

It had to be true. She was stunned. She
looked at her sisters. They were equally
dismayed. With as much dignity as she
could muster, she said, "Why don't we go
back?"

They didn't speak, either on the way to
the car or once Annette was behind the
wheel and leaving Downlee behind. Caroline brooded all the way, trying to understand why she was so upset, when she was
so distant from Ginny.

It wasn't until they turned onto Hullman
Road that she said, "I always thought
Mother was cool by nature. I chalked her
aloofness up to a personality limitation, and
that made it easier to accept. It wasn't
anything personal, right? It was just *her.* But
to believe this story is to believe that she
was perfectly capable of love. She just chose
not to give it to us."

"Either that," Annette said softly, "or it
was no longer hers to give."

Caroline felt a catch deep inside, and in

its wake an incipient sadness. She didn't have time to give it more than a cursory examination before they arrived at Star's End, and then the most important thing seemed to be locating Ginny.

No one answered at Lillian's house, or at the big empty house the St. Clairs had called home. The golf pro at the club hadn't seen her, nor had the maître d' in the dining room.

"She could be anywhere," Caroline said and, thinking that Leah might have more of a clue than either she or Annette, turned to her.

But Leah was already out the French doors and halfway past the pool.

SEVENTEEN

Leah was beyond the point of caring if her sisters saw where she was headed. She had to see Jesse.

Leaving the pool behind, she ran past the gardens and across the lawn toward the woods. When she didn't see anything resembling human form through the thick greenhouse glass, she swung open the screen door. He wasn't inside, or in the back mudroom, or out by his truck, which stood hot and idle in the afternoon sun.

Frantic, needing to find him fast, half-fearing that he had been nothing more than a figment of her imagination, planted in her mind by the ghost of Will Cray, she ran back in the direction of the house. She crossed the front drive and continued on, past the heather garden and its sculpted wildness, past the beach roses and their poignant scent. Jesse was nowhere in sight.

Fighting tears now, she ran into the woods

on an old path, a bald swath through white birch, spruce, and pine. His presence was an eerie certainty here, a woodsy familiarity. She followed twists and turns, over pine needles and exposed roots until the woods opened abruptly to sun, grass, and the untamed beauty of wildflowers. Jesse was weeding in their midst.

With the sight of him came the same melting deep inside, a craving so intense she thought she'd die of it. Pulled in every direction at once, she stood at the meadow's edge, taking short, shallow breaths. He looked up, started to smile, but stopped. In the next instant, he was striding toward her through the flowers, and she was suddenly frightened. Her feelings for him were *too strong.* The whole of her thirty-four years seemed funneled into this moment.

Instinctively, she backed up, but he broke into a run and caught her up before she made it into the woods.

"Don't," she pleaded when he wrapped his arms around her.

"I couldn't say anything, Leah," he said against her hair. "It wasn't my place."

"But you knew!" she cried, trying to pull away.

He held her fast. "Since I was nine, when my father explained why my mother left."

Leah barely heard. "The whole time I was asking about the legend, you knew the truth!"

"I never lied."

"You didn't tell me everything!"

"Because she hadn't told you!" he said. He shifted his arms to gentle his hold, though he wasn't letting her go. His voice was rough, urgent, vibrating through his chest by her ear. "I thought you'd have known, especially when she bought Star's End, then I started talking to you and realized you didn't. I figured she was planning to tell you, since she got you up here, but I didn't think it was my right to do the telling. I figured she had a reason for waiting so long."

"We had to hear it through the grapevine," Leah cried and felt his soft oath.

"I'm sorry." This time, when he shifted his arms, there was a soothing in his touch. The warmth of him crossed between her breasts, wound around her waist, cushioned her shoulders to calves. "If I'd known that would happen, I'd have told you myself, but you kept thinking your mother would be arriving any day."

She recalled the very first time she had seen Jesse. "You knew who I was even before I said my name that first day!"

"Hell, yes! Looking at you was like taking a body blow, like being hit in the gut, which was what my father told me he felt when he first saw your mother, and even if that hadn't been so, I'd have seen the resemblance. I have pictures, Leah, a stack of them that I only found after my father died."

She heard pain in his voice and realized with a start that he had suffered, too. She tried to remember what he had said about his childhood, about his mother, about his relationship with his father, and realized that it hadn't been much. She looked up at him, over her shoulder, with the question in her eyes. His face was dappled by the sun as it darted between pine boughs on the edge of the woods, but that did little to mute the anguish there.

"Oh God," she breathed in an expulsion of air. She couldn't be angry at him. He was a victim, too. Closing her eyes, she turned and put her forehead to his chest.

He let her stay that way for a minute, then drew her in closer and hugged her hard. When her legs began to tremble, he lowered her to the ground so that they sat Indian-style, facing each other, hands and knees touching. He spoke in a low voice.

"My mother stayed until I was old enough to go to school, then she left, just packed up and vanished one day. My father didn't tell me much, only that they had differences and that a son should grow up with his father. I took my cue from him, and because he wasn't upset, I wasn't either. One year passed, then a second. I started to miss her, but he didn't. He wasn't an emotional person. He got up in the morning, did his job, and went to bed at night. He never yelled, never cried."

"Oh God," Leah breathed. She *knew* how that was.

"But I was a child," Jesse went on, "and I did cry sometimes, especially when my mother sent me letters. She told me that she had remarried and had two more children. She kept saying that I'd visit her some day. She even sent me plane tickets for my ninth birthday. I wanted to go, but I couldn't. I couldn't leave my father alone. There was something about him — he was a tragic figure — sad in his lack of emotion. I was a child, sensing something I couldn't possibly understand."

"When did he tell you the truth?" Leah asked. She could see the pain in his eyes, a child's pain in grown-up eyes and all the more raw for it.

"When those tickets arrived. We argued. It was one of the few times he ever raised his voice to me. He told me to go. I said I wouldn't. He said he couldn't be a father because he was only a shell of a man. I said he wasn't, but he insisted. Then he told me about your mother."

"Were you angry?"

"I was sad. It was a sad story. He had loved her with all his heart. He still did then, fourteen years after she had left."

"Were you angry at my mother?"

Jesse gave a tiny shake of his head. "As my father told the story, she hadn't had much of a choice. She was a decent, upstanding lady. He didn't blame her for leaving, any more than he blamed himself for not running after her. In later years I was angry at her for coming along in the first place, but by then he was with her again."

Leah gasped.

"In his imagination," Jesse assured her with a sad smile, "that was all. They never met again, never communicated in any way. During the last years of his life he used to pretend she was there. Some people talk to themselves; he talked to Virginia. He always called her Virginia. Never Ginny. It was a beautiful, regal name, he said, and he was perfectly lucid about it."

"So sad," Leah breathed.

"He was a romantic. He said that he'd

been destined to love Virginia and lose her, and that even though they wouldn't see each other again, a part of him would always be hers. That was the part he couldn't give to anyone else. It was gone. He didn't have it anymore."

Annette had said nearly identical words. Leah shivered. How could she doubt Jesse's story, when it fit Ginny's so well? "Were there no other women?"

"None."

"Not even a meaningless fling?"

"He couldn't do it, Leah. He couldn't get it up."

"He did it with your mother."

"Obviously. That was when he was still trying to believe he could live normally without Virginia. After my mother left, he gave up the pretense."

"Why did she leave? What were their differences?"

"Commitment. Dedication. Love. He liked her. He respected her. But he couldn't love her."

"Many marriages survive without that." Lord knew her parents' marriage had.

But there was more to Jesse's story. "My mother wasn't from Downlee. She was up for the summer, like yours had been, and good-looking man that my father was, he caught her eye. They were married for a year or so when I came along, and by the time another two or three had passed, she'd had a glimpse of the future. It wasn't what she wanted."

"Is she still alive?"

"Yes. I see her once a year. Not here. She won't ever come here. She didn't love the place like your mother did. She didn't love my father like your mother did."

Leah was feeling numb. "It's such a new side of Ginny. So hard to accept."

Jesse rolled to his feet and brought her up beside him. "Come. I'll show you pictures."

She wasn't sure she wanted to see them. One part of her had seen enough for one day. The other part was starved for anything and everything that had to do with this warm, feeling, loving person her mother had been with Will Cray.

Besides, Leah needed to be with Jesse.

So she held his hand as they went back along the path. When they emerged from the woods, they bypassed the heathers and the beach roses, and cut down across the front drive to his cottage. There, after displacing a handful of magazines, a large candle, and a piece of driftwood, he opened a trunk and removed a large manila envelope. It was old and worn. Its metal catch had long since broken off.

There were nearly a dozen pictures, taken on different days, in different settings. Leah recognized the picture that had been re-printed in the newspaper. Aside from that one, the only other one with any kind of physical connection between the two was in a shot of them shoulder to shoulder, lean-ing on a wood rail at the town dock. Not that a physical connection was necessary. The photos were as powerful without.

But the pictures weren't alone in the large manila envelope. There was a wreath of dried beach roses, pressed between sheets of wax paper, and two leather rings, one small, one large.

"Wedding bands," Jesse said. "They used to pretend."

Leah was heartsick. Cradling the rings in her palm, she started to cry. He put an arm around her shoulder. "They should have stayed together," she said brokenly.

"Times were different. She was rich and married. He was a penniless laborer."

"But they paid an *awful* price." She wiped her eyes. "They were emotionally maimed."

"That's one way to look at it. There's another."

Ah, yes. *Far better to have loved and lost, than never to have loved at all.* Which raised the issue of what Leah was going to do about Jesse.

She started crying again.

This time Jesse brought her around and held her properly, which made her cry more deeply. She couldn't begin to sort out the parallels between their parents' affair and their own, only knew that they existed and were terrifying.

He held her until her tears slowed, then left her to get tissues from the bathroom. She had them pressed to her eyes when she said, "You told me he died of a broken heart. Do you really believe it?"

"Totally."

"Was he waiting for her to come back?"

"No. He knew she wouldn't. He just got tired of living without her." When Leah made a mournful sound, Jesse added, "I don't blame her for his death, or any of what came before. He might have gone after her, too. But there were all those other problems, and then, he loved Star's End. He's buried here. Want to see where?"

Leah dried her eyes. Yes, she wanted to see where. When a knot remained in her throat, she told him so with a nod.

Taking her hand, he walked her along the bluff, away from the house, farther than she had ever gone. Feeling trepidation, as though Will Cray's gravestone would be the final proof of an all too personal legend, she held Jesse's hand tighter, then even tighter when he led her over an outcropping of ledge. They moved inland a bit when they came to a grassy decline, half-walked, half-ran down it, then climbed the other side and mounted the rocks again.

That was when Leah saw it, not twenty feet ahead. The setting was breathtaking, another grassy patch bordered by rock, with a view of the open sea and the sound of gulls and the waves. Will Cray's grave wasn't the only one there. Leah saw a number of other markers, all of similarly weathered granite, but there was no mistaking Will's. It was the only one with a petite, white-haired figure kneeling before it.

Eighteen

Will loved this spot. He told me so on the single occasion when he brought me here. It was during the last week of my stay, when we knew that parting was imminent. He had wanted me to see the place where he hoped to be buried.

It hadn't changed over the years. The rocks were the same, the wind-whipped grass, the gulls, the snare-drum roll of the waves, the drone of the fog horn at Houkabee. I remembered thinking, that long-ago day, that death couldn't possibly be an ending if one were buried here. The sky was too large, the horizon too wide. They spoke of new worlds to explore in other lives.

Ahhhh, what a Will-like thought that was. And I did think that way when I was with him — not after I left, though it came back to me now. I suspected it had as much to do with the aura of Star's End as with Will.

I touched his name, each carved letter,

and enjoyed the intimacy of it. I enjoyed, too, the serenity of this spot, and the relief of finally being here. So often I had dreamed of my return, particularly in recent years. At times I feared I wouldn't make it. I feared that the anguish of other goodbyes would hold me back, or that I would die too soon.

But the other goodbyes were over and done, and I was alive. I had come back to Will, at last.

Hearing a sound, a small cry that was different from the gulls that soared overhead, I turned. A man and a woman had found me out. They were at the top of the rise. The incline of their bodies spoke of familiarity. Without a doubt they were good friends — and, in that, new to me. I struggled to my feet.

This was the first of my three moments of truth, after years and years, and countless imaginings. I had envisioned harsh words and accusations. I had imagined disapproval and scorn. I had dreaded rejection.

She offered none of those, still my heart ricocheted against too-fragile ribs. *Be strong, heart, just a little longer,* I prayed, and started forward. She met me halfway. I could see she had been crying.

I touched her cheek and smiled, because she was very beautiful. "Leah. You look like a different person." I touched her hair. "And to think we used to hide this away. It's lovely. You look wonderful."

When her eyes filled, I took her in my arms. It had been years since I had held her. Ours wasn't a physical relationship. None of my relationships were, after Will, and there was an awkwardness in it now. Still, I held her. Slowly, the awkwardness began to fade.

After a bit, I eased her back. I brushed the tears from one cheek while she did the other. She blushed and smiled. It struck me that I must be new to her, too.

"Will you introduce me to your friend?" I asked softly, though, of course, I knew who he was. There was no mistaking the wonderful brown eyes, the rough-hewn face, the one-hipped stance. He looked shaken. Clearly he knew who I was, too. I had wondered about that all these years, wondered what Will had told him. I deserved anger from him, too, but it seemed I'd been spared that, for now.

I extended my left hand as Leah and I approached. My right arm stayed around her waist. I found that I needed her support. I was feeling shaky.

"You look very much like your father," I said, admiring his rugged good looks as Will might have done, had he been there. I felt pride on Will's behalf. "And you're quite skilled. I saw the gardens. They are marvelous."

He nodded, but it was a distracted nod. He wasn't looking for compliments. He wasn't thinking about the gardens. His gaze was as penetrating as his father's could be. "I feel I know you. You look very much the same."

"Now that is a kind thing to say," I said with a short laugh, not that I believed it for a minute. My hair was white, my skin less firm, my body matronly even in spite of its slimness. Gravity spared no one, despite our attempts to fight it. Much as I prided myself on my posture, I was shorter than I had been forty-three years before.

"It's true," he insisted, staring intently. "The eyes are the same, and the smile."

"It's your Star's End smile," Leah remarked softly. "I saw it for the first time a few minutes ago, when Jesse showed me his father's pictures."

My heart skittered around inside me again. I willed it to steady. "Will kept them?" I asked.

"Yes. And the rose wreath, and the leather rings."

"Oh my," I breathed, fighting the odd

prickle of tears. I hadn't cried in years and years. I had assumed that my tear ducts had atrophied. This odd prickle was heady. "Perhaps later you'll show me?"

He nodded and looked at Leah to see how she was. I caught the way she returned his glance, and, in a flash that brought a budding warmth to my heart, realized why she wasn't angered by my secret. She was in love herself. She understood.

My daughter and Will's son — it was a lovely thought.

Leah was made for Star's End. The riot of hair, the relaxed features, the touch of color on her bare skin, the rapport with Jesse — I had never seen her like this. Even the crying. She was free with her emotions here — just as I was. She was finally herself.

I had prayed for this. Leah needed a home. God was good.

"Have you been to the house?" she asked.

It was a minute before my thoughts returned to earth. "No. I had to visit with Will first." I looked back at his gravestone, and felt a tight tug at my heart. "Such a beautiful setting. I'm glad you buried him here, Jesse."

"Star's End was his home from the time he was seventeen," Jesse said. "He wouldn't have been buried anywhere else."

"Have you lived here all this time, too?"

"Except for when I went to college."

I tried to imagine what life with Will had been like. I feared Jesse had suffered, as my children had, and felt more than partly to blame. "I'm sorry about your mother. It must have been difficult for her, living in a shadow. It's been hard on my family, too. I'm sorry about that." This I said to Leah, because the message was for her, and when I smiled this time, it was in pure relief. I coupled it with a pleased sigh. "All the times I wanted to say that and couldn't, yet it comes easily now. It's what I most wanted when I bought Star's End."

She nodded, tearing up again.

"Come," I suggested, eager to act while I was feeling brave, "let's tell the others I'm here."

I'll be back, sweet, I promised Will, then let Leah and Jesse help me over the grassy ups and downs and the ragged ledge to the more level bluff that led to the house. I knew they were wondering how I had made it out alone. Poor dears. They were still new to the power that came from wanting something more than life itself.

But I was still human, which meant that my bravery waned the farther we went from Will's grave. I was frightened of seeing

Caroline and Annette.

But this was my mission. I had been waiting a long time to complete it. Even in spite of that fear, there was the relief of approaching the end of the journey, the relief of being here at last.

And the excitement.

And the awe. I had wondered, all those years, how I would find the place, whether the breathtaking beauty I remembered would have faded, or perhaps have proven a figment of my imagination — but not at all. It was real. Indeed, it surpassed memory.

I couldn't keep my eyes on one place for long. They were enchanted by the lushness of the woods and the vivid color of the gardens, and then there was the house, which wore its new coat of paint well, and that was even before I looked at the pool and the porch, and the glassed-in family room that hadn't been there at all, so many years before.

I was startled when Jesse said, "I'll leave you now."

I started to protest. I wanted him with us. He was part of Will. His presence was reassuring.

But he added, "They don't know," and I realized that he was talking about his relationship with Leah. I also realized that this

360

was a time for my daughters and me. Perhaps Jesse knew that, too.

He set off toward the cottage that stood where Will's shed had once been. It looked to be a fine cottage, with its bump of a greenhouse on the side, but it wasn't the shed of my memories, which was probably just as well. Seeing the shed might have been one heart-tug too many.

Leah and I continued on toward the house. She held my arm the way younger women did older ones, with a hand lightly through the crook of my elbow. A cynic might have said she was restraining me, keeping me from running off. I believed she was simply offering support. And taking it, as well. This was an emotional time for her.

"How was your flight?" she asked.

"Very smooth."

"Are you tired?"

"Not at all. I always had more energy here." And my heart was beating soundly. "You do like it here, don't you, Leah?"

"I love it here."

I felt a moment's triumph, but it faded when Caroline stepped out on the deck. She was staring our way. Annette quickly joined her.

I waved. Neither of them waved back.

I sighed and for a minute, feeling old and

tired, wanted nothing more than to lie down, close my eyes, and shut out the world for a bit. Then I inhaled, and the air brimmed so with scents I had dreamed about long and hard, that I was revived. Will was with me. I could feel his silent strength.

"It's interesting," I remarked to my daughters when we came within earshot, "that summer so long ago, when I was grappling with my decision, I imagined having to tell my parents about Will. It struck me as being the hardest thing in the world, but I was wrong. This is."

"What about Daddy?" Annette cried. "I'd think the hardest thing would have been telling *him*. He was your husband."

I was set back by the force of her accusation, but only for a minute. Indeed, I hadn't been expecting a tea party. "Yes, he was. But my feelings for him were different from my feelings for my parents or my children."

"I'd have thought they would have been *stronger*," she argued, sounding confused. "He was the father of your children."

"Not back then," I reminded her gently. She was, of course, thinking of Jean-Paul, whom she adored. In eighteen years of marriage, she had never once, I wagered, entertained a single unfaithful thought. She was wondering how I could have been so weak and unprincipled and un*loving* as to have not only entertained the thought, but acted on it. "Back then we were two people who married for reasons that had nothing to do with love or romance. We were struggling with our marriage. That was what brought us here in the first place."

Their faces registered surprise. Clearly, their sources hadn't known of the struggle. No one had, except Nick and me. And, of course, Will.

"What was wrong with your marriage?" Annette asked.

"It was weak."

"Didn't you love Daddy?"

I hesitated, but only for a minute. This was a time for truth, perhaps the last such one I would have. Without pride, I said, "No, I didn't love him when I married him. That wasn't a prerequisite in my day."

"What was?" Leah asked. She had separated herself a bit from me.

"Name. Social standing. Money."

"That's incredibly cold," Caroline judged.

"Yes," I countered. "So were marriages that were arranged at birth, and mail-order marriages, and marriages of convenience, but those marriages weren't always bad. Many of them worked quite well. Not everyone married for love. Sometimes love came after the fact." Helpless to resist, I found myself looking around at the house, the deck, and the bordering flower beds. "This is delightful." I side-stepped the girls, approached the French doors, and peered inside, then opened the screen, and entered.

I heard footsteps behind me, then Annette asking, "In what ways was your marriage weak?"

But I was taking in the sights. "Just *beautiful.* And so inviting." I walked around the kitchen, touching the wood cabinets, the granite counter, the shiny stovetop. "She did a wonderful job. I'm pleased."

"In what ways was it weak?" Annette repeated.

As I swung around to see the rest, I said, "We weren't of the same mind, Nick and I. We couldn't communicate. We were awkward in each other's presence." I spotted the chair I wanted in the family room and headed for it. It faced the others but was slightly apart, which was fitting. I was the guest of honor, the main attraction, so to speak. I settled into it, folding my hands in my lap.

Annette and Caroline faced me from behind the buffer of the sofa. In the kitchen, Leah set to making a pot of tea.

"You're both looking well," I told them.

Caroline made a face. "That's irrelevant."

"Not to me. I care about you girls. I care deeply."

"You've never shown it very well."

"No." I took a breath. "I haven't." My heart thudded for an instant, during which I felt every one of my seventy years. Guilt was a natural ager. Regret, too. I wallowed in both just then.

But I had imagined this moment too many times in my life to want to postpone it any longer. Quietly, I said, "In order to understand what happened, you have to remember what my life was like as a child. My brothers and I were fourth generation money, and our lives reflected it. We had beautiful clothes and cars. We had a summer house and a winter house, and hired help to do everything we didn't want to do. We were listed in the Social Registry; we belonged to the country club; we went to all the best parties. I was raised looking forward to my debut — all my friends were — and once the parties were done, we turned our sights to marriage."

"What in the *world* then," asked Caroline, my feminist daughter, "was the point of college?"

But I wasn't a feminist. Nor were my friends. Indeed, feminism wasn't something we knew existed in those days. "College," I stated unabashedly, "was for people like me who hadn't found a young man to our liking from within our own social circle."

"With no thought to the education?" cried Annette, the mother of near-college-age children. "Do you know how many girls would *die* to go to Harvard?"

"In my day," I pointed out, "girls didn't go to Harvard. They went to Radcliffe, and the major entrance requirement was the ability to pay. I never claimed to be a genius. Yes, you may say I've wasted my life, with an education like that and no career, but women didn't have careers in those days, not as women do now. I'm not arguing the right or the wrong of it. I'm simply telling you how it was.

"I am a product of my age. If I couldn't understand why you wanted to be a lawyer, Caroline, it was because women didn't become lawyers in my day. We either became wives, or spinsters, and the latter was a harsh sentence, indeed, or so we thought. We couldn't imagine women finding reward in a man's profession."

"Can you now?" Caroline asked.

"Some. I'm not oblivious to the world around me. I see women doing things that once only men did. I've gotten used to it.

That isn't to say I completely understand. Certain ideas are deeply ingrained in me. A major one of those is that there is security in marriage."

"A professional woman doesn't *need* that security," Caroline argued.

"Maybe not," I conceded, though I wasn't being further diverted. "But I wasn't a professional woman. I met your father when he was finishing up at the business school, and he was a very nice man. There were no fireworks between us, simply a strong social compatibility. His background was similar to mine. His goals were similar to mine. And he was acceptable to my parents. Not all the men at Harvard were."

"Had you dated others?" Leah asked from the kitchen.

I smiled. "Times haven't changed all that much. I was living in a dormitory, away from home, and even though we had rigid curfews, there was some freedom."

"I can't picture you making the rounds of fraternity parties," Caroline remarked.

"I didn't. Nor, though, did I sit home every Saturday night."

"Had you fallen in love with any of the others, ones who might have been less acceptable to your parents?" Leah asked.

"No. Never. That's why I was unprepared

for Will." I'd had *no idea* that it was possible to be swept off one's feet that way.

"But how could you let it happen?" Annette cried. "You were already married. You had a responsibility to one man. How could you have become involved with another?"

"I didn't plan to," I said without apology. I had paid a price for what I'd done. I refused to be the chastised child. "It just happened."

"Didn't you think? Didn't you say to yourself, 'I can't do this. I'm married'?"

I sighed. "Annette, what would you have done if your father and I had hated Jean-Paul on sight?"

"That wouldn't have happened. He was too right for me in too many ways."

"But he was foreign-born. He didn't speak English well. He didn't know anyone in this country. If we had been short-sighted enough to let those things bother us, and we had forbidden you from marrying him, what would you have done?"

"I'd have married him anyway."

"What if we had warned you that you'd be a social outcast, marrying a foreigner?"

"I wouldn't have cared."

"What if we threatened to disown you?"

"It wouldn't have *mattered*. I was in *love*."

"Precisely," I concluded.

"You're saying," Caroline put in with obvious skepticism, "that you weren't thinking about right or wrong when you became involved with Will Cray?"

"No. I'm saying that I had stumbled onto something so strong that right or wrong simply didn't matter."

"Maybe if your relationship with Daddy had been stronger, you would have had more strength to resist," Annette suggested.

"Maybe."

"Why wasn't it stronger?" Caroline asked.

"Something was missing."

"For both of you?"

"Mostly for me. We'd been married for four years and nothing was happening. Children weren't coming. We weren't growing closer. The love that was supposed to be budding wasn't. I was frustrated because your father worked so much. I was convinced that there should have been something more." It had been a romantic notion that had crept under my skin and was chafing. "So we rented Star's End for the summer." A romantic notion, indeed. "It seemed the perfect place to concentrate on each other. Unfortunately, we only had the weekends."

"Then it turned out to be a *dumb* idea."

369

I answered Caroline's comment with a sharp look. "Sometimes the best laid plans go awry. Life isn't always black or white, bad or good, guilty or innocent. Sometimes we have to compromise." I caught a breath, closed my eyes for a minute, recomposed myself. Gently, sadly, as the memory moved me, I said, "We were indeed hoping to have more than just weekends, but it didn't work out that way. That summer the business made unexpected demands on your father. Four-day weekends became three-day ones, and then two-day ones. I was disappointed. I had wanted much more."

"Was it revenge then, your taking up with Will Cray?"

"Caroline," Annette said, giving her elbow a squeeze. "Let her tell her story."

Caroline, the lawyer, was leading the witness, while Annette, the mother and middle child, was making peace. Their personalities certainly suited their occupations, I had to say that.

I also had to say, because it was important that they know the truth as I understood it, "It wasn't revenge. It was sadness. And youth. And loneliness. And too much time to think about things that should have been but weren't. I used to spend hours walking the bluff. It was soothing, the ebb and flow

of the tide." Even *remembering* it was soothing, though, of course, I didn't have to
remember it. It was here and now, the
hypnotic rhythm of the waves, out beyond
the deck and the pool and the bluff. It was
muted where we sat inside, yet its soft beat
was unmistakable. It steadied me, sweeping
me back to the day that so changed my life.

"I had seen him from time to time, working around the property. I knew that he was
the groundskeeper, though, of course, since
we were only renters, it wasn't my place to
know more. Nick had talked with him
several times, but I had never come close
enough to see what he looked like until one
day, when I had gone into town and come
back with bundles, he materialized at the
car to carry them inside." I paused, search-
ing for words, desperate to describe what
that moment had been like, but nothing fit.
I looked from one face to the next, even to
Leah's across the room, trying to convey
the helplessness I had felt. Finally, reliving
that moment so long ago, I whispered, "I
lost my breath. It just went. I felt that I'd
been hit by something large and powerful,
something totally beyond my understanding."

Leah's eyes widened. So she had experienced it, too. I was pleased enough to laugh

— which gave nothing of Leah's secret away. For all outward purposes, I was mocking myself.

"Here I was," I said on the tail of that laugh, "trained from birth to know just the right thing to say at just the right time, and I was speechless. I'd had experience with businessmen and politicians, even a prince once. I knew how to handle plumbers and butchers and the man who filled my car with gas. But I had never met anyone like this man before."

"Daddy was good-looking," Annette argued in her father's defense.

"Very. But it wasn't Will's looks that hit me. It was the way he looked at me. It was what was in his eyes, what was coming from deep inside. There was an instant feeling."

"Physical attraction," Caroline said with a dryness I ignored.

"Yes. But the attraction was emotional and intellectual, too."

"Intellectual? He was the groundskeeper."

"*Caroline.*" It was Leah protesting this time, and I could understand why.

"It's all right, Leah," I said. "Caroline, does Ben have a law degree?"

"Of course not. He's an artist."

"Do you consider him intellectually inferior to you?"

"Of *course* not."

"Because he's a brilliant artist?"

"And because he grew up in an intellectually enlightened environment. He doesn't need a law degree to understand my cases. He has a natural grasp of things like that."

"So did Will. He was self-taught. He had a natural curiosity, and he knew how to satisfy it. He was a voracious reader. He knew far more about many things than you or I."

"You were attracted to his mind?" she asked, dryly again.

"I was attracted to the *whole* of him."

"In that one instant, when you saw him up close for the very first time."

"As improbable as it sounds, that's how it was."

"So you jumped right into bed with him."

"Caroline!"

"Caroline."

Caroline turned on her sisters. "Are you actually believing this?"

"I'm wanting," Annette stated as she rounded the sofa to sit down, "to hear the rest of Mother's story without your cross-examination. Can't you save it for later?"

I held my breath, fully expecting Caroline to lash out at Annette and make things worse. How well I remembered their bickering — all three of them — and not only as children. They had bickered their way into adulthood, defining each other in terms of their own grievances. It strikes me now that those grievances were with me, but at the time I couldn't see it. I simply turned a deaf ear to their squabbles.

Caroline didn't lash out. Nor, though, did she join Annette on the sofa. I was startled when Leah came to her side and put a reassuring hand on her arm — and even more startled when Caroline let that reassuring hand stay there.

"Go on," Leah urged me quietly.

I studied her, before broadening my study to include Caroline and Annette. Something had indeed happened during my absence. I was relieved by that, too.

I breathed more easily. My heart was behaving. Gratified, I slipped back into thoughts of Will again, and that first moment of realization. "The rapport was instant. He was my second half. But, no, we didn't fall right into bed. Women didn't do that in those days, at least, not women like me. It didn't even *occur* to me that Will and I might do something like that. I was innocent. Unawakened, you might say. Besides, I was married to your father, and I took those vows seriously."

I directed the last at Annette, because I did, indeed, know what made her tick. She had set out in life to be a woman totally devoted to her husband and children. But so had I, in my way. I had given my family all I could, considering the hole that was inside me. I wanted her to understand that. I wanted her to see that I had indeed tried, and to give me some credit for that. I wanted her to know what made me tick, too.

I wanted them all to know. I hadn't chosen to cheat on my husband. I had been drawn to it by a force so strong that all the resistance in the world was for naught.

"Will and I started slowly. We talked, mostly about things here at Star's End. He showed me parts of the estate that I hadn't seen. He showed me parts of Downlee that I hadn't seen. He understood that I was married, and respected it. So did I. I looked forward to your father's arrival each weekend."

I frowned and studied my hands. "Your father arrived late Friday and left early Monday, but those weekends weren't what I had hoped. We weren't communicating the way we should have been. Our relationship wasn't improving. And then there was Will. I was starting to look forward to seeing him more than I should. We were talking about

375

everything by that point. We always had so much to say to each other, even though we came from such different worlds." It had amazed me then. It amazed me now.

"That was the magic of our relationship. Then, too, there was the physical part." I looked up. Three pairs of eyes were glued to me, three pairs of ears hung on every word. I might have laughed, had the situation been less poignant. How did an old woman tell her grown daughters about the wildly passionate person she had once been?

"Will did something to me," I said, embarrassed but pushing on. "He unlocked wonderful little impulses. When I was with him I was free. I wasn't someone's daughter or someone's wife or someone's friend. I was a woman. He gave me confidence and courage. There were neither rules nor taboos. When I was with him, I was as uninhibited and adventurous as he was."

We were in the woods that first time. He had been showing me the mushrooms that grew in the moist darkness there, when it started to rain. We were protected, but only to a point. Hand in hand, laughing, we ran along the path, emerging nearer his shed than my house. He suggested we stop there for raincoats. I would have stopped in hell with him, so in love was I with him by this time.

Our clothing was soaked by the time we arrived, and it made more sense to wait out the storm there. He started a fire in the small potbelly stove, then removed his shirt and hung it nearby. He helped me out of mine, then my slacks.

I felt a tingling all over, remembering it now. Will's eyes on me were wondrous things. They dried me, heated me, lifted me. They caressed my body until it was aching all over, and that was before he had ever laid a hand on me — and when he was naked himself, any other reality that might have been simply faded away.

I took a shaky breath, emerged from the reverie, and whispered, "I shock myself still."

All was silent, save the muted coastal sounds. I blotted the tears that surprised me with their presence, and looked at my daughters. They were stunned.

I smiled. "It was a most beautiful time. But there was pain, right from the start. Everything about it was right, but it was very, very wrong. I loved Will more than I had thought it possible to love someone. Only I was married to another.

"I never forgot that fact. It's important

that you girls understand. I never forgot that I was married. I could put it aside during those moments when I was in Will's arms, but it was never gone for long. We didn't talk about it, at first. We were both thinking that what we had might just wear itself out by summer's end. But that didn't happen. It got stronger."

And stronger. And stronger. Even now, I felt the pull as though Will was over at the door, rather than in the graveyard way down along the bluff. He was, indeed, my second half. I had never been as whole before, or after.

I swallowed, reliving the quandary and tiring under its weight. "I had two choices. I could either stay with Will, or return with Nick. To stay with Will meant giving up everything — my husband, my name, family, friends, reputation. Nothing could be carried over. No one from my life with Nick would understand, much less accept my life with Will. To stay with Will meant renouncing everything I had been raised to value and expect."

I closed my eyes, feeling the pain so very freshly. I pressed two fingers to my heart, where the pain was centered. It eased, but slowly.

"Mother?" Leah asked.

I smiled. "I'm fine." Still, I took another minute to gather myself. "It was a difficult decision."

"What was it based on?" she asked.

"All of the above. At the time, I added duty. I told myself that I owed it to Nick and our marriage to return with him and try to make it work. I liked Nick — didn't love him, certainly not the way I loved Will — but I felt a responsibility to him. I told myself that staying with him was the right thing to do." I raised my chin, not in pride but in self-reproach. "Yes, that was what I told myself, but time has told me more. The fact is that I liked the kind of life your father and I had. I liked the approval of my parents. I wanted my children to have the finest and the best, all the advantages I'd had growing up. Will could offer me none of that. I imagined myself staying with him and coming to hate the limitations."

"But if you loved him —" Leah began, her eyes bright with tears.

Leaving my chair, I went to her, touched her hair, put an arm around her shoulder, drew her close. The awkwardness was even less now, the comfort of touching even greater. I wanted to cry for all that I had deprived myself and my girls of through the years.

Such irony. In the name of giving, I had taken away.

"I loved all the other things, too," I said sadly. "They were part of how I defined myself. I was materialistic. Foolish, perhaps. But that was the way I was at that time. And I did come to love Nick. We developed a relationship of shared experiences. When you girls came along, you bound us together, and by the time you were grown, we were so used to each other that any other kind of life seemed absurd."

As I had out on the bluff, I wiped at Leah's tears. In the process, I caught looks of astonishment on her sisters' faces. They didn't know me to be a toucher. They had no idea that my heart went out to Leah because she loved Jesse so.

"But you never forgot Will," Leah said brokenly.

"No. I never forgot Will. He was always part of my life, not necessarily a conscious part, but never far. Other friends have died over the years. I've mourned them, missed them, and moved on. But I never moved on from Will. He captured a unique part of me that no one else has ever touched."

A shrill whistle rent the air. I jumped, half-fearing that having said something so blasphemous, lightning was about to strike me dead. When Leah slipped out from under my arm, I realized it was the tea kettle. I left a supportive hand on my heart.

"Did Daddy know that?" Annette asked, looking up at me from a sideways perch.

"I never told him, not in as many words." I leaned against the sofa back. "He might have guessed."

"It's a wonder he didn't resent you."

"Actually not," I said fondly. "Your father was a kind man. We never talked about what had happened. We didn't have that kind of relationship. All he knew — all he cared — was that I'd decided to stay with him."

"What about trust?" Annette asked. "Didn't he get nervous when you talked with other men?"

"No. I had made my choice. He knew I would stick by it."

"Who else knew about that summer?" Caroline asked, looking paler than before. I fancied that she identified with Will and me, because what she experienced with Ben was a little like that.

"No one," I said.

"Not your parents?" Annette asked.

I shook my head. "They'd have been scandalized. Same with our friends."

"Did you live in fear of being discovered?"

I smiled. "No. I didn't fear that. The

people in Downlee knew what Will and I had done, but they were worlds away from my life with Nick."

"I'd have feared blackmail," Caroline said.

"Who would bother?" I asked with a shrug. "Nick already knew about Will. No, I didn't worry on that score. On others. But not that one."

"What others?"

I could smell the peach of Leah's tea and was craving a cup. "That smells divine," I told her as she reached for the china.

"What others?" Caroline prodded.

"The loss of feeling."

Leah set the cups down with a clatter. Annette and Caroline exchanged looks.

"You've all suffered it," I said quietly. "It's the source of my greatest regret."

"You regret not staying with Will?" Leah asked.

"I regret the price I paid for leaving him. I thought I could do it. I thought that I could resume my marriage and grow into it. But in leaving Will I found that I was emotionally maimed. The pain of the leaving was so great that I simply shut down. Rather than risk further pain, I separated myself from anything and everything of an emotional nature. I didn't express emotion. To some extent, I didn't feel it."

"You needed a shrink," Caroline remarked.

"I had one," I said and found some satisfaction in her surprise. "I saw one weekly for years. He helped me understand why I was the way I was, but he couldn't help me restore what I'd lost."

"Did you resent us?" Annette asked. "Did we represent the chains that kept you with Daddy? Was that it?"

"Lord, *no*," I cried, touching her shoulder. When it tensed, I took my hand away. In the next instant, consciously, I put it right back. "I never resented you in that sense. I might have resented you in other ways."

"What ways?" Caroline said.

I tried to express what I was only then coming to understand. "I was jealous. You three had the capacity to express things, and that made me look all the worse by comparison. What you took to be disapproval on my part, was self-defense. To approve of all you did in your lives would have been to admit to my own failings. I was feeling badly enough without that."

I patted Annette's shoulder, wanting to return to her question. "You girls were always a vital part of my life. Never once did I resent you. Chains? To the contrary. During those times when I asked myself if

I'd been right in choosing Nick over Will, you three were the overriding factors in the affirmative. If I'd stayed with Will, I'd never have had you."

"But you'd have had him," Annette said. "You'd have had his children. Didn't you ever wonder about that? Didn't you ever wish that you had?"

I shook my head. "I made my choice and never looked back. The only thing I regretted was not being able to give you more of myself. I could see each of you suffering at times, needing more from me, but I just didn't have it to give. It was gone."

"If that was so," Caroline said, "why are we here? Why did you buy Star's End?"

I took the tea Leah offered me. "I think you know the answer to that."

"Okay. You wanted us to know about Will. But wouldn't it have been simpler to invite us to Philadelphia and tell us outright?"

"Ah, but it wasn't only the knowing. It was the seeing. The feeling. The understanding. I wanted you to experience Star's End yourselves. Besides, I had to come back here. That knowledge has been lurking in my mind for years. I didn't give it much thought until after your father died, but then it wouldn't go away. I had to come back. I had to see Star's End. I had to visit Will."

"You didn't have to *buy* the place for all that," Caroline pointed out.

"This is where I want to die."

"Mother!"

"Don't *say* that."

"Good Lord."

"It is," I insisted, feeling confident in the face of death as women still in their prime couldn't possibly feel.

"But why?" Annette asked. "Your whole life was back in Philadelphia."

"Not my whole life. The major part of it, but not its entirety. As I see it, I've had five major achievements in my life. The first is my marriage to your father, the next three the creation of you girls, and the last my time with Will — and yes, that was an achievement. When I was with Will, I reached an emotional high that most people never, ever reach. In that sense, even in spite of the pain, I was fortunate."

I sipped my tea. It occurred to me that I might sit down again, but I was loath to put distance between me and my girls. I liked standing near them, being one of them. Besides, if I'd felt unburdened back at Will's grave, I was feeling all the more so now. Each loose end that was tied gave me strength.

"I've said goodbye to your father. There is no unfinished business on that score. There is, though, with you girls, and with Will. I wanted you to know him — through me and through Star's End. Only by being here can you begin to understand the kind of environment in which a love like ours could flourish."

I gazed out the window, past the flower beds and the bluff, toward the horizon. "And then there's the matter of apologies. I didn't have the taste for them in Philadelphia. This seemed the appropriate place."

I returned a slow, ready, anticipatory gaze to my girls.

It is late. I lie in bed, exhausted but at peace. I've been a mother this day, and it was quite a workout, but a thrill, too. We spent the evening talking, my daughters and I, over tea first, then dinner, then ice cream in a little shop in town.

What fun it was, piling into the Volvo and driving into Downlee. We've never been as content together, certainly not as adults. When the girls were children and we did things like that, there was a ceremony to it. Tonight, there was camaraderie. We were a family, relating to each other, perhaps for the very first time.

Was it Star's End at work? I like to think it was us. The potential was there. The setting simply enabled us to tap it.

Then again, by the time we made the ice cream trip, we were in need of a lighter moment. Unburdening the soul is heavy stuff, indeed. I retold the story of Will and me, and answered questions a second, third, and fourth time — and I didn't mind, really I didn't, it was such a relief to finally have it out in the open.

Perhaps that was what brought us closer, the simple fact of disclosure. The girls don't approve of what I did — I neither ask for, nor expect that — but I think they finally appreciate something of the earthshattering nature of my time with Will.

After the ice cream trip, when we returned to Star's End, we talked more seriously again. I faced other accusations — that I had neglected the girls in their times of need, that I pitted one against the other, that I favored Leah. I admitted to the first, was bewildered by the second, and clarified the third. I love all three of my daughters, always have, always will.

Love all three. Admire them. Want them happy.

There were tears, large, laughing, cathartic

tears, but they were good. So were the hugs. They came most often from Leah, though there were several from Annette, and those were gratifying, indeed. Annette and her family are huggers. I feel as though I'm finally one of them.

Only Caroline remains reserved. She thinks I betrayed her by keeping secrets all those years. I think her pride is wounded. In either case, time is the only healer. What happened today was just a beginning.

But a good one. Ah, yes. As I lie in the dark, I feel the satisfaction of that. The relief. The peace.

Inevitably, too, as I lie in the dark in this place I've dreamed about for so long, I think of Will. He never once slept with me in the big house, yet I feel him beside me now. It is the misty air, the rhythmic ocean song, the wonderful, wonderful smell that I've worn for so long. Beach roses lingering. They take me back.

I remember picnics on the rocks — crusty bread and cheese and homemade wine. I remember the early morning mist lifting off the water, and the hot noon sun hovering in ripples on the bluff. I remember the schooners slicing down east through the waves, and the monarchs flitting from iris to lily to Queen Anne's lace.

I remember Will's arms. Strong and brown. And Will's hands. Callused and nicked, but ever gentle on my soul.

I'm here, Will. I'm here.

I smile and sigh. Then sigh once more, deeply and contentedly.

NINETEEN

Annette held three pieces of paper in her hand. One was the note that had come with the flowers Jean-Paul had sent. The second and third were telephone messages, again from Jean-Paul. The first had come the day before, assuring her that Thomas was fine. The second had arrived that morning. It simply said that Jean-Paul missed her.

She hadn't called him back, initially because she had a point to prove, and after that, because events started unfolding that swept her up in their midst.

She picked up the phone now, held it for a minute, set it down. It was nearly one, midnight in St. Louis. Jean-Paul would be asleep.

But she wanted to talk with him. Standing on principle was one thing, bowing to heart and soul another.

This time she punched out the numbers before she could think again about the time.

The phone barely made it through half a ring when it was snatched up, but it wasn't Jean-Paul's deep, sleepy voice she heard. It was another deep voice, not sleepy, but breathless.

"Hi," it said.

Annette grinned. Imitating the breathlessness, she said, "Hi, yourself."

There was a pause — she imagined Robbie bolting up straight — then a far higher, "Mom?"

She was still grinning. "No. Jessica." At least that had been the love interest when Annette had left five days before.

"Mommm," he complained.

"Why is she calling this late?"

"We were talking a little while ago, and she had to get off to take a shower so her hair could dry, and she said she'd call back. Everything is fine here, Mom. We're all doing really good. You don't have to worry. There haven't been any more broken arms, Charlene's been here every day, and Dad's been great. He's sleeping. I'll tell him you called."

Annette knew Robbie wanted her off the phone, fast, before Jessica called — which was all fine and good, but fair was fair. If Robbie wanted to talk with his squeeze, Annette wanted to talk with hers. "Are you sure he's sleeping?" she asked. "Maybe the phone woke him."

"I just went down for a snack. He's dead to the world on the sofa. I turned off the TV."

"Didn't you wake him and tell him to go to bed?"

"I tried, but he looked at me like I was an alien and rolled over and went back to sleep. He's been doing this every night. He doesn't like going to bed without you."

"That's so *sweet*," Annette said. It was a reaffirmation, like flowers and phone messages, vouching for what Jean-Paul had said, what her sisters had said about true love lasting.

"Is everything okay there, Mom?"

"Fine." She took a breath and thought of the evening that had just been. "Great, actually. Your grandmother finally arrived. We've had an incredible time. I'm glad I came. I think this is really important."

"That's great, Mom. Can Dad call you tomorrow?"

"If he wants. You say Thomas is okay?"

"Thomas is a jerk, but his arm is fine."

Annette was sorry she asked. Instinct told her not to ask more. "Nat and the girls are okay?"

"Great. We're all great. How about I have

Dad call you first thing tomorrow?"

"It's not critical. He doesn't have to call first thing. He doesn't have to call at all, actually, if he's busy." She didn't *need* to talk with him; she just *wanted* to. She felt bolstered knowing that he didn't like sleeping in bed without her. "I just wanted to say hello."

"At midnight?"

"Why not?"

"It's late."

She refused to be chastised. "Excuse me?"

"It's late."

For you, too, young man, and still expecting a call. "Pardon me?"

There was a moment's silence, then a sheepish, "Okay. We won't talk long. 'Night, Mom."

" 'Night, Rob."

Pleased at how independently she was behaving, she hung up the phone.

Caroline couldn't sleep. It was this way when she was on trial, when her mind refused to shut down. Granted, she wasn't on trial here, but her adrenaline level was the same. Too much had happened for her body to settle, and her mind was three steps ahead.

She thought about having a cigarette, but

that was all it was — no craving, just a thought, and a distant one, at that. Cigarettes were for tension-filled meetings and power lunches. They weren't for Star's End.

What she wanted — the one thing that could calm her — was to reach Ben, but either he wasn't answering his phone, or he wasn't home. Neither possibility reassured her.

Throwing back the sheet, she jumped out of bed. She thrust a hand through her hair and made for the hall. The house was quiet, the others asleep. Her feet were soundless on the stair runner and little more than a soft padding on the wide-planked wood floor of the hall. She snapped on a small light in the kitchen, shook the tea kettle to make sure it held water, and turned on the gas. Just shy of the rolling boil that would have whistled, she removed the kettle and poured steaming water over the small holder that held the loose tea leaves together in her cup.

While they steeped, she went to the French doors. The moon was hidden behind a thin blanket of silver-deckled clouds. She saw a cluster of stars between them — here, gone, here again — and then a tiny light moving steadily across the horizon.

There was another light, this one moving

only by illusion, as tree branches swayed before it. It marked Jesse Cray's home, once the groundskeeper's shed where Ginny St. Clair had been wild and free. The image continued to astound her.

"Couldn't sleep?"

Caroline darted a glance over her shoulder as Annette joined her at the glass doors. "No. You neither?"

"I don't know why. I should be exhausted. What do you see?"

"The light at the edge of the woods. I'm trying to imagine it when it was the little shed Mother described. I'm trying to picture her running barefoot across the grass in the night."

Annette made a sound. "Bizarre. I never would have dreamed it."

"Me either."

"I wanted to tell Jean-Paul, but he was asleep."

"I wanted to tell Ben, but he isn't home."

"Where is he?"

"Beats me," she said with a nonchalance that wasn't nonchalant at all. "He wasn't home last night, either." She felt Annette look at her and couldn't meet her eye. "I've taken him for granted, I think."

"Has he been seeing anyone else?"

"No. But I frustrate him."

"He travels a lot. Maybe this is just another one of his trips."

"He would have told me he was going."

"Maybe he just took off — the frustration, and all."

Caroline knew it was possible. But he loved being at the cabin this time of year, when the days were long and the forest fertile. Those things inspired him, he said. Late spring and early summer were always productive for him.

"You really ought to marry him, Caroline. He loves you. I could see it way back at Dad's funeral, and if he's still hanging around, even with you turning him down, he must *really* love you."

"If we're together, what difference does it make whether we're married?"

"It makes a difference. It's a commitment. A *legal* commitment."

"Yeah, and I know how much of a hassle those can be."

"That's the point."

"What is?"

"Going out on a limb for someone you love. Mother didn't do it. She didn't want to give up the fine life, but look at the price she paid. Oh, she didn't say it in as many words. She said that she came to love Daddy, and that if she hadn't left Will, she

396

wouldn't have had us, but the fact is that if she'd stayed with Will, she'd have had a whole *other* kind of life. Who's to say it wouldn't have been richer?"

Startled, Caroline studied her sister. "But you were against what they did. You believe in fidelity. At least, I thought that was what you were saying before."

"I *do* believe in it. But I also believe in love. I'm not sure I could admit it to Mother, out of loyalty to Daddy and all, but I'm sorry she missed out on something so rare as what she had with Will Cray. I wouldn't want you to do the same." She held up a hand. "That's the end of my lecture. If I've offended you, I'm sorry, but that's the way I see it." Her expression softened. "We haven't always agreed on things, you and I, but you are my sister, Caroline. I do wish you happiness."

Caroline was appalled when her throat knotted up. But even if she'd been able to speak, she was spared a response because Leah chose that moment to burst into the kitchen. She drew up short when she saw them.

"Ooops. Sorry. I thought you were all asleep."

"Maybe we have the time wrong," Annette cracked, narrowing a gaze on the clock.

"Maybe it's only ten, or eleven. No. It's one-forty." She looked back at Leah. "I know my excuse and Caroline's excuse. What's yours?"

Leah shrugged. She had a brandy-colored afghan wrapped around her long nightgown and would have looked frail, had her cheeks not been so pink. Caroline guessed that she, too, had been wound up by the day's discoveries. "I couldn't sleep," she said unnecessarily, then added a quick, "I thought I'd go for a walk."

"At this hour?" Annette asked.

Caroline smiled at the maternalistic tone. "She's of age," she reminded Annette.

"But it's dark out there."

"I won't necessarily walk," Leah said with another shrug, an offhanded one this time. "I may just sit on the bluff. It's not dangerous. I've done it before."

Caroline stood back to let her out the door. "Want tea to go?"

"No, thanks," she said with a wave and was gone.

"Is she okay?" Annette asked.

Caroline wasn't sure. Through much of Ginny's confession, Leah had looked tortured. She seemed all right now, a little bright-eyed, perhaps, but all right. Still, it struck Caroline that Ginny had been right in defending what might have looked like favoritism. "She is more fragile, I guess. Maybe even a little lost. Does she call you much at home?"

"No. I probably should call her more. She could come visit."

Caroline was thinking the same thing. "She always liked Ben. Maybe he has a friend." She sighed. "Forget the friend. Where the hell's Ben?"

But Annette didn't have the answer any more than she did. She tried his number again when she went to her room, to no avail, then proceeded to toss and turn and imagine the unimaginable.

Ben had left for three months without a good-bye.

Ben had been killed riding his cycle.

Ben had taken up with another woman.

The first would dismay her, the second devastate her, the third cause the kind of pain from which she doubted she would ever recover. She could deal with her partners' betrayal; she didn't think she could deal with Ben's.

Funny. She hadn't thought about the office in hours and hours. Something was definitely wrong with her. But then, the office didn't deserve her thought. She'd been stabbed in the back for the sole reason that she'd dared take a vacation. And, probably, because she was a woman. Caroline doubted any of the men would have dared steal a case from another male partner. They were a bunch of two-timing hypocrites who weren't worthy of her worry.

Ben was another story.

She dozed off once, then again, only to awaken each time with a start. She imagined that her anxiety was similar to what Annette felt when she worried about her family, and felt a new respect for the woman. Okay, Annette took things to the extreme, still, worry went along with caring, Caroline supposed.

She also supposed that Ginny might have indeed worried about her daughters through the years, as she claimed. Worry came in different forms. With Annette, it was constant phoning. With Ginny, it might have been more subtle. Caroline knew from experience that the same evidence could be viewed one way by the prosecutor and another by the defense. A weekly phone call could be viewed either as dutiful, as in Mother felt she had to call, or restrained, as in Mother might have called more had she felt I would have welcomed it.

Mother. Ben. Annette and Leah. Holten, Wills, and Duluth. So much to consider. So much to *re*consider.

Dawn found Leah curled on Jesse's leather sofa, alternately looking from the pressed rose wreath and the old leather rings, to the loft where Jesse slept. They hadn't talked much. They had made love — always that, when they were together — and afterward he had held her until he'd finally dozed off.

She heard him shift in the bed, then heard a cautious, "Leah?"

"Down here," she called up.

The bed creaked again. Wearing only undershorts — gray knit boxers that hugged his flanks — he appeared on the steps. His hair was messed, his jaw stubbled, his body firm. As she watched him approach, she hugged her knees to her chest.

He hunkered down before her, pushing his fingers into her hair to draw it away from her face. "What's wrong?"

"I look at you and melt."

He brought her into his arms and shifted onto the sofa. She settled against him with her cheek to his chest and the palm of her hand before it, fingers splayed over his skin. It was warm, cushioned with a light layer of hair, and male-scented.

Ginny had wild roses, Leah had Jesse. She sensed that wherever she went in life, she wouldn't be able to smell that musky male smell without thinking of Jesse. She felt an ache in anticipation.

They didn't talk then, any more than they had earlier, just sat breathing in tempo with one another.

"I have to go," she finally whispered. She kissed him, then wove her arms around his neck and held him tightly. If there was an element of desperation in her grip, she refused to dwell on it. She wasn't leaving Star's End just yet. She had time.

She ran across the lawn in the pale purple light of the new day, ran past the pool and across the deck. She drew open the kitchen door and quietly slipped inside, intent on disappearing into her room undiscovered.

But the refrigerator door was ajar. Caroline stood in its light with a carton of juice in her hand and a startled look on her face, and no wonder, Leah mused in dismay. She could just imagine the picture she made. Her hair was a mess, her face was red, her breath short and shallow.

"Good Lord, Leah, have you been outside all this time?"

"I wasn't tired," Leah said without lying. "It seemed foolish to try to sleep. I may now, though. How about you? Just thirsty?"

"Mostly restless." She let the refrigerator

door drift shut and reached for a glass. "Want some?"

"No, thanks. I think I'll head up." She smiled. "See you in a bit." She slipped on through the room and up the stairs.

Only when she was in her bed with the comforter pulled to her ears did she wonder why she hadn't told Caroline about Jesse.

She wasn't ashamed of him. If anything, the reverse was true.

But she didn't trust what Caroline's reaction would be — or Annette's, for that matter — if they learned about him.

If? When.

But later.

Caroline remained in the kitchen, perched on a stool, watching the sun work its way over the distant horizon and trickle across the waves. She sipped orange juice or water, whichever happened to be in her glass, and thought about all she'd done wrong.

She had taken Ben for granted. It would serve her right if he disappeared for three months. He was a free agent. All her fault.

She had stereotyped Annette and Leah, had judged them to be shallow, when they weren't. Okay, so they didn't have careers like she did, but then, she didn't have a family like Annette or the ability to make friends like Leah, so maybe they were even. They had certainly been even yesterday. For all her professionalism, Caroline hadn't handled Ginny's startling revelation any better than her sisters.

Maybe worse, in fact. Leah had been able to listen to Ginny, understand what she'd done, and cry with her for what had been lost. Same with Annette. But not Caroline. She hadn't forgiven anything. Well, she had. At least, she thought she had. Only she hadn't been able to express it.

It struck her that she was like Ginny that way. But she had spent her whole life being *different* from Ginny. She had always detested Ginny's aloofness. She had always prided herself on being honest.

It struck her now that she hadn't necessarily been so, not where her emotions were concerned. Not with regard to Annette and Leah. Not with regard to Ben. Not with regard to Ginny.

Feeling a sudden urgency, she reached for the phone and punched out Ben's number, then listened to ring after ring after ring. She counted to ten to see if his machine would click on. When it didn't, she hung up, feeling frustrated and more restless than ever.

The clock said six-twenty. Leah had been

up all night and would no doubt be dead to the world. Annette, who had been in the kitchen with Caroline such a few short hours before, wouldn't be much better.

That left Ginny.

Caroline remembered once, when she'd been sixteen and bratty to the point that Ginny had taken to ignoring her, wanting to apologize but not knowing how. She offered to run errands. She offered to take Annette and Leah to a movie. She offered to pick up her father at the train station. When nothing seemed to work, she finally stole into Ginny's room one morning and sat on the bed until Ginny woke up. They didn't speak. Ginny simply touched her hand and smiled, and it was done.

Leaving the kitchen now, she crept quietly up the stairs. She knocked softly on Ginny's door. When Ginny didn't respond, she turned the knob, opened the door, and slipped inside. Ginny was asleep, looking so peaceful that for a minute Caroline stood immobile at the door. She couldn't begin to imagine what yesterday had been like for the woman. If it had been momentous for Caroline — seeing her mother laugh and cry, raise her voice, speak of passion and romance — it must have been even more so for Ginny. Unburdening one's soul was heavy stuff. And Ginny wasn't young.

She did look it, though, lying there with the worries of the world wiped from her face. She looked serene, even happy. But incredibly still.

Feeling a twinge of unease, Caroline quietly crossed the floor. Close up, Ginny's features were relaxed, eyelids lowered, mouth curved into a tiny smile. But she had no color, and there was a waxy sheen to her skin.

"Mother?" she whispered. She felt a bone-deep thudding, and touched a trembling hand to her mother's. It was cold. So was her cheek.

Timidly, she raised that trembling hand to Ginny's hair. Its short sweep was as neat and perfect as always, a proper cap beneath which to face one world or another. The cheekbones were pronounced, the jaw and chin sculpted. Ginny was a beautiful woman, even embalmed in this alabaster stillness.

Caroline's eyes filled with tears. She sank down on the edge of the bed and took that cold hand in hers. "Oh, Mother," she cried, "how *could* you." It wasn't fair! Ginny had been theirs for the very first time! Yesterday was just a *beginning.*

The urgency that had brought her upstairs

returned. Engulfed in a great surge of grief, she whispered a broken, "I'm sorry. I should have said more. I was stubborn and proud. I thought I had you all figured out, but I didn't, and that made me *angry*." She wept softly, holding Ginny's hand now in both of hers, jiggling it every so often.

"Wake up, Mother. We *have to talk*." She let out a long, ragged sigh and wiped her eyes on her shoulder, but tears welled back up. "We never talked. My fault, too. My responsibility as an adult. But I distanced myself. Like you did. Because it hurt less. Ignorance is bliss. Oh, *God* —" She made a large, loud, helpless keening sound as sobs worked their way up from deep inside her.

"Caroline?" came a voice from the door, then a frightened, "What is it, Caroline?"

She rocked on the bed, holding Ginny's hand to her thigh. She heard a gasp from just beyond her shoulder, then a short, anguished cry. Arms enfolded her. She leaned into them, crying freely with Leah.

"It's not fair," Caroline told her, wanting to scream and yell and turn back the clock.

"I know."

"There was so *much* still to say."

"I know."

"Yesterday was just a *start*."

"Or a harbinger," said a shaky Annette

407

from the door. Looking ash white, she approached. Her eyes were large, their lower lids heavy with unshed tears as she stared at Ginny. "It must have been her heart."

"But the doctor said she was fine," Leah protested.

"She was, that first time. I had Jean-Paul check. There have been more recent visits and an irregular EKG."

Leah gasped. "She didn't say a word. How could she have been so secretive about it?"

"She may have denied it. She had a prescription. She may not have used it."

"If we'd known, we would have *made* her use it."

Caroline rubbed Leah's back. It was easier to think clearly when someone needed you to. "No, Leah," she murmured. "It wasn't for us to decide. Ginny did things her way." She caught in another sob, then laughed through her tears. "I used to think she was weak. Dumb of me. She was iron-tough. She made decisions and stuck by them. She told us she wanted to die here, so she died here. She must have planned it this way."

"Look at her face," Annette whispered in awe. "So calm. So *pleased*."

"She's with Will," Leah said.

Caroline wasn't sure she believed in the afterlife. But that didn't mean it didn't exist. She had been wrong about other things. She could be wrong about this, too. Feeling humbled and drained, she let out a shaky breath. She wiped her face with her wrist, then took Ginny's hand again.

"Shouldn't we call someone?" Annette asked. "The police? A funeral home?"

"Not yet," Caroline said. She wasn't ready to let Ginny go, not this new Ginny who had been so colorful. "What if we had known sooner?"

"About Will?" Leah asked.

"We might have talked more. Had more time to get to know her. It's sad."

"Not if you take the position that she might have died last week or last month without us knowing *any*thing," Annette said. "She was hanging on for this. There's something triumphant in that."

"Do you think she bought the house with dying in mind?" Leah asked.

"She said she wanted to die here."

"Can people actually determine things like that?"

"Jean-Paul says the mind can heal as effectively as a surgeon in some situations. It's a powerful thing."

Caroline was just beginning to see that. "Kind of makes the law a crock."

"What do you mean?"

"Physical evidence. That's what we convict on. But it only tells half the story. How can a jury determine the extent of guilt or innocence with only half the story?"

"You address the issue of motive."

"Yeah, sure, but what do we know? We don't know what's going on in someone's mind. Not really. Take Mother. I assumed I knew what was in her mind, but I was wrong. I convicted her, I sure as hell did, on the merest of physical evidence." She wasn't all cried out, after all. Her tears returned.

Leah became the comforter then, wrapping a tighter arm around her shoulder. "You weren't the only one, Caroline. All of us did it."

Annette reached toward Ginny's still face, hesitated, then touched it. "She let us. She didn't argue. She didn't defend herself."

"Damn it," Caroline cried, "why not?"

Her question hung in the still, silent air. She knew that outside the ocean was rolling toward shore, the gulls screaming as they soared over the bluff, the fog horn droning its timed message by the Houkabee Rocks, but here all was hushed.

It was Annette who finally broke the stillness. "She thought she was doing the right thing. I guess we all do, in life. None of us

410

sets out to make mistakes. They're honestly come by. Mother thought she was doing the right thing in not telling us about Will Cray. She thought she was protecting Daddy."

"Maybe she was protecting herself," Caroline accused. In the next breath she added a bewildered, "Or punishing herself."

"We should call someone," Annette whispered.

"Wait." Not yet. Not yet. Caroline wasn't ready. "She would be pleased that we're all here with her. She wanted us to be close. It bothered her that we weren't."

"Why weren't we?"

"Because we've taken different directions in life."

"That's a pretty poor excuse."

"We never thought so before."

"We never *thought* before," Caroline realized. "Not together, at least. I really don't hate you guys."

"You just don't want to spend time with us."

That wasn't it at all. "You have your own lives, I have mine," Caroline said in her own defense, then added, "which is a dumb thing to say, too. Law is only one part of my life. Granted, the biggest part. Granted, the gargantuan part. Which may be dumb, too." She let out an uneven breath. "I think I have

411

thinking to do."

Another silence fell. The sun had risen enough to clear the windowsill. It spilled obliquely across the bed and crept toward Ginny's face, imbuing her features with an eerie glow.

Finally, Caroline said, "I guess it's time. She's earned her rest."

Annette was the resister now, pressing closer to the bed, crossing a hand to Ginny's far shoulder. Leah left Caroline and wrapped an arm around Annette's waist. Gently, reluctantly, but knowing that it wouldn't get any easier, Caroline set Ginny's hand back on the bed.

Lest she lose her resolve, she quickly rounded the bed and picked up the phone. Within minutes she had awoken Downlee's undertaker and alerted him to their need.

"He'll be along," she told Annette and Leah.

"Should we call her lawyer back home?" Annette asked. "Maybe she left written instructions."

"She might have," Caroline realized. "Then again, I think she'd have told us. She planned this all out so well. She wouldn't have left that to chance." Not weak at all, but tough, determined, smart. Caroline looked at her sisters. "I think we have a fairly good idea what she'd want."

"She'd want to be buried here," Annette said.

"Star's End has its own graveyard," Leah added. "It's down the bluff a ways. Will is there."

"What about Daddy?" Caroline asked, playing the devil's advocate.

Leah seemed about to say something, then stopped. It was Annette who said, quietly, "She gave Daddy all the years of her life from the time she left Will to the time Daddy died. She felt she owed him a responsibility. I think she's filled it."

So did Caroline. Leah's expression said she did, too.

That settled, there seemed nothing more immediate to do than to wait for the undertaker's arrival. Caroline sent Annette and Leah to get dressed while she sat with Ginny. She couldn't leave her alone, not in these few final minutes that she would be theirs. When they saw her again, it would be at the funeral home, and after that, at the graveyard on the bluff, with family and friends all around.

Holding Ginny's hand, she found herself crying again, but she didn't fight it. She didn't have the strength. Or the desire. She hadn't cried enough in life. Crying was good.

In time, she tried Ben again, desperate to hear his voice, but he didn't answer. She figured that once the funeral plans were firm — and morning reached the Chicago area — she would start calling friends who might know his whereabouts. Until then, she could only wonder and ache.

Leah returned, and even then Caroline would have liked to have stayed with Ginny. She was the oldest. It was her responsibility — but no, that wasn't it. The truth was that she had more making up to do with Ginny than the others did.

But she knew that she should be dressed by the time the undertaker arrived, and besides, Leah deserved time alone with Ginny, too. So she retreated into her room, where she eyed the bed in which she'd only slept in fits and starts during the night, and wondered at what point Ginny had died. It struck her as tragic that none of them had been with her at that moment. They'd all been nearby. So nearby. But not there.

It was, in a sense, the story of their lives as a family, and tragic in and of itself.

She was thinking about that when she returned to Ginny's room, where Annette had joined Leah in the vigil. The picture only underscored the tragedy — the three of them standing beside Ginny in death as they had never done while she'd been alive. There was a comfort in their being together, but it was a bittersweet one.

Caroline was feeling as though a rug had been swept out from under her, which was amusing, given that she hadn't thought herself dependent on Ginny at all. And she wasn't, with regard to everyday matters. Still, Ginny was her mother. In the back of her mind, Caroline had always known she was there. Now, suddenly and finally, she wasn't.

Shortly before nine, the doorbell rang. Caroline's eyes flew from Ginny's face to Annette's and Leah's. She swallowed and whispered, "This makes it real," which must have been exactly what they were thinking, if their convulsive nods meant anything.

Annette left to show the undertaker in. During the time that took, Caroline looked alternately from Leah's face to Ginny's. Leah looked terrified.

Caroline rounded the bed and held her. Twice, when she'd been with the prosecutor's office, she had been present during the removal of a body. She knew what to expect. Leah didn't.

The undertaker and his assistant, even in

as small a town as Downlee, were all neatly combed hair, pressed funereal suits, and polished black shoes. Beyond that, there were no similarities whatsoever to those other experiences Caroline had. By the time Ginny's body had been covered, transferred to a stretcher on wheels, and carried downstairs and out the door, Caroline was as distraught as Leah and Annette.

The three of them stood on the front steps while, beneath the porte cochere, the hearse accepted its burden. They followed it out into the sunlight and watched it cruise slowly down the drive.

Leah choked out an anguished cry. Caroline reached for her hand, but Leah wasn't watching the hearse. She was looking across the lawn.

Jesse Cray stood there, still at a distance but clearly not knowing whether to approach or turn away. When he started toward them, Leah gave another cry. Breaking free, she began to run toward him. Before Caroline could begin to understand, she was in his arms.

Dawning came then, a slow realization that stunned her. Yet it made sense.

Annette leaned close, sounding as stunned as she felt. "Leah and Jesse?"

"That's where she went last night."

"And why the story of Mother and Will tore her up so. Why didn't she *tell* us?"

"Would we have understood? Not the me who first arrived here."

"Nor the me. He's the gardener."

"He's also Will Cray's son. That makes him far more."

"Do you think they're in love?"

"They're something. Look how they're holding each other." Caroline was thinking how much she'd have adored holding and being held by Ben just then, when Leah and Jesse started their way.

Their hands were clasped. Leah looked frightened.

"I'm sorry about your mother," Jesse said. "She should have had more time at Star's End. She would have liked what the place has become. I would have liked getting to know her."

"Did you know *of* her?" Caroline asked.

He smiled a smile that was a little wry, a little sad, a little knowing. "For years she was all my dad talked about. She meant the world to him. He would have been pleased she came back."

Caroline had a feeling that Jesse had more to add to what they already knew of Ginny and Will. She had a feeling that he and Leah had already talked.

She had a feeling that he and Leah had done far more than talk. There was something about the way she stood, just slightly to his side and before him, leaning against him almost, sheltered by him almost.

"When you make funeral plans," Jesse said, speaking to the three of them now, "will you invite the town? They liked your mother. Word got around that she was back, after you all went for ice cream last night. They'll be sorry they missed her. They'd want to pay their last respects."

Caroline thought of all the other people who would, too. She thought of the phone calls to be made — to Gwen, to Ginny's sole surviving brother and a cousin, to scores of friends in Philadelphia and Palm Springs. She thought of calling Ben, thought of the phone he wasn't answering, thought of the steps she might take to track him down. She had the names of several top investigators whom she'd used on various occasions. If necessary she would call one of them.

Then she heard a noise that was incompatible with the sounds of Star's End. Her eyes flew toward the drive. She half-expected to see the hearse returning — indeed, had the insane hope that Ginny might have woken up from an absurdly deep sleep.

The sound wasn't smooth, like the hearse, nor well muffled. It was familiar, though. She knew it as well as she knew what his bare thighs felt like beneath her hands.

"Ben?" she whispered, afraid to believe as the motorcycle rounded the bend and emerged into the light. *"Ben."*

Leaving the others on the steps, she ran to the edge of the circular drive. He stopped the cycle several feet away, dismounted, and pulled off his helmet. His face was pale, his eyes concerned. He glanced back in the direction from which he'd come, then forward again, past Caroline, to Annette and Leah.

"Why was that hearse here?" he asked.

"I've been trying to call you for two days, *three* days."

"Your mom?"

She nodded.

He squeezed his eyes shut, threw back his head, then brought it forward again, closed the distance between them, and caught Caroline up. She wrapped her arms around his neck, locked them there, and began to cry again.

Ben had come.

TWENTY

"Jean-Paul," Annette breathed in response to his groggy hello. She knew she had woken him up. It was Saturday morning, the one morning when he slept late, and even then only until eight. It was barely seven in St. Louis. But she hadn't been able to wait a minute longer. Marriage was for sharing things like a parent's death, and that was only part of what she had to say.

It all spilled out on poor, unknowing, sleepy Jean-Paul, everything she had thought herself strong and independent enough to defer telling him last night. Now, strength and independence were irrelevant. The need to share momentous happenings in her life with her best friend was greater than either.

She told Jean-Paul about the legend of Star's End, then learning that the legend involved Ginny. She told of the closeness she had shared with her sisters during the discovery, and of Ginny's arrival and the subsequent outpourings. She told of the trip to the ice cream store and her late-night visit to the kitchen. Weeping softly, she told of returning to her room, oblivious to the fact that Ginny was breathing her last.

"It's heartbreaking, Jean-Paul," she cried. "Here we learn incredible things about our mother, things that help explain why she was the way she was all those years, and for the very first time in our lives the air is clear between us, and it is so incredibly *good* — and she dies."

"I'm sorry, sweetheart, I'm sorry."

"It isn't right that it should happen that way."

"No. Death is rarely right."

The words were spoken with quiet conviction, and such a total absence of criticism that Annette was ashamed. Jean-Paul saw death every day. He saw it in people decades younger than Virginia, people who left behind people even younger than that. He saw unexpected death, untimely death, cruel death. Virginia's had been none of those.

Gathering more positive thoughts, Annette said, "You should have seen her. She looked so different. Her face came alive when she talked of the time she had with this man. She had good color. She smiled, even laughed. Even *cried.* What an unbelievable thing *that* was. The first time it happened, the three of us looked at each other, totally floored. We'd never seen her cry before. We didn't think she had it in her. She's always been such a stoic."

"It is interesting that she was able to hold everything in and survive this long. That her heart didn't rebel sooner."

Annette gasped. She hadn't tied the ongoing heart problem to Ginny's keeping secrets, but it made tragic sense. "She paid the ultimate price for her decisions, then. They say Will Cray died of a broken heart. In a roundabout way, she did, too. We thought she simply didn't *feel* things. We were so wrong. You should have seen her. It was like someone had pulled the stopper on her emotions, and they all just spilled out."

"Was she enjoying herself?"

"Very much. Once in a while she seemed short of breath, but that fit in with the story she was telling. We were *all* short of breath. I guess hers was more symptomatic than ours."

"Was she taking her pills?"

"We found them by her bedside. The bottle looked full."

"She was warned against undue excitement."

Annette smiled fondly at that. Men were, after all, more mechanical than women. Even Jean-Paul, who was so much more sensitive than most, was that way, where medical directives were concerned. Like his fellow doctors, he wanted his patients to live. He had a hard time understanding that the price of staying alive was sometimes too high.

"How can you tell a woman in that situation not to feel excitement?" Annette asked. "She was relieved to be back here. She had gone out to see Will's grave. Her eyes were bright. She seemed more and more uplifted, as the night went on. She was so *nice* to be with, Jean-Paul." That fact continued to amaze — and dismay — Annette. "It isn't fair. We find her — then lose her — on the same day. *It isn't fair.*"

"I'm sorry, *cheri.* I wish I was there. How are Caroline and Leah doing?"

Annette steadied herself. "They're okay. Upset, naturally. Caroline even more so than Leah."

"Hmmm. Surprising."

"A week ago, yes. Now, not so much. I've had interesting glimpses of Caroline. She isn't as hard-nosed as she'd like us to believe. I think she's mellowed."

"Maybe she was never so hard-nosed, but

423

is only now letting you see that. Kind of like your mother letting you see that she was human after all. Do you or your sisters have any thoughts about a funeral?"

Annette hadn't made that analogy, the one between Caroline's professionalism and Ginny's stoicism. Tucking it away for later thought, she said, "Only that we're burying her here."

"There?"

Annette had to smile. "Shocking, huh? But you didn't hear her story, Jean-Paul. You didn't see her during the telling. There's no doubt about it. The three of us agree. She would want to be buried here."

"Rather than with Dominick?"

Annette took a deep breath and straightened her spine. Her room had only an oblique view of the water, but instead looked out over the lawn, down along the bluff, and its distant cloud of pink. The mere sight of the beach roses conjured their smell. They were part of her history.

She had to explain this to Jean-Paul, had to convey the importance of it in Virginia St. Clair's life.

"When I first learned about Mother and Will," she began, "I was offended on Daddy's behalf. Then Mother kept talking, and we understood all that she felt for Will and gave up for Daddy. If dignity and grace count for anything, she did the right thing by Daddy. She stayed with him and made him a fine home. She was his wife and the mother of his children, and if she lacked emotion in those roles, she still performed them better than many another woman."

There was a silence, then a quiet, "Whew," from Jean-Paul. "That's quite a concession."

Annette smiled sheepishly. "I guess." She was feeling stronger, braver. Connecting with Jean-Paul always did that to her. "Want to hear another? At first I identified with Daddy. Mother was married to him — I'm married to you — I wouldn't *dream* of taking up with another man. I kept thinking about the immorality of what she'd done. I kept thinking that it was one summer in her life that should have been over and done and forgotten. But she kept talking. She kept mentioning the ways that summer affected the rest of her life. She kept telling us little things that she had experienced with Will, not sexual things but passionate things, and you could see it in her face, the love." She caught her breath. "I felt it, Jean-Paul. *That's* what I identify with."

He made a soft, aching sound.

"I adore you," she hurried on, because it seemed the time to confess. "If I overdo it sometimes —"

"Shhhhh —"

"I don't intend to overdo. I'm just swept up in it."

"I love you, Annette."

"But you don't smother me. I'm trying to stop doing that. But I miss talking with you. I've been afraid to call."

Again came the aching sound. "Ah, no, no."

"Maybe you were right, and I was over-compensating for the way Ginny was, but, boy, do I see another side of that now. It's humbling. I always thought that our rela-tionship, yours and mine, was so much bet-ter than my parents'. I prided myself on it. We had done what they couldn't. But she had the same beautiful relationship with Will that you and I have. So yes," Annette concluded with a deep sigh, suddenly drained by the outpouring and by the hours of emotion that had followed Caroline's dawn discovery, "we're burying her here."

"Yes. That is right. Do you have a day and time?"

"Not yet. We'll meet with the minister this morning."

"Will you call me as soon as you know?"

"Yes." Her thoughts whirred. "But you don't have to come." It was the ultimate in letting go, she realized.

"Of course I do. I'm your husband. She was my mother-in-law. She was never anything less than lovely to me."

"Jean-Paul, this is really out of the way. It's a long trip. It'll be enough that I know you and the children are thinking of us. Besides, it's going to be out of the way for most of her friends. They won't understand why we're having it here, and I'm not sure we'll want to explain. If she didn't see fit to tell them during her life, I don't think they need to know now. So we'll simply say that she loved this spot from the summer Daddy and she were here, and we'll have some kind of memorial service next week in Philadelphia. You and the kids can be there. That makes so much more sense."

"I want to be with you."

She smiled. "That's all I have to know." How proud of herself she was. "The children need you this weekend. Do something wonderful with them, all of you together. Celebrate Mother's finally returning to the place she loved. She was happy. She died smiling." Her voice broke. That smile had been so very poignant. "Take the kids to church tomorrow and say a special prayer for her." More timidly she said, "I'll call you later, anyway. Just to hear your voice. Is that okay?"

"More than. I love you, sweetheart."

"Me, too," she said, growing teary-eyed. She dreaded hanging up the phone and severing the connection. Jean-Paul was her lifeline. "Jean-Paul? Thank you for making me come. I'd have regretted it if I hadn't."

"Shhh. Be with your sisters now. Help them through this."

"I love you."

"Go," he whispered.

Cornmeal. Flour. Baking powder. Honey. Leah assessed what was on the counter and quickly added butter, buttermilk, and eggs. She emptied a quart of blueberries into a colander and held them under running water while she picked out stems and bits of leaf. She did the same with a second quart, then a third.

"Leah," Annette approached from behind, "what are you doing?"

"Making blueberry corn muffins. I really wanted to do something with raspberries, but the season isn't right so the market didn't have enough." She began measuring cupfuls of cornmeal. "I'm making eight dozen. I figure I'll give four to Julia and keep four here for us. People will be stopping by. We'll need this to add to what Julia

428

will bring." They had set the funeral for Monday. That didn't leave much time to prepare.

"You don't have to do this now."

"I *do*." The busier she kept, the better she'd feel. "Since you and Caroline are making all the phone calls, this is the least I can do. It's much easier than having to call Gwen. How was she?"

"Not surprised. But very upset."

"And Mother's friends? I wasn't eager to talk with them. I know you thought I loved them all, but I really didn't."

"I think we should talk." This from Caroline.

"Where's Ben?" Annette asked.

"Sleeping. He drove the damn cycle halfway across the country with two six-hour rest stops. He's a crazy man."

"Incredibly sweet."

It was a meaningful minute before Caroline said a soft, "Yes." Leah spared them a fast glance, before returning to the cornmeal. But she had lost count of how many cups she had measured. She wasn't sure if she had reached five, or six. She stared at the mound in dismay.

"So while Ben sleeps, let's talk about Jesse," Caroline said.

Leah started again, scooping out one cup

from what was in the bowl and dumping it into a second bowl.

"Leah?"

"There's nothing to say," she murmured.

"It didn't look like nothing."

"It looked like a definite *something*," Annette put in.

Four cups. Leah measured out a fifth. "I suppose."

"Since when?" Caroline asked.

Then a sixth. "Since Monday. Sunday, if you count him creeping up on me while I slept on the swing Sunday night."

"What kind of something is it?" Annette asked.

Leah set down the near-empty cornmeal container and reached for the flour. "What kind of question is *that?*"

"One from a concerned sister."

"Make that two concerned sisters."

"This is something new," Leah remarked dryly.

"Yes."

"Put down the flour, Leah. Talk to us."

Sensing that they wouldn't leave her alone until she answered them, she set down the flour, gripped the edge of the counter, and said to the cabinet's pickled wood, "It's no big thing. We met. We started talking. He's an interesting man. But he's the gardener.

He lives here, I live in Washington. He wears denim, I wear silk."

"Not now you don't," Caroline pointed out.

Leah wiped a hand on her jeans. "Yes, well, this place is different and besides, I'm cooking — or trying to cook. Honestly, you're making something out of nothing. Jesse and I are wrong for each other in a million ways. Okay, forget denim and silk. Try beer and champagne, beef stew and crepes Suzette. He does his traveling in winter, I do mine in summer. I mean, I can't stay here. I'm going away."

"Where are you going?"

She had walked into that one. Improvising, she said, "Montana, I think. The plans aren't firmed up yet. But if it isn't Montana, it'll be somewhere else, and then I'll be back in D.C. to chair the Cancer Society gala, while Jesse's here mowing the yard. I'm light, he's dark, I'm opera, he's reruns —"

"Reruns of what?" Annette asked.

Leah had no idea. She had never seen him watch television. When she was with him, he was engrossed in her. But reruns sounded good.

"Funny," Caroline said, "I would have pegged him for 'Twenty-Twenty.' Or PBS. He seems articulate and bright. You said he was self-educated. You called him a horti-culturalist. That implies smarts."

Leah half-turned. "He is smart."

"And good-looking."

"And polite."

"He's all of those things —" she vowed, stopping short.

"And more," Annette finished for her.

Leah made a face. Tugging a garbage bag tie from the drawer, she gathered her hair and twisted the tie around it. Wild hair was fine and dandy for walking along the bluff, but it was definitely in the way when she cooked. She thought of cutting it short, but felt a twinge. What was it Ginny had said? *And to think we used to hide this away.* As though Leah's hair, unbound, reminded Ginny of all she had renounced.

Tears came to her eyes. She pressed several fingers to her forehead and said without turning, "Why does life have to be so complex?"

"Sometimes it only seems complex," Caroline offered. "With a little sorting and organizing, the complex becomes simple."

"Oh," Leah breathed, "I don't know. I've been trying to sort and organize since last Monday. No. I take that back. I've been *ignoring* the situation since last Monday, and all the while I've been getting in deeper and deeper."

"Love?" Annette asked.

Leah sighed. "I guess."

"Sex?" Caroline asked.

What the hell. "Oh yeah."

"That's incredible," Annette said. "Where were we all this time?"

"Sleeping. Or shopping."

"You did it while we were *shopping?*"

Leah shot a look over her shoulder. She spoke slowly and pointedly. "While you were shopping, we talked. We walked along the bluff. I watched him work." She grew less pointed, more bewildered. "Think of what Mother was describing of her relationship with Will. That's what I have with Jesse. It's both the most exciting thing that's ever happened to me, and the most terrifying. I mean, Mother and Will, now Jesse and me. It's eerie."

"What does he say?"

Leah rolled her eyes. "He says it was meant to be. He's a romantic."

"Like Will."

"Uh-huh."

"And you're like Mother."

"No, I'm not."

"In terms of social life you are, certainly more so than either of us," Caroline said.

"In looks," Leah conceded, anxious to put

the misconception to rest once and for all. She turned to face her sisters. "Maybe in general lifestyle, but that's it. Mother was obsessed with maintaining her place in society. She loved the invitations, loved the company she kept. She was a stickler for convention. I'm not."

"Leah, look at your life!"

"I am. I'm not driven to impress people. I dress stylishly because that's what I've always done. I shop because that's what I've always done. Same with having my hair done and getting a manicure. Same with sitting through board meetings. It's just *what I do.*"

"But not what you want?" Caroline asked.

"It's what I do," Leah repeated, at a loss for anything better to say. Her life in Washington was familiar. She knew what to expect. There were no surprises. She could handle herself.

"Oh, Leah."

"Mother chose it," she said in an attempt to sort through her thoughts. "I just woke up one day and it's what I was doing."

"What would you rather?"

In a moment of pique, Leah crossed her arms over her chest. "Bake. I'd rather bake. I feel productive when I bake. When I'm done, I have a product to show for it."

"So bake," Caroline said. "Start a catering service. Open a restaurant."

Leah sighed. "It sounds simple. But it isn't."

"Why not?" Annette asked.

"Because I'm a dabbler, not a trained chef, and I don't want to go to school to become one. School and I never got along. That would take the fun out of it, for sure. Besides, restaurants are a dime a dozen in Washington. Same with catering services."

"So leave Washington."

"But I *love* Washington," she insisted, and it wasn't wholly a lie. Washington couldn't be beat when it came to culture. And some parts of it were just beautiful. Of course, she could live without the social climbers, the bores, and the humidity.

"If you love Washington, and you love Jesse, something has to give."

"Exactly," Leah cried. She knew that she had to move on with her life — she and Ellen had discussed it at length — but she had never dreamed that moving on would entail such upheaval.

"Stay here and open a bakery," Caroline suggested.

Leah gaped. "You're kidding."

"No."

"I can't stay here."

"Why not?"

"I just told you. I love Washington. I have commitments there. Besides, now that Mother is dead, we'll be selling Star's End."

Caroline looked at Annette. "Did we decide that?"

"I don't recall we discussed it at all."

"Maybe we should."

But Leah was uncomfortable. Deciding on the future of Star's End would bring other decisions to a head. "Not now. It's too soon. I don't *think* we should think about it until after Mother is buried." She turned back to the counter and reached for the flour.

"What are you afraid of?" Caroline asked quietly.

Leah turned her head. "Are you talking to me?"

"Come on, Leah."

Forget the flour. She turned around again, but held her ground. "I'm not afraid of anything." Except change. Except failure.

"You say you love Jesse."

"You say you love Ben," she tossed back.

"So I'm starting to rethink things. Maybe you should, too."

"What things are you rethinking?" Annette asked Caroline.

Leah wanted to know, too, but Caroline

wasn't being sidetracked. "Do you think Mother made the right decision leaving Will?"

Leah shrugged. "She had Daddy, and she had us."

"But she lost Will. She did the noble thing. Was it the right thing?"

"How can I answer that, Caroline?" Leah cried, exasperated. "I'm not in her shoes."

"No. But close. You're in love with a man whose lifestyle is the antithesis of yours. Staying with him means making major changes in your life. So do you make those changes, or don't you? Nobleness isn't a factor. You don't have a husband. By your own admission, you do things more out of habit than choice. Maybe it's time you changed that. Make a *choice*, Leah."

"Jesse's the gardener."

"Oh, *please*," Caroline barked. "Why are you playing the snob? Are you trying to anticipate what we're thinking about him? Well, if you are, you're wrong. I meant what I said the other day — my problem with Ben has *never* been that he doesn't come with papers, like we do. Things were different in Mother's day. People didn't marry out of their social class, or religion, or race. Today, those things are less important. At least, they should be. The fact that Jesse is a gardener is irrelevant."

"If you love him," Annette said. Her voice trailed off.

Leah sighed. She raised bewildered eyes to the ceiling. "I'm having trouble believing it, I guess. It happened so fast." Her gaze fell. "And then, there are the parallels to Mother and Will. I don't want to mistake sentimentality for something else." Of course, she'd been falling for Jesse before she ever knew about Ginny and Will, but that was beside the point.

"Has Jesse said he wants you to stay?"

Leah's insides moaned. "In every look."

It was Annette's turn to sigh. "That's so *romantic.*"

But Leah wasn't being lulled into submission. "There's more to a long-term relationship than romance. Romance fades. I know. It happened to me twice."

"Those two were nitwits."

Caroline added, "She's right. I could tell it first thing."

Leah felt a stir of her old insecurity. She was the dumb one, the one with a head full of fluff. "Really? How?"

"I watched them at your weddings. They were more interested in looking at who was watching them than in looking at you. They wanted people laughing at their jokes, hang-

438

ing on their every word. You were a prize."
She shook her head. "Bad match. Both of
them. It was obvious."

"If it was so obvious," Leah charged, "why
didn't you tell me?"

"Would you have listened?" Caroline shot
back.

"You were in love with being in love,"
Annette said.

"Who knows I'm not still?" Leah asked
with a touch of defiance, but the defiance
was for show. She was haunted by her own
inadequacies, where love was concerned.
"I've known Jesse Cray for all of five days.
That's *pathetic*."

"Maybe you just need more time."

"That's what I'm trying to *tell* you."

Caroline held up her hands and backed
off. "Okay. Take more time. But I have to
warn you, I can't stay here forever. Regardless of what I decide to do with it, my life is
in Chicago. Another week, and I'll have to
go back. Same with Annette. The house is
yours."

"But we're not *keeping* the house," Leah
argued.

Caroline turned to Annette. "How far
down that list did you get?"

"About halfway. Lillian's helping by calling her circle of friends. She wasn't any

439

more surprised than Gwen was. She said that Mother was too thorough with her farewells."

"She's dead," Leah continued to argue. "We can't keep the house."

But she might as well have saved her breath, because Caroline was heading for the door, asking Annette, who followed, "Will Lillian be coming for the funeral?"

"Yes. They'll stay in Portland Sunday night and drive here early Monday. It may be a good-sized group."

"Guys?" Leah tried again.

Caroline turned back. "Gwen is on her way. Better make use of the kitchen before she arrives. She's apt to give you a fight."

Irked that they weren't taking her seriously, she called, "She can fight all she wants. The fact is that Mother *built this kitchen for me.* If I want to use it, I *will.*" This time she turned in earnest to her muffins.

Caroline sat at the foot of the bed, marveling at the nature of the man Ben was, as she watched him sleep. He had set his work aside during the height of his creative season and weathered the wind on his motorcycle for the better part of thirty-six hours, speeding eastward to be with her. He hadn't

440

known Ginny had died. He hadn't even known she had finally arrived at Star's End. He had wanted to be with Caroline. That was all.

As she watched him, her insides went soft and melting, aching in ways that went beyond physical attraction, though there was that, too. He was sprawled, face down, covered by a sheet from his buttocks down. Above was a long expanse of skin that was firm and tanned, freckled shoulders, sturdy neck, mussed hair. She could feel every muscle of his back, though she didn't touch a one. Not now. But she had. Many, many times.

He stirred, shifting beneath the sheet with a deep breath that undulated over his back. Twisting his head around, he cracked open an eye. When he saw her, he smiled and held out a hand.

She scooted closer and took it, holding it to her throat, then her mouth.

"Whatcha thinkin'?" he whispered sleepily.

"That you're a beautiful man. That I still can't believe you're here. I was imagining awful things."

"Like what?"

"Like you'd left me for another woman."

"Missed me that much, huh?"

She smiled. "Yeah." When he gave a tiny tug, she stretched out beside him. She kissed him softly and let her fingers linger on his mouth, then trail down his throat to his Adam's apple.

It was such a male thing, an Adam's apple. Like body hair and muscularity and erections that told of morning desire. Such a male thing. Such a Ben thing.

She felt the vibration in his throat when he said, "I want us married."

"I know. I think I'm weakening."

The Adam's apple bobbed. "Really? How come?"

"Because you're right about things. Like my firm." She told him about Luther Hines, all of which had happened while he'd been on the road.

"If *I'd* heard the news," he swore, angry on her behalf, "I'd have called you first thing."

"But then I wouldn't have known how loyal my partners are. You had them pegged, Ben."

"Um-hmmm." He unzipped her jeans, slipped his hands in back, against her skin, and pulled her closer.

Whispering by his jaw, taking in the scents of sleep and awakening sexuality, she said, "How come you saw it and I didn't?"

442

"You saw it," he whispered back, inching the jeans down. "You knew what they were."

She sighed. Her insides were starting to hum. They always did when Ben touched her. He had a way of reaching in and turning her on. "I hate the idea of going back there."

He was up on his knees, working the jeans lower. "Don't. Open your own place."

She raised her hips to help. "Where?"

"Near me."

"But I can't practice in the country," she protested, kicking jeans and panties aside. "Not my kind of law. I need to be near a courthouse. That's where things happen."

"Then live with me and commute," he said, bringing her up to straddle his lap. "Set up an office at my place for the days when you don't have to be in court." He rocked her against him.

She breathed his name. Oh, yes, erections were a male thing. Huge ones were a Ben thing. "Your place is tiny," she managed, struggling to cling to the thought.

"So build on," he rumbled against her cheek. "Renovate the tool shed."

"What about law books? Mmmmm, Ben." He had slipped inside and was filling her fuller, fuller, ahhhh.

"Buy the damn books," he ground out,

laying her back on the bed and following her down.

She wound her legs around his hips and took him deeper yet. "A secretary? Associ-ates?"

"Hire them," he said with a thrust that drove her up against the sheets.

She clung to his neck, panting, burning from the inside out. "What about . . . a partner?" She abandoned the thought when he drove into her again, because the outside world dissolved. Ben filled her senses, controlled her body, had her blushing and sweating and writhing, while he brought her from one level of pleasure to another. He had her crying for more and reduced to total dependency, before he finally allowed her release.

She might have been furious, if she hadn't known how mutual the dependency was.

"God, did I miss you," he whispered in the thread of a breath when his body finally relaxed.

"I wasn't gone long."

"Too much. Too far."

"You're gone longer and farther when *you* work."

"Too much. Too far. All of it. I think I'm getting old." He slipped to the side and rose on an elbow, still breathing unevenly, but

444

intent. "Find a partner. Find two. Find ones you can trust."

"What if I can't find clients?"

"With your reputation? Fat chance."

"Litigators don't work on annual retainer. We have a constantly changing clientele. We never know from one year to the next how much or little work we'll have, and the work comes in clumps."

"What else is new?"

"But it's different in a firm. The firm covers during the slow times."

"So I'll cover the slow times," he said with a grin. "You can live the artist's life with me, hand to mouth, struggling, starving, praying for a case to come along, any case —"

She put a hand to his mouth. They both knew money wasn't the issue. "I don't want to fail."

Ben took a deep breath and kissed her fingertips away. "None of us does," he said gently. "But failure is relative to whatever your goals are. If your primary goal is to show those bastards in the firm that you can play their game, and you resign your partnership, you've failed. On the other hand, if your primary goal is to be a good lawyer —"

"I haven't been in control, have I?" she

asked. "They have. I've been deluding my-self."

"No. You haven't once compromised your integrity. That's a critical form of control."

"Ben?"

"Mmm?"

"How would our lives change if we were married?"

"Outwardly, not a whole lot. I assume you'd want to keep your name, since it's the one the legal community knows you by. You'd keep your apartment, if you work in the city, and your car. The change would be more inside us. Knowing the other one's waiting. Wanting the other one to be wait-ing."

Caroline imagined herself preparing for trial, working long into the night and rising at dawn. She thought of all the lawyers she knew whose marriages hadn't survived that. "Won't that make you angry?"

"Nope."

"Why not?"

He gave a one-shouldered shrug. "I have work of my own to do. I can keep busy. Besides, trials end. Even the best litigators have to take breaks. As long as I know you're mine during those, I can wait."

"What about kids?" she asked without planning to, but she couldn't take back the words. She hadn't ever wanted kids, before. But she had never been as close to being too old to have them, before.

"That's up to you," Ben said.

"Do you want them?"

"I can live without them. Then again, they'd be nice. I can go either way, babe. What I can't go either way about is you."

Annette tried to keep busy. She finished calling Virginia's friends and family, so that Caroline might spend time with Ben. She called Portland to book hotel rooms for those who planned to attend the funeral, and called Downlee Taxi to arrange transportation for the same. She confirmed their plans with the minister, and passed word on to the undertaker.

The scents wafting up from the kitchen told her that Leah had finished her muffins and moved on to other things. She smelled apples baking. She smelled chicken frying. The latter, once cooled, turned out to be lunch, which was a quiet affair on the back deck, with Leah preparing and Ben serving, and the four of them sitting close, feeling the splendor of the setting and the sadness it brought. They talked of Ginny. They talked of flowers and the sea. They talked, openly and without apology, about wanting the funeral to be something Ginny would have approved of.

Caroline seemed quieter with Ben there, calmer, more peaceful. Annette felt an ache of envy as she watched them. They communed in subtle ways — with the touch of a hand, a shared glance — like old lovers whose familiarity bred contentment. It was the way Annette felt with Jean-Paul.

She missed him. The loneliness of losing Ginny seemed sharper for his absence. Still, it would have been foolish for him to come.

How lucky Caroline was to have Ben there.

It occurred to Annette that Jesse should have been there with Leah, but if Leah thought so, she wasn't saying. Rather, she sat with her back to the lawn and the flower beds, the places where Jesse might have been. Poor Leah. She was as confused as Annette was lonely.

When Caroline led Ben off to show him around and Leah returned to the kitchen, Annette went upstairs. She might have called Jean-Paul, had she not specifically told him to take the children out. She wondered what they were doing. She wondered if they missed her.

Curling up on her unmade bed, she fell asleep. When she awoke, it was nearly five in the afternoon. Leah was still at it, cooking different things now, if her nose was correct. She caught fleeting impressions of wine and tomatoes and curry, and imagined a stew of some sort. And vegetables. A robust soup. Gwen's specialty.

The smells were rich, as were the sounds of the sea, but still she felt empty. She sat on the edge of the bed and reached for the phone. Then she thought about the time difference between Maine and Missouri, and returned her hand to her lap.

She thought about Ginny, to whom time no longer held meaning. Rising, she went down the hall. Gwen must have indeed returned, because the bed had been neatly made, but everything else was as it had been at the moment of Ginny's death.

Annette touched the linen runner that crossed the dresser top. A gold-edged tray lay centered there. On it were a tiny vase with its spray of phlox, a delicate gold frame with a picture of Annette and her sisters as young children, and a beautiful perfume bottle.

She raised the latter to her nose and marveled at the exactness with which Ginny's perfumer had matched the scent of the beach roses. She tried to imagine what it must have been like for Ginny to have lived with the smell, year after year, to have with her always such a vivid clear picture of what she had lost.

Feeling that loss with a profundity that cut straight to her own soul, Annette made a mournful sound. She trailed her hand along the dresser, then the dressing table, then the back of the straight chair before it. She opened the closet and looked inside at the clothes the movers had brought, a collection of silk and linen and wool, all in Ginny's muted colors — with the exception of a brighter something.

She pushed clothing aside to reach that brighter something. It was a dress with floral splashes of yellow and red, and as she looked at it, she felt an odd sense of the familiar. She had seen it before, a long, long time before, as a child playing in forbidden places. She remembered thinking at the time that it was beautiful, but that since Ginny never wore it, it must have belonged to her mother.

Only now she understood — and in that instant knew that the ivory suit they had given the undertaker would never do at all.

She turned quickly, desperate to remedy the situation before a horrible mistake was made. Then she gasped. Jean-Paul was at the door, looking hesitant, but more beautiful than she had ever seen him.

Her eyes filled. Brokenly, thinking, absurdly, that if she didn't come up with a rational explanation for what she was holding, Jean-Paul might prove to be a mirage, too, she said, "Mother must have worn this that summer with Will. She should be buried in it."

"*Oui,*" Jean-Paul said softly.

Not a mirage at all, but *his* voice, so quiet and reassuring. "Jean-Paul?"

"Being independent is fine, but for another time, okay?"

She smiled through her tears. "Jean-Paul."

"You said to do something wonderful with the children to remember your mother, and I couldn't think of anything better. Nor could they."

Nor, with the wisdom of hindsight, could Annette.

TWENTY-ONE

Though the funeral was set for midday Monday, the townsfolk began dropping by on Sunday afternoon. If there were curiosity seekers among them, they didn't let on. No questions were asked. No stealthy eyes explored the house. Those who came were often shy, always pleasant and apologetic, and rarely stayed for long.

"Just offerin' our condolences."

"I remember your mother. She was all smiles."

"Shame she didn't have more time here."

Rarely did they come empty-handed, such that when dinnertime arrived, the dining room table was laden with casseroles, salads, and more goodies than Leah could have baked in a week.

Not that she stopped. If she stopped, she would start to think, and she didn't want to do that.

Mercifully Gwen understood, and while

she put her own grief to work coordinating last-minute details that neither Caroline nor Annette had the heart for, she yielded the kitchen to Leah, who continued to cook — a chilled soup to be put out the next day, a poached salmon with dill sauce, a fruit compote, rolls of every shape, size, and flavor.

"Hi."

The sound of his voice stirred a tingling inside. As confused as she was, as *frightened,* she couldn't help but smile. "Hi," she said without looking up. She was stuffing mushrooms. It was delicate work.

"Aren't you tired?"

"I'm okay."

"Your sisters are worried."

"Did they send you in?"

"No. I'm worried, too. There's plenty of food, Leah. You don't have to keep at this."

"But we've invited the whole town. If they come here after the funeral, we'll need all this and more."

"They'll bring more. Julia's bringing a truckload."

"Mother would like the sound of *that,*" Leah remarked in a high voice, close to laughter and tears, a breath away from hysteria. "Her greatest fear was that she'd throw a party and run out of something."

Jesse drew her close. Against her forehead, he said, "She would approve of all you've done. Now she'd want you to spend time with the others."

"But I have to do this now. I won't have time in the morning. I'll be doing the flowers then."

"I'll do the flowers. It's my job."

"But I want to," she said, only then raising her eyes. He was wearing a pair of gray slacks and a sweater, looking every bit as urbane as Jean-Paul or Ben. She started to say something but couldn't.

He gave a small hitch of his chin. "What?"

She swallowed. "You don't look like a gardener." He didn't act like one, either. In the course of the last twenty-four hours, he had talked light, shadow, and F-stops with Ben, debated ecosystem preservation with Jean-Paul, and taken Annette's kids on a tour of the rocks that had given the adults a welcome breather.

He was a remarkable man, able to slip from one guise to another with apparent ease. She wished she could, too, but change had never been her forte. She liked doing things she knew she was good at. She didn't like taking risks.

Loving Jesse was a *major* risk. Not that she could help it. One look at him and she ached inside for everything he was and might be in her life. The thought of it terrified her.

Not wanting to discuss it, not wanting to *think* about it, she asked, "What do you think of my family?"

"Nice people."

"A little overpowering?"

"Nah."

"*I* think they are."

"That's because you compare yourself to them. But you're different, Leah. Softer."

"Oh no. I'm the jet setter. I'm tough."

"You were made for this place."

"My friends in Washington would disagree. I throw the best parties around."

"Yes. I can see that."

"This isn't a party, Jesse. It's a funeral. It doesn't count."

"You could open Star's End to the town once a month and have a *great* party."

"But I have to be in Washington."

"You don't have to."

"*Want* to."

"Do you?"

Her dilemma in a nutshell. She made a small, bewildered sound and turned back to her mushrooms.

He didn't say anything else, simply kissed her forehead, and let himself out.

■ ■ ■ ■

Monday dawned the kind of brilliant June day that Virginia would have loved. Fighting the sadness of that, Leah was up early cutting and arranging flowers. She had a good eye and skilled hands, and found reward in what she did.

But she was tired. She hadn't slept much the night before, what with cooking late, then sitting wide-eyed at her bedroom window for hours until she finally gave in and ran across the lawn to Jesse's. Nor did she sleep there for more than a few minutes at a time. She couldn't. Her mind wouldn't settle.

By eleven, the out-of-town guests had arrived from Portland and were having coffee and danish on the deck. By eleven-thirty, the locals had started to wander up the drive. By eleven-forty-five, the minister arrived, and by eleven-fifty, the hearse. Flanked by those whose lives she had touched most closely, the casket was carried to the spot on the bluff where the beach roses bloomed.

At noon, with the sun high overhead, the gulls arcing widely and the waves spewing their froth up against the rocky headland, the minister said a few words, general words of love and attachment and return. Then began the slow walk along the bluff to the graveyard on the rise.

Leah barely heard the minister there. She was lost in thoughts of love and loss, drowning in them while tears filled her eyes and blurred the abyss of the grave and the vast horizon beyond.

She wept softly, pressing a tissue to her upper lip, leaning heavily against Jesse, who kept an arm around her. He was warm and alive, as nothing in a graveyard could be. She took the comfort he offered, able neither to resist it nor to hide it from anyone who cared to see.

Once back at the house, she was the hostess she had trained so long to be, greeting guests, generating small talk, seeing that the food was plentiful and the wine flowed. Later she couldn't say to whom she had talked or what she ate. She could remember the gut-wrenching sadness she felt at the moment her mother's casket was lowered into the ground, the roaring inside her head that was grief to the extreme, Jesse's warmth.

She remembered fighting that need as the day wore on and losing the battle at night. Jesse's cottage was a haven, a place where she could let the sensual blot out all else. There was forgetfulness in his arms, and love and security and excitement, and if she didn't sleep there either, her time was well spent.

Inevitably morning came. She returned to the main house to shower and put on fresh jeans and a T-shirt. Lacking the taste for makeup or the strength to do anything with her hair but run a brush once through the wet strands, she joined the crowd in the kitchen.

She let Annette make breakfast. She let Caroline make a pot of tea. Bone-tired and emotionally drained, she took refuge in a corner of the sofa, lay her head against its back, and tucked her bare feet beneath her. Eyes closed, she let herself be lulled by the banter between Annette and her kids.

"Are you okay, Aunt Leah?"

She opened her eyes to Devon and smiled. "I'm fine."

"You look tired. And sad."

"I am, both."

"Want some tea?"

"Mmm. That sounds good."

A short time later, a warm mug was nudged into her hand. A short time after that, the kitchen grew quiet. She heard the clink of dishes in the dishwasher and the splash of water in the sink. She heard silence, then soft footsteps. Then she felt movement beside her on the sofa.

"Leah? Let's talk." It was Caroline's voice, but Leah sensed that she wasn't alone. When she opened her eyes, she saw Annette perched on the coffee table.

She looked from one face to the other. "That serious?"

"That serious," Annette said. "You and Jesse. Important stuff."

Leah closed her eyes again. She wasn't up for a serious talk, particularly not one about Jesse. She could think of him as she'd last seen him, sprawled buck naked on his bed. She couldn't think further than that.

Caroline gave her knee a sharp shake. "Don't tune us out. This is your future."

"Right. *My* future. You needn't worry about it."

"If we don't, who will?"

"The same person who always has. Me."

"Well, you are clearly doing the worrying," Caroline observed, "since you look like you've been through a wringer. The question is whether it's getting you anywhere."

"You can't hold it in, Leah."

"Maybe we can help."

Ellen McKenna had tried to help. She had taught Leah to stand back and view her life

459

objectively. But it was more easily said than done. Leah couldn't be objective where Jesse was concerned. He stirred her so deeply and on such a visceral level that she couldn't separate out the elements of the attraction.

"I'm very tired," she said. She wanted them to go away. At least she thought she did. There was something to be said for having people care. Unless they pushed too much. Yes, she wanted them to go away. At least, for a little while.

When no one spoke, she wondered if they'd done just that, but when she opened her eyes, she saw them both there, waiting.

She sighed. "What do you want from me?"

"We want you to come to a decision."

"No," Leah corrected, "you want me to come to the decision you've already reached yourselves. But it doesn't work that way. You don't know what I want or need. You can't possibly know whether Jesse is right for me."

"He's right for you," Caroline said.

"How do you *know?*" Leah asked, desperate to be convinced.

"He looks only at you."

"For God's sake, Caroline, that's no basis for judgment."

"Sure, it is."

460

"Maybe it's an obsession. Like father, like son."

"Leah," Annette chided. "You know it's not. He's too normal. Too rational. Too . . . mainstream."

Leah knew all those things, damn it. She slid lower in the sofa and closed her eyes.

"You can't avoid it forever," Caroline warned.

Her eyes snapped back open. "Why not? You have."

Caroline shook her head. "No more."

"You've decided?" Annette asked expectantly.

Caroline scrubbed at her no-nonsense hair in a sheepish gesture. "Yeah. I think we'll do it. Nothing big, just a civil ceremony one afternoon."

"No floor-length gown with a long train and a dozen attendants?" Annette teased, but Leah could see that she was pleased, and Leah was, too. Ben was a wonderful guy. He had loved Caroline for a long time.

"What about the firm?" Leah asked, recalling all too well an earlier discussion. "You said it wouldn't work, being in the firm and being married to Ben."

"It won't."

"So, what are you going to do?"

Caroline thought for a minute. Then she

461

pushed out of the sofa and went to the kitchen phone. Leah heard a dial tone, followed by eleven melodious beeps, then a ringing. The voice that came over the speakerphone had a tinny edge. "Graham Howard's office."

"This is Caroline St. Clair. Is Graham around?"

Caroline looked speculatively at Leah and Annette while she waited to be put through.

"What are you doing?" Leah asked.

Caroline pursed her lips.

"Caroline," Annette cautioned.

Caroline folded her arms over her chest.

"Caroline!" Graham shouted. His testiness carried easily into the family room. "It's about time you called back. I've been trying to reach you since yesterday. Didn't you get my messages?"

"Didn't you get mine?"

"Yes, and I am sorry about your mother, but we have an emergency here, big problems with the FenCorp conspiracy case. Pete Davis has been representing the corporation for months now, preparing for trial, but he got himself in something of a fix —"

"What kind of fix?"

"It's nothing really —"

"What *kind* of fix?"

Graham sighed. "He was found in bed

with the wrong woman. It really was nothing —"

"A woman other than his wife?"

"A two-bit call girl who just happened to
be part of a ring that the government's been
watching. Pete was in the wrong place at
the wrong time. There wouldn't be any
problem if the *Sun-Times* hadn't listed
names, but now that it has, FenCorp doesn't
want any part of the notoriety. They say it
won't help their case, and they're right. So
we want you to front for Peter. He's done
all the work. He'll tell you what to do. You're
not sleeping with the mayor or anything,
are you?"

Caroline had approached Leah and
Annette. As he railed on about the evils of
the Fourth Estate, she said, "This is a
perfect example of what I've been dealing
with. The man doesn't care that Mother just
died. He doesn't care that I'm on vacation.
He had *absolutely* no sympathy when one
of his colleagues stole a case from me. And
he has the morals of a pig."

"Are you there, Caroline?" Graham asked.

Caroline took her time returning to the
phone. "I'm here."

"Would you pick up? The reception isn't
very good. I'm hearing background voices.
Better still, get on the first plane back here."

"Sorry, Graham. This is my vacation."

"You can vacation later in the summer."

"I'm mourning my mother."

"That's understandable, even admirable." The voice hardened. "But you also have a responsibility to the firm."

"Like they have a responsibility to me?"

"The firm's been good to you."

"Baloney," she said and let loose. "The firm's made money on me from day one. I wasn't a rookie fresh out of law school. No one had to train me. I was a lateral appointee. I came with my own skills, my own contacts, my own reputation. You people got a good thing when you got me, but you blew it."

"What are you saying?"

"I'm saying that you hired your token woman, then you tried to put her in her place. You made me wait longer than any of the others for a partnership. You scrutinized my time sheets more than you did any of the others. You criticized my work — don't deny it, Graham. I've heard more than one reference to PMS."

"Perhaps with good cause," he barked. "Clearly something's bothering you, but you aren't expressing it well."

"Let me be more blunt, then," Caroline said, grinning at Leah and Annette. "I quit."

There was a moment's silence from the phone, then a patronizing, "You're upset. It's an emotional time. You've just suffered a loss."

"Actually," Caroline leaned against the counter and crossed her ankles, "I'm feeling quite good."

"Look. Why don't we talk later this afternoon."

"No, Graham. We'll talk next Monday when I get back in the office, and the only topic of discussion then will be which of my cases stay with you and which come with me. Goodbye." She lifted the receiver, dropped it back on its hook, then turned and grinned even more broadly. "God, that felt good."

Leah was amazed. "I can't believe you did it."

"Are you sure it's what you want?" Annette asked.

Caroline gave a great sigh that suggested she had just released a heavy load. "Yes. It's what I want. I've done the big law firm thing. I've made it. They're just holding me back now."

"Holding you back," Leah echoed. "My God, what's *next*?"

Caroline approached the sofa. "I'm not sure. My own firm, I guess. Yeah, that sounds right. My own firm, my own hours, my own people. My own rules for a change."

Leah shot a glance at Annette. As far as she knew, Caroline had been living by her own rules for years.

Caroline intercepted the glance. "Funny, how you create an image for yourself. You even buy into it sometimes. I may have *thought* I was ruling myself, but I wasn't. I was being ruled by a grand image of the tough lady lawyer who conquers the world. And I did it, in a manner of speaking. At a price."

"Ben?" Annette asked.

"Ben. Mother. You. Me."

Leah was stunned. This was tough, arrogant, authoritarian Caroline. "But you're driven. You've always been driven. Can you suddenly change that?"

Caroline frowned toward the windows, then the floor. She wandered distractedly around the sofa and sat down. In a quieter voice, she said, "The drive seems dispersed. I can't get a grasp on it."

"Of course not," Annette said. "Not with everything else that's been going on around here."

"But that's it, I think," Caroline mused. "Mother is dead. Maybe the drive went with her. Maybe it was only rebellion."

Leah didn't believe that. "You couldn't be as good as you are, if that's all it was. You're the firstborn. The firstborn is always driven."

"But the edge is off," Caroline insisted. "Okay, so it's in my nature to go after things whole hog, so even if I start my own firm, I'll do it right, but I feel different now. I don't have to show Mother up." Her eyes grew moist. So did Leah's. "But hey, she'd probably approve more of this than the other. She'd love the idea of my getting married. Now that I know about Will, I can almost imagine that she'd like the idea of my marrying Ben."

And of my marrying Jesse, Leah thought. She would *love* that idea — approval, at last. But that didn't mean it was the best thing for Leah, and it was her life, after all. She dropped her eyes to her lap.

"So," Caroline announced, smugly patting Leah's knee. "That leaves you."

"Why don't we just bask in your happiness for a while?" Leah asked.

"Because we want yours, too."

"I'll handle it."

"We want to help," Annette joined in. "With Mother gone, we're all you've got."

"Mother never helped," Leah reminded her and seconds later felt the force of

467

Caroline's gaze.

"So we'll do better than she did. Isn't that what's driven all of us?"

Oh, yes. But *how* to do better? Leah didn't know whether Ginny should have given up everything and stayed with Will. She didn't know whether Ginny would have been happier that way. None of them did. None of them *could.*

"What are you afraid of?" Caroline asked more gently.

She sighed. "Failure."

"But if you love him —" Annette began.

Leah sent her a pleading look. "Love worked for you. It hasn't always worked for me."

"So if it doesn't, it doesn't, but at least you'll have tried."

"If it doesn't work, I'll be *destroyed.*"

"Because you love him so much."

"Because I love him so *weird.* It's different from anything I've ever felt. It scares me to death."

"Because it's all-consuming?"

"Because it's unreal?"

"Because the hunger goes on and on," Leah said. "The more it's satisfied, the worse it gets. Where does it end? What am I supposed to *do* with it? I have a *life.* I can't give it up."

Annette made a short, desperate sound. "That's what Mother said way back when."

Caroline sat back. "It's the all-or-nothing syndrome. It must run in the family. But does it have to, damn it? Do I have to be a lawyer to the exclusion of everything else? Do you have to be a wife and mother the same way, Annette? Does it have to be Washington or Maine, Leah? Why can't it be a little of both?"

"Because a little isn't good enough," Leah cried.

"Okay. Why can't it be a *lot* of both?"

"Because I can't *give* a lot of both. I don't have it in me."

"Who says?"

"I know."

"Have you ever tried?"

"How could I? I've never met anyone like Jesse before."

"He's all you've ever wanted," Annette said. "You can't throw it away."

Leah gave a high, slightly frantic laugh. "How do I *keep* it?"

"You're afraid of failure."

"That's what I said," she cried and with a burst of energy rose from the sofa.

"Leah!"

"Don't leave."

"I need air." She could hear them following and quickened her step.

"You have to talk about it, Leah."

"We want to help."

She spun around and held up a hand. When they stopped in their tracks, she said a quiet, "I need to think. Please?"

They remained still, in reluctant acquiescence.

"Thank you," she whispered and went out the door. Eyes low, she crossed the deck, passed the pool, and made for the front of the house. She didn't have a plan. Instinct led her on, through a world made surreal by a tepid mist.

She set off across the grass at a determined pace, her bare feet padding as rhythmically as the distant blare of the Houkabee horn.

I love him.

But I have a life in Washington. It's well defined. I'm comfortable with it.

I could cook here. I could garden. I could knit Jesse sweaters.

I don't know how to knit.

I could learn, but I might be lousy at it, and then Jesse would be disappointed.

I wouldn't want to disappoint him. Disillusion him. Fail him.

But I love him.

She began to run. The pebbles on the drive slowed her, but only for a minute. As

470

soon as she reached the grass, she was off again. She left the house behind, passed the shrubbery, the flowers, the heathers, the roses. She continued on down the bluff and came to a panting halt on the rocks.

A fog was in. She couldn't see a thing, this outside world as opaque and impenetrable as the other, the one inside.

Dredging up last bits of strength, she broke off toward the woods. She found the path and followed it, maintaining a steady pace, if more gingerly, over pine needles and roots. When the woods finally opened to the meadow, she lurched to a halt. Gasping for air, thinking about nothing at all except that the wildflowers were more beautiful than ever in the mist, she took another staggering step, then another. Finally, awash in a sea of blue, white, and yellow, she fell to her knees and sat back on her heels. She put her hands to the ground and took great gulps of air.

Gradually the gulping eased and her heartbeat slowed, leaving her devoid of energy and dead tired. She shifted to the side, then, uncaring that everything was wet, continued on down until she lay on her back among the wildflowers. She closed her eyes. The world around her was filled with the musk of damp earth and weedy grass. She breathed it in, breathed it deeply, let it spin a containing web around those other warring thoughts. Then she slept.

Washington was hot and humid. She had to wait twenty minutes for a cab, standing in the heavy air in city clothes, a skirt that cinched her waist and shoes that threw her weight onto the balls of her feet. The cab wasn't air-conditioned, and in deference to a presidential motorcade, traffic going over Arlington Memorial Bridge wasn't going anywhere at all.

She arrived at her townhouse to find it stifling. In her absence, the air-conditioning had gone on the blink. She called the company that held her service contract, but the servicemen were all on the road. She was promised a call the next day.

Resigned, she found brief relief in a shower. But when she toweled off and tried to put makeup on, it melted as quickly as she worked. Her hair was just as uncooperative. It insisted on curling. She pulled it back, knotted and pinned it, but wisps escaped and coiled. She wet them and pushed them straight. They kinked back up. She gelled them. They stayed. For five minutes. Then curled.

Despairingly she looked at herself in the

mirror. The chairperson of the Cancer Society gala couldn't go anywhere looking this way.

So she put on dark glasses and a floppy straw hat, and took a cab to the hair shop, where it was blessedly cool. Her hairdresser blew her hair straight, then, without a word of warning, took scissors to the long, flowing front and gave her bangs before she knew what he was about.

She hated it on sight. Dismayed, she tried to soothe herself by having her makeup done, but the artist put red on her cheeks and yellow on her lids. Leah was horrified. She *never* put red on her cheeks. Maybe pale pink or bronze, but never anything as harsh as red. And as for the yellow, her *hair* was pale yellow. She needed contrast, preferably smoky lilac or gray. Yellow made her look jaundiced.

Still she said nothing. If she threw a tantrum, the whole world would know. Gossip spread like wildfire in a town as hungry for it as Washington was, and it could be fatal. People were bumped from the A-list for far less than a temper tantrum.

Not that she was on the A-list. It was more like the A-minus list. Even the B-plus list. She had never been to the White House.

Feeling ugly, jaundiced, and socially

second-rate, she closeted herself in the booth with the pay phone, deposited a quarter, and punched out Susie MacMillan's number.

"MacMillan residence."

"Mrs. MacMillan, please."

"I'm sorry. Mrs. MacMillan isn't here."

"This is Leah St. Clair. I thought she was returning from vacation yesterday."

"She did. But she and the ambassador were invited to spend the weekend on the Dunkirks' yacht. They won't be back until Monday."

Leah deposited another quarter and punched out Jill Prince's number. "Jill. It's Leah. I just got back to town and am positively roasting in this heat. I thought I'd cool off over dinner at the Occidental. Want to meet me there?"

"Sorry, Leah, but I can't. We have a crowd coming over. It was a last minute thing — I mean, what with our just getting back from Quebec and all. I'd ask you to join us, but the table's already set with placecards, and the numbers are even. You know how it is."

"Sure. Okay. Another time."

Feeling *single* now, as well as ugly, jaundiced, and socially second-rate, she pushed in another quarter. This time she called Monica Savins. Monica was divorced. There

474

wouldn't be any even-number business.

"Hey, Monica, how are you?" she asked when Monica picked up.

"Leah? My God, Leah, you are the one person in the world that I absolutely have to talk to. I can't believe you're back in town. This is incredible timing. Totally fortuitous. You have to help me, Leah. I really messed up for tonight. I made a date with David — you know David, he's at Justice — and then I got a call from Michael — you don't know Michael, he's with the administration — and he invited me to the White House. I mean, we're talking an intimate little group — the president, the first lady, Michael and me — and a few others, but I can't pass it up. It's *the White House.* Only David's expecting me to go with him to a dinner at the Bolivian Embassy, and if he has to go alone, he'll be furious. You know him, Leah. Will you go?"

Leah knew him all right. She knew that he was overweight, that he talked about nothing but law, that he sweated too much, and that he smoked cigars.

"Ah, gosh, Monica, I can't. I have other plans. Maybe Donna Huntington can help you out?"

She slipped in one last quarter and made one last call. "Hi, Ellen. I need your help."

"No, you don't, Leah. You know what you have to do."

"I have to stand back and look objectively at my life, but *nothing* in my life prepared me for Jesse. He's like no other man I've ever known."

"Well, it's about time! You've picked some bastards, Leah."

"They weren't bastards."

"Then what would you call them?"

"Immature."

"What else?"

"Self-centered."

"Try one more time."

Leah sighed. "Bastards."

"Why did you pick them, then?"

"I don't know."

"Of course, you do. You were so desperate for love that you jumped the gun. You listened to your heart, but your brain was out to lunch. If it had been on the job, it would have told you to wait before you married either of those guys, but you were caught up in the romance of it, and scared to be without."

"I'm scared now, too."

"That's natural. You're taking a big step. Only this time your brain is saying the same thing as your heart. Do it, Leah. I can't do it for you. You're the one in the driver's seat."

"But I'm a *lousy* driver."

Ellen sighed. "I don't have time for this now, Leah. I have patients who need me. You don't."

Seconds later, Leah heard a dial tone. Feeling abandoned, she hung up the phone, threaded her purse over her shoulder, and set out on foot through the city streets. Within minutes her hair began to curl. Then her makeup began to run. She couldn't find a cab on Connecticut Avenue, so she kept walking until she reached Dupont Circle. She found a cab there, but by that time she was drenched with sweat, so she went straight home and got back in the shower.

Wrapped in a towel, she huddled in the dark of her apartment, more alone and lonely than ever before. The doorbell rang. On a wild burst of hope, she ran down the three flights and peered through the peephole, but the smell that crept beneath the door was a dead giveaway. She wasn't surprised to see a fat face, glistening with sweat, and a cigar.

She sank down against the door, hugged her knees to her chest, and in spite of the sweltering heat, began to shiver.

■ ■ ■ ■

Not heat, but cold. Not cold, exactly, but cool, on her arms and feet, both bare. She was lying on her side, her ear to something more giving than the marble in her hall. She opened her eyes to tall grass and flowers. Wildflowers. The meadow.

She felt a great swell of relief. Not Washington, but Downlee. Not heat, but mist. Not congested avenues, but pine-strewn paths. Not traffic circles littered with deviants and the homeless, but a large meadow heaped with plants. Not David, but Jesse.

Jesse.

She sat up and pushed the tangle of hair back from her face. It was curling as riotously as the Indian blanket bloomed, a tumult of red tipped in yellow, long blond waves, no bangs, as right for this place as they were right for her.

They were natural, those curls. They fit. She didn't know why she had fought them so long, couldn't think of a single reason that held any merit at all.

She put her head back and filled her lungs with the moist air of the meadow. It was fresh and clear, inspiring, nourishing, healing. Then she righted her head and saw him.

Jesse. Sitting some twenty feet away, head and chest above the flowers, watching her.

She went forward on her knees, parting patches of flowers, never once taking her eyes from his. She didn't stop when she reached him, but continued right on until she was wrapped around him, arms and legs.

His arms went around her and drew her in close.

"I don't know what it was about, all the agonizing," she whispered, "I don't want to be there. I want to be here."

"But you have a life there," he argued, as she had so many times herself.

"It's the one I fell into because I didn't have anything else, and I stayed in it because it was safer that way, but it's not the one I want." She remembered every discouraging detail of her dream. Yes, she loved Washington. But could she live there again? Knowing Jesse was here? "I kept thinking this wasn't real. It was too good, too strong."

"It still is."

"I know, but real or not, I want it." She became aware of her limbs. They hugged him, secure without being desperate. Like everything else about Jesse, they fit.

"Downlee is a parochial little town," he cautioned.

"Not parochial. Just little. But that's okay. I feel comfortable here." Yes, everyone knew everyone else's business, but there was something to be said for the intimacy of that, for the knowledge that people cared. No one in Washington cared, not the way she wanted them to. Gossip there carried a sting. Here it was a gossamer thread binding the town together.

"You may be bored."

"In a place that sells cappuccino makers? I have ten times more to do here, than I ever had in Washington," she said, realizing it was true. She drew back to look at him, to drink in a face that was rough-hewn and handsome, to drown in eyes that spoke of yesterday and tomorrow, of sunshine and mist and waves that exploded into brilliant bits of light, and she knew she was right. "Not bored. Never bored." She skimmed her fingertips over his cheekbone to his jaw, then his mouth. Then she smiled.

TWENTY-TWO

Wendell Coombs was scowling as he lowered himself onto the left end of the long wooden bench. His bones ached. It hadn't been a good day. Hadn't been a good week. Hadn't been a good month. Things were happening around Downlee that he didn't like one bit.

With a grunt of displeasure, he set his mug on his knee. The mug held vegetable juice. He had given up on coffee.

"Clarence," he muttered toward the right end of the bench.

Clarence Hart nodded. "Wendell."

"Gonna be a sticky one."

"Ayuh."

Wendell raised his mug, touched it to his mouth, put it down without a sip. He didn't want vegetable juice. He wanted coffee, but not the prissy stuff the grocery store was brewing. He wanted real coffee, like Mavis used to make. But Mavis had closed her door and moved to Bangor. To a retirement community. Damned if they'd ever get *him* into one of those things. Not that stayin' here was so great, what with Downlee goin' to the dogs. Every day there was less of the old and more of the new.

"Heeya the news?" he asked Clarence.

"Depends what it is."

"They ain't sellin' Stah's End." He was as dismayed now as when he'd first heard it.

"Ayuh."

He glowered at Clarence. "How'd you know?"

"Guessed."

"Dumb thing, if y'ask me. Place is a monstrosity."

It had been once. But the St. Clairs had fixed it up nice. At least, that was what Clarence thought. June thought so, too. And Gus, and Cal, and Edie.

"All that white wood and glass," Wendell muttered. "Fancy rugs. Funny food."

"Y'didn't have to go see."

"Yes, suh. Had to pay my respects like evra'one else."

Clarence drew on his empty pipe. He reached into his pocket for his tobacco pouch.

"My brothuh Bahney said the funeral cost ovah ten thousand dollahs," Wendell an-

482

nounced.

"Nah."

"Yes, suh. 'Coss, most of that was to pay Fathah to say somethin' nice."

"Father doesn't chahge. People just make a donation."

"And the moah they donate, the bettuh he speaks. Mebbe they paid him the whole ten — not that I believe all he said." He barked out a sound. " 'Gracious philanthropist,' hah. She was greedy. The wealthy always ah. Don't like what she did to Stah's End, eithuh. Kinda gaudy, if y'ask me."

Clarence opened his pouch, took the pipe from his mouth, and dipped it inside. "It wasn't so bad."

"Tell me that afta they been here five yeahs. Afta those kids'a been runnin' 'round town every summah. Afta the mob's taken ovah sellin' Christmas trees from the Vets."

Clarence pushed tobacco into the bowl of his pipe, returned the pipe to his mouth, and folded the pouch.

"Her death was a sign," Wendell warned. "She come up heeya, stepped foot in that house, and boom, that's it. They should be sellin'. We should be tellin' 'em to. If we thought we had trouble b'foah, we got big-guh trouble now."

Clarence lit a match. "Not many think so but you."

"Well, whadda *they* know. They ain't old enough to know much. Young kids an' ahtsies. And computahs."

Clarence was getting tired of listening to Wendell beat a dead dog. There were times when he thought of staying home with June. 'Course, she'd have him *doing* the wash, as well as carrying it out. He supposed he could stick it out here.

He drew on his pipe several times until the tobacco had caught, then put out the match with a flick of his wrist and blew a stream of smoke into the air.

Wendell waved it away and glared. "Got somethin' to say?"

"Ain't no computahs at Stah's End."

"Not yet."

"You evah work one?" He might as well have asked if Wendell had ever worn a dress, for Wendell's look of horror. But Clarence didn't feel any horror. "Howahd was showin' me what it could do. Got news the newspapuh didn't have. Got scoahs from late games out west. Red Sox lost."

Wendell grunted.

Clarence eyed him. "Bet'cha didn't know that."

"Could'a guessed," Wendell grumbled.

Clarence took a deep, satisfying draw. He had just finished exhaling a wide ribbon of smoke when Callie Dalton came up the steps. He touched a finger to his cap. "Mawnin', Callie."

"Mawnin', Clarence." She glided on past and disappeared into the store.

"Nasty woman," was Wendell's under-the-breath assessment.

Clarence didn't agree. Callie and George played Scrabble with him and June sometimes. Clarence liked them just fine.

Wendell was glaring at him again. " 'Coss, you probably like the St. Claya's, too."

Clarence looked out over Main Street. It was a peaceful morning, always a peaceful morning in Downlee. "Me an' lots'a othuhs. Face it, Wendell. Ya losin' the waw."

"Only b'cause people like you side with the enemy."

"I don't see no enemy."

"You wouldn't." Wendell snorted and angled himself away from Clarence. Then it occurred to him to wise Clarence up. Wendell happened to live next door to Potts, who happened to be the undertaker. Turning back, he said, "Heeya 'bout her dress?"

Clarence crossed one leg over the other.

"Potts said it was all yella' an' red," Wendell scoffed. "Imagine burying her in something like that." He gave a disdainful click of his tongue. "Good thing the casket was closed." He shook his head. "Poah Will."

"Will's dead. He won't know a thing."

"She shouldn't be buried theya."

"She had a right."

"Jesse should'a stopped it." Wendell made a sputtering sound. "Jesse. Lotta good he's gonna be. He's marryin' the youngest."

"Ayuh."

"How'd *you* know?"

Clarence sighed. "Wendell, it's all ovuh town."

"So why's he doin' it? Potts says it's the money. Chief says she's pregnant. Elmira says it's love," he snorted, "but what does Elmira know. Me, I say he's afta Stah's End. I would be, if I was him."

"Thank God you ain't," Clarence muttered with a flash of impatience, and looked off down the street. He was real tired of hearing Wendell's opinion. It was almost always sour.

"Got somethin' to say?" Wendell asked.

Clarence took the pipe from his mouth and looked right at him down the bench. "Thank God you ain't Jesse. If you were, the girl'd be doomed."

"We'a the one's doomed. She's gonna be livin' heeya, y'know. Know what she's gonna do? Throw awgies."

Clarence rolled his eyes. "Who told you that?"

"My cousin Haskell. She's from Washington. They pahty all the time theya." He glowered. "That's just what we need. Pols. Comin' up heeya, talkin' outta both sides'a theya mouths. I'll tell you somethin', Clarence. If she an' those pol friends think they can come in an take ovuh the town, they got anothuh think comin'. We don't need no pols any moah than we need the mob. We don't need no awgies, eithuh. And we *don't* need one'a ahs marryin' one'a theyas."

Clarence saw Hackmore Wainwright's pickup slip down the street and turn down toward the dock, and suddenly the dock seemed like a good place to be. He pushed himself up from the bench.

"Wheya you goin'?" Wendell asked with a frown.

"The dock."

"Whatcha gonna do theya?"

"Get some peace and quiet."

"You don't like what I say? Well then, go on down to the dock. Know what's theya? Buck Monaghan's theya. Know what Buck's gonna say? Buck's gonna say we gotta shell up the money to rebuild the dock, else the new fishin' boats he's buyin' won't be able

487

to tie on. Fact is, th' old dock's just fine. Problem's with Buck. His eyes'a bigguh than his stomach. So-phis-ti-cated e-lec-tronics. Bah! He don't need new boats. He's not gonna find the fish to fill 'em. Ocean's getting fished out in these pahts."

"Nah."

"Yes, suh. Fished out. Otta dry dock all the boats awhile, if y'ask me."

Clarence took a bold breath. "No one's askin' you, y'old coot," he said and, feeling a slow draft of satisfaction, walked off.

AFTERWORD

Straightening my shoulders, I close my eyes and breathe deeply of the morning-crisp September air. It fills my lungs, sending frissons of excitement up and down my spine. Surprising. After four years at Star's End, I should be used to it. But each day is still new and fresh.

Four years. Hard to believe. So much has happened, so naturally.

Jesse and I were married in August of that first year, in a simple ceremony in the meadow. Caroline and Ben, who had married quietly earlier that summer, were there, along with Annette and Jean-Paul and the children, and a handful of Jesse's closest friends.

Jesse's mother declined our invitation, and understandably so. Witnessing the marriage of the daughter of her nemesis to her son at the scene of the crime, so to speak, would have been difficult. I have seen her since.

Jesse and I make a point to visit her during our winter travels. All things considered, she has been cordial, even warm. I like to think that she's growing fond of me and that if the wedding were held now, she would come.

It was a wonderful day. Following the ceremony, we opened the house to the town, and what a party it was. There was dancing on the lawn, food and drink in never-ending supply, and a huge bonfire on the bluff. And that was just the first of many such parties. Jesse and I love having the townsfolk at Star's End. It is one small way we can thank them for their warmth.

"Mommy! Look, Mommy!"

The sweet sound of Joshie's voice brings me around. He is running toward me on sturdy, three-year-old legs, offering up a fistful of wild asters.

"Purple flowers!" he cries proudly.

I kneel down to accept his present, curling an arm around him to bring him close. "Very purple," I say just as proudly and point to the lighter flowers. "And pink ones. And lavender ones."

"I like this one," he decides, tugging a purple from the bunch and holding it to my nose. "Smell it?"

"Sure do." I turn the flower to his nose.

He gives an exaggerated sniff, then holds it away and scrutinizes it as though it were an intricate piece of machinery. I am, in turn, fascinated by his scrutiny, intrigued by imagining the thoughts milling about in his head.

Motherhood has taken me by surprise, literally and figuratively. Jesse and I had assumed children would be awhile in coming, but I conceived soon after our wedding and haven't regretted it once. I loved being pregnant, even loved giving birth — though if I told my sisters that, they'd rib me forever. Mostly, I love mothering Joshie. He has his father's sweet and even disposition. Jesse loves him to bits.

With a gleeful screech, Joshie hurls his fistful of flowers into the air. They rain down upon him, but not for long, because he is off and running along the bluff. He stops abruptly, then squats. Seconds later, he holds up a worm.

I hate worms. I hate crawly things, period. My sisters always thought that I gardened with gloves on to preserve my manicure. Not so. Though my nails are rarely polished now, I still wear gloves when I root around in the soil.

"Look, Mommy."

"I see, sweetheart." What I see are tiny

fingers holding a slimy something tighter than my stomach wants. "Are you being careful not to hurt him?"

"Yes. Look. He's moving."

"Worms like to move. What they *really* like to move on is earth. They wiggle through it and make it healthy. Daddy always says that. Remember?"

Joshie nods.

"Want to put him down?"

Joshie shakes his head, but the movement is enough for his eye to catch on a sprinkling of dandelions farther down the bluff. Dropping the worm, he takes off.

I stand there watching him, thinking that there can't be a sight much more beautiful than that of my son, in the jeans and sweatshirt that are miniatures of mine, kneeling on the grass, blowing at the dandelion fluff with the granite headland, the ocean, and the cloud-dotted sky as a backdrop. I feel a fullness inside that, yes, has to do with the new baby growing there, but even more with the overall state of my life.

Taking another deep, deliberately appreciative breath, I start on toward Joshie. By the time I reach what is left of the dandelions, he is scrambling up over an outcropping of ledge. Knowing the way, he leads me inland a bit. When we reach a grassy decline, he runs, then falls and rolls to the bottom, jumps to his feet and crawls up the other side. At the very top, on a patch of grass, he plops down and turns back on me a wide, waiting grin.

Can you see him, Mother? I think as loudly as I can on the chance that she might be able to hear. *He's a beautiful child, sweet enough to make you melt. Jesse sees Will in him. I see Jesse.*

Joining Joshie at the top of the rise, I bring him to sit inside the circle of my legs and put my mouth to his ear as we look out over the whitecapped waves. "Look at the boat. Isn't it pretty?"

"It's like Uncle Ben's."

Ben rented a two-master for the month that he and Caroline were at Star's End. It was great fun, what with Annette and her family here, too, and it wasn't the first summer we were all together. Since Ginny's death, we make a point to keep in touch. Thanksgivings are spent in St. Louis at Annette's, Christmases at a country inn north of Chicago, near Ben's cabin in the woods, and summers at Star's End.

Give or take.

It isn't always easy. Annette's three oldest are in college, Jean-Paul's schedule is unforgiving, and Annette herself has a part-time job in the social service department of the hospital. Caroline, ironically, has an easier time scheduling vacations. Now that she has her own practice, with three trusted partners and two reliable associates, she picks her cases with care.

Good thing. She and Ben are expecting. In December. With any luck the baby will be born while we're all there.

Annette and I both hope for that. Caroline is forty-four. If she has a hard time of it, we'd like to be there to help.

Then again, Caroline is a fighter. If any woman can have a first child at forty-four and do it well, she's the one.

"Where is Uncle Ben?" Joshie asks in a sad little voice. It isn't the first time he's asked. He and Ben became fast friends this summer. Parting was difficult for them both.

"He's in Chicago with Aunt Caroline."

"I wanna play with him."

"I know, sweetie." I give him a hug. "And you will. You'll see him on Thanksgiving and again at Christmastime. Before you know it, it'll be next summer, and he'll be back up here."

"With the boat?"

"Could be." I peer around at him. "Want to pick some flowers?"

The question is barely out of my mouth

when he pushes up out of my lap and races toward the marigolds that grow inland of the graveyard. Not far from these, a striking blue-violet against orange, are monkshood. This is the last of the color we'll have until spring, but the thought is far from discouraging. Winter at Star's End has charm. Granted, we aren't here for the worst of it, still, when life moves indoors, into the circle of a crackling fire, there is a coziness to it.

We pick flowers until our hands are full. Joshie knows this routine, too. In a singsong voice, he begins. "For Papa Will." He lays some at the foot of Will's stone, then at Mother's. "And Nana Ginny." With a moment's intense concentration, he shifts what is left into one hand, then smiles up at me. "For *us.*"

Concentrating again, he singles out one of the marigolds, and in a gesture that he has never made before, a pure imitation of Jesse, he comes to me and pushes the flower into my hair.

I choke up, catch the flower when the breeze knocks it out, and anchor it more firmly in the riot of my curls. "For me?"

He nods, wraps his little arms around me and gives me a hug, then breaks away and dashes off. I think how blessed I am to have such a child, before I collect myself and follow.

We head home, down the grassy decline and up, moving inland a bit. Joshie is skipping now, or trying to. The end result is more a trot, but the bottom line is contentment. He is a happy child, particularly in anticipation of seeing his father.

Jesse will be back soon. He is in town, dropping my breads and muffins at Julia's and buying fall bulbs at the supply store. Joshie and I would have gone along — we usually do, both to be with Jesse and to see friends — but the thought of a morning walk on the bluff was too much to resist.

Later, while Jesse plants his bulbs and Joshie naps, I'll drive in for coffee with Julia. We're planning another spying trip, this time to restaurants in the Berkshires. While we're in the area, we thought we might sneak in a day at the spa.

What better way to prepare ourselves for a night of espionage. Right?

Soon after that, Jesse and I will be off to Washington to pass final papers on the townhouse and clean it out. We simply aren't there enough to justify keeping it, what with plenty of fine hotels nearby. We love the city, but my ties to it have loosened. I've put down roots in Downlee, and they've taken hold. I can't imagine calling any other place home.

Nor, obviously, can Jesse. He continues to be the gardener, and though he hires others to do the more tedious chores, he supervises it all. Star's End is a source of personal pride for him, and rightly so. It is a dream that keeps getting better and better and better.

As does my life, I realize, as I watch Joshie scramble over the outcropping of ledge and run on. I keep thinking things are so good that they can't possibly improve, then they do. Either a shower throws a rainbow over Star's End to breathtaking effect or Joshie puts a flower in my hair or Jesse looks at me in a way that touches my soul more deeply than ever.

I think back to my life before him. It was filled with finery, yet barren and stark. And I agonized about leaving it behind.

I was a fool.

Then again, not so. I made the right choice in the end.

Mother said, in that last day we had together, that she didn't regret her life's decision. But not a day passes when I don't give thanks that my own life's decision was different. I have the love she grasped so briefly, and it keeps multiplying upon itself.

Ahead of me, Joshie begins to sprint. When his legs can't keep up with his excitement, he stumbles, but in little more than a continuation of the same motion, he's up and off again. And no wonder. He sees Jesse.

I stop to watch. Joshie launches himself toward Jesse, who catches him up in a hug. They draw back. They say something to each other. Then Joshie is hoisted to Jesse's shoulders, and they are striding toward me.

They are such a pleasing sight — father and son — that I don't move. And then there's the matter of the father alone, making my insides hum with his simple approach, even stronger after four years together — incredible.

"Hi," he says as he nears, and, incredibly, too, I feel tongue-tied. Melting brown eyes, tanned skin, long legs, fluid walk — not even Joshie's inadvertently grasping his hair into pigtails can detract from his rugged good looks. He is devastatingly male. I don't think I'll ever get used to it.

He knows that and grins. "Have a nice walk?"

I nod. "Get your bulbs?"

"Yup. Julia says thanks for the goodies. She also says she's looking into seaweed wraps." His eyes twinkle. "A new business?"

He knew damn well that it wasn't, but far

be it from me to call him on it. I grin. "Could be."

When he throws an arm around my shoulder, I fall into step beside him. "Queasy?" he asks.

"Nope. Breakfast helped."

"Think it's a girl?"

I look up at him with a grin and a shrug. "Could be. Then again . . ."

Our arms draw each other closer. As we walk on, my senses come alive to the extreme. I hear the gulls, the waves, the wind. I smell the salt of the surf, the tang of the pines, the musk of man. I feel the chill of September and the warmth of Jesse. And more. A glow. It isn't tangible. Or external. But it's very much here, leading us home.

ABOUT THE AUTHOR

Barbara Delinsky, a lifelong New Englander, was a sociologist and photographer before she began to write. There are more than 30 million copies of her books in print. Readers can contact her c/o P.O. Box 812894, Wellesley, MA 02482-0026, or via the Web at www.barbaradelinsky.com

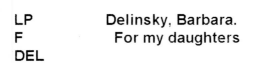